Praise

"Griggs delivers the
adventure and laug
charming, quirky a
—*RT Book* ... *ney*

"Griggs really outdoes herself in her latest Texas Grooms story, with outstanding characters who are developed strongly."
—*RT Book Reviews* on *The Holiday Courtship*

"The final Texas Grooms story is a delight to read, and readers will be sad that it is the last book."
—*RT Book Reviews* on *Lone Star Heiress*

Praise for Victoria Bylin

"Readers will get caught up in the characters' pain, joy, sorrow and anger and believe there's hope and forgiveness for them as well as for the characters."
—*RT Book Reviews* on *The Maverick Preacher*

"*The Bounty Hunter's Bride* is a sweet love story, with rough edges, filled with hope, love, forgiveness and redemption. Victoria Bylin has written enough historical novels to know what readers expect, and she delivers on all levels."
—*RT Book Reviews*

"*Wyoming Lawman* is a tender, charming love story filled with strong, memorable characters…. Don't miss this talented author."
—*RT Book Reviews*

Winnie Griggs

and

Victoria Bylin

The Hand-Me-Down Family

&

The Maverick Preacher

ISBN-13: 978-1-335-65280-5

The Hand-Me-Down Family & The Maverick Preacher

This edition published by arrangement with Love Inspired Books.

www.Harlequin.com

Printed in U.S.A.

CONTENTS

Winnie Griggs is a city girl born and raised in southeast Louisiana's Cajun Country who grew up to marry a country boy from the hills of northwest Louisiana. Though her Prince Charming (who often wears the guise of a cattle rancher) is more comfortable riding a tractor than a white steed, the two of them have been living their own happily-ever-after for thirty-plus years. During that time they raised four proud-to-call-them-mine children and a too-numerous-to-count assortment of dogs, cats, fish, hamsters, turtles and 4-H sheep.

Winnie retired from her "day job" and now, in addition to her reading and writing, happily spends her time doing the things she loves best—spending time with her family, cooking and exploring flea markets.

Readers can contact Winnie at PO Box 14, Plain Dealing, LA 71064, or email her at winnie@winniegriggs.com.

Books by Winnie Griggs

Love Inspired Historical

The Hand-Me-Down Family
The Christmas Journey
The Proper Wife
Second Chance Family
A Baby Between Them

Texas Grooms

Handpicked Husband
The Bride Next Door
A Family for Christmas

Love Inspired

The Heart's Song

Visit the Author Profile page at Harlequin.com.

THE HAND-ME-DOWN FAMILY

Winnie Griggs

For we are God's masterpiece. He has created us anew in Christ Jesus, so we can do the good things He planned for us long ago.

—*Ephesians* 2:10

To each of the following, my most sincere gratitude:

My agent, Michelle Grajkowski,
who has always been upbeat about my work and
has never allowed me to give up or get discouraged.

To the members of the "I Told You So Club,"
Cathy, Laura, Margaret and Lenora, who gave me
some not-so-gentle nudges toward taking this
leap-of-faith path for my writing. Thank you, ladies,
and I hereby admit publicly that you were oh-so-right.

To my "first readers," Joanne, Cathy and Renee—
your feedback was invaluable.

I am truly blessed to have each of you in my life.

Chapter One

California, May 1888

"Hey, Jack!"

Jack bit back an oath at the hail, then turned in a slow, controlled movement. He pinned the foreman's errand boy with a cold stare, holding his peace for three long heartbeats, just enough time to set the unthinking messenger to fidgeting in his saddle.

Finally, Jack pulled the sliver of twig from his mouth. "You got a death wish, Dobbins? Or didn't you see those yellow flags marking off this area?"

The young man's expression faltered. "Yes, but you're still—"

Jack snapped the twig and tossed it away. "I'm inside the perimeter because I'm setting charges. Which means I'm working with enough explosives right now to blow you, me and most of this pile of rock to smithereens."

Dobbins's Adam's apple bobbed, but he stuck out his chin and pulled a paper from his pocket. "A telegram came for you. Mr. Gordon wanted—"

Jack's jaw muscle twitched. Fool kid. "I don't care

if it's a set of executive orders from President Grover Cleveland himself. When I'm in the middle of a job, you don't cross the perimeter unless it's life or death." He narrowed his eyes. "Because it just might turn into that."

A quick nod signaled understanding.

Jack wiped his brow with his sleeve, already regretting his harsh tone. The heat and the hours were starting to wear on him. He waved the intruder forward. "Well, now that you're here, you might as well give me the thing."

Dobbins nudged his horse forward and handed the folded paper to Jack. His eyes rounded when he saw Jack slide it into his pocket without so much as a glance. "Aren't you gonna read it?"

"Not 'til I'm done here. I don't need any more distractions right now." He raised a brow. "Anything else?"

Dobbins got the message. "Guess not." With another nod, he jerked on the reins, turned his horse, and headed back in the direction of the base camp.

Jack frowned as he watched the messenger gallop off.

A telegram. Now who would—

He was doing it already, he realized.

He shoved the telegram out of his mind. Right now he needed to focus on the work at hand. Like he'd just told Dobbins, he couldn't afford distractions while he was on the job.

Twenty minutes later Jack stood and tilted his hat up. He stepped back far enough to take in the remainder of what just a week ago had been a steep, rocky hillside. He drew his elbows back behind him, stretching the kinks out of cramped muscles.

Then he mentally reviewed the placement of all four charges one more time. You just couldn't be too careful.

Satisfied everything was in order, he headed back toward the stand of scrub he'd designated as the meeting spot for his two-man team. Hopefully they were already waiting for him. He was more than ready to wrap up this job.

As he crossed the uneven ground, Jack fingered the folded sheet of paper tucked in his pocket. The only people who'd be likely to send him a telegram would be his sister or brother.

He'd just gotten a letter from Nell a few weeks ago. She hadn't had anything new to say—just updates on what was going on back home and sisterly admonitions to visit soon, coupled with a bribe to bake up one of his favorite apple pecan pies.

No, he couldn't picture either Nell or Lanny sending a telegram. At least not to deliver good news.

The back of his neck prickled and his step slowed.

Putting off reading the thing was becoming more of a distraction than whatever news the telegram contained could possibly be.

Jack jerked the crumpled paper out of his pocket and read the four stark lines written there.

And as surely as if someone had detonated the charges prematurely, he felt the world rock under his feet.

Chapter Two

Texas, four days later

Callie studied the man seated across from her as the stagecoach swayed and bounced, bringing her ever closer to her new life.

She placed a finger to her chin. No, he wasn't a sea captain. The hat was all wrong and he had an air about him that seemed more akin to earthiness than saltwater.

She scrunched her lips to one side as she examined his features more closely. He was actually quite handsome, in a dangerous, rugged sort of way. Rather than detracting from his looks, that faded scar on the left side of his chin served to lend him an adventurous air. She refused to believe a man who looked as he did was anything so mundane as a farmer or shopkeeper.

He could be a Texas Ranger. Yes, that would fit. He had that lean, grim-purpose look about him.

She settled into her mental tale-spinning. So, if he *was* a ranger, what was his story? Perhaps he was returning home for a well-earned rest after grueling weeks of tracking down desperate outlaws. Or maybe he was traveling to Sweetgum on official business in search of—

Callie straightened in her seat. Was it her imagination, or had they slowed down a bit? A quick glance out the window confirmed that the tree-lined countryside had given way to scattered farms. And if she wasn't mistaken, the edge of a small town was just up ahead.

This was it. Her new home—Sweetgum, Texas.

She adjusted her poke bonnet with hands that weren't quite steady, then laced her fingers tightly together and closed her eyes.

Heavenly Father, I'm truly grateful to You for getting me all the way here from Ohio without a hitch. But we both know that was the easy part compared to what comes next. And since this whole undertaking was actually Your idea, I know You're going to help me figure out what to say and do when I step outside and come face-to-face with my new husband for the first time.

Bolstered by that thought, Callie began gathering her belongings. Then she paused and slanted a glance toward the object of her former musings.

Her unsociable traveling companion seemed completely unaware of their arrival.

Should she say something to him?

He'd climbed aboard at their last stop and, after the briefest of greetings, settled into the opposite corner, closed his eyes and hadn't moved since. Not that she resented his lack of attention.

After all, being this close to such a man was a new experience for her, and his closed-off demeanor had given her an opportunity to study him unobserved. Besides which, trying to concoct a history for him from only the hints provided by the rough and calloused look of his hands, his weathered complexion and his firm, wiry build had been an interesting way to pass the time.

One thing she'd decided about thirty minutes into her story-weaving was that, whatever his profession, he was not someone at peace with his world. There was something about his very stillness, about the hint of tension in his stubble-covered jaw, that pointed to a weary or troubled spirit.

Before she could make up her mind whether or not to disturb him, his eyes opened and their gazes collided. The lack of any residual drowsiness in those startling blue eyes made her wonder whether or not he'd truly been asleep.

The heat rose in Callie's cheeks. How mortifying to have been caught staring so rudely! She tugged on the edge of her bonnet again. Thank goodness it already hid most of her face.

"We're here," she blurted, then mentally cringed. Why did she always feel compelled to rush in and fill the silences?

He straightened. "So I see."

The hint of dryness in his tone warmed her cheeks even further. But the driver opened the door, rescuing Callie from more embarrassment.

As she rose to leave the coach, the glimpse of the dusty street and plank-lined sidewalk forcibly reminded her that she had left her familiar world behind. A bubble of panic rose in her throat.

What if Mr. Tyler was disappointed when he met her?

What if she couldn't learn how to adjust to life in this rural community?

What if—

Callie took a deep, steadying breath. *Forgive me, Lord. I know we already wrestled with my doubts be-*

fore the wedding. This is the ministry You gave me. Mr. Tyler and his daughter need me, and I need them. I—

"Ma'am? Are you all right?"

Her companion studied her with a worried frown, no doubt wondering why she wasn't moving. After her earlier actions, he must think her completely addled.

Callie offered an apologetic smile. "Yes, I'm fine, thank you. Just making certain I have all my things." She adjusted her bonnet once more, squared her shoulders and stepped down from the stagecoach onto the sidewalk's dusty boards.

Pasting on what she hoped was a confident smile, Callie waited for her husband to step forward and introduce himself. But, while she received curious glances from some of the passersby, no one greeted her.

Her smile faltered. Where was he?

She continued scanning the sidewalk even as she moved aside to allow her fellow passenger to exit the stage.

Why wasn't Mr. Tyler here? Surely he wouldn't keep her standing alone in foreign surroundings where she didn't know anyone…

I will never leave thee, nor forsake thee.

The remembered verse calmed her. She wasn't alone. God was with her.

Mr. Tyler had undoubtedly been delayed. Poor man. He was likely as nervous about this meeting as she was. And he had little Annabeth to tend to as well. It must be difficult for him to care for a child and a farm all on his own.

Well, he wouldn't have to any longer.

Trying to ignore the stubborn prickling of anxiety that wouldn't quite go away, Callie turned to study the community that she would now call home. These people would be her neighbors and, hopefully, her friends.

The town itself was just as Julia had described in her letters. The stage had stopped in front of the Sweetgum Hotel and Post Office. To her left she could see an apothecary shop and the mercantile with a long wooden bench out front. On the other side of the hotel stood a bank, and past that the doctor's office.

Callie glanced across the street and frowned in dismay. About a block down the road, one of the buildings had been reduced to charred timbers. She immediately offered up a prayer that strength and healing be afforded to the lives that had been touched by that calamity.

What business had it housed? It was next to the barber shop, so—

The sight of a gentleman hurrying toward the stage jerked Callie's attention away from the puzzle.

Her heart stuttered a few beats.

Was this him?

She stood straighter and adjusted her bonnet. But instead of approaching her, he absently tipped his hat in her direction and stopped in front of her fellow passenger.

"Jack, welcome back," he said as the two men shook hands. "I just wish it were under happier circumstances."

Callie turned away, deflated. It wasn't Mr. Tyler.

Well, at least now she had a name for her traveling companion. Jack. A good, solid name. And, if the greeting he'd received was any indication, she'd apparently guessed right as to his troubled spirit.

The two men spoke in low tones and Callie immediately focused on other sounds, avoiding the temptation to eavesdrop.

A buckboard clattered down the street accompanied

by the muffled clop-clop of horses' hooves. A shop bell jingled as a woman emerged from the mercantile with a loaded basket. Two boys raced down the sidewalk, a yipping dog at their heels.

Such bustling normalcy all around her. Yet she felt isolated, apart from it all, like a stranger peeking in through a window at a family gathering.

The minutes drew out as the driver unloaded luggage and parcels from the back of the stagecoach. It was hotter here in Texas than it had been in Ohio. Callie longed to loosen her tight-fitting bonnet, or better yet, take it off altogether, but she dared not. Not until she was away from prying eyes and safely inside her new home.

A number of townsfolk stopped to speak to Jack, but though she received a few friendly nods in addition to more curious glances, no one stepped forward to greet her.

Finally, the last of the baggage and cargo was unloaded and the driver stepped inside the hotel with a mail sack. The man, Jack, lifted two of the bags, easily hefting the larger one up to his shoulder.

Callie couldn't help but wonder—would Mr. Tyler be as fine and strong a figure of a man as this Jack?

As if feeling her eyes on him, the man paused and met her gaze. His expression was gruff and a muscle twitched at the corner of his mouth. "Is someone meeting you?"

She smiled, grateful for his show of concern, reluctant though it might be. "Yes, thank you. I'm certain my husband will be along soon."

Something akin to surprise flashed across his features but it was gone in an instant.

"Good." He nodded and allowed his friend to take

one of his bags. "If you're sure you don't need any help..." He tipped his hat and turned.

As she watched him walk away, it was as if the last link to her old life were being severed. A foolish notion, since she really didn't know this man at all. But before she could stop herself, Callie took a small step forward. "Excuse me."

Both men turned, facing her with questioning glances.

"Ma'am?" Jack prompted.

"I was wondering if perhaps either of you know a Mr. Leland Tyler? He was supposed to..." Her voice tapered off as she saw their startled reactions.

Jack's jaw tightened visibly. "Why would you be looking for Lan— Leland?"

Callie noticed his familiar use of her husband's name. "So you *do* know him."

That tic near the corner of his mouth made another appearance. "Yes." He didn't expand on his one-word answer, and his expression remained closed, unreadable. "But you didn't answer my question. How do you know Leland?"

Callie offered up a quick prayer that Mr. Tyler would arrive soon. He should be the one making the introductions to his neighbors and friends. "I'm Callista Johnson Tyler, his wife."

"Wife!" Jack set his bag down with a loud thump and sent a sharp look his companion's way. "You know what she's talking about, Virgil?"

The other man shook his head. "Lanny never said anything about a new wife."

They certainly were reacting strongly to her news. She knew Julia had only been gone about four months, but it wasn't unusual for a widower to remarry so soon, especially when he had a young child to care for.

For that matter, why didn't they already know about her? Surely Leland wouldn't have kept such momentous news from his friends and neighbors? Unless he'd worried she wouldn't show up.

Or was there another, more disturbing reason? Her heart beat faster as possibilities whirled through her mind.

Realizing the men were watching her, Callie tried to hide her confusion behind a confident air. "I'm not certain why Mr. Tyler chose to keep this a secret. Perhaps he was planning to surprise everyone. But be that as it may, I assure you, I am indeed Mrs. Leland Tyler. If you'll be so good as to tell me where my husband can be found, I'm certain he'll verify my identity."

Jack took another step forward. "Perhaps we should introduce ourselves first." He swept an arm toward his companion. "This is Virgil Wilson."

She smiled and nodded acknowledgment. "Mr. Wilson." The name was familiar. Oh, yes, he and his wife owned the farm that adjoined Leland's. Perhaps he could transport her there if Leland didn't show up soon.

The farmer touched the brim of his hat, ducking his head respectfully. "Ma'am."

When she turned back to Jack, he was studying her intently, as if trying to read something from her countenance. Holding her gaze, he extended his hand. "And I'm Lanny's brother, Jack."

Brother! Of course—Jack Tyler. Julia had mentioned Leland's brother in many of her letters. It had grieved her friend deeply when the breach had grown up between the brothers, and even more so when Jack had left Sweetgum and all but cut himself off from his family and friends.

No wonder he was startled by her news. If he was

just now returning to Sweetgum after all these years, of course he wouldn't know about Leland's second marriage.

Feeling her anxiety ebb, she grasped his outstretched hand eagerly. "Then you are my brother-in-law. I'm so very pleased to meet you."

She smiled, relieved and happy. Jack Tyler. Perhaps he was part of her mission here—maybe she could help heal whatever rift existed between the two brothers. Julia would have wanted that.

When her newfound relation released her hand, Callie adjusted her bonnet again. "If I'd realized who you were, I would have waited before I said anything. I'm certain your brother wanted to tell you himself."

"No harm done." His expression, however, hinted that all was not well. Did he resent hearing about the marriage from a stranger?

"Well, it's a wonderful circumstance that we should arrive together." She was more certain than ever that the Lord's hand was in this. "Since your brother is delayed, perhaps you would be so kind as to escort me to his home." Surely he couldn't refuse her request, no matter what rift existed between himself and Leland.

But Mr. Wilson intervened, clearing his throat. "I'm afraid that—"

Without taking his eyes from Callie, Mr. Tyler interrupted whatever his friend was about to say. "Leland isn't at home right now."

The hairs at the nape of Callie's neck prickled.

There was something strangely intense about the look he was giving her.

And how would he know Leland wasn't at home when he'd only just arrived in town himself?

Chapter Three

"I don't understand."

Jack saw the uneasy flicker in the woman's expression. Fair enough. He wasn't sure he knew what to make of her, either.

How was he supposed to believe her claim that Lanny had married again, had replaced his first wife with someone so unlike the vibrant, delicate and pretty-as-a-spring-meadow woman Julia had been?

Not that this woman was unattractive. He couldn't see much of her face, but she had a nice enough smile and a trim figure.

But she wasn't Julia.

In Nell's last letter she'd mentioned how hard a time Lanny was having dealing with Julia's passing. It was one of the reasons Jack had been thinking about making a visit home.

This remarriage thing just didn't make sense.

"Excuse me, ma'am." He tried to keep his voice even. No point fanning her distrust. "I know you have questions. To be honest, I have a few for you as well. But it's a mite hot out here on the sidewalk."

He nodded toward the open door to the hotel. "Why

don't we step inside and find a more comfortable place to talk." Not to mention less public.

He saw her hesitation and spoke up again before she could object. "I'm sure Virgil won't mind watching our bags while we figure this out."

"Uh, yes, ma'am." Virgil gamely followed his lead. "I mean, no, I don't mind at all. You two just go right ahead. And take your time. I mean, you have a lot—"

"There, that's settled." Jack used his best take-charge tone to cut off Virgil's rambling. He wanted to give her the news his way, in his time.

He pointed to the trunk and carpetbag still sitting on the sidewalk. "So, are these yours? We'll just set them with mine over here out of the way."

Once he got her inside they could sort through her story without the whole town looking on. It was a pretty sure bet that once he told her why Lanny wasn't here to meet her there was going to be a scene of some sort.

Which was another good reason to get her inside—it would be right handy to have her already seated in case she decided to swoon. He just hoped she wasn't one of those melodramatic females who were prone to hysterics.

But her lips compressed in a stubborn line. "Just a minute, Mr. Tyler. I'm not going anywhere until you tell me where my husband is." She tugged on that bonnet again. "And what exactly did you mean by 'figure this out?'"

Just his luck—she was going to be muleheaded. "Ma'am, trust me, you really don't want to have this conversation out here in the middle of town." He crossed his arms and raised a brow, trying a bit of intimidation. Couldn't she see that he just wanted to make this easier on her?

Rather than backing down, though, the obstinate woman tilted her chin even higher. "It's a simple question, sir, requiring a simple answer. Where is my husband?"

Jack dropped his arms and narrowed his eyes. At another time he might have admired her spirit, her stubborn resolve. But not today. He was too tired from four days of travel and frustrating delays—four days of trying to absorb the impact of what had happened—to continue this argument.

She wanted to know where Lanny was, then so be it. "Have it your way. I'll take you right to him."

"Huh?" Virgil almost dropped the bag he held. "Jack, what are—"

Jack raised a hand. "No, no, it's okay." He gave his friend a tight smile. "I planned to pay a visit when I got here anyway. No point putting it off, and this lady might as well come along."

Virgil shot a look toward the far end of town, then shifted his gaze uncertainly from the woman back to Jack.

Jack clapped him on the shoulder before he could protest again, or worse yet, blurt out something that would set off a scene. "You don't mind seeing to our luggage while the lady and I take a little walk, do you?"

"No, of course not. But—"

"Good." With a short nod, Jack turned back to Lanny's self-proclaimed bride and swept his hand out in a gesture that was more challenge than good manners. "Shall we?"

She didn't answer immediately. Instead, she drew her lower lip between her teeth and gave that odd-looking bonnet another tug forward.

Jack's flash of irritation turned inward. There he went, taking his frustrations out on someone else.

Again.

He rubbed the back of his neck, feeling wearier than he ever had in his twenty-nine years. He hadn't had more than the odd thirty-minute nap here or there since he'd gotten that telegram.

And he still hadn't figured out what he was going to do now that he was here. Just the thought of—

He shook his head, trying to focus on the current issue. That other business was his problem, not this woman's. Given the circumstances, she deserved better treatment. "Look, ma'am, I—"

"Very well." She spoke over his attempted apology as if he hadn't opened his mouth. Her spine was rail-spike stiff, all signs of hesitation and uncertainty replaced by an air of determination. "Lead the way."

It was Jack's turn to hesitate. He could tell she was still a bit uneasy and admired her pluck, but maybe this wasn't such a good idea after all. Yes, taking her along would give them a bit of privacy, but it would also put him alone with her when he broke the news. He wasn't good at dealing with emotional women. And he certainly wasn't in any shape to deal with one today.

Then he shrugged. She had to be told, and his gut said she wouldn't get all hysterical on him.

"This way."

They started down the sidewalk, Jack matching his pace to her shorter stride.

They walked in silence. Jack kept his eyes focused straight ahead and refused to slow his step, halting any would-be greetings from the folks they passed with a short nod. He wasn't ready to talk to his former friends and neighbors right now.

He had to get this over with first.

He carefully avoided looking at whatever was left of Nell and Jed's café, but as they drew even with it he could smell the acrid odor of scorched wood and ashes that still lingered in the air, threatening to suffocate him.

Jack shot a quick glance at the blackened remains in spite of himself.

A definite mistake.

Loss and guilt slammed into him again, harder this time, like a fist in the gut. It was as if he'd tossed a stick of explosives into the building himself, leaving this grotesque skeleton of charred timbers and debris.

He scrubbed a hand along the right side of his face. Perhaps if he'd made plans to come home before now, to make amends. If he had been here when—

"Pardon me."

His companion's breathless words interrupted his thoughts. A quick glance her way revealed she was struggling to keep up.

He slowed immediately. "Sorry, ma'am. My mind was on something else."

She glanced over her shoulder at the charred rubble, then back at him with dawning dismay. "That building, it was the café, wasn't it?"

He felt that betraying muscle in his jaw twitch. "Yes." And just how did she know that?

Unspoken questions tumbled across her face, a growing dread clouding her eyes. Apparently she knew of the café's significance to him.

And to her as well, if she was who she said she was.

How did she know enough to read the situation from a burned-out building she'd never seen before?

Had Lanny *really* married this woman, this apparent stranger to Sweetgum and everyone here?

Twice her mouth opened then closed again. For a change she seemed to have nothing to say. Instead, she gave him an assessing look, nodded and increased her pace.

He spared a moment to ponder over the puzzle this woman presented. In the short time he'd been in her company she'd proven herself to be more stubborn, outspoken and full of spit and vinegar than might be seemly for a female. Yet just now she'd seen no-telling-what in his expression and held back her questions. Not at all the reaction he'd expected.

The walk through town seemed endless. The closer they got to their destination, the tighter the tension inside him coiled. Everyday sounds like dogs barking and harnesses jangling seemed both magnified and distant. He felt eyes focused on them from every angle. It was as if the two of them were the main characters in some sort of stage play, only he'd forgotten all his lines and even which role he was assigned.

"Watch your step." He automatically took her elbow as the sidewalk ended. As soon as they stepped down onto the well-packed dirt path, she withdrew her arm. But not before he felt the slight trembling of her muscles.

So, the lady wasn't as composed as she wanted him to think. Was it because she'd already figured out what had happened?

Or because she still didn't trust him?

The main section of town gave way almost immediately to greener expanses. Up ahead was Sweetgum's schoolhouse. The church was just beyond, close enough that it was difficult to tell where the schoolyard ended and the churchyard began.

Both of these places had been a central part of his world, his life, at one time. But no more.

He'd outgrown the schoolroom at sixteen.

He'd outgrown the church a few years later, when he'd decided it was finally time to get away from Sweetgum and strike out on his own.

Jack shook off those memories as he led his companion across the schoolyard, past the church building and up to the white picket fence that marked the boundaries of the cemetery.

He paused and turned to her, removing his hat and raking a hand through his hair.

She stood there, rooted to the spot, her eyes wide, her gaze fixed on the neat rows of grassy mounds.

"Ma'am?"

She started, and her gaze flew to his.

Her pallor roused a protective response in him. She looked nearly as white as the ribbon on her bonnet. Jack could see the shock, the inner battle she was fighting between denial and a sickly acceptance.

Was he going to have to deal with a swooner after all?

"Steady now." He took her elbow. "I'm sorry to break it to you like this. But I thought it was better to have a bit of privacy. I—"

She raised a hand. "No, I understand." Her gaze slid back to the somberly peaceful green, and she swallowed audibly. "Was it the fire?"

He nodded.

"And your sister?"

Ah, Nell. His sweet, peacemaker of a sister. To die like that…

Not trusting himself to speak, he pulled the crumbled telegram from his pocket and handed it to her. He didn't have to look at it again to know exactly what it said.

The words were burned into his memory.

Café fire. Nell, Jed, Lanny killed. Please return to Sweetgum earliest possible. Children need you.

Callie tasted the bile rising in her throat as she read the terse missive. These people were her newly acquired family, the people she had so eagerly looked forward to meeting and befriending. To learn that they had died under such horrific circumstances…

Everything seemed to go silent, to pull back from her. A heartbeat later her vision clouded over and the earth swayed under her feet.

"Whoa, there."

Mr. Tyler's hand was under her elbow, steadying her, lending her a measure of strength.

Sounds and objects came rushing back into focus, racing to keep pace with the emotions that careened through her like water rushing over a fall. Horror at the thought of their deaths, confusion over what this meant for her future, and a guilty relief that her husband had not deliberately shunned her after all.

She attempted to smile at her concerned brother-in-law. "Thank you. I'm okay now."

He raised a brow. Probably worried she'd faint on him.

"Look, there's a bench over yonder under that cottonwood." He nodded his head in the direction of a tall leafy tree. Then he cleared his throat. "Why don't we sit for a spell? It'll be cooler in the shade and you can tell me the story of how you came to be married to my bother."

Callie glanced toward the cemetery, then nodded. She could pay her respects to Leland after she and his brother had their talk.

Then she realized how selfish she was being. These people were his family, his siblings and the people he'd grown up with. "I'm sorry to have made this more difficult for you, Mr. Tyler," she said softly. "And my condolences on your loss."

He nodded silently, leading her across the grounds.

"When did it happen?" Callie was still trying to take it all in. "The fire, I mean."

He released her arm as they reached the bench. "Four days ago." Both his face and voice were controlled, giving no hint of whatever emotion he might be feeling.

Then it hit her. She plopped down onto the bench. Could it be?

She clasped her hands tightly and stared up at him. "Do you know what time?"

His brow wrinkled in confusion. "Pardon?"

"At what time did your brother die?" She heard the shrillness of her tone, saw his brow go up. No doubt he thought her hysterical. But right now she didn't care.

He lifted a hand, palm up. "I don't know. I wasn't here. I only—"

"Do you have any idea?" she pressed. "Morning? Afternoon? Please, this is important." Her heart beat with a dull thumping as she waited for his response. A few hours one way or the other could make all the difference in the world.

The thing was, she didn't really know what answer she wanted to hear.

He scratched his chin. "Virgil did mention the café was nearly empty because it was after lunch..."

"I see." She sagged back in her seat, not sure whether she was relieved or disappointed.

Help me to see Your will in this, Father. Because right now, all I feel is confused and adrift.

"And just why does the time matter so much?" Jack asked, interrupting her silent prayer.

Callie dug in her handbag and pulled out a packet of papers. She stared at them for a moment, then held them out to him. "Because, as you'll see if you look through these documents, your brother and I were married by proxy four days ago. At exactly ten o'clock in the morning."

She gave him a humorless smile. "Which means, since the ceremony occurred before the fire, I am indeed a widow without ever having met my husband."

Chapter Four

As he took the papers from her, Callie closed her eyes, trying to absorb the fact that she had become a widow without ever knowing what it meant to be a wife. Yes, it was true that Leland had meant this to be a marriage in name only, but she had secretly hoped that, given time…

Stop it! Callie gave herself a mental shake. She should be mourning the man, not the end of some foolish daydream.

More to the point was the fact that she no longer had a reason to be here.

Had she come all this way for nothing?

Heavenly Father, I thought this was Your answer to my prayers. But was I too impulsive yet again? Was this mere wishful thinking on my part rather than Your intent for me? Please, help me understand what it is You want me to do now.

The sound of rustling papers drew her attention back to her companion.

He leaned forward, pinning her with that intense gaze again.

Her skin prickled. Even though they were out in the open rather than closed up in a stagecoach, being alone with him suddenly felt much more dangerous than it had earlier.

"So tell me," he asked, "how did this proxy marriage of yours come about?"

She bristled at his suspicious tone, forgetting her previous discomfort. Then she softened as guilt washed over her.

How could she sit here feeling sorry for herself while he dealt with such pain? He might seem gruff and overbearing, but how could she blame him? He'd lost his family less than a week ago, and now he was confronted with a sister-in-law he hadn't realized existed until just a few moments ago.

At the very least he deserved an explanation, something to help him make sense of the situation.

No matter how humbling it might be for her to tell him the story.

"Your brother was in need of someone to help raise his daughter," she said evenly. "And I wished to find a husband and household of my own. It was a mutually beneficial arrangement.

"As for why we did it by proxy…" She shrugged. "My family wouldn't hear of my leaving Ohio without ironclad assurances that the wedding would actually take place, and this seemed the best solution."

His eyes flashed with an emotion she couldn't identify. "Forgive my bluntness, ma'am, but why you? I mean, you just admitted the two of you never met. And, unless things around here have changed more than I realized, I'm sure Lanny could have found a local girl more than willing to marry him and help raise Annabeth."

She gave the edge of her bonnet a little tug. He was treading on uncomfortable territory. "Your brother is—was—a good-hearted, God-fearing man. He was very open about the fact that he wasn't looking for, nor could he offer, a love match." She brushed at an imaginary speck on her skirt. "He loved Julia very much and was certain he would never feel the same about another woman. I understood and accepted that."

Callie titled her chin up as she met her inquisitor's gaze. "I think he found it easier to say those things in a letter, and to someone he hadn't grown up with."

At his raised brow, she looked down at her clasped hands. "Besides which, as I said, your brother was a very kindhearted man. He knew I would receive his offer in the same spirit in which it was given, and as the possible answer to a long-standing prayer of my own."

He handed the papers back to her. "Ma'am, you just raised a whole wagonload more questions than you answered with that statement."

His tone had lost some of its belligerent edge. He seemed to be leaving it up to her as to whether she continued her story or not.

And his consideration lifted some of her reluctance to explain. "So ask your questions."

"It sounds like, in spite of what you said a moment ago, you and my brother knew each other."

"Knew *of* each other would be more accurate." She tucked her marriage papers back in her purse. "Through Julia."

He made a small movement of surprise. "You knew Julia?"

Callie nodded. "Yes. Her family lived next door to mine when we were children. We were best friends, closer than sisters, and almost inseparable. It was one of the saddest days of my life when I learned they were packing up and moving to Texas. She and I kept in touch after that through letters." She smiled. "Julia wrote the most wonderful letters. I feel like I already know the people and the town here."

He sat up straighter. "Wait a minute. You said your name was Callista. You're Callie."

Her brow furrowed at his abrupt statement. "Yes."

"Julia talked about you all the time when she first moved here. Really looked forward to getting them letters from you, too."

Her smile softened. "As I said, we were close. Even after she moved here, I always felt I could confide anything to her. Julia was that kind of friend."

He rubbed his chin. "So that's how my brother knew so much about you."

She nodded. "Once Julia was married, she shared some of the things from my letters with her husband. She asked first, of course, and I didn't mind. And naturally her letters to me were sprinkled with references to him."

"Naturally."

She wondered at his dry tone, but continued with her story. "Julia assured me she and Leland often included me in their prayers, a consideration I cherished. It also let me know that Leland was familiar with both my dreams and my situation."

"Situation?"

Callie took a deep breath and loosened the strings to her bonnet.

This was it.

Time to get it all out in the open. How would he react? Would he be as understanding as his brother? "Yes, my situation. The reason why I'm nearly twenty-six years old and unmarried. The reason why I always wear this stuffy bonnet when I'm in public. The reason why I would probably have remained a spinster the rest of my days if your brother hadn't made his generous offer."

Slowly she pushed the confining bonnet back until it hung loose behind her neck. She'd thought she was past feeling self-conscious. She shouldn't care what this man thought of her appearance, but somehow she did.

She lifted her head and waited for his inevitable reaction.

Jack watched her remove her bonnet and got his first good look at her face. He wasn't sure what he'd expected after her dramatic lead-in, but it wasn't this.

While not beautiful, she was passably fair, pretty even, at least in profile. Her hair was sandstone brown and her green eyes were brighter now that they could more fully reflect the sunlight. She had a small crook in her nose, but that added interest to her appearance rather than detracted from it.

So what was this "situation" she'd mentioned? "I'm sorry, ma'am, but I don't—"

Then she turned to him and he stopped cold. He winced before he could stop himself.

Along the left side of her face, from mid-cheek to hairline, her skin was stained by a palm-sized blotchy patch of a deep red color. It was difficult to see past such disfigurement to the pleasant picture she'd presented a few seconds ago.

Her gaze drilled into his, allowing him to look his fill, waiting for him to say something.

But he had no idea what to say.

She finally turned away, presenting him with her unblemished profile again. Her shoulders drooped slightly, but she gave no other sign that she'd noted his reaction.

"So now you know." Her voice was steady and surprisingly unemotional as she reached back and pulled her close-fitting bonnet up once more. "Your brother understood what he was taking on by marrying me. And he also understood why I would see his offer as a welcome opportunity to finally have a family of my own."

Her acceptance of his unguarded reaction made him feel like a complete oaf, like the worst kind of mannerless fool. "I "

She raised a hand, palm out. "There's no need to say anything, Mr. Tyler." She faced him fully again, her smile perhaps a little too bright. "I assure you I'm quite accustomed to such first-time reactions."

It was good of her to give him an out, but his momma raised him better than that. "Look, ma'am, I'm sorry I was so rude. You caught me by surprise, is all. And, well, I don't believe in fancy speeches or anything, but I want you to know I admire you for agreeing to my brother's scheme and coming out here on your own the way you did. I'm sure it wasn't an easy decision."

At least the whole situation made more sense now. It was exactly the kind of grand gesture Lanny would make.

Her smile warmed a bit. "You'd be surprised." Then she brushed at her skirt. "Now, if you don't mind, I think I'm ready to pay my respects to my—our—family."

Jack recognized her desire to change the subject. "Agreed." He helped her rise, then offered his arm as they made their way across the churchyard.

Once through the cemetery entrance, he led her around the inside perimeter, past the graves of his parents, to three freshly turned mounds with markers. Nell and Jed rested side by side, and Lanny was buried a few yards away, next to Julia's grave.

Jack stopped in front of Nell's grave while his companion trudged the last few steps to Lanny and Julia's resting places.

Somewhere nearby a blue jay squawked his displeasure. A heartbeat later Jack caught a flash of movement as a squirrel raced down the trunk of a nearby pecan tree.

Other than that, everything was hushed, still.

He frowned at the half dozen or so pink roses someone had placed on his sister's grave. That wasn't right. Daisies were Nell's favorite flower.

The memories pelted him, one after the other, piercing him with their clarity, battering his attempts to hold them at bay.

He could see his little sister, skipping along the fence row, pigtails bouncing, picking armloads of the yellow blooms. Then she'd sit under the oak tree in their yard and make braids and crowns and other little girl treasures for hours on end.

Ah, Nell, I'm so sorry I didn't come home sooner like you kept after me to. You always warned me I'd be sorry I waited so long, and as usual, you were right.

He twisted his hat brim in his hands.

I'll find you some daisies tomorrow, I promise. Bunches of them.

A leaf drifted on the breeze and landed on the grassless mound. Jack stared at it as if memorizing the nuances of color and the tracery of its veins were vital.

About those young'uns of yours. You know I don't know anything about being a father. And they sure deserve a lot better than me. But I swear to you, what-

ever happens, I'll do my level best to see that they're taken care of proper.

He wasn't sure if mere seconds or several minutes passed before he finally looked up and took his bearings again.

The woman, Callie—easier to think of her as Julia's friend than Leland's wife—stood between the markers that served as Lanny and Julia's headstones with her head bowed and her eyes closed.

Was she feeling faint?

Or praying?

As if she felt his gaze, she looked up and drew in a deep breath, then let it go on a sigh. Jack joined her and stared silently at his brother's grave.

Lanny, the big brother who was good at just about everything he attempted, who could be bossier than the day was long, but who bent over backwards to lend a hand where it was needed.

Regret threaded itself through Jack's feeling of loss. Why hadn't he come here sooner, made peace with Lanny, offered him the apology he deserved?

Now he would never have that chance....

Movement drew his gaze to Julia's grave. He watched as a butterfly, its wings the same deep blue that Julia's eyes had been, landed briefly on her marker, then fluttered toward them. It rested momentarily on Callie's bonnet before drifting away on the breeze.

When he looked back, he found her watching him. He straightened and shoved his hat back on his head. "Ready?"

She nodded and took the arm he offered. Their silence was companionable this time, all of the tension that had been there when they marched through town earlier having evaporated.

He was surprised to realize how glad he was that she'd been here these past few minutes. Somehow it felt right to have her share this graveside visit, to mourn alongside him for a few moments over their mutual loss.

"Those poor little ones," she said softly. "They must be so confused and frightened by what's happened."

The mention of the children brought back his earlier worries. Was he up to the job of playing nursemaid to three confused and frightened young'uns?

"Who's been looking out for them since the accident?" she asked.

"Mrs. Mayweather." At her questioning look, he elaborated. "Sweetgum's schoolteacher. She offered to take them in until I could get here."

"How kind of her. Does she have children of her own?"

Jack smiled at the thought of the major general of a woman that was Alberta Mayweather having a husband to "take care of her." "The 'Mrs.' is more of a courtesy title," he explained. "She never married. But Mrs. Mayweather's been schoolteacher here since before I was born, and she knows what she's doing when it comes to watching over young'uns."

Unlike me.

Jack's gut tightened. He had quite a tangle to deal with, and it kept growing. He still hadn't figured out what he was going to do about the three kids, and now he had to add Lanny's widow to the mix.

Of course, he probably wouldn't have that added worry for long. Now that Lanny was gone, she'd likely head back to Ohio where she'd be amongst people she knew.

"Then they're lucky to have someone like her looking out for them." Her steps quickened slightly. "But the sooner they can settle into a permanent home again with family around them, the better it'll be."

Hah! Easy enough for her to say. She didn't have the responsibility of making it happen.

Her sigh interrupted his thoughts. "I just pray that, with God's help, I can be a good mother to Annabeth."

Mother? Jack stopped in his tracks.

"Wait just a minute. You can't honestly believe you're going to take charge of my niece."

He might not know how to be a father, but he'd just made a solemn promise to Nell and Lanny to give it his best shot. And there was no way he'd break a promise like that. No sir, he wasn't about to hand any of those kids over to a stranger.

No matter who she'd been married to.

Her eyes widened, but she didn't back down. "In case you've forgotten, helping to raise Annabeth was the reason Leland asked me to come here. I'm still Annabeth's stepmother. Of course I'm going to take care of her," she said as if it was the most logical thing in the world.

"Stepmother!" He rubbed the back of his neck, more to keep himself from reaching out to shake some sense into the woman than anything else. "You were married to my brother for less than half a day. Why, I'll wager you've never even laid eyes on Annabeth, have you?"

She crossed her arms and he saw a flash of temper in her eyes. "Have you?"

He didn't much care for the ring of challenge in her tone. "I'm her blood kin," he argued, sidestepping the question. "It's my responsibility to—"

She yanked the marriage papers from her handbag and held them in front of his face. "Not according to these documents."

The woman was downright maddening. If she

thought for one minute he was going to let her lay claim to Annabeth, she was going to be mighty disappointed.

He was maddening! Why couldn't he see that this was something she needed to do, was meant to do? It *had* to be why God had led her here.

That reminder drew Callie up short.

There she went, making assumptions again.

"I'm sorry." She offered a conciliatory smile. "I don't believe either of us is thinking clearly right now. I'm certain we both have Annabeth's best interests at heart, and that's what counts. We just need to make certain we understand what those are."

His expression didn't soften a bit. "The best thing for her right now is to be with her family. And that's me and her cousins."

Callie took a deep breath and tried again. "Mr. Tyler, why don't we call a truce for the moment. At least long enough to pray about it. I'm sure God will help us resolve this if we just look to Him for guidance."

Her oh-so-stubborn brother-in-law didn't answer right away. Instead, he gave her a peculiar look.

A prickly unease stole over her, engulfing her like a scratchy woolen cloak.

No. She must have misinterpreted his expression.

Leland and Julia had been such steadfast Christians. Surely Leland's brother...

She forced her lips to form the question.

"You *do* believe in God, Mr. Tyler, don't you?"

Chapter Five

Callie watched as Jack paused, rubbing the back of his neck. Then he gestured back the way they'd come. "My dad helped build that church and my mother was the organist there for years."

She frowned. What his parents did or didn't do had nothing to do with—

"It's just, well, I'm not really the praying sort."

The words shocked her. "I don't understand."

He shifted his weight. "Look, I don't have anything against folks praying if they've a mind to. It's just that I don't believe in asking for handouts myself. I cotton more to the 'God helps those who help themselves' way of thinking."

Callie blinked. Surely she'd misunderstood. "Mr. Tyler, asking for guidance and direction from our Heavenly Father is *not* the same as asking for a handout." She saw the skepticism in his eyes and tried again. "Besides which, there is absolutely nothing wrong with humbling ourselves before the Almighty."

He waved his hand as if to brush her words aside. "Ma'am, you just go right ahead and pray for guidance if that makes you feel better." Then he folded his arms across his chest and his eyes turned flinty. "But I'm telling you right now, there's nothing on earth—or in heaven, for that matter—that's going to convince me to turn any member of my family over to a stranger, no matter how strong that stranger might think her claim is."

Callie pursed her lips, not trusting herself to respond immediately. It wasn't about just Annabeth now. All three youngsters deserved to have a proper Christian influence in their lives. It was what their parents would have wanted for them, and it was the right thing to do. Actually, it was the most important thing.

She might not be the best person to fill that role, but God could use even the most flawed vessel to do His work. She was more determined than ever to have a hand in raising these children.

She focused again on Leland's brother. He seemed to have nothing in common at the moment with the compassionate, generous man she'd come to know through years of correspondence.

Not the praying kind indeed!

Time to try another tack. "Mr. Tyler, I find myself quite weary from the day's events, and would prefer not to stand here arguing with you. I'd like to meet Annabeth and then find a place to refresh myself, if you don't mind."

His eyes narrowed and she wondered for a minute if he would continue to argue despite her request. But he gave a quick nod. "Of course. This way."

As he offered his arm he gave her a warning look. "Just don't think this means I've changed my thinking. You're welcome to stick around if you've a mind to. But the care of the children—*all* of the children—is my responsibility."

We'll just see about that. After the briefest of hesitations, she placed her hand on his arm, giving him her sweetest smile. "I must admit, your concern for the well-being of the children does do you credit, Mr. Tyler."

Jack escorted his suspiciously compliant sister-in-law to Mrs. Mayweather's home. The woman wasn't fooling him with that winsome smile and those sugar-coated words of hers. He knew good and well she hadn't given up the battle yet.

Well, she could scheme and plot all she wanted. It didn't change his mind one jot about his duty to Annabeth, Simon and Emma.

But as they drew closer to Mrs. Mayweather's home, his thoughts turned from Lanny's widow to the three children.

What was he going to say to them? He was their closest living kin, but he'd never laid eyes on them before—not since Nell's oldest was an infant, anyway—and they certainly didn't know him.

How much had their parents told them about him? Or had the subject of their absent Uncle Jack ever even come up?

How would they react when they met him? How would he deal with their grief when he was still trying to absorb the loss himself?

His free hand clenched and unclenched. How could this woman walking beside him talk about looking to God for guidance when that same God allowed such a thing to happen in the first place? If the Almighty had wanted to take another Tyler, it should have been him. His passing, unlike that of his brother and sister, wouldn't have left a hole in anyone's life.

His face must have betrayed some of what he was thinking because Callie cast a questioning glance his way. Luckily, they had finally reached Mrs. Mayweather's front gate.

"Here we are," he said, cutting off any comment she might have made. He opened the gate without meeting her gaze and gestured for her to precede him up the flagstone walkway.

Before they'd made it halfway to the porch, a tall, spare woman stepped out to greet them.

Age had definitely not interfered with Mrs. Mayweather's commanding presence. From the top of her tightly wound, steel gray bun to the hem of her no-frills, severely cut skirt, she still had that force-to-be-reckoned-with schoolmarm look that could quiet a classroom full of rowdy children with just a raised brow.

"Hello, Jackson. It's good to see you back in Sweetgum again. My condolences for your loss."

Facing her, Jack felt like a ten-year-old schoolboy again. "Thank you, ma'am." He quickly turned to Callie. "This is " He paused for the merest fraction of a second and she immediately stepped forward.

"Callista Tyler, ma'am. I am—was—married to Leland Tyler."

Mrs. Mayweather nodded. "Yes. Virgil stopped by to explain the situation. Most astounding." She paused a minute. "I must say, you seem to be holding up remarkably well under what must have been a terrible shock."

"It's kind of you to say so, ma'am." She gave her bonnet a tug. "I'm afraid the full impact of the situation hasn't entirely sunk in yet."

"Understandable." Mrs. Mayweather tilted her head thoughtfully. "Callista. Unusual name, that. You wouldn't by any chance be Julia's friend Callie."

"Why, yes." Her smile warmed and some of the tension eased from her stance. "It seems my fame precedes me."

"Well then, that explains quite a bit." The schoolteacher nodded in satisfaction as if she'd solved a puzzle of some sort. "Julia always spoke of you in such glowing terms. It's no wonder Leland turned to you for this special kind of help after she passed on."

She waved toward the far end of the porch. "By the way, since we weren't certain how things would sort themselves out, I instructed Virgil to deposit your baggage here for the time being."

"Why, thank you, I—" The widow seemed a bit overwhelmed by their hostess.

Jack knew the feeling. He stepped forward. "Where are the children?"

"They're upstairs, digging through an old trunk of mine. I'll call them down shortly, but I thought it would be best if we had a chat first."

"Of course." Jack felt a guilty surge of relief at being able to put off the moment of truth a little longer.

Mrs. Mayweather stepped aside. "Now come on in to the parlor. You both look as if you could do with a cool glass of lemonade, and we have matters to discuss."

Callie nodded. "Thank you. That sounds lovely."

Jack removed his hat and followed the ladies inside.

"You may set your hat on the hall table there, Jackson." She turned to Callie. "Feel free to set your bonnet and handbag there as well."

He tensed in sympathy. What would Callie do? How would she handle this?

Once again, she surprised him. Though she moved with a sort of deliberate slowness, her initial hesitation was so brief he doubted Mrs. Mayweather noted it.

With steady hands, she loosened the strings to her bonnet and let it fall behind her head.

Mrs. Mayweather studied her for a minute. "A birthmark, I presume?" At Callie's nod, she pursed her lips thoughtfully. "Yes, indeed. I'm beginning to understand why Julia had such respect and admiration for you."

Callie was startled by the woman's words and didn't know how to respond, so she said nothing. She pulled her bonnet back up, wondering exactly how much Julia had said about her and to whom.

Mrs. Mayweather raised a hand to stop her. "No need to do that on my account."

Callie smiled, but firmly tied her ribbons. "Thank you, but I'd rather that not be the first view the children have of me."

"As you wish." A slight nod accompanied the words. "But I think you would be surprised by how accepting children can be."

A few moments later, they were seated in the parlor and Mrs. Mayweather was pouring glasses of lemonade.

"I know a man of the world such as yourself would probably prefer something stronger," she said as Jack reached for his, "but I'm afraid you will have to make do with this for now."

"This will do just fine, thank you." He took a long drink, then set the glass down. "So how are the young'uns doing?"

Mrs. Mayweather's face softened in concern and Callie saw a whole new side of her.

"About as one would expect. They went through such a horrid experience. At least they didn't have to witness the fire firsthand."

Callie sent up a silent prayer of thanksgiving. She'd worried…

"As it happens, Simon had taken Emma and Annabeth down to the livery," Mrs. Mayweather continued briskly. "He wanted to show them a new foal that had been born the day before. When they heard the alarm, they headed back to the café. Luckily, the O'Connor sisters spotted them and had sense enough to keep them from going anywhere near the fire."

Callie saw past the woman's businesslike tone. "And so you took them in."

Mrs. Mayweather nodded. "I had the room and the time to see to them, since school had let out for summer the week before."

Jack stood and moved to one of the windows. "Still, I'm very beholden," he said without turning around.

"I just thank the Lord I had the means to step in." She refilled Callie's glass. "But back to your question. The tragedy has affected each of them differently. Simon has turned from an active, outgoing boy to one who is belligerent and aloof."

She waved a hand. "Emma has always been a quiet child, but now she clings to Simon like bark to a tree. She can barely stand to have him out of her sight for more than a few minutes. Simon is taking his role of big brother seriously—too seriously, if you ask me. He insisted I set his cot in the room with the girls when Emma balked at separating from him even in sleep."

"And Annabeth?"

Mrs. Mayweather sighed. "I'm not certain. Bless her, she was just beginning to move on from the loss of her mother, then this happened. She misses her father terribly, of course. But the child, who's normally quite the little chatterbox, has barely said a word since the accident, except in answer to a direct question."

Callie twisted her hands nervously in her skirts. "Do you think she knows? About me, I mean."

Mrs. Mayweather gave her a sympathetic smile. "If so, she hasn't given any sign. But, as I mentioned, she hasn't said more than a handful of words since her father passed. Besides, even if Leland did say something to her, she may not have understood. She's only four, after all."

Jack turned to face them and crossed his arms. "It doesn't matter whether she knows or not. Like I said, Annabeth is my concern now."

Callie carefully set her glass down, resisting the urge to retort in kind. *Lord, give me patience. Please!*

She caught a measuring look Mrs. Mayweather gave the two of them.

The woman stood. "Well, I can tell the children certainly won't want for family willing to take them in. You two help yourselves to more lemonade while I let them know you're here."

Jack's expression gave nothing away, but she saw him rub the back of his neck. Was he as nervous about facing the children for the first time as she was?

Moments later, Callie's entire being focused on the sound of footsteps tromping down the stairs.

Simon entered first, looking both ready to take on the world and achingly vulnerable at the same time. His sister, Emma, was close by his side, her arm wound tightly with his, her eyes wide and uncertain.

But it was the third and youngest of the children that captured Callie's attention. The little girl hung back a bit while still holding on to Emma's other hand.

Callie would have been able to pick Annabeth out of

a ballroom full of little girls. She looked so much like Julia it made her heart ache. The same bouncy blond curls, the same bright blue eyes, the same pink bow of a mouth.

Mrs. Mayweather spoke up first. "Children, remember I told you that your Uncle Jack would be coming?" She made a flourishing movement with her hand. "Well, here he is."

Then she gestured toward Callie. "And we also have a surprise visitor."

Annabeth stared at Callie with wide, questioning eyes. Was it possible the child was expecting her after all?

Simon, however, seemed to be the designated spokesman for the trio. He completely ignored Callie as he gave Jack an assessing look. "So you're our Uncle Jack."

Jack strode to the middle of the room. "That's right. And I've come to take care of you." He smiled at the two girls. "All of you."

None of the three returned Jack's smile.

"Momma talked about you some." Simon's tone hadn't softened. "And she read your letters to us when they came." His eyes narrowed. "It made her sad that you never came around."

To Callie's surprise, Jack didn't attempt to make excuses.

Instead he nodded and walked right up to his nephew. "I'm sorry about that—more sorry than you can rightly know. I should have been a better brother to both her and your Uncle Lanny." He laid a hand on Simon's shoulder. "But I'm here now."

Simon didn't seem appeased. "She said you had to move around a lot 'cause you work for the railroad." The boy put a protective arm around his sister's shoulder.

"Does that mean we have to travel around the country with you?"

Callie found herself as interested as Simon was to hear Jack's answer.

Jack took a minute, stepping back and crossing his arms again. "Well, now, I plan to stay right here in Sweetgum for the time being. We're going to stick together, just like families are supposed to."

Emma sidled closer to her brother's side, drawing Annabeth with her. "But where are we going to live? Our house is all gone now." Her voice was so soft Callie had to lean forward to hear her.

Jack nodded solemnly. "I know, and I've been giving that some thought. Your house may be gone but Annabeth's house is still sound. And I'll just bet she'd be glad to let us all live there with her."

Annabeth, who hadn't yet taken her eyes off Callie, turned to Emma. "Oh, yes," she said, nodding her head emphatically. "There's lots and lots of room there. You could even bring Cookie and nobody would care how much he barked out there."

"There now." Jack gave Emma an encouraging smile. "You've been to Annabeth's house before, haven't you? It's the same house your momma lived in when she was your age."

Emma nodded, tentatively responding to Jack's smile.

But Simon was far from won over. "Annabeth's house is on a farm way out in the country. All of our friends live here in town."

Annabeth's face crumpled into a hurt expression. "But Simon, it's a very nice house. Don't you want to come live with me?"

Emma gave her young cousin's hand a squeeze.

"Simon didn't mean anything by that. Of course he likes your house." She gave her brother a little nudge. "Don't you?"

Simon gave a grudging nod.

Appeased, Annabeth turned her attention back to Callie. She let go of Emma's hand and took a tentative step forward, her head cocked at a questioning angle. "Are you going to come live with us, too?"

Callie clasped her hands together tightly, fighting the urge to reach out for the child. She didn't want to frighten her. "Would you like for me to?"

Annabeth crossed the room and stopped directly in front of her. With pudgy fingers that weren't quite clean, she reached up and started to push aside Callie's bonnet.

Callie's first instinct was to pull back, to stop the child from revealing the hidden ugliness. But something about the hope in the little girl's expression changed her mind.

Forcing herself to sit completely still, Callie held her breath and waited for Annabeth's reaction.

Chapter Six

As soon as the bonnet fell back, Callie heard a startled gasp from Emma and peripherally noted the way Simon's eyes widened.

But Annabeth's response was entirely unexpected.

A large smile blossomed on her face and she touched the discolored skin almost reverently. "It's you," she said, her voice tinged with delight. "You finally came."

Callie's heart hitched painfully as she expelled the breath she'd been holding. "Annabeth, do you know who I am?"

The child nodded emphatically. "Oh, yes. You're the lady Daddy said was going to come live with us, to be my new mommy." Her face took on a more somber expression. "I was so scared you wouldn't come since Daddy wasn't here anymore."

"Oh, sweetheart, there wasn't any reason to worry." Callie smoothed the child's hair. "I came here as much to be with you as with your daddy."

Callie's heart lightened at this further evidence that Leland had never wavered in his commitment to keep his promise. "So, your daddy told you about me?"

"Yes, ma'am." Annabeth smiled. "He said we were

lucky you were coming to stay with us, that you were a friend of Momma's ever since she was my age. But it was supposed to be a secret so he could tell Aunt Nell and Uncle Jed first." She gave Callie an anxious look. "I didn't tell anyone, I promise."

Callie touched the child's cheek. "I know you didn't, sweetie. Your daddy would be very proud of you. But how did you know I was the one?"

"Because of what daddy said about you. He told me you were very special because you have angel kisses on the side of your face."

A lump formed in Callie's throat. That's what Julia used to say when they were little girls. It had always made her feel so special.

Annabeth stared deep into her eyes. "Do you think my daddy is up in heaven getting angel kisses, too?"

Callie pulled the child onto her lap. "Of course I do. And your mommy is right there with him. I imagine both of them are watching you and smiling at how brave you are."

Annabeth gave a satisfied nod and then threw her arms around Callie in a tight embrace.

Callie buried her face in the child's curls, feeling an immediate bond with her. The fierceness of her desire to cherish and protect Julia's child was almost frightening.

Dear God, please don't put this sweet child into my life just to separate us again. If it be Your will, help me make Lanny's brother understand that I need to be here.

She glanced up to find Jack staring at her, frowning uncertainly. Surely he could see how right it was that she have some hand in the child's upbringing, couldn't he?

But Annabeth wasn't the only child who needed reassurances here. Callie gave Julia's daughter one last squeeze. Then she put her down and stood, looking at the other two children. "You must be Simon and Emma

Carson. I'm a very good friend of your Aunt Julia, and I came here to live with Annabeth."

Neither child said anything, but their gazes remained locked on the red splotch that marred Callie's face.

Callie drifted closer, casually pulling her bonnet back in place and tying the ribbons as she did so. "Your Aunt Julia and I used to write to each other. Her letters were quite long and wonderful. She shared all kinds of things about this town and her favorite people here. And that included you two, of course."

"It did?" Emma seemed more at ease now that Callie's bonnet was back in place.

"What kind of things did she say about us?" Simon's voice held a note of challenge.

"Well, I know you're eleven years old, that you're a good student, and that you're also good at building things."

Simon seemed surprised by her words, but she noticed his chest puffed out with pride a bit.

Callie turned to Emma. "And as for you, young lady, you are eight years old and your Aunt Julia thought you were a very fine artist. She said you were always drawing her the prettiest pictures. Her favorites were the ones with flowers and rainbows."

"I like to draw," Emma acknowledged. She finally met Callie's gaze. "Why do you call it angel kisses?"

Callie was relieved the girl was comfortable enough to talk about it. As Mrs. Mayweather had said earlier, children were usually much more forthright in confronting the subject than adults.

"I was born with this mark," she explained. "Sometimes, when your Aunt Julia and I were little girls, she would tell me that she thought it was there because just before God sent me down to be with my parents, one of his angels bent over and kissed me on the cheek."

Emma studied Callie's face, as if trying to see past the bonnet. "Does it hurt?"

"Not at all. It's always been just a part of who I am." Callie gently touched a spot near the corner of Emma's mouth. "Just like this little mole right here is a part of you."

"Oh." Emma's hand reached for the spot Callie had touched. "And like my friend Molly's freckles?"

"That's right. But I tell you what. I know it's a little scary right at first. So why don't I just keep this bonnet on for the time being, at least until we get to know each other better."

Emma nodded. Then her brow furrowed. "What are we supposed to call you?"

Caught off guard, Callie glanced up at Jack. She had no real claim on Simon and Emma. But, then again, she *had* been married to their uncle. She turned back to Emma. "Why don't you just call me Aunt Callie?"

"Aunt Callie." Emma tried out the name, then nodded approval. "That's nice."

"That's settled then."

"So you *will* be living at the farm with us." Annabeth made the pronouncement with all the confidence of a self-assured four-year-old.

Jack cleared his throat and Simon started to voice another protest.

But Mrs. Mayweather stepped in before either of them got very far. "Children." With that one word, she claimed everyone's attention. "Why don't the three of you go outside and check on Cookie. Simon, there is a bone left over from yesterday's supper on the kitchen counter that you may take to him."

Once the children left the room, Jack turned to Mrs. Mayweather. "I want to thank you again for taking them in until I could get here." He rubbed the back of his neck again. "I suppose I should ask them to pack up their things so we can head on over to the farm."

Callie sat up straighter. No! He was *not* going to sidestep her claim that easily. Those children needed her. "I don't believe that is your decision to make, Mr. Tyler."

He frowned. "We've already—"

She cut off his attempt to play the kin card again. "As your brother's widow, I believe I should have some say as to who will be staying at the farm."

"Are you saying you want to go out there yourself?"

"I don't—"

Mrs. Mayweather held up a hand to halt their discussion. "It appears to me that the two of you have some things to work out in respect to the children's future. After all, you only learned the full extent of the situation a few hours ago."

"It seems pretty cut and dried to me," Jack groused.

Mrs. Mayweather drew herself up. "Jackson Garret Tyler, I will thank you to mind your tone when you are in my home."

Apparently it didn't matter how old Jack was—he would always be a recalcitrant schoolboy to Mrs. Mayweather. Callie carefully swallowed a grin.

Jack mumbled an apology, chafing under Mrs. Mayweather's obvious censure.

He wasn't sure what was wrong with him today. One minute he was breaking out in a cold sweat at the thought of taking sole responsibility for the three kids, and the next he was ready to fight to the death against anyone who'd dare try to take that privilege from him.

Mrs. Mayweather smoothed her skirts and gave them both equally stern looks. "Now, you've had a long day, both physically and emotionally. This is probably not the best time for you to make any major decisions."

Callie nodded. "I agree. It would be best if we spent a little more time seeking guidance in this matter."

Jack bit back a retort. There she went with that "seeking guidance" talk again. Didn't the woman know how to make a decision on her own? Or did she think her delaying tactics would give her some sort of advantage in their tug-of-war?

Mrs. Mayweather, however, didn't give him an opportunity to voice his objections. "Quite sensible. I insist the children stay here with me another night or two, while you two get everything worked out. It would be criminal to uproot them again before there is some certainty as to where they will live and with whom." She looked from Callie to Jack. "Are we agreed?"

"Yes, ma'am." Callie's response was quick and confident.

No surprise there. It was exactly what she wanted—time to build her case. But he couldn't come up with an argument that didn't sound petty, so, under Mrs. Mayweather's stern gaze, he had no choice but to follow suit. "Yes, ma'am."

"Very well. Jackson, you are welcome to stay for supper. The more time you and Callista spend in the children's company, the better for everyone. Afterward, I suggest you spend the night at the farm. It will relieve Virgil of the responsibility of taking care of the chores in the morning. You may use my horse and buggy to get there."

She rose as if the matter were settled. Which he supposed it was.

His brother's widow stood uncertainly. "I suppose I should get a room at the hotel."

Mrs. Mayweather frowned. "Nonsense. You'll stay here with me and the children."

She held up a hand, halting any protest Callie might make. "This is no time to stand on ceremony. Your presence has already made such a difference to Annabeth. She's spoken more in these past few minutes than she has the last four days."

Jack frowned at this point in Callie's favor in their battle for guardianship of the children.

"Besides," Mrs. Mayweather continued, "you can help me with some of the extra chores that have resulted from the presence of the children."

That seemed to seal the deal for Callie. "Of course. Thank you."

There was a feeling of feminine conspiracy to this. Not that the arrangement didn't make sense from a strictly logistical standpoint. The only problem was, it let his sister-in-law have free rein with the kids while he was exiled to the farm. Which gave her a leg up in winning the children's favor.

He'd have to find a way to level the field.

Callie had mixed emotions that evening as she watched Jack walk out Mrs. Mayweather's kitchen door.

Just as when he'd started to walk away from her beside the stagecoach this afternoon, she felt as if a lifeline was slipping away from her, leaving her stranded in unfamiliar territory.

Strange. As stubborn as the man was, she felt they'd formed a connection of sorts. After all, when he wasn't being so pig-headedly combative over the matter of the children, he was actually nice. And even in that matter, one had to admire a man who was willing to take his perceived responsibilities so much to heart.

Callie turned away from the door with a tired sigh.

So much had happened today. It had begun with her looking forward to starting life as a wife and a mother, and ended with the discovery that she was a widow who would have to fight to maintain her claim on her stepchild. What a welcome to Texas. Her father would—

Oh, no! She raised a hand to her mouth and spun around to face her hostess.

"My goodness, dear, you look as if you just burned Sunday dinner and the preacher's at the door. Whatever is it?"

"I promised my family I'd send a telegraph when I arrived so they would know I was safe. It slipped my mind until just now." She grimaced. "I hate to impose, but would you have a piece of paper and a pen I could use?" Silly of her to feel this sense of urgency since she wouldn't be able to send the telegram until tomorrow. But doing this would provide a small bit of normalcy to a day that had spun out of control.

A few minutes later, Callie sat at a small desk tucked in the parlor. She dipped the pen in the inkwell, then paused.

What would she say? How much *should* she say?

Her family worried about her so. No good would be served by adding to their concerns. After all, she had confidence that God would see her through this.

But she couldn't lie to them.

Best to keep it short and non-committal for the moment. Nodding to herself, she quickly jotted down three sentences.

Have arrived safely in Sweetgum. Already made new friends who have welcomed me warmly. Will send a letter with further news soon.

As she set the pen down, Callie's thoughts turned to resuming her battle of wits with Jackson Garret Tyler in the morning.

Surprisingly, her feeling about this was not dread—but anticipation.

Chapter Seven

Jack clicked his tongue, encouraging the horse to pick up the pace as the sun edged lower on the horizon. Not that he needed daylight to find his way. Even after eleven years, the road was as familiar to him as his own face.

He'd already made a quick stop at Virgil's place to let him know he wouldn't need to worry about handling the chores at the Tyler farm any longer. Luckily he'd caught Virgil out in the barn so he hadn't had to spend time on pleasantries with his friend's family. There'd be time enough for neighborly visits in the days to come.

Jack didn't really consider himself a sentimental man, so the little kick of expectation that hit him when he turned the buggy onto the familiar drive surprised him.

As soon as the house came into full view, he tugged on the reins, halting the horse and buggy. The sight that greeted him was at once soul-deep familiar and strangely foreign.

The same two-story gabled structure sat on the lawn like a fat hen guarding her nest.

The same large oak tree spread its made-for-climbing branches over the left side of the lawn.

The same red barn pointed its cupola to the sky.

But Lanny and Julia, not to mention Father Time, had made noticeable changes. There was now a roomy swing on one end of the wraparound front porch. The oak tree was several feet taller and its branches shaded a much larger patch of ground than Jack remembered. And the gray-and-black speckled dog that came bounding from behind the barn was nothing like ole Clem.

With another flick of the reins, Jack directed the horse around the house and into the barn.

There were several changes in here as well. The old buggy had been replaced with a roomier one and it seemed Lanny had invested in some interesting-looking tools and equipment. It might be worth his while to do a little exploring in here when he had some time.

But for now he had to take care of bedding down the animals while there was still light enough to see by. He gave the energetic dog a bit of attention, then unhitched the horse and patted the animal as it moved past him toward the water trough.

As he worked at the chores that had once been second nature, his mind wondered over the day's happenings.

Callie was a puzzle to him. Her intentions and determination were admirable, but he didn't believe she understood what she was up against. Such an obviously sheltered city girl would have a hard time adjusting to life in a place like this. Especially now that she didn't have a husband to smooth the way for her.

Still, there was something about the woman, something about the way she faced a fracas head-on rather than shying away that he found intriguing.

Had her life back in Ohio been so terrible that even with what had happened, she—

Jack gave his head a shake. He'd let her get under his skin. He had to remember that her personal problems were no concern of his. She wanted to challenge his claim to Annabeth, and that made her his opponent.

He gave the carriage horse one last brush with the currycomb then patted her again, sending her into an empty stall.

Once he'd fed and watered the other animals and taken care of the evening milking, Jack headed for the house. As he climbed the porch steps he ran a hand over the familiar support post. The etched image of a rearing horse his father had carved into the wood one rainy summer afternoon was still discernable, even under the layer of new paint.

Family mattered. Shared history mattered. That was something only he could offer those kids.

Jack stepped inside, noting the addition of a new screen door as he passed. He wandered through the first floor, feeling strangely disoriented by the mix of the familiar and the new. Everywhere he looked he could see where Julia and Lanny's lives together had left a lasting imprint on the Tyler family home. New curtains here, a new chair there. A tin type picture of Julia's parents now shared space on the mantle with those of the Tyler family. There was also a tintype of Lanny and Julia. Julia held an infant on her lap.

He soon discovered a room had been tacked on to the back of the house. Inside sat a shiny porcelain bathtub and some new-fangled laundry equipment. A hand pump stood against the far wall, sprouting from the back lip of a large metal sink. Next to the sink, a small iron fire box supported a large kettle, ready to heat the water when needed. Large windows set high on three of the four walls would provide ventilation without sacrificing privacy. Someone had even strung a cord below the rafters, no doubt to be used for hanging wet laundry when the weather made it uncomfortable to do so outside.

Not for the first time Jack admired his brother's ingenuity. He could see how this setup would have been a great convenience for Julia. And it would make his life here with the kids that much easier, too.

Jack climbed the stairs, curious to see the bedchambers.

The first room he stepped into was the one he and Lanny had shared as children. Gone were the rock collections, pouches of marbles and patched overalls that had once marked it as the room of two active boys.

Now, everything was clean and neatly arranged. A number of subtle feminine touches had been added, too, no doubt thanks to Julia.

Still, if one looked close enough, the memories were there, lurking in the shadows. Memories of horseplay and fights, of discussions in the dark long after they were supposed to be asleep, of the big brother he'd adored and resented by turns.

Jack stepped farther into the room, looking for the wooden chests his father had built for them. He and Lanny had used them to store their few personal possessions.

Lanny's was nowhere in sight but Jack found his tucked below the window sill with a lace doily and a needlework picture of some flowers on top.

Inside were the things he'd treasured growing up, the few items that had been his alone, that had never belonged to Lanny. He lifted out a leather pouch with a grin. It contained exactly twelve marbles—two nice sized aggies and ten immies. Lanny had given him two of these and taught him how to use them, but the rest Jack had won for himself from schoolyard games.

Of course, he'd never beaten Lanny. Lanny had been good at just about everything he tried. Much as Jack loved his brother, growing up in his shadow hadn't been easy.

Which was one of the reasons he'd left Sweetgum. Only he'd never intended to stay away so long.

Jack shut the lid on the chest and left the room. Too bad he couldn't shut out his feelings of guilt so easily.

He walked across the hall and opened the door to Nell's old room. It still had the stamp of a little girl occupant—lace and frills and brightly colored hair ribbons everywhere. This had to be Annabeth's domain now.

A rag doll lay on the bed. He should bring it to her in the morning, to give her back a little bit of her home.

Jack reached for it, but his fingers curled back into his palm. There was no similar memento he could bring to Nell's kids. How would they feel as they watched Annabeth enjoy her piece of home?

He turned and left the room empty-handed.

Jack skipped the room next to Annabeth's and moved instead to the one across from it. This used to be his mother's domain. Its main function had been as a sewing room, but it had served a multitude of other purposes, too. A pull-down bed had turned it into a guest room when the rare overnight visitor came calling. Spare odds and ends had been stored on shelves that lined two of the walls. And his mother had also hung dried flowers and herbs in bunches from the rafters.

As soon as Jack pushed the door open, he was assaulted by the familiar smells of his childhood. Floral scents mingled with dill, mustard and mint. He could almost imagine his mother working in here, humming in that off-key way she had.

As he looked at the room, he noticed a nearly finished lap quilt attached to the quilting frame, patiently waiting for the seamstress who would never return.

A moment later it hit him that it wasn't a lap quilt but one made for a baby's bed.

He turned abruptly and left the room, closing the door firmly behind him.

The only room left to visit was the one that his parents had slept in. Except it would now be Lanny's room, the one he and Julia had shared when she was alive. The one he had, no doubt, been prepared to share with Callie.

Jack decided he'd faced enough ghosts from his past for one night. He took the stairs two at a time and headed straight for the front door. Stepping out on the porch, he took a deep, soul-cleansing breath. Leaning his elbows on the rail, he listened to the night sounds and stared out at the shadowy forms of the landscape.

So many reminders, so many pieces of his family's history—and dreams for the future—encompassed in this building, this place.

Did it all really belong to Lanny's widow now? Just because of some quirk of timing that had her married to his older brother for a few short hours before his death?

If a person really decided to press the matter, he could argue that you couldn't even call it married.

But it seemed mean-spirited to challenge her claim. After all, she'd come out here in good faith, pursuing her own dreams, and none of what had happened had been her fault.

It might be better for all concerned if he offered to

buy out her claim on the farm. That way she could either purchase herself a place in town or head on back to where she came from with a nice little nest egg in hand.

As for the guardianship of Annabeth, Callie would come around on that once he talked to her again. Sure, he didn't know exactly how he was going to handle raising the youngsters on his own, but he'd find a way. After all, there was no arguing that it was his responsibility to take care of Simon and Emma, so it just made sense for him to take Annabeth as well.

How much extra work could one little girl be?

The crux of the matter kept coming down to the fact that he and the kids were blood kin. Even a woman as stubborn as Lanny's widow was proving herself to be couldn't deny that they belonged together.

Yes, that was the best way to go.

And hang it all, he still believed someone like her just didn't fit in here in Sweetgum, especially not all on her own. She'd be as out of place as a canary in a hen house.

Not that the woman lacked spirit. It had taken a lot of gumption for her to make it this far. And she certainly didn't let the thought of what others might think of that birthmark stand in her way. Yes, all in all, quite a spirited woman.

Too bad she was so all-fired muleheaded.

Jack pushed away from the porch rail and jammed his hands in his pockets.

He'd never met a woman like her. True, it had been a while since he'd spent much time in what his mother used to call "polite company," but he figured things hadn't changed all that much. Callie was...well...hang it all, he hadn't quite figured out what she was, besides being a thorn in his side. And just plain wrong about her rights in regard to Annabeth.

On the other hand, could he really say the kids would be better off with him than with her?

Rather than pursue that thought, he decided to turn in for the night.

Callie gently eased her armload of dirty breakfast dishes down on the counter next to the sink. She started rolling up her sleeves, then paused at the sound of a knock on the back door.

Mrs. Mayweather, who'd just placed a large kettle on the stove, glanced over her shoulder. "Callista, would you see who that is, please?"

Callie had a pretty good idea who was on the other side of the door, and she was certain Mrs. Mayweather did as well, but she dutifully wiped her hands on her borrowed apron. "Of course."

As expected, she opened the door to find Jack standing there. He had a pail in one hand and a basket in the other.

"Ah, Jackson, there you are." Mrs. Mayweather waved him in from behind Callie. "We saved you a bit of breakfast."

"Thanks. It sure does smell good." He lifted his offerings. "I brought some eggs and fresh milk for your larder."

Studying his easy smile and friendly manner, Callie decided the man could be something of a charmer when he set his mind to it.

Mrs. Mayweather obviously agreed. She beamed approvingly as she held out her hands. "Wonderful. I'll take those and put them away. You go on to the sink and wash up."

She nodded to Callie as she passed. "Would you hand him a plate, please?"

Callie nodded and stepped past Jack, reaching into the cupboard. "Mrs. Mayweather brewed a pot of coffee. Would you like a cup?"

"Yes, thank you."

There was a formality about their interactions today, a sort of stiff truce. But at least it *was* a truce.

She watched him heap a pile of eggs and two biscuits onto his plate, then he took a seat at the long kitchen table. Simon was still picking at his own breakfast but the girls had finished theirs.

Annabeth immediately moved to Jack's side. "Did you see Cinnamon and Taffy and Pepper last night?" she asked before he'd even settled in.

"Cinnamon, Taffy and Pepper." Jack drawled the words as he smeared jam on his biscuit. "Some of my favorite flavors. But I'm afraid I didn't look in the pantry."

Annabeth giggled. "They don't live in the pantry, silly."

"They don't?"

Callie smiled at the teasing tone in Jack's voice. Perhaps she'd been wrong about his ability to relate to the children. Maybe she should just step back and let him—

The memory of his declaration that he wasn't "the praying kind" interrupted her move toward retreat and stiffened her resolve. It just plain didn't matter how charming he could be, these children needed her in their lives, too.

But for now, she'd give him his share of time to create a connection with his nieces and nephew.

"They're animals, not food," Annabeth explained with exaggerated patience. She began to tick them off on her fingers. "Cinnamon is my pony and Taffy is the big yellow cat who lives in the barn and Pepper is our dog."

"Oh!" Jack did a good job of sounding surprised. "Well, in that case, yes, I saw all three of them."

The child twirled a curl with one pudgy finger. "Do you think they miss me?"

"I'm certain they do."

Emma set her elbows on the table next to Simon. "I have a dog, too."

Jack turned his attention to his other niece. "Do you?"

She nodded her head. "He's a beagle and his name is Cookie."

"Now, would he by any chance be that fine looking animal I saw outside next to Mrs. Mayweather's carriage house?"

Emma beamed at the compliment. "Uh-huh. And I had a bird, too. Mr. Peepers. But he…" Her lower lip began to tremble.

Callie caught the panicked look on Jack's face and quickly stepped in. "Emma, would you please bring me the empty platter from the stove?"

"Yes, ma'am."

Jack gave her a small nod and she felt a warm glow at this ever-so-slight sign of gratitude. Maybe he was finally beginning to see how she could help with the children. Perhaps they could work this whole matter out amicably after all.

A few moments later he carried his dishes to the sink. Then, without so much as a glance her way, he turned back to the children. "I plan to head back out to the farm to take care of some chores. Why don't you all come with me? Annabeth, you can visit with your animals. And Emma and Simon, you can take Cookie along and let him run as far and as long as he wants to."

Callie stiffened, the glow quickly evaporating. Was he actually planning to take the children and not her?

Annabeth clapped her hands in excitement. "Oh, yes! Do you think Mrs. Mayweather will let me bring some of her sugar cubes for Cinnamon?"

"We'll ask her," Jack answered. "But I'm sure it'll be all right."

"And Aunt Callie can come, too, can't she?"

Bless Annabeth's innocent little heart.

Jack cut her a quick glance, that stiff formality firmly back in place. "Yes, of course. That is, if she wants to?"

Was it her imagination, or did it sound as if he'd rather she declined the invitation?

She lifted her chin and smiled sweetly. "I need to make a stop at the telegraph office first, but I can't think of any place I'd rather be."

Chapter Eight

"Here we are."

Callie breathed a small sigh of relief, glad that she would finally be able to escape the confines of the buggy. The only men she'd been in such close proximity to before were her father and her sisters' husbands. Jack was a different sort of man altogether, and she wasn't exactly certain how to talk to him.

Not that he'd seemed to want to talk. The only conversation during the entire carriage ride had been among and with the children. The two adults had barely said three words to each other.

She certainly hoped the children hadn't picked up on the tension between her and Jack. They had enough to deal with at the moment without this added burden.

She leaned forward as Jack brought the carriage to a stop, forgetting her discomfort in her eagerness to view the homeplace Julia had written about in such loving detail over the years. The house, fronted by rosebushes and shaded on the left by a venerable oak, was as charming as she'd imagined it to be. An oversized swing hung from one end of the roomy front porch, and

Callie could picture Julia sitting there with Annabeth beside her, reading stories or doing a bit of needlework.

And surrounding the place were acres and acres of open farmland, God's handiwork, uncluttered by people or crowded buildings. Callie wanted to hug herself for the pure joy and sense of freedom it gave her.

The carriage had barely stopped before Annabeth scrambled down. A gray dog, his coat sprinkled with black spots, bounded up to meet them. Tail-waggingly ecstatic to see a familiar face, he nearly knocked Annabeth over in his eagerness to lavish her with dog kisses.

Annabeth giggled as she knelt down and hugged the dog. "That tickles."

Cookie barked at the duo from the safety of the buggy.

"Stop that," Emma chided, scratching the animal's ears. "You know Pepper is just playing with Annabeth."

Annabeth stood up. "Aunt Callie, this is Pepper. Don't be afraid, he won't hurt you."

"My, but he certainly is an exuberant animal."

The girl wrinkled her brow. "Zu-ber-ent?"

"Ex-u-ber-ent. It means joyful, active in a playful sort of way."

Annabeth grinned proudly as she stood up. "Yes, Pepper is *very* zuberent. If you come to the barn I'll show you my pony Cinnamon. He's not as zuberent as Pepper, but you'll like him."

Callie hid a grin. Annabeth had obviously found a new favorite word. "You go on. I'll be along in a minute."

By this time Simon and Emma had climbed down as well. Pepper and Cookie took a moment to check each other out, then started vying for the youngsters' attention.

The children ran off toward the barn, the dogs at their heels. Callie watched that beautiful sight until they disappeared around the corner. "It's wonderful to see them acting like the carefree children they're supposed to be. Bringing them out here was a good idea."

Jack merely nodded as he moved to help her down. Despite the tension between them, his touch was solicitous. There was protectiveness and assurance to be found there.

But as soon as her feet touched the ground he stepped back and gave her a challenging look, dispelling any notion she might have that his feelings had changed. "So, how much do you know about running a farm?"

His tone dripped skepticism.

She refused to let it throw her. "Your brother and I agreed that, besides caring for Annabeth, I would be responsible for the house and vegetable garden, and he would take care of the rest." She lifted her head. "It was always my intention, however, that with Leland's help I would learn more over time so I could be a proper helpmeet to him."

Jack nodded. "If you plan to live out here, there's definitely a whole lot more you'll need to learn. For one thing, there's the care of the animals. This place has two cows that'll need milking twice a day, a yearling and a young calf, a half dozen laying hens and a rooster, a mule and a horse—not to mention Annabeth's pony, the dog and at least one barn cat."

He tilted his hat back. "Then there's the haying, the constant maintenance, like fence mending and upkeep of the house and yard. And how do you feel about mucking out the barn and cleaning out the chicken coop?" He raised a brow. "Of course, if you had the means, I guess you could always hire someone to help out."

She lifted her chin, quite aware that he was trying to scare her away. Well, she was made of sterner stuff than that, as he'd soon find out. "Or I could just sell the whole place," she said giving him a challenging look of her own, "lock, stock and barrel." She tapped her chin with one finger. "With the proceeds I'm certain I could buy a nice little house in town for me and the children. Something cozier, with no animals and less upkeep."

It had been an idle threat, of course. She had no intention of selling the farm. Quite the contrary. She planned to hold on to this little parcel of solitude for all she was worth.

But to her surprise, he gave an approving nod. "Just what I was thinking. Rather than fight over who has the stronger claim, I think it would be better for all of us if I just bought it from you." He waved a hand. "As you said, lock, stock and barrel. I'm sure we can reach an agreement over a fair price."

Callie frowned. Surely he knew she hadn't been serious.

"Besides," he continued, "this is more than a farm. It's a Tyler family legacy. My granddad and dad built this place with their own hands. I don't intend to stand by and see it fall into some stranger's hands."

Did that include her? "Mr. Tyler, I'm very sorry if I gave you the wrong impression just now. I'm embarrassed to admit that I said what I did in a fit of pique." Which should teach her to guard her tongue more closely. "Selling this place is not an option I'd seriously consider."

She tugged her bonnet forward. "I'll admit I don't know anything about running a farm—*yet.* But I'm not afraid of hard work, and I consider myself very teachable."

He faced her head-on. "You're right. You *don't* know

anything about running a place like this." He took hold of both her hands and turned them palms up.

Her pulse jumped. When was the last time anyone, outside of her family, had held her hands so deliberately?

She couldn't remember.

And it certainly hadn't been with hands as large and calloused as these. Hands that seemed to contain a tightly leashed power and an ability to protect.

She gave her head a mental shake, trying to rid herself of the fanciful thoughts. Whatever his intentions, there was no affection in his touch, just a sense of purpose and tried patience.

But for a heartbeat, as her gaze locked on his, she saw his resolve falter, saw his expression shift into something she couldn't read. Had he felt that same off-balance feeling that she had?

Then the moment passed and his expression hardened again. "Look at these hands." His tone said clearly that he didn't approve of what he saw. "Not a callous in sight. These are *not* the hands of a person used to hard work."

Callie snatched her hands back, trying to ignore the unexpected feelings his touch had evoked. "I may not have callouses, Mr. Tyler, but that doesn't mean I'm a stranger to work." She clasped her still-tingling hands tightly in front of her, and drew herself up, both physically and mentally. "I ran my father's household for ten years and I pride myself on the very high standards I maintained in doing so. I have every intention of staying here and making a go of this."

She couldn't bear to face returning to what she'd left behind in Ohio. And moving into a town full of strangers, even a town as small as Sweetgum, didn't sound much more appealing.

No, she'd been looking forward to the freedom the open expanses and relative privacy of farm life could afford her. She wasn't about to trade it away without a very good reason.

He dusted his hat against his leg. "Then it seems this is another topic we're at odds over."

Callie managed to hold her shoulders back, though the temptation to slump was strong. "Mr. Tyler, I truly don't want to fight you over any of this." How could she get through to him? If only he was the kind of man his brother had been—solid, caring, patient. Julia had used those words and more to describe Leland. "There must be some way we can make things work to everyone's benefit."

"You're the one who's been doing all the praying. You get any answers?"

Callie winced at his flippant attitude. "Surely you know that God's timing is not always our own," she said calmly. "His answer will come if we wait on it."

The reappearance of the children forestalled whatever response he might have made.

Annabeth skipped up to them and latched on to Callie's hand. "Cinnamon was very happy to see me."

"I'm sure she's missed you this past week."

"And Clover's new calf has really gotten big. Simon says we should name him Buster."

"That sounds like a fine name for a growing calf." Callie smiled at the bubbly chatter coming from the little girl. "How would you like to show me the inside of your house?"

"Okay." She tugged on Callie's hand. "Just follow me."

"Mind if I tag along?"

Callie noted the determined set to Jack's jaw. Was he afraid she'd try to stake her claim while he wasn't looking?

As the three strolled toward the house, Emma joined them. Simon, however, chose to stay outside and play with the dogs.

Callie felt at home as soon as she stepped across the threshold. Everywhere she looked she saw the stamp of Julia's presence. Everyday things her friend had written about were all around her, as if a favorite storybook had sprung to life.

While the girls continued down the hall, Callie stepped inside the front parlor. She was immediately drawn to the large, leather-bound Bible that sat in a place of honor on a table next to the window. Opening it, she found a listing of the Tyler family tree going back to Jack's great-great-grandparents. She remembered Julia writing to tell her what a proud moment it had been for her when Leland added her name to the lineage chart as his wife, and later, how special it had been for them to add Annabeth's name together.

Jack peered over her shoulder. "Thinking of adding your name?" he asked dryly.

"No, of course not." The thought hadn't even entered her mind. Her short-lived marriage to Leland would have absolutely no impact on the Tyler lineage. It didn't deserve so much as a footnote.

She turned and realized he was no longer focused on her.

Instead, he studied the open Bible, a tight expression on his face. "I guess I should update the entries on Nell and Lanny."

It took Callie a second to realize he was referring to notating the date of their deaths.

She placed a hand on his arm. "There'll be time enough to take care of that later."

He stared at her hand, then gave a quick nod and

turned away. "Come on," he said, his tone once again easy. "The kitchen's this way."

But before Callie had a chance to do more than glance around, Annabeth reappeared at her side and tugged her impatiently from the kitchen to the next room. "This way. I want to show you the new room Daddy built."

Callie smiled as she entered the washroom. "Julia was so proud of this. She wrote to me when they were building it."

"Of course she did."

Callie ignored his dry tone. "She asked me for suggestions, but Lanny pretty much designed and built the whole thing himself. She was very proud of him, and of this." Callie ran a hand along the clothes wringer. "It made life a lot easier on her, especially once she...well, what I mean is, during those last few months."

But Annabeth, as impatient as ever, didn't let them linger long in this room, either. "Let's go see my room."

As soon the child was certain she had their attention, she darted ahead of them up the stairs.

"Here it is." Annabeth opened the door to the first room on the left and made a beeline for her bed. She scrambled up on the mattress and hugged the doll sitting there. "Hello, Tizzy. Did you miss me?"

Callie's smile faded when she saw the way Emma looked at the doll with longing, the way her eyes ran over the other items in the room, pausing to study each of her younger cousin's possessions with an almost bittersweet hunger.

Callie felt as if a hand had reached inside her chest and was squeezing her heart. That Emma and Simon had lost both their parents at once was an unthinkable tragedy. To have also lost every jot and tittle of their former life, including mementos of those dear loved ones—it added a poignancy that absolutely broke one's heart.

All they had left from their old life was each other.

And God's love.

Callie's arms ached to gather Emma up and hug the child for all she was worth. But that would serve no purpose right now, other than drawing attention to the child's heartache.

"Ready to see the rest of the rooms up here?" Jack seemed impatient to move on.

Callie nodded, glad for the distraction.

Keeping a tight hold on her doll, Annabeth skipped ahead of them to the room across the hall.

"This used to be my daddy's room when he was a little boy," she said as Jack opened the door. "And you, too, Uncle Jack, wasn't it?"

"That's right, Little Bit."

Callie tried to picture Jack as young boy, spending time in here with his older brother. Perhaps this was what had taught Leland that deep patience Julia always spoke of.

Annabeth bounced onto the closest bed. "Daddy was getting it ready for you, Aunt Callie. See the pretty vase and lamp he set here?" She fiddled with her doll's dress, very carefully not looking up. "That's when he thought you were going to be my mommy instead of my aunt."

"He did a very nice job." Callie tried to ignore the heat creeping into her cheeks. Jack had no doubt suspected that the marriage between her and Leland was supposed to be a platonic one. But having this stark evidence blatantly revealed was mortifying. And somehow, having it revealed to Jack himself made it more so.

To his credit, Jack gave no clue that he noticed anything out of the ordinary. And he didn't linger in this room, either. With only a cursory look around, he herded them down the hall.

"This was Mommy's workroom," Annabeth explained before Jack had so much as opened the door.

As soon as Callie stepped inside and saw the nearly finished baby quilt, she stopped in her tracks. It was such a painful, unexpected reminder of her friend's death. Julia had slipped and fallen just one month before the baby was to be born. The ensuing early labor had killed both her and the baby.

"Momma was making this for my new baby brother or sister." Annabeth was standing beside her.

Callie rested a hand on the child's shoulder. "Yes, I know." She stepped forward and fingered the lovely bit of piecework. "I tell you what, sweetheart. Why don't we take this beautiful quilt and put it somewhere safe? One day, when you're old enough, perhaps you can finish it yourself. Would you like that?"

Annabeth nodded vigorously.

Callie decided the girls—not to mention she herself—needed something more cheerful to focus on. She looked around the room seeking inspiration and found it hanging among the rafters.

Jack drifted toward the window, listening to Callie and the girls chatter. They seemed to be making a game out of identifying all the varieties of flowers and herbs hanging from the ceiling.

Callie was probably trying to lighten the mood a bit. He'd sensed the tension in her earlier. Was it because she was picturing the life she would have had here had Lanny not died? A life that was lost to her now?

Unbidden, the memory of that moment when he'd taken hold of her hands returned. He had felt the pulse jump in her wrist, had suddenly become aware of her as feminine, small and vulnerable, yet full of warmth and a woman's strength. It had taken a full measure of resolve to push that unwelcome awareness aside and move forward with the point he'd wanted to make.

A pair of girlish giggles from across the room broke into his thoughts. Callie's doing, no doubt. Jack rubbed his chin as he stared unseeing out the window.

How was it she always knew the right thing to say and do with the kids? Maybe Lanny hadn't been so crazy after all in choosing her to be Annabeth's stepmother. The woman sure seemed to have a knack for the job.

And apparently that's all Lanny had been looking for—more of a glorified nanny than a wife. Had sticking her down the hall in the guestroom been her idea or his?

Not that it was any of his business. Or that it even mattered.

Still, he'd give a pretty penny to know whether her embarrassment back there had been due to his finding out about the arrangement or from being faced with the proof of Lanny's expectations.

The muffled sound of Simon's voice caught his attention.

He opened the window, but before he could call out he saw what had caught the boy's notice—a wagon leading a cloud of dust down the road was headed their way.

"Somebody's coming," Jack said.

He heard Callie step up behind him. "Do you think they're coming here?"

"Only one way to find out." He turned to the girls. "Looks like we might have visitors. What say we head outside to see who it is?"

Chapter Nine

The girls clattered down the stairs while he and Callie followed at a more sedate pace. As they stepped onto the porch, Jack sensed her nervousness. For the second time in as many minutes she tugged that ever-present bonnet forward. That telling betrayal of self-consciousness always surprised him. She certainly didn't seem to lack gumption when it came to anything else.

"Who is it?" she asked, interrupting his train of thought.

He shaded his eyes, following her gaze to the approaching wagon. "It looks like Virgil and Ida Lee with their kids. You met Virgil yesterday when the stage arrived. He's been taking care of this place since Lanny died." Jack gave her a meaningful look. "These folks aren't just good friends, they're also the closest neighbors to this place."

"I know."

Now how would she know something like that?

She must have read the question in his expression. "I told you, Julia's letters were like chapters in a book, and the people of Sweetgum were the main characters."

That comment set Jack back on his heels. If Julia had

been so all-fired gabby, what had she written about *him* in those letters over the years? More to the point, did Callie know about that botched proposal?

He pushed that uncomfortable thought aside as the wagon pulled to a stop. "Hi, Virgil, Ida Lee."

Virgil acknowledged the greeting with a nod. "Sorry if we're intruding. As soon as Ida Lee saw your carriage go by she insisted we head out here to welcome you home, proper-like." He gave Jack a just-between-us-men grin. "Not to mention she's been dying to meet our visitor ever since I mentioned her arrival."

Ida Lee didn't seem at all put out by her husband's words. "Just wanted to extend a neighborly welcome," she said calmly.

Four kids scrambled down from the back of the wagon. Ida Lee made shooing motions. "You all go along and play with the other kids. Just stay out of the house."

Jack offered his hand to help Ida Lee down.

"Hi-dee, Jack." Her expression softened. "I'm right sorry about Lanny and Nell. They were good people."

She patted his hand then smiled that broad, toothy smile he remembered from their childhood. "It's been much too long since we saw you. Now that you're back, I hope you plan to stick around for a while."

He accepted her quick hug. "I'm not figuring to go anywhere for the time being."

"Good." She smoothed her skirts and turned to Callie. "And you must be Julia's Callie. It's good to finally meet you. Julia used to go on about what a sweet friend you were. I'm sorry you got such a sorrowful introduction to Sweetgum."

Ida Lee reached for Callie's hand and Jack was hit

again with the memory of how Callie's touch had made him feel.

Callie was trying to reconcile the mental image she'd formed of Ida Lee from Julia's letters with the reality standing here in front of her. She'd never realized before that Julia's descriptions had actually focused more on people's character and manner than their physical attributes.

Which was probably why folks around here didn't know anything about her birthmark.

And which was also why she hadn't realized Ida Lee was such a big-boned, sturdy-looking woman. The kind you could picture handling farm chores with ease.

But Ida Lee's smile, as big and hearty as the woman herself, was infectious.

"Thank you." Callie found it easy to respond to her warmth. "I apologize for not having any refreshments to offer you."

Ida Lee waved a hand, flopping it from the wrist. "Oh, land's sake, girl, we didn't come here to put you to any trouble." She reached under the buggy seat and lifted out a covered basket. "In fact, I brought you one of my maple pecan pies."

"How very kind."

There was nothing dainty about Ida Lee's laugh. "Truth be told, it's a way to repay you for all the prying I'm about to do." She turned to her husband. "You menfolk go off now and take care of the horse and wagon while Callie and I have us a nice little chat."

Jack and Virgil didn't need to be told twice.

Callie nodded toward the house. "Why don't we get out of the sun?"

"Now that sounds like a mighty fine idea." Ida Lee

chattered on about the heat until they reached the porch. Then she plopped down on the rocking chair.

Callie took a seat on the swing.

"Imagine that, Julia's friend Callie right here in Sweetgum. And you're Lanny's widow to boot. If that don't beat all." She shook her head in wonder. "The Lord does work in mysterious ways."

"That he does." Callie glanced over to where the children were engaged in a boisterous game of tag.

"Now don't you go worrying about the kids. The big ones'll keep an eye on the little ones. They'll be just fine." She loosened the strings of her bonnet, letting it hang loose against her nape. Then she picked up a leaf-shaped fan and waved it in front of her face. "Goodness, but it's a scorcher today." She gave Callie a friendly smile. "We don't hold much to suffering for the sake of appearances hereabouts. No point sweltering underneath that bonnet of yours now that we're out of the sun."

Callie weighed what she knew about Ida Lee, both from Julia's letters and from her few minutes of personal acquaintance. "How much did Julia tell you about me?" she asked carefully.

Ida Lee paused in her fanning. "Not a whole lot. I mean, we all knew she had a friend she left behind when she moved out this way. 'The sister of my heart,' she used to call you. But she never did go into any specifics."

"So she never mentioned my birthmark?"

"Birthmark?"

Callie loosened her bonnet and let it fall back just as Ida Lee had done. Out of habit she had sat on the woman's left side, so she had to turn her face for Ida Lee to get the full effect.

The woman winced. "Oh, my."

"I'm sorry." Callie reached for her bonnet. "I'll cover it."

Ida Lee resumed her fanning. "Don't be a ninny. It's too hot for that and you sure don't have to hide your face on my account. Just takes some getting used to, is all."

Callie smiled as some of the tension eased from her spine. The woman's words might be less than genteel, but there was no doubting her sincerity. "Thank you."

"Oh, fiddlesticks, girl. No need to thank me for something like that."

In spite of Ida Lee's assurances, Callie tucked her hair back under the bonnet but let the ribbons hang loose. She didn't want to do anything to make the children feel awkward or nervous if they should join them.

To her relief, Ida Lee let the subject drop. Instead, she leaned forward conspiratorially. "So, let's get down to talking. Having you show up in Sweetgum is the most interesting happening since goodness-knows-when. What do you plan to do now?"

Callie wished she had the answer to that question. "I married Mr. Tyler, Mr. *Leland* Tyler, that is—" why did she feel the need to clarify this? Callie hurried on "—because he wanted me to help raise Annabeth. If anything, she needs me even more now."

Ida Lee frowned. "You're not thinking of taking that child back to Ohio with you, now are you?"

"Oh, no. This is her home." Callie raised her chin. "And I plan to make it my home, too. In fact, I'd also like to play a part in Simon and Emma's lives if I can."

Ida Lee nodded. "All children need a mother's touch. Lanny knew that. And I think Nell and Jed would be grateful to you as well."

Callie waved a hand. "Yes, but it's more than just

mothering. These children also need someone to look after their spiritual upbringing."

The rocker halted. Ida Lee opened her mouth as if to speak, but said nothing. Finally she set the rocker in motion again. "What does Jack have to say about that?"

Callie shifted in her seat, searching for a diplomatic response. "Mr. Tyler and I are still trying to work out how to deal with the situation."

"He's wanting to take charge of it all, isn't he?"

"His concern is understandable." Callie felt oddly defensive of Jack's stand. "I mean, not only am I a stranger, but I have no knowledge of the workings of a farm." She fiddled with the edge of her bonnet. "Even if I do have a claim to the place."

"Why, that's right," Ida Lee gave a bark of laughter. "I guess this place is rightly yours now. Don't that beat all. I reckon Jack is fit to be tied. He never could abide having to share what he thought was rightfully his." She gave Callie a probing look. "He's fighting you over who gets those three young'uns, isn't he?"

"He is their uncle, after all. It's only natural that he'd want to be a part of their lives."

"No need to mince words around me. Jack Tyler no more knows how to care for three kids on his own than you can run this farm. He's just too ornery and prideful to admit it."

"I think perhaps you're being a bit harsh."

Ida Lee shrugged. "Maybe you're right. Lanny and Nell's deaths must have hit him hard." She leaned forward and patted Callie's knee. "I know he stayed away all this time, but deep down he's a family man. Always has been, even if he won't admit it, even to himself. And right now, those young'uns are the only real family he has left."

The words struck a chord with Callie. She couldn't deny the man his right to be close to his family. But she couldn't abandon those children if God had truly sent her here to minister to them.

There had to be a way to make this work. *Lord, please help me find the path You want me to follow in this matter.*

She looked up to find Ida Lee staring at her. "I wish I knew the answer." She tucked a few more stray hairs under her bonnet. "I've been praying about it ever since I found out about Leland."

Ida Lee nodded approval. "Then you're on the right track. I'll add my own prayers. The right answer will come."

"So, how are you and the widow getting along?"

Jack grimaced. "She's one stubborn woman. I can't believe this is the same gal Julia spoke of with such admiration. The two are nothing alike."

"It's not being alike that makes people friends. Look at me and you."

Jack plucked a stem of grass and slid it between a thumb and forefinger. "She's trying to stake a claim on the farm. Not even willing to let me buy her out."

Virgil gave Jack a puzzled look. "I'm surprised you let that bother you so much. Lanny was always the one with farming in his blood, not you."

One more thing he'd never be as good at as his brother.

Virgil rubbed his chin. "I figured you'd be heading back off to your work with the railroad as soon as you settled matters here."

Not a far cry from the truth. At least that had been the plan when he first headed back to Sweetgum.

"I'll admit the idea of staying put and working a farm isn't something I'm looking forward to. But I'm the last of the Tylers, except for them kids. Taking care of this place and those three young'uns is my responsibility, and it ain't one I intend to shirk."

"You aiming to handle the farm and the kids all on your own?"

Jack heard the doubt in his friend's voice, but refused to admit he shared it. "Don't see why not. Other men have done it. And Simon's old enough to help."

"Sure, it's been done." Virgil gave him a hard look. "But it ain't easy, even if you've had some practice. Why, even Lanny figured he needed help raising that little girl of his."

Virgil raised a hand before Jack could do more than stiffen. "I know you don't like being compared to Lanny, but I'm just saying it ain't as easy a job as you seem to think."

Jack flicked the blade of grass away. "I didn't say I thought it would be easy. But that's my worry. And I'm sure I'll get the widow to come around. So that'll be one less person for me to look out for."

He rested his arms on the paddock fence and stared off toward the far tree line.

"So, tell me about the fire."

Virgil hesitated, then joined Jack at the fence rail. "Nell hurt her ankle two days before," he said quietly. "Jed naturally insisted she stay in bed and let him run the café on his own. But you know Nell. She wasn't going to stand that for too long."

Jack knew Nell, all right. She'd been the sweetest person he ever knew. But when she'd set her mind to something, there'd been no stopping her.

"Anyway," Virgil continued, "on that Tuesday, she

insisted on hobbling downstairs to help Jed cook for their lunch crowd. Lanny showed up after most of the customers had cleared out, and he helped Jed convince Nell that they ought to close up for the afternoon. Mr. Dobson from over at the mercantile stopped in about then to buy one of Nell's pies. According to him, Lanny told Nell he had some big news to share but he wasn't going to tell them anything until she was settled upstairs in her rocking chair."

Big news, huh? Well, that one was easy to figure out. Jack found his gaze wandering back to where Callie sat chatting with Ida Lee. Nell would have liked her, he was sure of it. In some ways, they were a lot alike.

"They sent Mr. Dobson on his way and closed up," Virgil said. "It was probably thirty minutes later when the fire started."

Virgil cut Jack an apologetic look. "'Fraid we couldn't figure out what started the thing. But best we can tell, it started in the café kitchen downstairs."

Jack clenched his jaw, determined to hear Virgil's story without interrupting.

"They probably didn't realize anything was wrong until it was almost too late." He teased a splinter from the fence rail. "We found Jed and Nell near the foot of the stairs, pinned down by a beam. Jed still had his arm around her." Virgil swallowed hard. "Lanny was there, too. Looked like he was trying to free them before he was overcome himself." Virgil straightened. "I just thank God the young'uns were down at the livery when it happened."

"I can't see as how God deserves much gratitude for any of what happened."

Virgil leaned forward, his brow furrowed. "Look, Jack, I know you're upset, and no one could blame you for that. But you need to keep in mind that they're all in a better place now." He clamped a hand on Jack's shoulder. "None of them would want to hear you talking like that."

Jack pushed away from the fence, ready to change the subject. "Thanks again for keeping this place going for me the last few days. If there's anything I can do—"

Virgil shook his head, still studying Jack with that sober expression. "Ain't no need for thanks. Lanny helped me out many a time and I'm glad I could do something to return the favor, though it's little enough, considering..."

Jack nodded, then forced a smile for Virgil's sake. "While you're still feeling so neighborly, come over to the barn and let me know what you think about this yearling."

Chapter Ten

At supper that evening, the children regaled Mrs. Mayweather with their adventures of the day. Callie was pleased to see they had truly enjoyed themselves. Even Simon seemed more animated.

"And Aunt Callie said I could move back to my house soon," Annabeth said toward the end of the meal. She looked around the table. "Does that mean all of us?"

Callie ignored the look Jack sent her way as she took a sip from her glass.

Mrs. Mayweather shook her head. "If you were including me, I thank you for the kind invitation, but I shall have to decline. I have my own house and I happen to like it very well here."

"But you don't have other houses, do you, Aunt Callie and Uncle Jack?"

Callie set her glass down. "Why, no, but—"

"Good. Then you can come live with us. Like a family."

"They aren't really our parents, you know," Simon said sullenly. Seemed his change of temperament had only been temporary.

"No, we aren't," Jack said calmly. "No one can ever

replace your mother and father. But I'm your uncle and I'd like to try to take care of you if you'll let me."

"As would I," Callie chimed in.

"But we *are* going to all live together, aren't we?" Emma's voice was a timid counterpoint to Annabeth's enthusiasm and Simon's anger.

The girl was obviously looking for some kind of reassurance that her life would regain a sense of normalcy. And she wasn't the only one. Annabeth looked from Jack to Callie with troubled eyes.

Callie wanted to give all three of them the reassurance they needed. But what Emma was asking for was impossible. How could she explain that it would be highly improper for both her and Jack to live under the same roof?

Callie glanced Jack's way but found no help there. She took a deep breath. "Your Uncle Jack and I haven't quite worked everything out—"

Mrs. Mayweather stood, interrupting Callie's floundering attempt to answer Emma's question. "It sounds as if you children have had a full day. Why don't you go on and get ready for bed. The grown-ups will take care of the meal clean-up tonight."

"Yes, ma'am." The children excused themselves and scampered out of the room as if afraid she would change her mind.

Callie pushed her chair back, concerned about the impression their discussion had made on the children. "Perhaps I should go with them."

Mrs. Mayweather stopped her with a look. "They'll be fine. You're needed down here." She turned to Jack. "You may help Callista clear the table while I prepare the wash water in the kitchen."

"Yes, ma'am."

Even Jack didn't argue when she used that schoolmarm tone.

As they worked at clearing the table, Emma's last question lay between them like a sleeping bear—something to tiptoe around and avoid poking or prodding at all costs.

As usual, Callie couldn't stand the silence. Hugging a large serving bowl to her chest she managed to catch Jack's gaze. "Perhaps I should help Mrs. Mayweather while you finish in here." He hadn't so much as completed his nod before she fled to the kitchen.

Mrs. Mayweather raised a brow at her precipitous entrance, but merely asked her to fill the kettle and set it on the stove.

Callie studiously kept her gaze focused on the water flowing into the kettle as Jack, his arms loaded with dishes, made a more sedate entrance a few moments later.

"Place those over there with the others." Mrs. Mayweather wiped her hands on her apron as she turned to Callie. "Would you mind washing tonight?"

Callie set the kettle on the stove. "Not at all."

"And Jackson, you may dry."

As the two took their assigned posts, Mrs. Mayweather crossed her arms and watched them with a prim expression. "I want to know what your intentions are."

Callie glanced sideways, watching as Jack quirked a brow, a humorous gleam lighting his eye. "Intentions? Why, Mrs. Mayweather, I had no idea you had such tender feelings for me."

"Don't be impertinent, Jackson."

Was there a hint of a smile lurking in the reprimand?

"I mean," she said sternly, "what do the two of you have in mind for the children's future. They've been hurt quite enough already. I won't allow you to trifle with their feelings while you circle around each other like a pair of dogs fighting over a bone."

Jack's demeanor closed off immediately. "We still haven't worked that out yet."

Mrs. Mayweather nodded. "I take it you both feel you have a claim to Annabeth, and to the family farm."

"As Leland's widow—"

"As a Tyler, I have—"

The school teacher gave an inelegant "Harrumph!" Jack and Callie fell silent. "I understand a great deal has happened to you in a short period of time," Mrs. Mayweather continued, "but you cannot put the children in the middle of this tug-of-war. A few more days like today and those three will be forming attachments and making assumptions. In fact, unless I'm mistaken, they've already started."

Callie knew she was right. It wasn't fair to the children. But no matter how much she prayed and pondered, the solution eluded her.

"I've enjoyed having them spend time with me, but they need a more permanent home, a sense of normalcy and family in their lives again. So let's start with you, Callista."

Callie braced herself and turned.

"I know you already feel something for the children," the schoolteacher began. "I watched you put them to bed last night, sing them lullabies, tuck them in. And I could tell by the way you helped with their prayers that you are a God-fearing woman. That's an important quality for someone who's going to take on the care of young children."

"Thank you." Callie couldn't resist a quick glance Jack's way.

His glower was back and the plate he held was getting an extra vigorous rubbing.

"You talk to them without talking down to them," Mrs. Mayweather continued. "Children notice and respond to such things. You are a natural mother figure, and those children need a mother figure in their lives."

A tingle of pride warmed Callie. It was nice to have her actions recognized and appreciated.

Then Mrs. Mayweather straightened and the look on her face erased all trace of the smugness Callie had felt a moment earlier.

"On the other hand, besides having no idea how to run a farm, you have no claim on Simon and Emma. This tragedy has formed a bond among those children, a bond that runs deeper than that of most natural-born siblings. It would be a terrible blow to them if you split them up now."

She adjusted her shirtwaist. "Then there is the matter of the markings on your face."

To Callie's surprise, almost before she herself could react, Jack spun around and focused his glower on Mrs. Mayweather.

Jack couldn't believe he'd heard right, especially not from Alberta Mayweather. The woman had never been one to judge others by their appearance.

But he'd barely opened his mouth to protest when she held up a hand.

"Come now, Jackson, we must face facts, even unpleasant ones. While I do not feel Callista's birthmark lessens her suitability, there are more narrow-minded folk who may hold it against her."

"She's right." Callie's tone was flat and matter-of-fact. "Even the children have some reservations about seeing me without my bonnet."

"Only because you took them by surprise," Jack argued. "They'll get used to it."

He caught Callie's startled look and pulled himself up short. She sure didn't need to be reading anything special in his defense of her. He was simply being fair-minded, that's all.

"Then we have you, Jackson," Mrs. Mayweather said as she shifted her focus to him. "I know family is important to you. But more to the point is knowing how important family is to those children, especially right now. You are their uncle, the only tangible connection to their parents they have left, *and* you have a claim of sorts to all three of them. Also, unlike Callista, you are perfectly capable of running the farm yourself."

Jack nodded in agreement. About time somebody saw things his way.

"However, while I know your love for these children will grow, I don't think you are as comfortable in the role of parent as Callista is. Not to mention how awkward it might be for you to try to raise two young girls alone." She gave him a direct look. "I have always believed it is more difficult for a man to raise daughters than it is for a woman to raise sons."

That comment hit home, but Jack refused to admit it. "That's not necessarily true for all men."

She raised a brow, then moved on. "Even so, I don't believe you can manage the farm and properly care for the children on your own."

He didn't plan to. "I'm sure there's someone here in town who'd be willing to take on the job of housekeeper."

Callie stiffened. "Those children need a mother, not a housekeeper."

"That's a matter of opinion."

"Putting that and everything else aside," Mrs. Mayweather said firmly, "we still have the matter of your wanderlust, Jackson. Can you honestly tell me that after a few months back here you won't feel any inclination to leave again?"

Jack resisted the urge to squirm. To be honest, he didn't know how he would handle setting down roots, or even if he could.

No point in announcing it to the world, though. "Despite what I may or may not want, I'll honor my responsibility to Lanny and Nell's children."

"I wouldn't expect anything less. But if your heart is not in it, if your desire is to be somewhere else, the children will sense it. And what they desperately need right now is to be with someone who will make them feel wanted and cherished."

Not liking the turn this was taking, Jack took the offensive. "It sounds like you've given this quite a bit of thought. Do you have a solution to offer?"

She met his gaze head on. "I do."

That set Jack back on his heels. It wasn't the response he'd expected.

"And what might that be?" Jack prompted.

Mrs. Mayweather folded her hands in front of her with a self-satisfied air. "Isn't it obvious? I believe you should consider making the same decision Leland did, Jack. For the good of the children, of course."

Chapter Eleven

It took a moment for the meaning to sink in, but when it did, Jack nearly dropped the dish he was drying.

"What?!"

Callie looked just as stunned as Jack felt. "You can't mean—"

The schoolteacher raised hand to halt their outbursts. "Far be it from me to dictate what you should do."

Hah! That was *exactly* what she was trying to do.

"Only the two of you can decide on the best course of action." She gave them both a stern look. "And by that I mean the best course for the children."

The woman had obviously lost her senses. Jack tried to take back control of the conversation. "What seems best for the children today is not necessarily the right thing to do in the long run. I think this decision requires an objective, analytical perspective."

"I agree."

Before Jack had time to feel any sense of victory, however, she continued. "And if you consider this objectively, I don't see why either of you should have any serious objections. Marriage to each other seems the ideal solution."

Jack heard what sounded suspiciously like choking coming from Callie's direction, a reaction she tried to cover by clearing her throat.

"Callista, unless he has changed significantly since leaving Sweetgum, Jackson is a hardworking, forthright fellow, every bit as fine a man as his brother. Seeing his determination to do his duty by the children should assure you of that."

Nice of her to give him that small shred of praise. She'd actually put him on even footing with Lanny.

"In fact," Mrs. Mayweather continued, "this proposal is not so different from what you and Leland agreed to."

"I'm sorry, but I believe it is." Callie's voice was respectful but firm.

Not that he didn't agree with her, but why did she have such a problem with this proposition? Did she think he wouldn't be as good a husband as Lanny?

"How so?" Mrs. Mayweather asked the question for him. "If I recall correctly the bargain was struck for the purposes of providing Annabeth with a mother. That need still exists, only in triplicate."

"True." Callie tugged on her bonnet. "But this situation is different in a number of ways. For one, Leland *wanted* to marry me. He wasn't begrudging, much less outright resistant. For another, though we never met, I believe I knew him well and, more importantly, he knew me. We felt we'd get along comfortably together." She paused and glanced at Jack as if uncertain whether or not to continue.

She had a point there. Getting along "comfortably together" was not something he could see the two of them doing.

"Is there something else?" Mrs. Mayweather prompted.

"Please," Jack said dryly, "don't feel the need to spare my feelings."

She tilted her chin up. "Very well. Since we are being frank, my impression of Leland, based on Julia's letters and my own recent correspondence with him, was that he was a deep-rooted family man and one who had a close walk with the Lord. Those are two qualities I believe to be very important."

"And you don't feel the same is true of Jackson?"

Callie shifted uncomfortably. "He admits he's in no hurry to set down roots. As for the other, well, I won't claim to be qualified to judge another's relationship with God. I just don't know."

Jack's jaw clenched. How self-righteous! Did she think that his faith was weak or false just because he didn't spend time praying every day the way Lanny apparently did? So what if he didn't feel the need to bother God every time he needed something?

He believed in God, all right. He just knew better than to count on him to take care of things in his life. He'd made that mistake before and paid for it with outright rejection and shredded pride.

Mrs. Mayweather lifted a brow as she turned to him. "Jackson, do you have anything to say to that?"

What he *wanted* to say was more appropriate for a railroad camp than ladies' ears. But Jack gritted his teeth, tempered his thoughts and chose his words carefully. "The widow is quite right. She's not qualified to judge the depths of my faith or lack thereof. It's a personal matter between me and God, and one not open to debate or discussion."

Her face reddened slightly and she gave him an apologetic look. "You're right, Mr. Tyler. Forgive my presumption." She leaned forward. "It's just that I feel very deeply that it's important for parents to set the proper example and direction in spiritual matters for their children."

Mrs. Mayweather nodded. "Very true." She turned back to Jack. "Well, what about you? For all your posturing and blustering about being able to take care of everything yourself, you know quite well you are not able to raise those children on your own. And Callista not only has the right qualifications, she's agreed to do this very thing once already."

She paused and gave him a considering look. "Unless… Your affections are not already otherwise engaged, are they?"

Jack cleared his throat. "No, but—"

"We already know Callista was Julia's trusted friend and Leland's choice for his second wife. That gives us a firm basis to believe she'll make a good wife and mother. So surely you don't object to her on those grounds."

"As someone has already pointed out," Jack said, cutting a hard glance Callie's way, "I'm a very different man than my brother, so his choice is not necessarily a good indicator of my own preferences."

Mrs. Mayweather waved away his objection. "Even so, a marriage between you two would solve all of the problems. Callista, you could take care of the children and the house, and Jackson, you could provide for them and take care of the farm. The children would have both a mother and a father to provide the guidance they'll need."

Jack and Callie avoided looking at each other.

"And if you do feel the need to return to your job again, you can do so knowing the children are in good hands, Jackson. Really, this does seem to settle matters nicely for everyone concerned."

Jack's hands balled into tight fists. The woman had definitely overstepped her bounds.

"However, as I said, this is merely a suggestion. You are free to pursue another course of action if you wish. But you need to decide quickly, for the sake of the children. Now, I'll go check on them while you two discuss your options."

Once she'd left the room, Callie stood there, acutely aware of Jack standing beside her, mechanically handling the dishes, the minutes drawing out between them in brittle silence.

Marry this man! How could Mrs. Mayweather expect her to seriously contemplate such a step? Did the woman think she'd be willing to marry just anyone who seemed in need of a housekeeper and nanny?

Callie remembered her first impression of Jack back on the stagecoach—a ruggedly handsome, dangerous sort of man. Not at all the type of fellow to be comfortable setting down roots and nurturing a family. And not at all the type of fellow who'd be looking for the likes of her in a wife if he did.

His aversion to the whole idea of marrying her, in fact, had been immediately obvious. No, Mrs. Mayweather had been wrong—this wasn't the answer.

Actually, she'd been right about one thing. They couldn't keep going the way they were.

Finally, as she handed him a saucer to dry, Callie broke the silence. "She's right, you know."

His brow raised.

"Not about the marriage thing." Goodness, but this was awkward. She tried to ignore the heat rising in her cheeks and push on. "But about the need for us to reach a decision."

Callie reached for the next dish on the stack. "I agree with her that it's not fair to keep the children in limbo.

Annabeth doesn't understand why she can't go back to her own house. And Simon and Emma need a place to set down new roots."

Jack placed the dry saucer in the cupboard and held out his hand for the next one. "So what do you suggest?"

Callie dipped a plate in the rinse water and handed it to him without meeting his gaze. "Perhaps we could divide the responsibilities the way she described—I manage the children, you run the farm—but do it without a marriage. I mean, it is a big house after all."

He gave a grunt of cynical amusement. "Not if you want to be able to show your face in this town." As soon as the words were out of his mouth he gave her a penitent look. "I'm sorry, I meant—"

"That's all right, Mr. Tyler, I know what you meant. Please don't feel like you have to watch your words with me." She wiped her brow with the back of a wet hand. It was almost amusing the way he tried to bend over backwards to make her believe her birthmark wasn't an issue. "I suppose you're right. Conventions can be bothersome at times, but they are there for a reason."

She plopped the last bowl in the dishwater with a splash. "So, do you have an alternative to offer?"

"I'm still not convinced I couldn't handle this on my own. I might have to hire a housekeeper to help out, but otherwise we'd be fine."

The man didn't seem to know the meaning of the word compromise. "That's not a solution."

"Why not?"

He knew very well why not, but she refused to let him goad her into losing her temper. "Well, for one thing it cuts me out of the picture and I refuse to let that happen."

She handed him the bowl then wiped her hands on

her apron, maintaining eye contact with him the whole time. "But even if that weren't the case, a housekeeper is not the same as a mother. There's nothing to hold her to the children but a wage. That's one of the reasons Leland discarded that option in favor of marrying again."

She finally turned away and took a seat at the table, her hands twisting in her skirts. This was impossible!

He joined her, taking a seat directly across the table. "Lanny and I didn't necessarily share the same views on everything."

She wondered at his tone, but now was not the time to try to figure out his personal issues. "So you said. Still, you have to agree that it's not what their parents would want for them."

He tilted his chair back, letting it balance on the two back legs. "So what do you suggest?"

Callie stared down at her hands, clasped together on top of the table. *Heavenly Father, if it is truly Your will for me to be a part of these children's lives, You're going to have to help me work this out.*

She finally looked up and met Jack's gaze. "I don't have one yet."

"Then it seems we're back at square one."

Callie wondered again at his tone. Did he object to marriage in general, or just tying himself to her? After all, he wasn't Lanny. He hadn't known of her disfigurement for years, nor had he gotten to know her through her letters and the filter of Julia's love.

Even given his pronouncement that her birthmark didn't bother him, it was a far cry from wanting to tie himself down to her. A man like him would want a woman who was pretty, vibrant, worldly. She was none of those things.

Did he still use Julia as his gold standard for judging women?

Gathering her courage, Callie forced her voice to remain even. "If it's me you object to, I mean, if there's another woman you'd prefer to marry, to help in raising the children."

"No."

His protest was too quick, too sharp. Perhaps he was trying to spare her feelings. Or maybe he didn't want to admit the truth, even to himself.

He rubbed the back of his neck, something he seemed to do whenever he was uncomfortable. "I mean, if marriage is really the only answer—and that's a big 'if'—then of course it should be between the two of us. We're the ones who share a feeling of responsibility for the children's well-being."

Fine sounding words, but she wasn't buying it.

His face got that closed-off look again. "I'm just not convinced yet that it *is* the only answer."

But what if it was? Could they live with such an arrangement? "If we do this, it would strictly be for the sake of the children." She traced a circle on the table with one finger, avoiding even so much as a glance his way. "I mean, we would naturally agree that it would be in name only."

Jack let the chair fall forward. "Of course."

She forced herself to continue. "And we would need to come to a clear understanding of what we would be agreeing to."

"For instance?"

She finally dragged her gaze up to his. Seeing the intense look on his face almost doused her resolve. Almost. "Do you intend to go back to your old job?"

He folded his arms. "Not right away," he said slowly.

"I mean, if we did get married, I'd stay around as long as you and the kids needed me to. But once things settled down, say after a month or so, then I don't see why I wouldn't." He rested his still-crossed arms on the table. "I'm good at my job and I make good money at it, more than I could make off of the farm."

"Money isn't everything, Mr. Tyler. Lanny and Julia, for instance, seemed to do quite well on the farm alone."

A muscle at the corner of his mouth jumped. "Let me put this another way. I'm not Lanny and that's not the life I planned for myself."

Apparently she'd said something to ruffle his feathers again. No, theirs could never be a simple, comfortable relationship.

Even with the bonds of matrimony.

That unbidden thought brought heat to her cheeks. Luckily, Jack didn't seem to notice.

"If you're worried I'm going to abandon you and the kids, though," he continued in that tight voice, "you can put your mind at rest. When I go back to doing demolition work, I'll make a point to come back several times a year."

"I see. In that case, if you're really willing to stay here long enough to teach me how to take care of the place, we could probably make this work."

One eyebrow went up. "Even if I gave you daily lessons for a month, do you really think you could learn to run the farm by yourself?"

His lack of confidence in her abilities stung. "Julia was a city girl like me and learned to do most of the chores as well as any girl born to this life."

"But Julia started her learning at age eleven, not twenty-five."

She refused to back down. "That just means I'll have

to work harder, not that I can't learn. And, as Mrs. Mayweather said, we can hire someone to help out a few days a week."

"So you admit you'll need help."

She let out a huff of irritation. "I'm not a ninny, Mr. Tyler. I know my limitations. I will freely admit that I'm not capable of caring for the children and a farm on my own." She studied the back of her hands. "There is one other thing."

"And that is?"

"I intend to raise these children to know and delight in the teachings of the Bible. You profess to be a Christian, just not the 'praying sort.' While I don't understand how this can be, I won't attempt to judge you. Each person must wrestle with his beliefs in his own way." She sat up straighter. "But, while you are here, I ask that you support me in providing the proper encouragement and example to the children. Surely you agree that bringing them up in the Word is important?"

She waited for his nod, then continued. "So you understand that we have a big responsibility before us. As the head of the household, your influence on the children would be strongest. I'd expect you to take part in family Bible readings and to accompany us to Sunday services. And of course we'd say grace at every meal and make certain the children say their prayers when they go to bed at night."

He didn't say anything at first, and Callie held her breath. Surely he wouldn't balk at such a request, would he? "I believe it's what your brother and sister would have wanted for their children."

His jaw clenched, but he finally nodded. "You're right. Such things are important in bringing up children."

Such things were not just for children, but now was not the time to push that issue.

Callie felt a sudden fluttering in her stomach as the import of what they were contemplating sunk in. At some point they had moved from talking about it in abstract terms to figuring out how to make it work.

She gave him a weak smile. "We're really going to do this, aren't we?"

His answering smile held a touch of self-mockery. "It appears so."

"When?"

"No point putting it off. We can talk to the preacher tomorrow and set a date."

Not the most romantic of proposals. Callie kept her hands tightly clasped in her lap, trying to remain anchored in this suddenly shaky reality.

Heavenly Father, is this really what You desire for me? Jack is nothing like his brother. Can he truly be the life partner You prepared for me?

She turned to Jack, trying to picture this new turn her life seemed to be taking, trying to see through the emotionless façade he'd erected, to figure out his true feelings. But it was no use. "So what now?"

A hint of her inner turmoil must have communicated itself to him because his demeanor changed and some of the hardness left his face. She was struck again by his ability to set his own worries aside. Here he was, being pushed into a corner, being forced to give up much of the freedom and footloose independence he obviously craved. But he was ready to do it without further complaint.

All for the sake of the children.

He stood and held out a hand to help her rise. "I guess now we tell Mrs. Mayweather that, once again, she was right."

Chapter Twelve

"We have something to tell you."

Breakfast was over and all three children sat side by side on the parlor settee, looking equal parts apprehensive and curious.

Callie caught her bottom lip between her teeth and risked a quick look Jack's way.

He gave her a barely perceptible nod, but seemed content to let her take the lead for now. Almost as if he were saying this was all her doing so she should handle it.

She turned back to the children, making a point to capture the gaze of each of them in turn. How were they going to react to the news?

Annabeth suddenly sat up straighter, her expression hopeful. "Are we moving back to my house today?"

"Not today," Jack answered, "but very soon."

"Then what's the news?" Simon's surly response indicated he wasn't expecting to like whatever it was.

Callie said a silent prayer for the right words and plunged in. "Your Uncle Jack and I had a long conversation last night. We decided we would like for all five of us to live together as a family. But if we are *truly* going to be a family then we need to start acting like one. So," she took a deep breath, "the two of us are going to get married."

Annabeth wrinkled her brow as if not certain what to make of the news. "You mean, just like a real mommy and daddy."

Simon stiffened. "They're *not* my mom and dad, and no stupid wedding is gonna change that."

Callie leaned forward. "Oh, Simon, we know that no one can ever take the place of your parents in your heart." She looked at the girls, including them in the discussion. "But they're up in heaven now and you all need someone to look out for you until you're grown up enough to take care of yourselves."

She waved a hand in Jack's direction. "And we would dearly love to be those someones."

Simon leaned back, crossing his arms tightly over his chest. He obviously wasn't taken with the idea.

She tried a different approach. "And that also means you need to start thinking of each other as brother and sisters, not just cousins. How does that sound?"

The girls nodded, but Simon remained closed off.

"Simon, this is especially important for you. You'll need to be a big brother to Annabeth as well as Emma, which means looking out for both of them. Do you think you can manage that?" She held up a hand before he could say anything. "It's a very important responsibility. Don't say yes unless you mean it."

"Simon already takes care of us," Annabeth said quickly. "Don't you, Simon?"

Simon nodded. "Don't worry." He thrust his chin out. "I'll look out for them, same as I've been doing since the fire."

"When are you gonna get married?" Emma's quiet question gave no hint as to what she felt.

"We're going to talk to Reverend Hollingsford today." Jack had apparently decided to get involved in the conversation. "If he's agreeable, we'll have the ceremony sometime in the next couple of days."

"*Then* can we move back to my house?" Annabeth seemed to have a one track mind.

"Yes, we can." Jack leaned forward. "But it won't be just your house any more, Little Bit—it'll be a home for all of us together."

There he went again, surprising her by dealing with the children's concerns in a straightforward but sensitive manner.

She gave him a quick smile, then touched Annabeth's hand. "You won't mind that, will you, sweetheart?"

"No." Annabeth twisted one of her ringlets around her finger. "But do I have to share Cinnamon, too?"

"Cinnamon is all yours," Callie said. "But it would be nice if you would let Emma and Simon ride him sometimes."

The child nodded. "I can do that."

Jack stood. "And since we're all going to be living at the farm, your Aunt Callie and I thought it might be a good idea to take another trip out there this afternoon to start getting things ready."

Annabeth bounced up and down with excitement. "Oh, yes! And I can visit with Cinnamon and Taffy and Pepper again."

Seeing the little girl's enthusiasm, some of Callie's uncertainty faded. This might just possibly work.

As Jack escorted Callie through town to Reverend Hollingsford's place, he mused over the turn of events.

Now that he'd had a chance to sleep on it, this marriage really did seem to be the ideal solution.

If you looked at it right, it gave him the best of both worlds. He'd be making sure Lanny and Nell's kids were well taken care of, aided by Lanny's hand-picked candidate, no less. And he'd still be free to leave Sweetgum and return to the life he'd so carefully built for himself for the past eleven years.

It wasn't a love match, but that had never seemed to be in the cards for him anyway. The only thing that stuck in his craw was that he would be marrying Lanny's widow, which felt irritatingly like making do with another of his brother's confounded hand-me-downs. But that wasn't Callie's fault and he was man enough to not blame her for that unpalatable piece of this pie.

He could do a whole lot worse, he supposed. That stubborn streak of hers was offset by an unintimidated mettle that was growing on him. And she *was* good with the kids. Add to that the fact that she was going into this with her eyes open and it seemed to be a can't-miss proposition.

"The children appeared to take the news well," Callie said, interrupting his thoughts.

"No reason why they shouldn't."

"Simon seems a bit sullen, though."

The woman sure did like to talk. "He'll get over it."

They walked on in silence and he hid a grin, wondering how long it would take her to say something.

"How well do you know Reverend Hollingsford?"

Three minutes. "I've known him all my life. He's been the preacher in these parts for nearly forty years. He performed the ceremony at my folks' wedding. And at both their funerals. I guess he'll do the same for me—wedding ceremony, that is."

She tipped her head to one side. "Sounds like you're surprised."

He shrugged. "Guess I just never thought that much about getting hitched." Not in a long time, anyway.

"You mean not since Julia turned you down."

He paused. So she did know.

When he resumed walking, he'd hopefully erased any emotion from his expression. "Julia wrote you about that, did she?" he asked as casually as he could manage.

"Yes." Callie gave him a sympathetic look. "She was worried you wouldn't understand and asked me to add you to my prayers."

"Well, she needn't have worried. I survived." But it had taken a long time to get over the bitter taste her rejection left in his mouth.

"Did you love her?" The question was soft, almost wistful.

Jack thought back to the boy he'd been. It seemed a lifetime ago. "I thought I did at the time." He shrugged. "But I was only seventeen. And as it turns out, she loved Lanny." That was what had stung the most. It had seemed the ultimate betrayal—by both of them.

"Yes, she did. Very much." She bit her lip and cast him a sideways glance.

He resisted the urge to roll his eyes. "Whatever it is, you might as well tell me."

"It's just, well, it was more than the fact that she loved Leland. It was also that she knew he loved her. And she was fairly certain you didn't."

Jack absorbed the words as if they had been a body blow. Julia had thought he didn't love her?

"I'm sorry, maybe I shouldn't have said anything."

She was able to pick up on his moods—he'd have to watch himself around her. "Don't be ridiculous. It was a long time ago. It's not like I've been carrying the torch for her all this time." Not a torch, but maybe some resentment.

"Of course not."

Her tone conveyed doubt, but he refused to dwell on the subject further. "There's Reverend Hollingsford's home. Prepare yourself for a boxcar load of questions."

That afternoon, when the buggy turned into the drive that led to the farm, Callie looked at the place with fresh eyes. Yesterday it had been Annabeth's house and the place where Julia once lived. Today it was her soon-to-be home, where she would belatedly start her married life.

Strange what a difference one day could make.

Once Jack had taken care of the horse and wagon, and Annabeth had a chance to say hello to her animals, they trooped into the house.

"First thing we need to decide today is where everyone will sleep," she announced.

"I already know where I'm going to sleep," Annabeth said confidently. "In my own room."

"Well, let's just think about that for a minute." Callie gave Annabeth an encouraging smile. "Remember how we said we were all going to have to make some changes in order to help us come together as a real family?"

Annabeth nodded cautiously.

"Since there will be five of us living here now, you'll need to share a room with Emma."

Annabeth shot a quick glance at Emma. "I guess we can put another bed in my room." There was a definite hint of martyrdom in her voice.

"But the room across the hall from yours already has two beds," Callie reasoned, "and it's also bigger than yours. Don't you think it makes more sense for you and Emma to share that one and for Simon to have the smaller one?"

Annabeth's lower lip jutted out. "But why does Simon get a room all to himself?"

Jack finally stepped in. "Because Simon is a boy and he's the oldest," he said firmly.

"But I like my old room," Annabeth said petulantly.

"I know, sweetie. But you want to do your part to make this work, don't you? And you can bring all your things with you to your new room."

Annabeth plopped down on the sofa with a grudging huff. "I guess it'll be okay."

"I don't want a frilly ole girl's room." Simon, arms crossed over his chest, looked ready for battle.

"Don't worry." Callie ignored his churlish attitude. "It won't look like a girl's room once we move Annabeth's things out and put yours in."

"I don't have any stuff."

Callie felt a pang at this reminder of their loss. That was the real root of the boy's rebellious attitude and she needed to make allowances. "You do have a few things. And you'll get more over time." She deliberately lightened her tone. "And this way you'll be able to make it into anything you want it to be."

But Simon didn't return her smile. "I liked living in town. That's where my friends are. And I don't know anything about farm chores."

"Well, you'll have your sisters to play with here, and you can visit with your friends whenever we go to town. And of course you'll see much more of them when school starts."

"But it won't be the same."

She touched his shoulder. "No, it won't. Not for any

of us." She withdrew her hand but gave him a smile. "And I don't know anything about farm chores, either. Your Uncle Jack will have to teach both of us."

"What if I don't want to learn?"

Jack stepped forward. "You'll do your share of the work around here, whether you feel like it or not. Just like everyone else." His tone was brook-no-arguments firm.

"And another thing," he continued. "You'll speak with respect when you're addressing your Aunt Callie, or any adult for that matter. Understand?"

"Yes, sir."

Callie sat back and stared at Jack. He'd done it again—employed a firm hand with the children without being overbearing. Just the kind of loving discipline they needed. The fatherly skill seemed to come so naturally to him.

How could a man to whom family was so important not have married before now? Had his feelings for Julia been so strong? Had he been holding out for someone like his first love?

Her pleasure in the day dimmed as she realized he was now settling for her.

"My word, Callista dear, you're nervous as a cat who's been tossed in a kennel."

Mrs. Mayweather's prodigious understatement managed to tease a smile from Callie as they sat side by side at the kitchen table, shelling peas.

It had been a long day. Today's visit to the farm hadn't had the playful, exploratory atmosphere that yesterday's had. They'd spent most of the afternoon moving furniture around, scrounging forgotten pieces from the attic and generally rearranging things, trying their best to satisfy everyone. An impossible task, of course.

In the end, the place likely felt as unfamiliar to Anabeth as it did to the rest of them.

Now supper was over, Jack had returned to the farm, and the children were playing quietly in the parlor.

"It's only natural for a bride to be a bit nervous," Mrs. Mayweather continued. "What you need is something to take your mind off of the upcoming nuptials."

"No offense, ma'am," Callie said, attempting to keep her tone light, "but I don't think there's anything that can distract me from that particular event right now."

She knew all about prenuptial jitters. She'd watched all four of her sisters go through it. This was something entirely different. This was a feeling of wrongness that came from the certain knowledge that she was about to enter into marriage with a man who not only didn't love her, but who felt as if he'd had a gun held to his head to agree to it.

Not the most comforting of feelings for a bride-to-be.

"Come now." Mrs. Mayweather seemed blissfully unaware that anything was amiss. "You've prayed about it and I've prayed about it. It's in God's hands now."

"You're right." Callie grimaced. "And I know it shows a lack of faith on my part, but I can't help but wonder if we're doing the right thing. Marriage is a sacred institution, not to be entered into lightly."

"From where I'm sitting, neither one of you seems to be entering into this lightly."

Callie sensed a touch of dry humor in the woman's tone.

Mrs. Mayweather dropped another handful of peas into the bowl. "You've both given it serious thought.

And you're both committed to making it work for the children, are you not?"

"Yes, of course." That was the only thing that had gotten them to this point—the thought that they both had the interests of the children at heart.

"Well, there you go. I'm certain God will see fit to bless what you two are doing."

Callie fervently hoped she was right.

"Oh, by the way."

The very casualness of Mrs. Mayweather's tone set Callie on the alert. "Yes?"

"I've invited some of the local ladies to come by for tea tomorrow afternoon. I thought it was high time you became acquainted with a few more of your neighbors."

Callie froze. Her heart seemed to pause for a moment before stuttering painfully back to life. *"Tomorrow?"*

"Of course. I sent the invitations out while you and Jackson were talking to Reverend Hollingsford this morning."

"How many?" Callie was too appalled to be embarrassed by the croak in her voice.

Mrs. Mayweather lifted her shoulders in a genteel shrug. "A couple of dozen, more or less."

A couple of dozen! Would Mrs. Mayweather's parlor even hold that many?

"It's a last minute thing, but I expect most everyone to accept." She gave Callie an amused look. "You must know the whole town is abuzz with your remarkable story. Rather gossipy of us I know, but I also know you're charitable enough to overlook and forgive us our curiosity. We don't get much excitement in our little corner of the world."

Callie rallied enough to attempt a protest. "But the wedding is the day after tomorrow. There are things I need to take care of and I need to get the children ready to move." All true statements. "Perhaps now is not—

"Balderdash! Everything for the wedding is taken care of. And sadly, there's not much for the children to pack." She patted Callie's hand. "I thought it best that folks meet you before the wedding so they can see what a fine person you are."

Callie tried again. "Thank you, but—"

"No need to thank me." She settled more squarely in her chair. "Now, let's finish with this little chore and we'll plan out our menu."

Callie added peas to the bowl with hands that weren't quite steady.

This was a disaster in the making. Crowds, especially crowds of strangers, made her nervous. She'd wanted to ease her way into this community, to give folks here a chance to get to know her one or two at a time before she unveiled herself—the way she had with Mrs. Mayweather and Ida Lee.

Of course, it wasn't as if she'd show her birthmark to them tomorrow. That would be a true disaster. They would likely have a negative reaction, and that reaction would affect Jack's perception of her.

She knew theirs wasn't a love match, but she'd at least hoped to build a life with him that was based on mutual respect.

All of those hopes could be summarily dashed if tomorrow did not go well.

Chapter Thirteen

The next day, Callie stood in Mrs. Mayweather's parlor, surrounded by at least twenty-five ladies of varying ages.

The children had escaped to the backyard, where Jack and Virgil had engaged them in a game of horseshoes.

Callie envied them. She couldn't remember ever being in the midst of such a crowded room, much less finding herself the center of attention at such a gathering.

Her family would never have allowed it. One of her sisters would have stood beside her at all times, keeping her company while shielding her from undue attention. Far from serving in that capacity, Mrs. Mayweather was busy circulating amongst her guests.

During a lull in the ever-shifting conversation, Callie stole away to the corner table where a punch bowl sat. Her head spun from all the introductions. How in the world was she going to remember all those names, much less which faces they went with?

But at least she hadn't made any embarrassing missteps yet. Perhaps Mrs. Mayweather's plan hadn't been so dreadful after all. Callie filled one of the delicate crystal cups and took a fortifying sip before turning to face the room again. She found herself nearly toe-to-toe with two of the ladies she'd met earlier.

The women were Alma Collins, president of the Sweetgum Ladies' Auxiliary, and her vice president, Jane Peavey. But Callie couldn't remember which was which.

"Mrs. Mayweather makes the most delicious apple peach cider, don't you agree?" the one in the blue dress asked.

Callie moved aside to allow the women to refill their cups. "Yes, quite delicious."

"We hear you're a friend of Julia's," the one in the yellow dress added.

"Yes." Perhaps she could carry on this conversation without using names. "We lived next door to each other as children and kept in touch after she moved here."

"Well, I must say, I do so admire you. It must have taken so much courage to agree to marry a man you'd never met." Mrs. Blue Dress placed a hand to her heart. "And then to travel all this way by yourself! Why, land's sake, I just don't know if I could have done such a thing."

"Actually, some friends of the family accompanied me on the train ride." Another of her father's precautions. "It was only when I boarded the stage at Parson's Creek that I was without an escort."

"Still, Alma's right, that was mighty brave of you."

Aha! That meant Mrs. Blue Dress was Alma Collins, which made the speaker Jane Peavey.

Callie smiled, glad to have navigated past that conversational pitfall. "It's kind of you to say so, but I'm afraid I truly can't claim to have much in the way of courage. In fact I was quite nervous every step of the way. It was faith that brought me through. I felt God's presence with me all the way here."

"What a wonderful attitude." Mrs. Collins sketched a toast with her cup. "It does you credit, my dear."

"And it's so compassionate of you to take all the children in," Mrs. Peavey added.

"Not at all." Callie resisted the urge to bolt from the room. She could barely stand being the focus of these women's attention. "I'm looking forward to caring for the three of them. I only pray that I'm up to the task."

Mrs. Peavey took a sip of her punch and gave Callie an arch smile. "I must admit, I am surprised you were able to convince Jack to join forces with you. He's always been so footloose. Why, even when we were all running about the schoolyard, Jack would talk about how he wanted to travel the country. And from the looks of things he certainly hasn't let anything tie him down since he left."

Callie's back stiffened, but she kept her smile firmly in place. "People change. And to be honest, Mr. Tyler was quite insistent that he have a hand in raising the children."

Mrs. Peavey raised a delicate brow. "Is that so?"

Callie's discomfort was quickly changing to irritation. "Absolutely. He's going to make an excellent father."

The women shared an arch look that caused Callie's grip to tighten around her cup.

"That's a wonderful sentiment, dear," Mrs. Collins said. "And perhaps you're right. It has been eleven years, after all."

She was spared the need to respond by the appearance of Mrs. Mayweather. "I have something I want to show you."

Callie smiled, grateful for the excuse to change topics.

When Mrs. Mayweather opened the box she was holding, however, all thoughts of the previous conversation fled. Inside, elegantly displayed on a bed of black velvet, was a lustrous strand of pearls with a matching set of earrings. "It's beautiful," Callie breathed.

"My father gave these to my mother on their wedding day." Mrs. Mayweather brushed a finger against the pearls, then met Callie's gaze. "I'd like you to wear them on your wedding day."

"Oh, I couldn't possibly—"

"Nonsense. I know you didn't come prepared for a wedding. And it would make me very happy to see someone put it to such meaningful use again after all these years."

"I don't know what to say, except thank you." She was truly touched by the gesture. Her first wedding had been little more than a formality. No one, not even her sisters or her father, had done anything to try to make it a special day for her.

Of course she hadn't really expected them to. It was a proxy ceremony for a marriage to a man she'd never met. How could she blame her family for not bothering to celebrate her wedding day?

"Why don't you try it on?"

Mrs. Collins's question pulled Callie back to the present. She reached out a hand to touch the heirloom piece. "May I?"

"Of course." Mrs. Mayweather lifted it from the box. "I'm afraid the catch is broken. But don't worry, it's long enough to slide over your head, if you remove your bonnet."

Callie's hand drew back as if scalded.

Remove her bonnet? In front of all these strangers?

Had Mrs. Mayweather forgotten why she wore the less-than-stylish piece in the first place?

"Perhaps I should wait."

Mrs. Mayweather gave her a look that said she knew exactly what Callie was thinking. "I insist." Her voice carried that combination of the compassion and firmness that was peculiar to schoolteachers. "I really do think you should try it on now so everyone can see how lovely it will look."

Callie searched her hostess's face. She hadn't considered the woman cruel. So why was she attempting to force Callie to unmask so publicly?

But there was no getting around it. Explaining why she'd prefer not to would be almost as awkward as actually doing it. This was her worst nightmare. She thought about Jack, out in the backyard. What would he want her to do? He said her appearance didn't matter, but would he feel the same once all his friends and neighbors knew?

She took a deep breath and sent up a silent prayer for courage and decided to trust Mrs. Mayweather's instincts. "Very well."

Quickly, before she could talk herself out of it, Callie reached for her bonnet strings. Her fingers were trembling. The look of approval Mrs. Mayweather sent her way, however, gave her a much needed boost of support.

"I believe it only fair that I warn you all of something." Callie was surprised at how calm her voice sounded. "I have a rather prominent birthmark on the left side of my face."

With that, she removed the bonnet.

There were several muted "Oh, my"s and a sharp intake of breath or two, but Callie refrained from trying to identify the sources. Such initial reactions were normal, and she had learned long ago that it served no useful purpose to harbor resentment.

Instead, she moved to a mirror hanging in the foyer and gently eased the strand over her head, trying to ignore the sounds of shifting and clearing throats and even one nervous titter that was quickly shushed. Fidgeting with the necklace long enough to give everyone time to compose themselves, she finally turned to Mrs. Mayweather and pasted on a bright smile that hopefully masked her embarrassment. "Thank you for the loan of such a treasure. I promise to take very special care of it."

"You're welcome, my dear. And I think it looks absolutely lovely on you."

Callie removed the necklace and tucked it back in the box. Then she donned her bonnet once again and gazed around the room.

Suddenly there was a rush of voices, nervously eager to fill the silence. No one, except for Ida Lee and Mrs. Mayweather, met her gaze.

Perhaps Mrs. Mayweather had been right. Painful though it had been, maybe it was best that she got this revelation over with all at once. She just hoped she'd never have to go through such an ordeal again.

The question was, now that everyone knew her secret, how big a difference would it make in their eagerness to welcome her into the community?

And what difference would it make to Jack and the children, and how they felt about her?

Callie's second wedding day dawned clear and beautiful.

She had lain awake long into the night, praying and searching for answers that wouldn't come.

And wondering about the repercussions of her unveiling at Mrs. Mayweather's tea party.

It felt strange, dreamlike. For so much of her life she'd accepted that she would never marry and have a family of her own.

Now, in the space of a few short weeks, she was preparing to say her wedding vows for the second time. And again it was to a man who wanted a mother for his children, not a wife for himself.

The morning dragged on interminably. Callie helped the children pack the few possessions they had with them. That, along with most of her own belongings, were loaded into Mrs. Mayweather's buggy.

Once the ceremony was over, the newly formed family of five would proceed directly to their new home together.

Home.

Callie let out a wistful sigh. Would that farmhouse ever truly feel like the home she'd dreamed of when she'd imagined her life with Leland?

No matter. Just thinking of the alternative strengthened her determination. She didn't want to go back to Ohio, and it made no sense for her to stay here and *not* do her part to help this family. And she so looked forward to the sense of freedom country life promised.

Even if she did have strong reservations about her ability to manage the place on her own once Jack left. Just the thought of taking on such a task twisted her stomach in knots. Perhaps Jack would change his mind, decide to stay and work with her to make this a real family.

Callie squelched that thought before it could take root. He'd been very clear on what he was and was not willing to give up when they'd struck this bargain. Expecting him to do a sudden turnaround now was unrealistic and unfair.

No, better to draw comfort from the knowledge that the good Lord wouldn't have set her feet on this path if He hadn't had a purpose for her.

The question was, did she really have the fortitude to see it through?

Callie barely touched her lunch. Later she couldn't recall what was served.

And suddenly it was time to go to the church. Callie donned her best Sunday dress along with the pearls Mrs. Mayweather had loaned her, clutched the flower bouquet Emma and Annabeth had picked for her, and piled into the carriage with Mrs. Mayweather and the children. Simon proudly handled the reins.

Once they arrived, Mrs. Mayweather escorted the children inside while Ida Lee stood with Callie at the back of the church.

A few moments later the piano signaled it was time, Ida Lee gave her hand a squeeze, and Callie stepped from the foyer into the small auditorium.

For a split second she froze, unable to either move forward or retreat, uncertain which she wanted to do more. Every pew was packed. It looked as if all of Sweetgum wanted to see the town's Prodigal Son and the blotchy-faced widow get hitched.

Callie took a deep breath and tugged her bonnet forward. By now everyone would know about her birthmark, but at least she didn't have to bare it to them.

With a quick prayer, she looked straight ahead and began placing one foot in front of the other. She told herself it was perfectly natural for the bride to be the center of attention on her wedding day. But this felt like something very different.

Her hand itched to reach up and tug her bonnet forward again, but she resisted, hoping to portray a serenity she didn't feel.

When her gaze latched on to Jack, her world shifted once again. He looked so different in that Sunday-go-to-meeting suit, so dashing and distinguished. It hit her again that this was not the kind of man who was used to settling for anything, much less a wife.

Her steps faltered. What had they been thinking? Jack didn't really want this. She should—

He met her gaze and a crooked smile curved his lips.

Then, without quite knowing how, Callie was at his side and they were turning to face Reverend Hollingsford.

As the reverend began the service, Callie couldn't help but compare this wedding with her first.

This time it was a solemn church ceremony instead of a rushed civil one.

This time there was a community of neighbors and friends to witness her big day rather than just a few family members.

And this time, instead of some disinterested stand-in, the actual groom stood beside her, gazing intently into her eyes, vowing to honor, cherish and provide for her, as long as they both should live.

And to her surprise, he had a simple but beautiful gold band to slip on her finger as he said those vows. That gesture alone added a special touch to the ceremony.

It might all be for the sake of the children, with no real affection between the two adults, but for the space of time it took to repeat their vows, Callie felt a shiver of emotion.

What would it be like to have someone truly love and cherish her, not as a matter of convenience, but as a matter of the heart? She yearned for that experience with every fiber of her being.

As they turned back to face Reverend Hollingsford, regret sliced through her as she realized that that one brief, mirage-like moment would likely be her only taste.

Chapter Fourteen

They didn't leave for the farm immediately as Callie had expected. When she and Jack stepped outside, they found several tables set up on the church grounds, most of them laden with food. Ida Lee approached them, her generous smile broadcasting that she was pleased with the surprise she'd had a hand in.

"Well, Mr. and Mrs. Tyler, seeing as how you've had to plan this wedding all quick-like without much time for celebrating, the members of the Sweetgum Ladies' Auxiliary decided to throw you this little shindig. Just our way of letting you know we're tickled pink to have you as part of the fold, so to speak."

At the sound of "Mr. and Mrs. Tyler," Callie felt that shiver. Even after her proxy marriage to Leland, most everyone had continued to address her by her first name rather than as a married woman.

It took her a moment to realize Jack was leaving it up to her to respond. "I—I'm certain Jack shares my appreciation for all of this." She stumbled over the first few words, then saw all the friendly, smiling faces beaming at the two of them. That made it easier to speak from the heart. "You've made our special day so much brighter with your outpouring of support and kindness. I know now why Julia always wrote of Sweetgum and its people with such affection."

"Well done." Jack spoke so low she was certain no one else heard him. But the compliment added an extra bounce to her step as they descended the church stairs.

They stopped at the bottom and stood there while a parade of townsfolk came by to offer well-wishes. The faces and comments swirled about her like schools of fish.

"Wouldn't be right for the new bride to have to cook her own supper on her wedding day."

"We want to make sure you feel welcome here."

"Just wait until you taste Helen Beaman's peach cobbler."

"It's what Lanny and Nell would have wanted for you."

It was all so overwhelming. First the gathering at Mrs. Mayweather's yesterday, then the wedding itself, and now this. Who would have thought she'd feel more hemmed in and crowded in a small town than she'd ever felt in her big city home?

Callie resisted the urge to fidget, or worse yet to bolt and run. Being on display this way was excruciating, but she didn't want to appear ungrateful when these folks had worked so hard to make her feel welcome.

Finally, the last of the wedding guests shook their hands and she and Jack were free to lose themselves in the crowd. They became separated almost at once, drawn into different groups as they began to mingle.

Callie felt some of her tension ease. Better to be part of a milling crowd than to be the center of attention. But after five minutes, she found an opportunity to slip into the church unobserved. Sitting in one of the pews, she closed her eyes and breathed a sigh of relief.

Thank You, Father, for setting me among such neighborly people. Help me remember that it truly is a blessing. And give me the strength and fortitude to accept with good grace their outpourings of friendship, even when it isn't comfortable to do so.

She sat there for a few more minutes with her eyes closed and her head resting against the back of her pew. Muted sounds of conversation drifted in from an open window, punctuated now and then by the drone of insects. She really should return to the reception before her absence was noted. But it was so nice sitting here unobserved, drinking in the peace.

Callie let the serenity of the small country church refresh her spirit a minute longer, then she straightened. The murmur of conversation was drawing closer. It was time she rejoined the others before she was discovered hiding in here like a coward.

Then one of the conversations sharpened, as if the speaker stood right under the window.

"…sakes. Did you see her face yesterday?"

"That poor thing. I suppose it's understandable why she'd rather hide behind those frumpy bonnets."

Callie froze.

"Bless her heart," the voice continued. "No wonder she came all this way to marry a man she'd never met. I wonder if Lanny even knew about that birthmark when he proposed."

"Well, Jack's the one I feel sorry for. I mean, at least Lanny had his time with Julia. But Jack, well, all I can say is, it's very noble of him to go through with this, for the sake of the kids and all."

Callie's face burned with mortification. This was the

sort of thing her family had always warned her about, had tried to shield her from.

And she recognized the voices. How could she face these women now that she knew how they viewed her?

Heavenly Father, I know I should turn the other cheek, but sometimes it's so difficult.

"You know Jack. He might not have been as gentlemanly as Lanny, but—"

"Ladies."

Callie stiffened. That was Jack's voice. And she'd thought this couldn't possibly get any worse.

"Uh, hello, Jack."

Callie heard the caught-in-the-act tone in the woman's voice.

"Have either of you seen my bride in the last few minutes?"

"Why, no."

"I'm quite a lucky man to have found such a fine woman to marry, don't you agree?"

"Yes, of course." There was the sound of a throat clearing. "Why I was just saying what a wonderful thing the two of you are doing for those children."

"I'll tell you ladies a secret. Callie took a bit of convincing. Why, I'm almost embarrassed to admit how much arm-twisting it took to convince her to have me."

"Is that so?"

"Yep. But it was worth it. In fact, I'd be mighty put out if I learned someone said something to make her sorry she decided to stay in Sweetgum."

"I'm sure you have nothing to worry about on that score." The rustling of skirts filled the short pause. "Well, if we see her, we'll let her know you're looking for her."

"Thank you kindly, ladies."

Callie's heart warmed at Jack's defense of her. Whatever else he might be, Jack Tyler was an honorable man with a good heart.

Jack watched Alma Collins and Jane Peavey hurry away. It had been all he could do to keep his tone pleasant while he dealt with them. If they'd been men…

That pair didn't seem to have changed much from the adolescent babblers he remembered. They thrived on gossip and were always on the lookout for ways to stir things up. Hopefully he'd managed to nip in the bud any further attempts to target Callie.

Thank goodness Callie wasn't that sort of woman. She might have some less than docile qualities that got under his skin, but at least she was forthright and fair-minded.

Just where was she anyway? He glanced around, his gaze honing in on Ben Cooper heading for one of the food tables. Time for a quick detour.

"Hey," he said as he clapped Ben on the shoulder, "I've been meaning to talk to you." Virgil had informed him it was Ben, the town's young undertaker, who'd seen that everything was done all right and proper for the funerals after the fire.

"Well, hi there, Jack. Is there something I can do for you?"

Jack shook his head. "You've already done more than expected. I wanted you to know I appreciate your taking care of the three burials for me. And that I intend to pay you back for every bit of your time and expense. Just let me know how much."

Ben shook his head. "I just did what needed doing. And your wedding day is not the time to be talking business. You can stop by my place one day next week."

Ben glanced up past Jack's shoulder. "Right now you have a bride you should be tending to."

Jack followed the direction of Ben's gaze just in time to see Callie step out of the church. So that's where she'd disappeared to. Truth to tell, he didn't much blame her. He could do with a bit of peace and quiet right now himself.

Then he frowned. Something wasn't right, though he couldn't explain how he knew. She wore a serene smile and her stride was unfaltering.

And then it hit him. If Callie had been in the church, she may have heard the conversation between Alma and Jane. And if she had, she'd no doubt be feeling pretty low right now.

"Excuse me, Ben, I do need to speak to Callie for a minute."

Ben gave him a knowing smile. "You go right ahead."

Jack rolled his eyes at the implication. Nothing could be further from the truth.

Could it?

He caught up to Callie before she'd reached the thick of the crowd and took her arm. "Are you okay?"

Her eyes widened in surprise. "Of course." She glanced back at the church. "Sorry for slipping off like that. I hope no one noticed. It's just that I'm not used to crowds and so much attention."

"No need to apologize. I'm pretty sure no one else noticed." He studied her face, or at least the part of it he could see. Had he read her wrong? "Are you sure you're okay? We can leave now if you like."

"I'm fine, really."

That little tug she gave her bonnet said otherwise.

She laid a hand on his arm. "Please don't break this up on my account. Everyone has been so neighborly and they worked hard to put this together." She made a shooing motion. "Now go on back to our guests and I'll do the same."

Jack watched her walk away, more certain than ever that she'd caught at least part of the conversation.

He raked a hand through his hair as he moved toward the food tables. If she'd heard his defense of her, he sure hoped she wasn't reading anything into it. He'd merely been doing what any decent man would do—taking care of his own.

And like it or not, that included her now.

Callie had mixed emotions later that afternoon as she stood on the porch and watched the day draw to a close. They'd left the reception a little over an hour ago, the buckboard loaded down with not only the luggage from Mrs. Mayweather's, but also with the choicest leftovers from the reception.

Now everything had been taken into the house, at least as far as the front hall, and the sun was just kissing the horizon.

Jack was somewhere inside. Emma and Annabeth sat on the porch swing playing with Annabeth's doll. Simon was out in the yard, throwing sticks for both dogs to retrieve.

Callie wrapped her arms around herself. She'd always liked this pre-dusk moment. It was a restful time of day, one that usually brought her a sense of peace and a renewed appreciation for her many blessings.

But the events of *this* day, and the fact that she'd been on display for most of it, left her drained. Overhearing that bit of conversation hadn't helped much.

But Jack had defended her, and so deliberately. That

was almost as disquieting, though in a different sort of way. It turned all her ideas of him upside down.

But most of all, the thought that she was now responsible for these children, and that she not only shared that responsibility, but also this house, with Jack Tyler—a man she was beginning to see in a new light—left her unsettled and jittery.

No, she wasn't in any frame of mind right now to appreciate the quiet majesty of the day's close.

Enough of that kind of thinking. Callie pushed away from the porch rail. There was unpacking to do, and food to sort through and put away. And this being their first night together as a family would mean dealing with everyone getting used to a new routine and new sleeping arrangements.

She turned to the front door, but before she could move further, Jack stepped onto the porch. "I'm going to get the animals settled in for the night."

"Yes, of course." She tugged on her bonnet. "I've some chores to take care of myself."

He paused and gave her a long, considering look. "You've had a busy day," he said gruffly. "Whatever you have to do will likely wait until tomorrow."

His concern surprised her and she smiled. "Thank you, but I'm fine. And I'll sleep better knowing things are in apple-pie order, as my mother used to say." She clasped her hands together. "When you come back inside, we can select a Bible verse to read before we get the children ready for bed."

He merely nodded.

"And you do remember that tomorrow is Sunday?" She didn't want to be a nag, but it was important that they get off on the right foot in this matter from day one.

An annoyed furrow creased his forehead. "I know

what day it is. That's all the more reason for me to get as many chores done this evening as possible."

As she watched him cross the yard in ground-eating strides, Callie nibbled at her lower lip. Was she being too pushy? Was there some other approach she should use with him?

It was just so important that they set the proper example for the children. On the other hand, if it was obvious that his heart wasn't in it, that could do more harm than good.

As promised, Jack read from the family Bible that evening. He asked Callie to pick the verse, and she selected Isaiah 43:18-19. A passage about new beginnings seemed appropriate.

His reading voice was pleasant, strong and authoritative. A bit like the man himself. And he didn't stumble over the words once. It showed a familiarity with the scriptures she hadn't expected.

Afterwards, as Jack carried the Bible back to the stand by the window, Callie rose. "Before you children go to bed, I have a surprise for you. Stay where you are and I'll be right back."

Callie returned a short time later with four parcels, her insides fluttering. She hoped she had gauged their interests well. "This is the first day of our life together as a family," she said. "And I thought it would be nice to mark the occasion with something special. So I have a little gift for each of you."

The children sat up straighter, a gleam of anticipation firing their eyes.

Callie, feeling a bit of anticipation herself, handed the parcels out. She caught the flash of surprise in Jack's expression as she handed him his. Did he think she would leave him out?

Annabeth opened hers. "It's a book."

"That's right. It's called *The House That Jack Built* and it has some wonderful pictures in it."

Annabeth giggled. "He has the same name as you, Uncle Jack." She turned the pages, her eyes sparkling in delight at the illustrations. "Will you read it to me?"

"Of course. But let's save it for when I tuck you in tonight."

Callie held her breath as Emma slowly unwrapped her parcel. This was the one she'd most looked forward to.

When Emma lifted the lid off the box, her reaction was everything Callie had hoped for.

Her eyes grew round and her mouth formed a little *O* of surprise. "She's beautiful." The words were breathed more than spoken. Emma lifted the doll gently out of the box, smoothing the dress and golden curls. "What's her name?"

"She doesn't have one yet. She's waiting for you to name her."

Emma squeezed the doll in a fierce hug. "Then I'll call her Dotty, just like my other doll."

"That sounds like a perfectly lovely name."

Annabeth clapped. "Now Tizzy will have a new sister to play with, just like me."

Emma nodded, then turned to her brother. She gave him a nudge with her shoulder. "Your turn."

When he didn't move right away, Annabeth offered her own encouragement. "Don't you want to see what's inside? I know I do."

Simon finally untied the string with a great show of disinterest. Once the paper was removed, he stared at the small wooden box as if uncertain whether or not to open it.

Annabeth prodded him again. "Why do you have to go so slow? Let's see what it is."

Simon slid the lid off the box to reveal a neatly arranged group of tiles, each decorated with a series of dots.

"It's a set of dominos," Callie explained. "They're made with real ivory. Have you ever played the game before?"

Simon frowned. "I've only ever seen old men playing it over at the mercantile."

"Well, it *is* usually played by adults. But I thought, since your Aunt Julia told me what a good student you are, that you might be able to learn it anyway."

She leaned forward. "But if you don't want it..."

He moved back slightly, fingering one of the smooth tiles. "This is really ivory?"

Callie nodded. "I found it in a little shop that specializes in items brought to this country from all around the world. The box is made from sandalwood, a tree that grows in India."

She saw the acceptance in his eyes. Deciding not to press the point, she leaned back. "I'm sure your Uncle Jack has played before. He can teach you how."

Jack nodded. "Anytime you're ready."

Annabeth turned curious eyes toward the last package. "What about you, Uncle Jack? Aren't you going to open your gift?"

Jack stared at the parcel as if it might blow up in his face. He still hadn't touched it. With a smile that seemed a bit forced to Callie, he slowly opened it.

He stared at the pocket watch nestled inside for a

long minute, then looked at Callie. A small muscle at the corner of his mouth jumped.

Her pleasure in the gift-giving deflated. Something about the watch had upset him. "I know it's not brand-new. It belonged to my grandfather. If you don't like it—"

"No, it's a fine piece," he said quickly. "Thank you."

"You're welcome." She'd never heard a less convincing expression of gratitude.

Annabeth popped up from her seat and stood in front of Callie, her lips drawn down in a melodramatic frown. "But we didn't get you anything."

Callie forced her thoughts away from Jack's disappointing reaction, and smiled at the little girl. "Of course you did," she said, taking both of her hands.

The child's nose scrunched in confusion. "We did?"

"Most certainly. Don't you remember?" She released Annabeth's hands and gave her tummy a gentle poke. "You and Emma picked that beautiful bouquet of flowers for me to carry during the wedding. And Simon drove the carriage to get me there on time."

She held up her left hand. "And your Uncle Jack gave me this lovely wedding ring. So you see," She smiled, determined to end their first evening on a happy note, "I've had plenty of gifts today."

Only she had hoped the watch would mean as much to Jack as the ring had meant to her.

Apparently she'd failed.

Chapter Fifteen

While Callie herded the reluctant children upstairs, Jack stepped out on the front porch.

He pulled out his pocketknife and hefted a thick chuck of wood he'd pilfered earlier from the woodpile for just this purpose.

Sitting on the top step, he placed the pocket watch she'd given him on the porch floor beside him. Then he shaved a long thin curl of wood from the block.

Whittling was something he enjoyed doing at the end of the day, or anytime he just needed to be quiet and think. Sometimes he ended up with a whistle or a crude animal shape, but more often than not, he just ended up with a pile of shavings to use as kindling for the cook fire. In fact, even his better carving efforts usually ended up tossed in the fire.

What use did he have for such trinkets?

Married.

He sliced off a particularly thick chunk as he thought about the woman tucking the children in upstairs. The woman he'd vowed just a few hours earlier to cherish and protect until death should part them. The woman he knew next to nothing about.

Except that she was stubborn enough to stand up to him.

And that she genuinely cared about the kids.

And that she seemed dead set on cramming religion down his throat.

What she didn't understand was that he and God had an understanding of sorts.

For years he'd prayed for all he was worth that God would give him the chance to come into his own, to be something other than Lanny's not-quite-as-good little brother. He'd prayed even more desperately for Julia to say yes when he'd proposed. None of those prayers had been answered.

And he'd finally realized why. It was because he was so full of jealousy and pride that he wasn't good enough even for God. At least not so far as being worth His special attention.

That's when he'd realized that he was the kind of person the adage "God helps those who help themselves" had been penned for.

And it had worked for him so far. He was well-traveled, independent and respected in his field.

Sure, he had a few regrets—not making things right with Lanny was the biggest of them. But there probably wasn't a man alive who didn't have regrets of one sort or another.

Jack leaned back against the porch post.

Speaking of regrets…

He glanced down at the pocket watch and winced. His lack of enthusiasm had hurt Callie's feelings. But trying to explain that accepting a gift she'd selected for Lanny would leave a sour taste in his mouth would have only made matters worse.

Better for both of them that she just think him ungrateful.

Jack ran a thumb over the surface of the wood. He had to hand it to her—passing out those gifts had meant a lot to the kids, especially Nell's.

Seems his new wife had been quicker than him to see that those kids needed things to call their own, things to help them rebuild their sense of belonging.

Jack planed another long curl from the block of wood. He should have been the one to realize that, to take care of their needs.

Mrs. Mayweather had been right. The kids needed a mother, a mother like Callie.

The question was, was he the right man to play the role of their father?

The door opened behind him.

"The children are all settled in for the night."

And why aren't you? "Good." Kicking himself for not putting away the watch, Jack kept his voice even and his attention focused on whittling.

She took a few steps forward, halting just behind him. "I think today was a really good start."

He glanced over his shoulder and gave her a long, steady look. After a minute, he went back to his whittling. "Today was merely recess. Tomorrow the real work begins."

"I agree. And I'm ready."

"Are you now?"

Her sigh conveyed a sense of sorely tried patience. "Mr. Tyler, I—"

"Jack." He glanced up and saw her confused frown. "We're married. Might as well use first names."

"Very well. Jack, I know you think I'm too green for

farm work, but with you to teach me, and God to help me, I'm certain I can learn what I need to."

"Then I suggest you turn in. Your lessons start tomorrow, which means you'll need to be up before sunrise in the morning."

"But tomorrow is Sunday."

"Lesson number one. The animals don't know what day of the week it is. They still need to be fed, the cows milked, the eggs gathered." He pointed his block of wood in her general direction. "And that's in addition to fixing breakfast and getting the kids ready for church service."

"Very well." He heard the swish of skirts as she turned. "I'll see you in the morning."

Twenty minutes later, Jack turned down the bedside lamp in his room and plopped onto the mattress, his fingers laced behind his head. It wasn't exactly the cozy marriage bed a man normally slid into on his wedding night.

Not that he wanted it any other way. This whole marriage thing had happened way too fast. This might have been their only option, but he still felt as if he'd been backed into a corner.

He rolled over on his side and punched his pillow into shape. He'd keep up his end of this bargain.

She'd have to be satisfied with that.

Callie slipped under the covers in the four poster bed that had been Julia and Leland's. She'd heard Jack come upstairs a few moments ago and she felt guilty enjoying the comfort of this large bedchamber while he made do with the smaller bed in the room across the hall.

But he'd insisted on those arrangements, arguing that in a month or so he planned to be gone anyway, and that the spare room accommodations were a step up from what he was used to while on the job.

Much as he would deny it, the man really did have a kind heart beating somewhere under that gruff exterior of his.

Too bad he didn't let it show more often.

His insistence that she would have a difficult time with the farm chores was worrisome. Surely he was being overly-pessimistic. She could make this work. She had to.

After all, wasn't this where God intended her to be?

Jack had been as good as his word when it came to the family bible reading. Though he'd asked her to pick out the verse, he'd done the reading himself and then asked Simon to lead them in prayer afterward.

Her heart warmed at the thought that God might be using her to help Jack find his way back.

Dear Heavenly Father, help me to be the sort of example You desire me to be.

And with that, she snuggled down into her pillow. But thoughts of Jack's insistence that he'd be moving on in a month or so made it hard for her to find the easy slumber she'd hoped for.

Chapter Sixteen

Callie woke to the sound of someone tapping at her door. Glancing toward the window through slitted lids, she saw a glimmering of gray pushing out the black of night. It was dawn, way too early to—

Dawn! Her sluggish brain suddenly flared to life.

Oh no! She'd overslept. Callie popped upright and tried to untangle herself from the covers. "I'm awake," she called out.

"Good." Jack's tone was dry, as if he could see her frantic rush to get out of bed. "Meet me in the barn when you get dressed."

Finally kicking off the covers, Callie quickly made her morning ablutions and dressed. She was still tying the strings to her bonnet as she hurried down the stairs, determined that their first full day together go as smoothly as possible.

As she passed through the kitchen she noted that the stove had already been stoked. Jack must have been up and about for some time.

Her guilt for oversleeping deepened a notch.

She quickened her pace as soon as she stepped outside, and fought the urge to pause when she stepped off the back porch. Normally she'd take an extra second or two to appreciate God's exquisite handiwork in the first glimmerings of sunrise. But today she'd have to admire it on the run. Already a blush of color seeped past the horizon, reminding her that time was slipping away.

Lifting her skirts, Callie sprinted across the last few dew-dampened yards toward the barn. She arrived breathless and all but stumbled across the threshold.

Jack sat on a stool, already at work milking one of the cows. He spared the briefest of glances over his shoulder, then went back to work.

"I apologize for oversleeping." Though how one could call it oversleeping when you were up before sunrise…

He ignored her apology. "I'm almost finished milking Belle." He nodded toward the other stall. "As soon as I'm done, I'll let you try your hand at milking Clover."

Feeling duly chastised, Callie nodded. Curious, she moved closer so she could watch Jack at work.

It didn't look so hard. He merely squeezed on the cow's teats and the milk squirted into the bucket. The animal stood placidly eating from a waist-high mounted feed trough while Jack worked. The animal didn't even seem to notice what Jack was doing, much less mind.

A few minutes later Jack stood and patted the cow. "Thanks, girl." He carefully set the bucket of frothy white liquid on a wooden table next to the barn door, then returned and untied the cow.

Finally, he turned to Callie. "Ready to give it a try?"

She gave a confident nod.

"All right. First, add a bit of grain to her feed trough." He handed her a large chipped bowl filled with corn and some other type of grain. "Always approach her from the right side. That's also the side you're going to milk her from." He set the stool in place. "Cows are creatures of habit and you want to approach her the same way every time."

Callie nodded and dutifully poured the grain into the feed trough.

"When you're ready, take a minute to pat her side and talk to her so she knows you're there."

What did one say to a cow? She decided to pretend Clover was just a big dog. "Hi there, girl." She patted the animal's side. "I'm Callie and I hope you're going to take it easy on me this morning."

The cow turned her head, looking at Callie with big, soulful brown eyes as if to reassure her. Callie smiled. So far this didn't seem so difficult.

"All right," Jack said. "Now take these two pails." He handed her an empty pail and one with fresh water and a rag.

"Scoot your stool up next to her, then sit at a right angle." He watched carefully as she complied. "You might want to lean your head or shoulder against her flank, just to keep the two of you anchored to each other."

Callie gave him a startled look. Was he serious? But then she remembered that he'd been sitting that way earlier. She leaned forward, her shoulder touching the cow.

"Now take this bucket," he said, pointing to the one filled with water, "and wash down her udder. That'll make sure you don't get any dirt in the milk."

Callie did as she was told, all the while feeling Jack's assessing eye on her.

"That's good. Take the milk pail and place it directly under the udder. Okay. Now you'll want to use your left hand to hold the pail steady. These two cows seem pretty tame, but you never know when one of them will have a bad day. You don't want them stepping in the pail or kicking it over."

"Kicking?"

He shrugged. "It happens. Hurts like h—" he cleared his throat "—like fire if you get in the way. Just keep your eyes open."

Callie shifted uneasily.

He stooped down beside her. "Watch me, then you try it. What you need to do is take one of the teats into the palm of your hand, like this. Starting at the top, squeeze with your thumb and forefinger. Then squeeze with your next finger, then the next, until your entire hand is curled around it. Then you release and do it all over again."

Sounded simple enough.

He straightened. "Think you have it?"

She nodded.

"Then give it a shot."

Callie took a deep breath, then reached up and positioned her hand as he'd instructed. She mentally reviewed his directions as she squeezed.

Nothing happened.

"Let's go over it again." He repeated the instructions, then crossed his arms and waited for her to follow through.

Feeling slightly less confident, Callie tried again.

Still nothing.

Jack stooped down until his head was level with hers. "One more time."

She did, with the same dismal results.

"I think I see what your problem is. Here, let me show you."

Jack shifted forward until they were shoulder to

shoulder. He wrapped his hand around hers, encompassing it in a firm yet not unpleasant hold.

Callie was startled by his nearness, by the solid warmth of his hands on hers. She'd felt it before when he held her hand—that something protective in his touch, strong and gentle at the same time.

It took her a few seconds to realize he was speaking again.

"...need to apply a bit more pressure and make your movements smoother, firmer." He used his fingers to manipulate hers and like magic the milk pinged into the bucket. "Do you feel the difference?"

"Y-yes." She cleared her throat, clearing her head at the same time. "That was very helpful. Thank you."

With a nod he released her hand and glanced up. For a moment their gazes locked and she saw something flicker to life in his eyes. Whatever it was, though, it was gone almost as quickly as it had come.

"Well then," he sat back on his heels and broke eye contact, "let's see you give it a go on your own."

"Of course."

To her immense relief, the milk spurted into the pail with a satisfactory splish.

Jack stood. "Better. Now, you just keep that up until nothing more comes out. Then you move on to the next one. Clover's calf needs to be fed so you'll just milk out two teats. The calf will get the rest."

Callie nodded as she continued to work. There was a rhythm to this and she'd almost found it. It helped if she concentrated on what she was doing rather than on Jack.

It took her nearly twenty minutes to complete the task, but Callie felt an immense sense of satisfaction when she'd finished. She turned to share her accomplishment with Jack, only to find him busy spreading fresh hay in the vacated stalls.

Looking around, she realized he'd turned out Belle and filled the water troughs already. And probably a few other things she wasn't yet trained to notice.

And here she'd been feeling so smug about having milked a cow in that time, and only halfway at that.

She stood, stretching her back and flexing her sore hand muscles.

Jack leaned on the pitchfork, giving her an almost sympathetic smile. "Harder than it looks, isn't it?"

"I imagine it'll get easier with practice." She set her pail on the table next to his. "What's next?"

"You take this milk on up to the house." He cocked his head to one side. "That is, if your hands aren't too sore to handle the pails."

She wasn't going to let him see how cramped her hands and arms felt. "I'm fine."

"Good." He wiped his brow. "Morning's getting on. If we're going to get everyone fed and ready for church, you need to get breakfast started and see to the kids. I'll finish up in here and take care of gathering the eggs."

He took a firmer hold of the pitchfork, then paused again. "And don't forget to strain the milk. There ought to be some cheesecloth in the kitchen or laundry room."

She nodded and grabbed the pails.

"Don't worry," he said cheerfully, "tomorrow you'll get a real taste of what farm life is all about."

Jack rubbed the back of his neck as he watched Callie trudge through the barn door with the pails of milk. What was it about holding hands with this woman? There'd been a moment earlier when—

He tamped that thought down and focused instead on what they'd accomplished this morning.

Callie might have more than her fair share of determination, but now she'd gotten a small taste of what she'd be up against. How would she feel about things after a few more days of this? Would her resolve to stay out here waver? If it did, could he really, in good conscience, leave her and the kids here on their own?

He let the calf out of its pen and it immediately trotted over to its mother and began suckling.

He snatched the cloth-lined wicker basket from the workbench and trudged toward the hen house.

As he methodically reached into each nest and plucked out the still warm eggs, Jack began pondering alternatives. Like it or not, these four were his responsibility and leaving them in the lurch was not an option. But neither was his staying here in Sweetgum. So what could he do to make certain both their interests and his were taken care of? Surely he was resourceful enough to come up with something.

Because he was as determined as ever to return to his former life as soon as possible.

Callie set the milk pails on the kitchen counter and went to the washroom to clean up and fetch the cheesecloth. The day was barely started and already she was sore. And Jack implied he'd gone easy on her! Could she really do this?

Father, give me the strength I'll need to see this through. I desperately want to stay here in this place, but help me to not let my selfish desires blind me to what is best for the family as a whole.

It took more time to prepare breakfast and get the children ready than Callie had expected, but finally they were all dressed in their Sunday best and seated in the buggy. She'd have to do something about Emma and Simon's clothing. With the exception of what they'd been wearing the day of the fire, everything had been destroyed. Mrs. Mayweather had found them a few extra items to wear, but they needed more.

Jack flicked the reins and set the wagon in motion. Callie faced the road with a smile of satisfaction. She'd made it through the first morning without any notable disasters. And with any luck they would make it into town before the church service started.

The silence drew out. This wouldn't do at all.

Callie turned to face the children. "Have any of you ever played the Endless Story game?"

Three sets of eyes stared at her blankly.

"It's a game my sisters and I used to play for hours at a time," Callie said.

"You have sisters?" Annabeth's eyes were round with surprise.

"Yes, four of them, actually."

"I like stories," Emma offered.

"Then you'll enjoy this."

Annabeth propped her arms and chin against the back of the front seat. "How do you play?"

"Well, one person starts telling a story." Callie waved a hand. "It can be about anything at all. But at the end of two minutes they must stop, even if they are in the middle of a sentence. Then the next person picks up the story where the first person left off, taking it in any direction they want. After two minutes, they stop and the next person starts, and so on."

Annabeth clapped her hands. "Ooh, let's play."

Callie looked at the other two. "How about you? Do you want to give it a try?"

Emma nodded somewhat hesitantly. Simon merely shrugged.

"All right, then, I'll start." She turned to Jack. "Can we borrow your pocket watch?"

He hesitated a fraction of a second, then slowly pulled his watch out of his pocket and handed it to her.

She stared at it. It wasn't the one she'd given him.

She did her best to ignore the stab of rejection. Perhaps this one had some sentimental value to him, had come from someone who mattered.

She swallowed her hurt and gave him a smile. "Thank you."

Then she quickly turned to the children. "Now, let's see. In a land far away, there was a castle situated next to the ocean. And in this castle lived many people, including a girl named Flora and a boy named Hawk. Flora's favorite pastime was working in her garden where flowers of every color and scent grew, and where butterflies and insects added color and nature's own music.

"Hawk, on the other hand, preferred to roam through the forest, exploring caves and gullies, discovering new trails and fishing in the many streams..."

While Callie wove her tale, she kept a close eye on the watch. As the two-minute mark approached, she deliberately stopped in mid-sentence. "While Flora was busy deciding what to do about the wilting flowers, Hawk had discovered—" She halted. "Uh-oh, looks like my time is up. Who wants to go next?"

Annabeth raised her hand. "I do."

"So, tell us what happens next."

"Hawk had discovered...he was lost." The little girl tossed her head, dismissing the hapless Hawk. "Back at the castle, Flora looked under her pink rosebush and found a puppy..."

Annabeth happily chatted on about Flora and the menagerie of pets she discovered hiding in her garden until Callie signaled that her two minutes were up and tapped Emma to take over.

Jack listened to the story unroll from each of his passenger's perspective. Callie even managed to coax shy Emma and surly Simon to participate. How did she do that?

He declined when she asked if he wanted a turn, and without missing a beat, she took her turn again.

Her very lack of reproach over both his refusal to participate in their game and his rejection of the gift she'd given him had him mentally squirming.

Shaking that uncomfortable feeling off, he listened to the story as it was reshaped by each speaker in turn.

Interesting.

Annabeth concentrated on Flora and her interaction with the numerous animals she invented for her to play with.

Emma tied the two characters together as brother and sister. She also set the boundary of the garden right at the edge of the forest so that Flora and Hawk could take time out to visit with each other as they went about their activities.

Simon, of course, focused on Hawk's adventures, setting him off in search of lost treasure.

Whenever it came back to Callie, however, she would deftly weave the threads of the story back together and set it dramatically off on a new course before her two minutes were up.

They were still going strong when the outskirts of town came into view.

As the wagon rolled past the burned out remains of the café, all talk ceased.

Jack cast a quick glance at the three children and saw Simon's clenched jaw, Emma's downcast eyes and Annabeth's quivering lower lip.

He should have come into town by a more roundabout route, he realized with regret. So what if they were a little late?

The kids shouldn't have to face this reminder again.

Another black mark on his parenting record.

Chapter Seventeen

Jack cleared his throat, not quite sure what to say, but knowing the kids needed a distraction.

A quick glance Callie's way confirmed that she shared his concern. She pasted a smile on her face and turned back to the children. "Well, there's the church and it looks like we made it on time. Simon, isn't that your friend Bobby there by the steps?"

As if to reinforce her words, the bells started pealing and the small crowd that had been gathered out front began to make their way inside.

Callie adjusted her bonnet, facing forward again. "Thank you, children. You are amazing storytellers. And thank you," she said turning back to him, "for the loan of your watch."

He accepted his timepiece back, mouthing a quick, "Thank you."

She merely nodded as she smoothed her skirt.

A few other latecomers were still making their way inside when Jack pulled the wagon up to the hitching rail.

"Simon, you help the girls down," Jack instructed as he secured the horse.

He knew what his role was today and he was determined to play it well. If only to prove that Callie wasn't the only one capable of making the best of an uncomfortable situation.

He helped her down, then offered his arm. He placed his hand solicitously over hers as he escorted his new family into the church. The fourth pew on the right, the one the Tyler family had occupied all during his growing up years, was vacant. Apparently the townsfolk still favored their same seats, Sunday after Sunday.

Jack sat through the opening of the service, fighting the urge to leave. The only thing he actually looked forward to was the singing. With his mother serving as church organist, there had always been music in his home, especially hymns. He remembered many an evening spent with her playing their old upright piano while the family sang along.

It looked like one of Mrs. Friarson's daughters played the organ now. Was it Cora or Ruby? They were both several years younger than Jack and he hadn't ever been able to keep them straight, even when he lived here. He reached for one of the hymnals and held it so that he and Callie could share it. But when the Friarson girl struck the first few chords and the congregation launched into song, Jack forgot all about identifying the musician.

Callie's voice was amazing. Strong and clear, it had an almost haunting purity to it. There was beauty there, beauty that went beyond any surface definition. He found himself using the shared hymnal as an excuse to lean closer, brushing shoulders with her as he let that wonderful voice wash over him.

It was only when the music had stopped and he saw the faint blush on her face that he realized how transparent he'd been. Jack adjusted his jacket as he faced forward.

No real harm done. If anyone in the congregation had noticed, they would put it down to the fact that he and Callie were newlyweds. And hopefully Callie would assume that he was just playing his part.

But he'd have to watch himself. That little twitch of attraction had been a mite too real for comfort.

Later, as they exited the church, Reverend Hollingsford shook Jack's hand. "It was good to look out over the congregation this morning and see you seated in your brother's place with your family all around you."

Jack nodded, trying to keep his smile friendly. So, even the pew had become Lanny's rather than the Tyler family's.

As soon as they made it past the reverend, the kids ran off with some of their friends, and Virgil called Jack over to join a discussion with several of the other menfolk.

While he talked, Jack kept a close eye on Callie. Just to make sure she didn't feel abandoned or lost in the crowd, he told himself.

But Mrs. Mayweather and Ida Lee had drawn her into discussion with a circle of friends, and as long as they stayed close, he knew Callie would be all right.

"By the way," Mr. Dobson said, claiming his attention, "Lanny had talked to me about placing an order for a new strain of corn he was thinking about planting next year. We were all pretty interested in watching how it went. You planning to follow through with that?"

"I don't know. Hadn't really given it any thought." Jack wasn't ready to tell these folks he wouldn't be sticking around that long. It somehow didn't feel fair to Callie to announce the day after their wedding that he was planning to leave in a few weeks.

Then again, it was probably better to start dropping a few hints so folks could get used to the idea and not think anything objectionable had happened between the two of them when the time came. "Besides," he said, choosing his words carefully, "I may end up going back to my old job once I get Callie and the kids settled in. I have a family to support now, after all."

Mr. Dobson shrugged. "Well, farming was always more Lanny's strong suit, I suppose."

"That brother of yours was both smart and good with his hands," another of the men added. "Always finding ways to improve his crop yield or make life easier for him and his family."

"I'll bet you've seen some exciting things in your travels," Virgil interjected.

Jack could always count on his friend to try to snuff out any "Ain't Lanny wonderful?" conversations before they got too thick. "I don't know about exciting," Jack drawled, "but yes, I've happened on some sights. I've seen the Rocky Mountains and the Grand Canyon. I've seen the Pacific Ocean and I've seen a tree so big it would take twenty men to circle it."

One of the men let out an appreciative whistle. "That must be some tree." Then he turned to someone else in the group. "That reminds me. Didn't Lanny say he'd planned to put in a peach orchard next spring?"

And as quick as that, the conversation turned to Lanny once again.

Jack let the conversation flow around him. He was well-traveled and experienced. Still, to these folks, he was Lanny's shadow of a brother. Nothing had changed for him here.

Nothing ever would.

A few minutes later, the womenfolk began to signal that it was time to go. As the groups reformed into family clusters and headed toward their wagons or moved to the sidewalk that led into town, Jack saw Annabeth run up and take hold of one of Callie's hands.

Simon left his friends grudgingly to join them, and Jack noticed that the boy's surliness had returned.

"Where's Emma?" Callie looked around the dwindling crowd, a frown on her face.

"I saw her picking flowers back behind the church," Annabeth said. "You want me to go fetch her?"

Jack waved them forward. "Y'all go ahead and get settled in the buggy. I'll fetch her."

He headed toward the side of the church, nodding to friends as he did so. But before he'd covered more than a couple of yards, he spotted his niece leaving the cemetery, traces of tears on her cheeks.

Wishing he'd asked Callie to search Emma out, he stood there as the girl caught sight of him and hurried over.

"I'm sorry," she said as she drew close. "I didn't mean to keep y'all waiting."

"That's okay. We're not in any big hurry." Feeling awkward, Jack put a hand on her shoulder. "Any time you want to come out here and visit, you let me know. Okay?"

Emma nodded and offered him a grateful smile.

Jack felt a flash of relief. Apparently he wasn't completely without the skills needed to handle this parent thing.

Callie sat in the parlor, pen poised over a sheet of paper.

Lunch was over and the kitchen cleaned up. The sound of the children playing with the dogs drifted in through the open window. Jack was upstairs doing heaven only knew what. The man was certainly not one to voluntarily share any personal information.

There was absolutely nothing to keep her from finally writing that letter she'd promised her father.

Yet she'd sat here for ten minutes now, just staring at the blank sheet of paper. How could she possibly explain all that had transpired in the few short days since she'd arrived?

The sound of footsteps descending the stairs provided a welcome distraction. But when Jack came into view, he looked dressed for work.

"Where are you going?"

He paused with his hand on the screen door. "There's a section of fence out behind the barn that needs attention," he said as if she had no business asking. He pushed open the door. "I thought I'd—"

She set her pen down. "It's Sunday."

They stared at each other for a long minute. Finally Jack shrugged and let the door close. "All right." He headed toward the parlor and leaned against the doorjamb, crossing his arms. "So what do you suggest we do with this perfectly good afternoon? I'm not much good at just sitting on my hands."

"Well, we could have a talk." She'd like to learn more about this man she was married to.

"Talk about what?"

He made it sound as if she'd asked him to eat a dung beetle.

She'd better start with something safe. "It's not as if we know each other well," she said. "I'm certain there's lots of information we could share to help us get to know each other better."

"Actually, I figure we know all we need to about

each other." He crossed one booted foot over the other. "The less personal we make this whole arrangement, the better it'll be."

The words were like salt on a cut. Why was he so determined to keep that wall up? "Very well, then, we should do something with the children, something to help them feel like we're coming together as a family."

"What do you suggest?"

The man was determined not to make this easy.

Remembering the items still packed in her small trunk, Callie stood, a grin spreading across her face. "Actually, I have just the thing." Why hadn't she thought of this sooner? "You gather the children. I'll meet you out on the porch."

Callie was thrilled. She'd found something they could all enjoy together, something that brought them one step closer to being a true family. Now if she could just do the same for her marriage.

When she stepped outside, four pairs of eyes looked at her with varying degrees of wariness and expectation.

She held up the item she'd retrieved from her room. "This book is called *The Swiss Family Robinson*. I thought I might read a part of it to you this afternoon."

Annabeth's eyes lit up. "Is it like our story about Flora and Hawk?"

"It's a different kind of story." Callie sat on the porch swing, where she was immediately joined by the two girls. "But I think you're going to like it every bit as much."

Simon held back, wrinkling his nose. "I'll bet it's just some sappy fairy tale about princesses and such."

"Actually, it's an adventure story. My father read it to me when I was about Emma's age. And I enjoyed it so much I read it on my own when I got older."

Simon looked far from convinced. "What kind of adventure?"

"It's about a family who's shipwrecked and stranded on a deserted island. They have to find ways to survive all on their own." She turned to Annabeth, tweaking one of her curls. "And along the way, they encounter lots of strange and exotic animals."

Annabeth bounced up and down on her seat. "Ooh, that sounds exciting."

"It is." Callie opened the book. "I tell you what. I'll start reading. If any of you get bored, feel free to return to whatever it was you were doing before."

Turning to the first page, she began reading. "Already the tempest had continued six days; on the seventh its fury..."

Thirty minutes later, she closed the book. "Well, that's enough for one sitting."

She smiled at the clamor of protest. Even Simon had edged closer while she read.

Her glance snagged on Jack's and she felt her grin widen at the look on his face.

He'd enjoyed the story, too, had he?

As soon as he realized she'd noticed, Jack stood and stretched as if bored by the whole thing.

"I'm glad you enjoyed it so much," she said, turning back to the children. "But the book is much too long to finish in one sitting. If you like, we'll plan to read a little every day."

Chapter Eighteen

That evening, Jack sat on the porch again, whittling by the light of the moon.

Callie sure didn't fit into any kind of box he knew of. Hiding behind that bonnet and avoiding the limelight the way she did made her seem timid. And the woman was absolutely out of her element when it came to handling the farm chores.

But then again, she didn't seem to let much stand in her way when she wanted something, at least not for very long. In fact, when she happened on an obstacle, she easily went over or around it.

And she hadn't murmured a word of protest this evening when he'd told her it was time to get the animals in for the night. She just asked what she could do to help.

There was no denying she was good with the children. They'd hung on to her every word as she read that story. And to tell the truth, he'd been almost as taken in by it as they were.

The tale itself was part of it—nothing like a rousing adventure to keep you wanting to find out what happens next. But it was more than that. The way she'd breathed life into the words—the animation in her voice and face—had been just plain entertaining. He could see the whole thing playing out as if it were on a stage.

And her singing in church today. She had an amazing voice, using it as a good musician used his instrument. And he was pretty sure he wasn't the only one who'd noticed. In fact he wouldn't be surprised if the choir didn't try to recruit her next time they showed up for Sunday service.

The door opened behind him and she stepped out on the porch.

"Thank you for going to church with us today."

He ran his thumb over the edge of the wood. Did she think he'd done it just to get her approval? "I keep my promises."

"Yes, of course. I didn't mean to imply otherwise."

Jack changed the subject, moderating his tone as he glanced over his shoulder. "Interesting book."

Some of the stiffness left her spine, and she sat on the bench behind him near the door. "I've always enjoyed it. I probably read that story a half dozen times before I turned twelve."

"Seems an unusual choice for a girl."

"Does it? I've always liked books that could carry me off to exotic destinations."

At least that was something they had in common. He turned just enough to see her without turning his neck. "So, you like to travel."

She laughed. "I'm afraid the only traveling I'd done before coming here *was* through books." She tugged on her bonnet. "My family was always good about keeping me close—you know, sheltering me from strangers and large crowds."

Hmm. Couldn't tell much from her tone, but he got that sense again that something wasn't quite right. Was that so-called sheltering something she'd appreciated or chafed at? Or had there been other motives that drove her family to keep her close?

He leaned back and studied her a moment. "You know, you don't need to wear that bonnet around the house."

The smile she gave him was one part wistfulness and three parts resignation. "I think it's probably best I keep it on until the children get to know me a little better."

"They're all in bed now."

She took her bottom lip between her teeth, studying his face as if not certain of his intention.

He felt a stubborn impulse to push the point. "You insist that this is your home now, that me and the kids are your family. Did you wear that thing constantly when you were just among family?"

"Not growing up. But—"

She halted abruptly.

Now wasn't that interesting? He'd give a pretty penny to know what it was she'd been about to say.

Whatever it was, though, she apparently decided against elaborating.

"Very well." With a small nod, she untied the ribbons under her chin. After only a slight hesitation, she removed the bonnet completely and set it in her lap.

It never ceased to amaze him how different she looked without that shield she hid behind.

Sure, she had that birthmark. But she also had rich green eyes and high cheekbones that gave her profile a classic beauty.

Why had God seen fit to mar such a face with that angry-looking stain? As far as he could tell, she was a good and dutiful member of His flock, not a rebellious scapegrace like himself. Surely she'd earned some measure of mercy.

Realizing he'd been staring, Jack went back to whittling. "So, what do you think about Texas so far?"

She smiled as she fanned herself with the bonnet. "It's certainly a lot hotter than Ohio. But I can see why Julia came to love it so much." She gazed off into the night, her smile turning dreamy. "There's a wild sort of beauty here, an untamed quality, that gets under your skin. God's majesty seems closer, more visible somehow."

"Don't you miss your home just a little bit?" Jack asked.

Her grin had a teasing quality to it. "If you're trying to hint that I should go back, I'm afraid it's too late for that. To answer your question, though, of course I miss my family and former home. But my life has taken a new path now and I'm quite happy with it."

He leaned back, resting his spine against a support post. "Speaking of family, you know a lot about mine, but I don't know anything about yours."

She gave him a look he couldn't quite read. Was she remembering that he'd refused her earlier offer to have this conversation? If so, she chose not to throw it back at him.

"There's not a lot to tell. I have four sisters, two older and two younger. All four are married, two have children. My father is a tailor, one of the best in Hallenton."

He heard the touch of pride in her voice and remembered her saying her father had read to her as a child. Theirs was obviously a close relationship.

"And your mother?" he prodded.

"She died of a fever when I was fourteen." Callie paused, seeming to go inside herself for a minute.

"About six months ago, my father married a very sweet, lovely young woman whom he met while on a business trip to Philadelphia. Sylvia, my stepmother, has made him quite happy."

The very neutrality of her normally expressive voice hinted that there was more to the story.

"And how do the two of you get along?"

Her expression closed off further and he wondered for a minute if she'd tell him to mind his own business. But she leaned back against the wall, putting her face deeper in shadow.

"Sylvia is a gently raised woman with very delicate sensibilities. She's been nothing but kind to me. In fact, she went out of her way to make certain I knew I would always be welcome in my father's home, even though she was now the 'lady of the house.'"

Was that it? Had there been tension between the women over that position of power? Or did it have more to do with her stepmother's "delicate sensibilities"?

Suddenly her earlier half-finished answer—when he'd asked about wearing her bonnet in her old home—made sense. He felt a surge of anger that anyone would make her feel she was a burden or someone to be tolerated.

But before he could press further, she turned the tables on him.

"What about you?" she asked. "I know something about the boy you were, but Julia and Lanny never heard from you after you left Sweetgum. What did you do during those years?"

Her words reminded him again of the advantage she had over him because of Julia's letters. "As you said, not much to tell. I drifted around for a bit, seeing different parts of the country. Went to work for the railroad. Joined up with a demolition team and learned the trade. Eventually formed my own team. I've been blowing things up ever since."

"What an odd way to describe it." She tilted her head slightly. "Don't you sometimes wish you were building something rather than destroying things?"

Her question got his back up. Was she judging him again?

"Actually, I'm proud of the work I do. And I'm d—I'm good at it. I've built up a reputation for precision and safety that few others in the business can match."

He shaved another curl of wood from the block in one quick motion. "And I don't think of it as destroying things. What my team does is clear the way so others can come behind and build new things, important things, like the railroad lines that connect people and places."

"I hadn't thought of it that way." Her brow furrowed thoughtfully. "So you enjoy your work?"

"Yes, I do." Time to change the subject. "By the way, I plan to spend some time in town this week clearing away the debris left from the fire."

Her face lit up with approval. "That's a fine idea. It's not good for the children to face that every time they go to town."

"My thoughts exactly."

"And I'm certain the townsfolk will appreciate it as well." Her smile shifted to concern. "But you're not planning to tackle it alone, are you?"

He shrugged. "Normally I would. But I'd like to get most of it taken care of before we go to town for market day on Friday. I asked Virgil after church service this morning to spread the word that I was looking to hire some help. I'll spend the day around here tomorrow making sure everything's in order, then get started on Tuesday."

"Will that be enough time to get it all done?"

"If I get a couple of hard-working youths to help out it shouldn't be any problem. But even if I have to do it all myself, I'll see that it gets done."

Jack watched from the corner of his eye as she twisted her hands in the folds of her skirt. Something was on her mind.

"I wanted to speak to you about Emma," she finally said.

Emma? Of the three children she seemed to be adjusting the best. Sure, she'd been crying at the cemetery this morning, but there was nothing so unusual in that. The girl had just lost her parents, after all. "What about her?"

"She's just too quiet, too closed in."

Wasn't quiet a good thing? "Mrs. Mayweather did say she's always been on the shy side."

"I know." Callie tucked a strand of hair behind her ear. "But this seems like something more than just shyness."

How could she know that after so short a time? "The kid's been through a lot these past few days. Seems to me it's only natural for her to mourn for a time."

"Maybe you're right." Callie didn't sound entirely convinced.

"I'm sure that's all it is." Jack rested his arm on his knee. "I would have thought you'd be more worried about the way Simon's been acting."

She smiled sadly. "Simon is just angry at the world right now. No chance of him hiding how he's feeling. He'll get it out of his system eventually. He just needs a firm hand until he learns to trust us and feels some sense of security again. And thankfully, a firm hand seems to be your specialty."

Before he could respond, she stood. "I guess I'll turn in."

He nodded. "I think I'll sit out here a spell longer."

Once Callie was inside, Jack continued absently shaving on the block of wood.

So, she thought his parenting methods were something to be thankful for, did she? That was a surprise.

What was even more of a surprise was the warm feeling of pleasure brought on by simply glimpsing the light of approval in her eyes. He'd never had a woman look at him quite that way before.

And, in spite of himself, he found he liked it.

Chapter Nineteen

The next morning, Callie had already kicked off the covers and swung her feet to the floor when she heard Jack's rap on her door. "I'll be out in a minute." At least he hadn't caught her still asleep this time.

"I'll meet you in the barn."

Again, when Callie hurried through the kitchen, she saw the stove had been stoked. Just how early did that man get up, anyway?

She entered the barn to see Jack already seated beside Belle with several inches of milk in his pail.

He glanced up. "Think you remember how this works?"

Callie nodded. So much for morning pleasantries.

"Good. You'll find the grain in that sack over there." He nodded his head toward an empty stall. "Scoop up some for Clover's trough, but keep an eye out for rats."

Callie had her hand halfway in the sack before his warning sunk in and she drew back. "Rats?"

"That's right."

Was that a hint of amusement she heard in his tone? Maybe he was just teasing.

"The barn cats do a fair job of keeping them run

off," he elaborated, disabusing her of the notion that rats weren't a real possibility, "but every once in a while they slip in past the cats. The feed sacks draw them like a candy store does a youngster."

She swallowed, trying to work up the courage to stick her hand into the sack.

The rhythmic pinging of milk squirting into the pail stopped. "Just knock on the side a couple of times with the handle of the hoe or pitchfork and wait a couple of seconds. If there's one in there, he'll come scurrying out."

Not an altogether reassuring thought. Callie did as she was told, certain he was laughing at her all the while. When nothing stirred, she gingerly scooped up a generous portion of grain and hurried over to Clover's trough.

Jack nodded approvingly. "Once she starts eating, you can get to work. Don't forget to wash her udder and to save some milk for her calf."

Callie found the correct rhythm quicker this time, getting the milk to squirt into the pail on her second try.

Once the milking was done, she set her pail beside Jack's on the worktable and let Clover's calf out of his pen.

She and Jack worked together until they were finished in the barn, Callie filling the silence with a quiet humming. This work was different from what she was used to, but it wasn't much harder than scrubbing floors or doing piles of laundry, both of which she was intimately familiar with.

Jack finally dusted his hands on his pants and shot her a challenging look. "So, do you want to try your hand at gathering eggs this morning?"

"Of course." That chore *had* to be easier than milking cows.

Callie let him lead the way.

First he scattered grain in the chicken yard. "Just throw this about on the ground and let them scratch for it. Most of them will come out to eat, which makes the egg gathering a lot easier. Of course, a few might stay on the nest."

"And what do you do then?"

"You carefully reach under them and slide the egg out." He handed her the basket. "But before you reach into a nest, whether a hen is there or not, it's a good idea to check for snakes or other critters."

"Snakes!" First rats and now snakes?

"For the most part, any snake you find in the nest will be a chicken snake. It might give you a scare, but it won't hurt you. What it *will* do is swallow your pin money."

"Pin money?"

"They eat the eggs. Not to mention baby chicks, if you're trying to hatch some. Eggs aren't just food for our table. Any extras you have at the end of the week can be taken to town on market day and traded for other things you need."

"So what do you do if a snake is in there?" Poisonous or not, there was absolutely nothing that could convince her to touch a snake.

He must have seen the look on her face. "Don't worry, it doesn't happen often. We'll just cross that bridge when we come to it. So, assuming there's no snake, if the chicken is still sitting on the nest, you're gonna have to reach under her to collect the egg. Sometimes they'll let you do it without much fuss, but other times, they'll take exception."

"How?"

"You'll have to watch out for the sharp beaks—I've gotten my hands pecked more times than I care to remember. Or they might try to fly into your face, so be ready to duck. Just don't drop the eggs."

Callie swallowed hard. She'd accepted that farm work would be difficult. But she hadn't realized it could also be hazardous.

She sent up a quick prayer for courage. She was determined not to embarrass herself in front of Jack

"Good breakfast." Jack set his fork down and stood. "Girls, you help your Aunt Callie clean up the kitchen. Simon, you can help me take care of some chores outside."

The boy met his glance across the table with a guarded look.

"Have you ever chopped firewood before?" Jack asked.

Simon sat up straighter. "No, sir."

"Ever handled an ax at all?"

Simon shook his head again.

"Then I'd say your education has a few holes in it. It's high time we fixed that."

"Yes, sir." Simon stood and gathered up his dishes. Obviously the idea of wielding an ax sounded better than kitchen chores.

Jack saw the protest forming on Callie's lips and gave her a look that silenced whatever she'd been about to say. Last night she'd said she appreciated his firm hand with the kids. She'd just have to remember that and trust him to know what they could and couldn't handle. These three had to learn to take some responsibility, especially if she was to have any chance of making a go of things here once he left.

She certainly couldn't do it all on her own, and there were lots of things the kids could handle with the right kind of training.

Jack carried his empty plate to the sink. "Why, by the time your Uncle Lanny and I were your age," he told Simon, "we were chopping firewood, milking cows and helping with the plowing."

Callie turned to the girls. "All right, ladies. Annabeth, you finish clearing the table. Emma, you can wash the dishes. I'll dry and put them away." She handed Emma a clean apron, then fetched hers and tied it around her waist.

"It's laundry day," she continued, "so I'm going to the washroom to set the water to boiling while you two get started in here."

Jack raised a brow. How about that—Callie was actually taking his cue on something. Maybe he'd been wrong about her teachability after all?

Jack hefted his sledgehammer as he watched Simon. The boy hit a chunk of wood dead center, splitting it into two nearly equal pieces. They'd been at it for almost thirty minutes now and both of them were sweaty and tired. But Jack finally felt that his nephew was getting the hang of it.

He clapped Simon on the shoulder. "That's probably enough for today. Good job."

Simon added his contribution to the woodpile and wiped his brow. "You're planning to go back to work with the railroad, aren't you?" The boy leaned on the ax handle and gave Jack a dark look.

Jack's temper rose in response, then he remembered what Callie had said last night about the likely cause of Simon's orneriness. "Eventually," he said as matter-of-factly as he could. Then he led the way to the barn.

Simon hefted the ax and marched along behind him. "And you're going to just leave us stuck out here on this hayseed farm."

"I'll be coming back for visits every few months. And it's not such a bad place to be, Simon, if you just give it a chance."

"If you think it's so great, why'd you leave Sweetgum as soon as you could?"

Jack put away the wedge and sledgehammer. *Remember, he's just a confused kid.* "That was different. I was a grown man and your Uncle Lanny and Aunt Julia were moving in here to help my mother after my pa died." He held out a hand for the ax. "It was time for me to strike out on my own."

"Momma said you wanted to get away from here ever since you were a kid."

"True. But I don't regret growing up here or learning all the skills my daddy taught me." At least not now when he looked back on it. "I still use a lot of what I learned back then."

"Well, that's where we're different. My pa taught me town skills 'cause that where my home is."

What in Tom's back forty were town skills? "I'm sorry, son, but it's time for you to accept that that place doesn't exist any more."

Simon's expression darkened. "Don't call me that. I'm not your son." He crossed his arms over his chest. "Besides, the land the café and our house was built on is still there. And it belongs to Emma and me. We can rebuild it."

"Maybe. But then what? You and Emma can't live there by yourselves. And your Aunt Callie and Annabeth will need your help whenever I'm away."

Simon's hands clenched at his sides. "That's not fair."

Jack shrugged. "Maybe not. But that's the way it is."

Simon wasn't giving up. "Then they could live with Emma and me."

Jack folded his arms. His patience was growing thin. "And do what? How would you live? At least here there's fresh milk and eggs. There's a vegetable garden out back and meat in the smokehouse."

"I could get a job." Simon met Jack's gaze head on. "I'll bet Mr. Pearson down at the hotel would hire me to run errands."

The boy didn't know when to cut bait. "It wouldn't be enough to support all of you." He placed a hand on the boy's shoulder, trying a different approach. "Simon, when I'm not here, you're going to be the man of the house. I need to know that I can count on you to take care of the womenfolk and always think about what's best for the family, not just for yourself."

Simon shook off Jack's hand and stepped back. "And is that what you're doing when you think about leaving?"

"That's different." Was he really trying to justify his actions to an eleven-year-old? "Look, I need to return to my old job. It's important work, I'm good at it, and my crew and my customers depend on me. And like I said, I'm not abandoning you. I'll come back to visit on a regular basis and I'll be sending money to help Aunt Callie with the expenses."

"So that makes it all okay?"

"Yes, it does," Jack snapped.

He watched as Simon spun on his heel and stalked away.

Jack raked a hand through his hair. So much for holding on to his temper. But confound it, what was it going to take to make that boy see reason?

Chapter Twenty

Jack sat on the top step of the porch, listening to the familiar night sounds while he mulled over an idea that had been taking shape in his mind for the last few hours. It seemed one good thing had come out of his discussion with Simon this morning after all. The boy's idea about rebuilding on that plot of land in town had given him the backup plan he needed.

He wasn't at all surprised when the door opened behind him. In fact, he'd been waiting for her.

"They're all tucked in."

"Good." He glanced up and frowned at her bonnet, pointing his knife at it.

"Aren't you forgetting something?"

He watched the play of emotion on her face. She obviously thought he was being unreasonable. And maybe he was. But he just didn't like to see her constantly imprisoning herself in those uncomfortable-looking headwraps.

Callie moved closer, leaning against one of the support posts that flanked the steps. The one with his father's carving.

With slow, deliberate movements, she removed the

bonnet. It was strangely mesmerizing to watch her unveil in the silvery moonlight.

When she was done, she raised her face to the stars and shook her head, as if to make the most of her newfound freedom. But he noticed she had positioned herself so that her "good" profile was presented to him.

He decided not to press her on that point. Not tonight.

"I dug out all of Julia and Leland's old clothes this afternoon," she said. "I was wondering if you wanted any of Leland's things. For your own use, I mean."

Just what he *didn't* need—more of Leland's hand-me-downs. He shaved a thick curl of wood from the block in a sharp movement. "No, thank you. I'm sure you can find some other use for them."

"Actually, I already have."

He glanced up, intrigued.

"Emma and Simon's wardrobes are sadly lacking," she said, her voice rushing over the words. "I'd like to take the cloth from these garments and fashion them some new things."

One step above a hand-me-down. Would the kids mind?

"Wouldn't it be a lot easier to just buy some new fabric and start from scratch?"

"Maybe. But that would be so wasteful when this cloth is readily available. And I can fashion the clothes so that they look like new, made for children their age. I told you, my father is a tailor. I learned quite a bit from him."

A practical-minded woman. And once again she'd recognized a need that had slipped right by him.

He rubbed his chin, not sure if he felt admiration, jealousy or some combination of the two.

"Suit yourself," he said, then changed the subject.

"Don't forget, I plan to work on clearing out the rubble from the fire tomorrow. I'll probably be gone most of the day."

"I'll make sure I get up earlier."

Did she think he planned to leave without taking care of things here first? "Don't worry. I won't head out until the morning chores are done."

"That wasn't what I meant." She turned to face him fully, possibly forgetting she'd removed her bonnet. "What you're planning to do in town is important. And it'll be hard work. I just don't want to hold you back or add to your work."

"Don't worry, you won't." He rested an elbow on his thigh. Time to mention the new plan. "I'm thinking, once I get the place cleared, I might build something new there."

"Oh?" Her unspoken question hung in the air between them.

"Yes. Simon reminded me earlier that that bit of property is his and Emma's legacy. I was thinking, if I put up a new structure, it would give you and the kids a place to go if you decided life out here was too hard."

She crossed her arms. "That won't happen."

"Maybe not." He didn't want to argue with her over this. He was going to provide a safety net for her and the kids, whether she wanted one or not. Yep, by August he could head back to his old life with a clear conscience and the confidence that he'd done his duty.

But right now he'd soothe her ruffled feathers. "Even if you do decide to stay here, we could always rent the place out and have another source of income."

She relaxed, letting her arms drop to her sides. "That makes sense. But how will Simon and Emma react to having someone else live in what they think of as their place?"

"It might be hard for them to get used to at first, especially Simon. But I'll make sure it doesn't look anything like the old place. And as long as we lease it, it'll still be there for them to do whatever they please with once they get old enough."

She brushed a stray lock of hair off her forehead. "Building a new place will be a lot of work."

"Most things worth doing are."

"I agree. But won't it delay your departure?"

Was she disappointed or glad? He caught himself—the answer to that question was irrelevant. "It might delay things a bit. But I think in the long run this will be better for all of us."

It would give him a clearer conscience when he left, that was certain.

Jack arrived in town the next morning to find three youths lined up in front of what was once his sister's home and workplace. He gave them an assessing look as he set the brake on the wagon. One of them was a big lad, probably seventeen or eighteen, and obviously used to hard work. The second was not quite as big or as old, but he still looked like a worker. The third hopeful was slimmer and not near as muscled. But if the kid was willing to work, he could probably still get some use out—

He frowned, taking a second, closer look as he neared the trio. Unless he was mistaken, the third youth was a girl dressed in boy's overalls.

Now who in tarnation had let their daughter out like that?

He stopped in front of his would-be work crew and

folded his arms. "So you all want to earn a bit of money, do you?"

Three heads bobbed in unison. "Yes, sir."

"What're your names?"

The biggest of the three spoke up first. "Calvin Lufkin."

"You Walter Lufkin's boy?"

"Yes, sir."

Walter Lufkin was a farmer with a big place and an even bigger brood of children. The man was as honest as the day was long and knew the meaning of hard work. Chances were, he'd passed those traits on to his son. "You'll do."

He nodded to the second boy. "And you?"

"Albert Hanfield. I'm Charles Hanfield's son," he added before Jack could ask.

Charles Hanfield owned a pig farm just outside of town. Albert likely knew the meaning of hard work as well. "All right, Albert, you're hired."

Next he turned to his third candidate.

"Jessie Mills." She offered the name before he even had a chance to ask.

"And would that be short for Jessica?"

The two boys snickered, but stopped abruptly when she flashed a glare their way.

She turned back to Jack and the tilt of her chin reminded him strongly of Callie. "Actually, it's short for Jessamine."

"Well, Jessie, I'm afraid—"

"You didn't ask about my dad," she said, cutting him off. "He's Joe Mills, and he runs the livery and smithy. I'm used to hard work, just ask anyone here in town."

"I'm sure you are, but knocking these timbers down

and carting them off is not only hard work, it can be dirty and dangerous, too."

"I work around a smithy and horses that ain't been broke yet. I don't mind getting dirty and I know how to handle dangerous jobs."

There was something about the girl, an edge of determination beneath her bravado, that kept Jack from refusing her outright. He rubbed his chin. "I tell you what. I'll hire you for just this morning and see how you do. After lunch we'll talk again."

"Yes, sir! I promise you won't be sorry."

Jack wasn't so sure of that—he was already second-guessing his decision. But he'd given her his word and he'd stick by it.

He stepped back and spoke to the group as a whole. "The pay is four bits a day, and I expect you to earn every cent of it. I don't have any use for laggards and lay-abouts. I want to have every bit of this wreck dismantled and the whole lot cleared out by Thursday evening. And I want it done without anyone getting hurt in the process. Understand?"

There was a chorus of "Yes, sir"s.

"Good. Then you'll find tools in my buckboard. Calvin, I want you working with me, knocking down these timbers. Jessie and Albert, while we're working on this end, you get a wheelbarrow and start carting off everything that's just laying about down on that end. And that means shoveling the ashes as well. Make sure you keep your eyes open for jagged bits and shaky timbers."

He grabbed a sledgehammer from the back of the wagon. "Take the bigger timbers and stack them in the middle of the back lot. We'll go through 'em later to see what can be reused and what should be tossed on someone's woodpile." He paused. "If you happen across anything that seems salvageable—anything at all—set it aside for me to look at."

The three nodded and set to work.

All through the morning, Jack kept an eye on Jessie. He had to admit, the girl definitely knew how to get things done. She was nimble and quick, and she didn't complain about the dirt or the work.

When he called a break at lunchtime she sauntered over with a smug smile. "Do I pass the test?"

He took a bite of the sandwich Callie had packed for him, studying her thoughtfully while he chewed.

After a moment some of her cockiness faded and she jammed her hands in the pockets of her overalls. "Well?"

He swallowed and tilted his hat back. "You'll do."

Relief shone in her eyes. "Thanks, Mr. Tyler. I'll do you a real good job this week, you'll see."

He watched as the girl raced off in the direction of the livery stable, wondering what her story was.

That evening, Jessie held back as the two boys headed home. "Mr. Tyler, I want to thank you for taking a chance on me today."

Jack nodded. "Thank you for not disappointing me."

She watched as he dipped his bandanna in the horse trough and washed his neck. "People say you've traveled all over the country."

Jack laughed. "Not all over, but I've visited my share of places."

"That's what I'm gonna do someday." Her voice lost its hard edge. For the first time he saw something of her feminine side. "And not just this country, either," she continued. "I'm gonna travel to Europe and Africa and all those places Mrs. Mayweather talks about in school."

He remembered having those yearnings to see what existed outside the narrow confines of Sweetgum. "I wish you well."

"That's why I'm working so hard. People make fun of me 'cause I'm not like other girls. I'll do most any old job to earn a few pennies, so long as it's honest labor. But it doesn't matter what they think of me. Once I leave here I can become whoever I want to be."

He heard echoes of his own childhood in her words. His eagerness to leave Sweetgum had been tied up in his desire to be looked at differently, to become someone other than Lanny's little brother.

What was her reason?

Not that it was any of his business. He squeezed the water from his bandanna and put his hat back on. Then he had another thought. "How would you like to earn some extra money?"

Her eyes lit up. "Just tell me what you need done."

"This job requires someone with keen eyes who doesn't mind getting more than a little dirty."

"Then I'm your girl."

"I told y'all earlier to keep an eye out for anything salvageable. I know it may be a lost cause, but I'm looking for anything that survived the fire that would have some value or meaning to Emma and Simon. It'll mean digging through all the soot and ashes to see what might be buried underneath."

If there was any piece of Emma and Simon's home or belongings that remained intact, he intended to find it.

"I'll be doing some looking myself, of course, but it would be good to have another set of eyes."

"I think that's a mighty fine thing to do. The Carsons were always good to me and I'd be right honored to help you do something nice for their kids."

With a nod, she headed home, whistling off key.

He watched her a moment, then climbed into the wagon, ready to get back to his family.

As the wagon passed out of town, he let the mare have her head. She knew the way home as well as he did.

Jack rolled his shoulders and stretched his neck muscles, trying to work some of the kinks out. Clearing the burned out shell of his sister's café was hard work. Demolition, of course, was his stock and trade. But this was not like his usual jobs.

Making sure he got those scorched walls and timbers down without allowing the whole thing to collapse in on him and his young crew made it much trickier.

Despite that, they'd made a lot of progress today. But they'd have to keep up the pace to meet his deadline.

Jessie, especially, had surprised him. The girl was a hard worker with a lot of grit and determination. She had big dreams and wasn't content to just sit back and *hope* they came true—she was doing everything in her power to *make* them come true.

Had she learned that from her parents—both the dreaming big and the working hard? What would his nieces and nephew learn from him? He wouldn't be around much, but when he was, he'd have to make sure he took his role as father figure seriously.

Of course, they had Callie to look to. And he'd challenge anyone to find a better example for a child to follow, especially when it came to a willingness to dig in and get the job done.

Remembering the way she'd tackled the farm chores these past few days brought a smile to his lips.

But only for a minute.

His shoulders slumped at the thought of tending to

evening chores when he got back to the farm. It was like having two jobs at once. But it was only for about five weeks, give or take.

At least he'd have a home-cooked meal waiting for him when he finished up, something that was hit or miss at camp. One thing Callie could do well was cook.

The sun hadn't quite set when the horse turned into the familiar lane and Jack pulled her up short. Surprise washed away his fatigue. Callie and the kids were herding the cows into the barnyard.

Seems he'd underestimated the woman once again.

Chapter Twenty-One

Jack stepped out on the porch and drew his shoulders back, watching the fireflies play hide and seek in the front yard.

Callie was putting the children to bed, but he knew she'd be out to join him soon. It had become routine.

When he'd arrived home this evening, she'd only allowed him to take care of the horse and buggy, insisting that she and the kids could handle the rest of the chores while he went inside and washed all the soot and grime away before supper. There'd even been a kettle of water already warming on the firebox for him in the washroom.

A man could get used to that kind of treatment.

He stopped himself once again. It wouldn't do for him to get *too* used to it. He couldn't afford any ties that would make it harder on him or them when the time came for him to go.

He moved toward his usual seat on the top step, then paused.

Maybe he could repay the favor, even if only in a small way. After all, he didn't like being beholden to anyone.

If Callie was going to join him out here every night...

Acting on impulse, he grabbed the bench from its place by the door and moved it up against the porch rail. He studied it a moment, then slid it slightly to the left.

There.

She'd have a place to sit if she wanted to, but could still stand at the rail if that was her preference.

He stared at the bench, rubbing the back of his neck. What if Callie read something into the gesture he hadn't intended?

Maybe he should just put things back the way they'd been.

He bent over the bench and then halted, a self-mocking smile curving his lips. For a man who prided himself on being decisive, he was certainly acting like a waffley whelp.

Jack left the bench where he'd placed it and pulled out his pocketknife.

Five minutes later, Callie finally stepped out on the porch.

Jack studiously sliced another curl of wood to add to the pile of shavings at his feet. He felt rather than saw her pause a moment before stepping forward. But she took a seat on the bench without comment.

"How did the work go today?" she asked.

He looked up and attempted to hide his surprise. For once, he hadn't had to prompt her to remove her bonnet.

A good sign.

"Better than expected. Three able-bodied workers showed up to help this morning." He resumed his whittling, watching her from the corner of his eye. "One of them's a girl."

She raised a brow. "How did that come about?"

"Jessie Mills is the blacksmith's daughter. She's got

a burning desire to earn enough money to travel around the world."

"So, a soul mate of sorts."

He shrugged. "Let's just say I sympathize with her dreams. But she's earning her pay every bit as much as the two guys."

Callie merely smiled that wise-woman smile of hers.

Jack shaved another long curl of wood from the block. "I think we'll get everything cleared out by Thursday evening."

"You're doing a good thing for the children," Callie said, worry in her voice, "but don't push yourself too hard in the process."

"It's just for a few days—I know what I'm doing." He changed the subject. "So how did your day go?"

"We did all right. Today was ironing day, of course, so that took up a big part of the morning. While I worked on that, I had Simon and the girls drag the rugs out to give them a good beating."

"Sounds like you kept busy." He found himself wondering if they missed having him around at all.

"Oh, it wasn't all work. The girls had a tea party after lunch. And Ida Lee's son Gil came over to deliver some of her peach preserves. He stayed and spent some time with Simon."

"Good. Having a kid around here to spend time with might help Simon lose that chip on his shoulder."

Callie leaned back against the porch rail. Her neck looked longer, leaner without that bonnet.

"I overheard Simon telling him about the story we've been reading. They spent most of the afternoon playing shipwreck." She glanced over at him. "I'm afraid Cookie and Pepper were drafted to play the part of the goats," she said dryly.

He laughed, then pointed the wood at her. "I suppose you went ahead and read the latest chapter without me."

"Sorry, but I'm afraid so."

"An apology won't do it," he said with mock-sternness. "You'll have to fill me in on what I missed."

"Really?"

"Of course. You don't think you can abandon me in the middle of the adventure do you?"

Jack half-listened while she launched into a summary of the latest trials and triumphs of the shipwrecked family.

Yes, if he wasn't careful, a man could definitely get used to treatment like this.

Callie drew the brush through her hair, relishing the soothing, rhythmic movements.

She'd enjoyed reciting the high points of the latest chapter of *Swiss Family Robinson* to Jack tonight. His request meant he was enjoying the story, which in turn meant they did have a shared interest or two after all.

A promising sign.

Even more promising was the fact that he'd gone to the trouble of moving that bench for her this evening. Giving her a place to sit while they chatted was an unexpectedly thoughtful gesture. Was he beginning to enjoy those quiet moments together as much as she?

If only he didn't insist she remove her bonnet every evening. Callie stared at her reflection in the mirror, facing the ugliness head-on, something she rarely did. At least outside in the fading light her birthmark wasn't quite so obvious. Maybe that's why he was insistent about the whole thing. In the twilight it must look like more of a shadow than anything else. So he could at least pretend she looked okay.

Yes, that must be it. Having her sit there without her

bonnet in the moonlight while they discussed the day's events probably lent a sense of normalcy to what—to him at least—must be an uncomfortable situation.

She set the brush down and reached back to separate her hair into three thick ropes. But before she could begin braiding, the door opened behind her.

"Aunt Callie?"

She turned to see Annabeth peeking through the doorway.

"What is it, sweetheart?"

The little girl stepped inside the room. "I had a dream about Daddy."

Callie held out her arms, which was all the incentive the child needed. Annabeth rushed forward and snuggled into her lap. Callie picked up her brush and drew the bristles through the child's sunny curls. "Was it a good dream?"

"Uh-huh. He was leading me around on Cinnamon like he used to, and telling me how pretty I was, that I looked just like Mommy."

"That sounds very nice."

"It was. But then I woke up and I remembered he wasn't here anymore."

"And that made you sad?"

Annabeth nodded.

"It's okay to be sad, you know. My own mommy died when I was fourteen, and I was very sad, too. But do you want to know a secret?"

Annabeth nodded again.

"I was sad for me because I missed her so much. But I was also very happy for her."

The little girl's eyes widened. "You were?"

"Yes. Because I knew she was in heaven, and heaven is such a wonderful place, more wonderful than we can even imagine. I knew Mother was happy there and that nothing could hurt her or make her cry ever again."

"Oh." Annabeth thought about that a minute. "And that's where my daddy and mommy are, too."

Callie heard the question in her statement. "That's right. They're both there together. And your Aunt Nell and Uncle Jed are with them."

"And your mommy, too?"

"That's right. And you know, they're probably watching us right now."

Annabeth snuggled deeper into her lap. "That's nice."

"So even though it's okay to miss them, we can also be very happy for them."

"Okay." The word ended on a yawn.

"Now, it's time for you to get back to bed, young lady." Callie set the brush down and allowed Annabeth to slide from her lap. "Would you like me to tuck you in again?"

Annabeth nodded and slipped her hand in Callie's.

Callie led her down the hall to her room. The child was already rubbing her eyes as Callie pulled the covers up to her chin. Callie leaned down and kissed her forehead. Before she could rise again, Annabeth lifted a hand and stroked Callie's left cheek. "I don't care what Simon says," she said sleepily. "I like your angel kiss."

Callie stood, feeling both warmed and chilled by the artlessly uttered words.

What had Simon been saying?

Careful not to waken the still-sleeping Emma, Callie glided from the room and quietly closed the door behind her. She turned to find Jack standing at the top of the stairs, staring at her with a strange look in his eyes.

He stepped forward, his expression changing to concern. "Is something wrong with one of the girls?"

He spoke in a stage whisper, his voice oddly husky.

"No." She tucked a strand of hair behind her ear. "Annabeth was troubled by a dream she had, but I think she's okay now."

"Good." He cleared his throat. "Well then, I guess I'll say good-night. Again."

"Good-night." Callie, feeling as nervous as a schoolgirl under his peculiar stare, hurried across the hall and into the sanctuary of her room.

Jack closed the door to his chamber. Now why had he just reacted so strongly to the unexpected encounter? Even if he and Callie hadn't been married, there'd been nothing the least bit improper or suggestive in her appearance. In fact, that prim, buttoned-to-the-chin wrapper she had on would have looked at home in an elderly spinster's wardrobe.

He supposed it was the sight of those waves of unbound hair. Every other time he'd seen her without her bonnet she'd had her hair up in a tight bun or a braided coronet. He'd had no idea it was so long and fluid. She appeared to be a whole different person with her hair down—softer, more feminine.

But there was something else that had tugged at him just now. He'd seen a hint of pain in her eyes, in the slight droop of her shoulders. He itched to find out what had caused it, to see if there was a demon he could slay for her.

Jack shook his head. Now that was a blamed fool way to be thinking.

He splashed water from the bedside basin onto his face. Of course, it *was* natural for a man to want to protect his family. And Callie was part of his family now, the same way the kids were.

No more, no less.

Chapter Twenty-Two

It was already dark Thursday evening when Callie heard the sound of Jack's return. His work hours seemed to get longer with each passing day.

Twenty minutes later she watched him leave the barn and head toward the house. Despite his apparent weariness there was a jauntiness to the set of his shoulders.

Did that mean he'd finished clearing the lot? She hoped so, and not just for the children's sake. He'd worked so hard to make his deadline, it would be a shame for him to feel he'd failed.

As she set him a place at the table, she heard him step into the washroom, whistling. Where did the man get that kind of energy?

By the time Jack entered the kitchen, hair still damp, she had the meal ready for him.

He inhaled deeply as he took a place at the table. "Smells good. And boy, am I hungry."

"You put in a long day today."

"Yep, but we finished all the clearing out work." He scooped up a forkful of potatoes. "In fact, we did better than that. We set down the plank floor for the new building. Those kids won't even see the scorched earth when they go to town tomorrow."

No wonder he seemed so pleased with himself. "My goodness, you *did* get a lot done."

"It wasn't just me and my crew. Apparently word got around about what I was trying to do and why. Virgil came out today, along with several of Lanny and Nell's friends."

"And you're okay with that?"

He shrugged. "I'd rather have done it myself. But there wasn't time and these folks were doing it for the kids more than for me."

Well, well, Mr. I Don't Need Anybody was finally learning to accept a bit of help from others.

When the buckboard turned onto Main Street the next morning, Callie's gaze immediately locked onto the empty lot where the café used to stand. Instead of ashes and charred timbers, a platform of fresh lumber now marked the spot. In fact, several of the town's children were using the place as a makeshift playground.

It was indeed a remarkable transformation. Callie turned to Jack, touching his arm.

Simon also turned to Jack, disbelief and hope on his face. "You're rebuilding our house."

"Not your house." Jack's tone was firm. "It won't be anything like the building you remember. But yes, I've decided to erect a new structure where the old one stood."

Simon leaned forward, clutching the back of their seat. "But we can move back to town when it's finished, can't we?"

"I didn't say that."

"But—"

"One thing at a time, Simon," Callie said quickly. She didn't want to mar this outing with bickering and sullen pouts.

Especially not today.

Simon's eyes narrowed rebelliously, but he settled back in his seat without another word.

Callie closed Mrs. Mayweather's front gate behind her. Jessie Mills had volunteered to take Annabeth and Emma down to the livery to see Persia, the frisky young colt. Simon had disappeared somewhere with his friends, and Jack was working on his construction project.

So, once the shopping was done, she'd taken advantage of the free time to visit with her friend, as a gift to herself. The schoolteacher had been as warm and welcoming as ever, and had seemed genuinely interested in the progress the newly-formed family was making. They'd had a lovely talk over a tasty snack of tea and cake.

But now it was nearly noon. Time to gather the family and head back to the farm.

Callie found herself humming as she walked along the sidewalk toward the center of town. The day was gorgeous, the family had made it through this first week and God had proven once again what a faithful, loving Father he was.

So what if she were the only one who knew what day today was? She had blessings enough to make her content without any added fanfare.

She approached the hedge-lined border of the Pearsons' front lawn. Unless he'd already joined Jack at the work site, Simon was supposed to be here or at the Thompsons' home.

"You really learned how to milk a cow?"

Callie smiled at the sound of the boyish voice coming from the other side of the tall hedge.

"Sure, nothing to it."

Was there a touch of bragging in Simon's voice? Quite a change from the tone he'd used when she tried to teach him the skill a few days ago.

But the other boy laughed. "Next thing you know you'll be mucking out stalls and pulling stems of hay from your hair."

What a snide thing to say! No wonder Simon was so dissatisfied with life on the farm if his friends felt this way. How could she help him learn to—

"So how is life with Old Miss Splotchy-Face?"

Callie stopped in her tracks, stunned by the unexpectedness of the name-calling.

"Oh, you know, she keeps one of those horse-blinder bonnets on all the time." The sullen tone was back in Simon's voice.

"Bet you don't have problems with varmints on your place." There was an ugly snicker underlining the words. "All she'd have to do is take off that contraption and anything with eyes in its head would run for the hills."

"Yeah. She could scare the sweet out of sugar with that face, all right."

Heaven help her, that was Simon's voice. Was that how he really felt about her?

She heard the sound of spitting. Then Simon spoke again. "I have to keep an eye on things so she doesn't pull that bonnet off and scare the girls. You know what scaredy cats they can be."

There was more laughter and talk of how silly girls were, then one of the other boys spoke up. "So, are you going to be moving back to town when your Uncle Jack gets done with that new building?"

"*She* doesn't want to."

Callie had no doubt the "she" Simon referred to with such venom was herself.

"But I think Uncle Jack will get her to come around once he's done. Hey, why don't we head over to where they're working? I'll bet Uncle Jack would let us help if we asked."

Callie had only a few seconds to compose herself before the boys came racing out through the break in the hedge a few yards ahead of her. But she managed to school her features, determined not to let them know she'd heard anything amiss.

Simon saw her first and halted in his tracks. The look on his face was a hodge-podge of embarrassment, defiance and bravado. And maybe just the merest touch of remorse. Or was that only wishful thinking on her part?

As soon as the other boys saw her they pulled up short as well.

Bobby Pearson kicked at a clod of dirt with the toe of his shoe. Then he dug his hands in his pockets. "I just remembered, my maw wanted me to refill that old birdbath out back."

Abe Thompson looked from Simon to Callie, his eyes as round as saucers and his Adam's apple bobbing visibly. "Uh, yeah, I probably ought to help you with that."

Within seconds it was just Simon and Callie on the sidewalk, facing each other. All through that short exchange, she'd felt Simon's eyes on her, studying her, no doubt trying to decipher what she might or might not have heard.

Well, he'd just have to continue guessing.

She spoke up first. "I'm glad I found you. It's time we headed back to the farm. Do you think you could run down to the livery and fetch the girls?"

Guarded relief flashed across his face. Then, with a quick nod, he turned and ran off in the direction of the livery.

Callie watched him go. She reminded herself of all that the boy had been through, told herself his display was at least partly show for his friends and that he might not actually feel that way, but her rationalizations didn't erase the sting of those hurtful words.

She resumed her walk toward the center of town, but the bounce had gone from her step, and she no longer had the urge to hum.

Callie tromped past the barn, heading toward the tree line just north of the open field.

All of the goods from the market had been put away, lunch was long past, and supper simmered on the stove. Emma was sketching. Annabeth was looking at her picture book. Simon and Jack were playing dominoes.

No one had bothered to do more than glance up and nod when she'd announced she planned to take a walk.

Which was just as well. She needed to find a place where she could be truly alone, where she wouldn't be overheard or interrupted. Because she could feel emotions swirling around inside her, emotions that needed to be let out before they overwhelmed her.

And when she did let loose, it would not be a sight for public viewing.

Callie reached the tree line and easily found the well-worn trail that provided entrance to the wood. Julia had written about a spot back this way where the trees opened up on a small grassy meadow fed by a narrow stream.

Sure enough, several minutes later she discovered the flower-dotted swath of green. The stream was little more than a trickle at the moment, but it was sparkling and clear.

Callie sat near the bank, removed her bonnet and hairpins, and shook her hair free as she raised her face to absorb the warming rays of the sun. Closing her eyes, she deliberately opened her other senses to her surroundings.

Birds, insects and gurgling water provided lyrical background music. The scents of crushed grass, pine needles and wildflowers perfumed the air. The warmth of the sun and the slight kiss of a breeze caressed her, filling her with a lazy comfort.

It was peaceful here, every bit as lovely as Julia had described it, and it was a sweet testament to God's artistry.

She hugged her knees to her chest and rested her chin on the makeshift prop.

And found she couldn't hold back the doubts and dark thoughts any longer.

Simon's hurtful words, Lanny's untimely death, the letter she'd expected from her father that hadn't come—all this and more tumbled round and round in her mind.

What if her presence here had actually made things worse for this family instead of better?

Was she really the mother these children needed or had she stubbornly stood in the way of a more worthy candidate? Had she done them a disservice by making it easy for Jack to eventually leave rather than stay and learn to be a real, day-in-day-out father?

Oh, but she missed Julia so much.

Missed being able to pour her heart out to someone who would understand and not judge. Missed getting those wonderful letters with her pithy responses and uplifting advice.

Missed with a deep-down ache knowing that there was someone in this world who loved her just the way she was.

Father, I know You love me unconditionally. I know You are with me always and that that should be enough to carry me through the hard and lonely times without complaint. But I'm a wretchedly weak creature. I want to be loved by someone who will share my walk here. Not just be deemed useful or acceptable, but be truly and deeply loved.

Did admitting such feelings mean she'd failed God as well?

And then the pent-up sobs came.

Jack covered the trail in fast, long strides. Where was she? He hadn't really been paying attention when she'd mentioned going for a stroll. It was only later, when his game with Simon was finished, that he'd thought about how unaccustomed she was to the hidden dangers in this part of the country.

He wasn't worried about her getting lost. Even the greenest of city girls could find their way out of so small a wood, and Callie had a good head on her shoulders. But other things could happen out here—a trip and fall that resulted in a twisted ankle or worse, an unexpected encounter with a snake or other critter, a tangle with some painfully spiky thorns.

He should have known better than to let her wander off by herself.

Jack stepped into the meadow and paused for a moment as memories intruded of past picnics and games played here with Lanny and Nell. But the sight of Callie seated near the stream quickly brought his thoughts back to the present.

She was hunched over and her shoulders were shaking. Even from this distance he could hear her sobs.

Within seconds he'd crossed the meadow and was kneeling at her side.

Putting a hand at the small of her back, he scanned her form, looking for injuries. "Callie, what's the matter? Are you hurt?"

Her head came up like that of a startled doe. The pain he saw reflected there wasn't physical, but it was real and bone-deep.

She made a visible effort to stop the flow of tears, to compose herself.

As gently as he could, he brushed the hair from her forehead. "It's all right," he whispered. "Let go."

And with a ragged breath, she surrendered her effort, buried her face in his shoulder and let the tears flow.

Chapter Twenty-Three

Jack held her as she cried, feeling the tears dampen his shirt, feeling the sobs well from deep inside her.

Had something happened in town today?

Had he done something to upset her without even realizing it?

Or was she beginning to realize she wasn't cut out for this kind of life?

Whatever it was, it seemed to be tearing her up.

And this gut-wrenching weeping was killing him. He had to do something—anything—to comfort her. He found himself whispering soothing nonsense to her, stroking her hair, rocking her in his arms.

Anything to bring her misery to an end. No one deserved to be this unhappy.

Finally, with one last shuddering gasp, she stilled. He continued to hold her, letting her rest. He liked the feel of her in his arms, the trusting way she clung to him, the way her unbound hair tickled his chin.

Mostly, he liked the feeling that she needed him, felt safe with him.

They stayed that way for another long minute, the

beating of their hearts the only sounds besides nature's chorus.

At last she gave a little sigh and gently pulled out of his embrace. "I'm sorry." Her gaze didn't meet his. Instead she raised a not quite steady hand and touched his shoulder where her head had rested. "I've gotten your shirt all wet."

"It'll dry." He titled her chin up with his fingers, forcing her to look at him. "You want to tell me what that was all about?"

"It's nothing."

He leaned back on his heels. "It takes a mighty powerful nothing to have an effect like that."

She waved a hand. "I was just feeling a bit sorry for myself, is all."

"Why?" He stood and pulled a bandanna from his pocket, moving toward the stream, giving her a chance to compose herself.

"I don't know." Her voice was husky from all of that crying. "I suppose, with everything that's happened, I hadn't really taken the time to mourn Lanny's passing."

The little kick of jealousy Jack felt was unexpectedly sharp. But he was sure there was something else eating at her.

He squeezed the water out of the bandanna and returned to her side, stooping down next to her again.

She reached for the bit of cloth but he began to wipe her face himself. "Are you sure that's all it is?" he asked.

The flair of guilt in her face was all the answer he needed.

"I was expecting a letter from my father to arrive today," she added, twisting her hands in her lap.

Homesickness then?

She tried to turn the blemished side of her face away,

but he had her chin cupped in his hand and he refused to let her. "You realize you only just sent off your own letter a few days ago," he reasoned. "Give him time. I'm sure he'll respond."

She gave a little half smile then. "It's not a response to my letter I was looking for."

He paused in his ministrations, lifting a brow. "Then what?"

She sighed. "This is going to sound foolish, I know. But today is my birthday."

That set him back. He hadn't marked his own for quite some time, but he knew occasions like that were important to women. "I'm sorry," he said awkwardly. "I didn't—"

She touched a finger to his lips. "Don't be silly. I didn't expect anyone here to even know, much less make a fuss. I just expected the few folks in the world who did know to mark it somehow."

She pulled her hand away and tucked a strand of hair behind her ear. "Actually, it was quite selfish of me to feel that way since my family celebrated the occasion in advance, before I left Ohio." She gave him an overly bright smile. "As I said, I was just feeling sorry for myself."

Jack could still feel the gentle touch of her finger on his lips, could see the vulnerability behind her smile, could hear the wistfulness beneath her sensible tone. Something strong and instinctive welled up inside him.

Almost of its own accord, his thumb stroked her chin, and he bent down to give her a kiss. He had intended it to be a quick gesture of comfort and reassurance, nothing more. But her little gasp of surprise caught him off guard, turning it into something altogether different.

A moment later, he reluctantly pulled back. "Happy birthday," he whispered.

He saw the soft wonder in her expression, the way her eyes searched his, looking for answers.

Answers he suddenly realized he wasn't ready to give, even to himself.

What had he been thinking? He didn't need complications like this in his life.

Handing her the still-damp bandanna, he stood. "We probably should be getting back to the house. The kids'll be wondering where we got off to."

Callie was confused, by both the kiss and his abrupt change of manner afterward.

Her first real kiss.

Her mind was awhirl with the unexpectedness of it, with the still-tumbling sensations. His rush to distance himself only added to her off-balance feelings.

Was he regretting the kiss? Or embarrassed by it?

Had she reacted improperly?

Callie fumbled around for her bonnet and hairpins, trying to gather her thoughts at the same time. She accepted his hand to help her up, but released it as soon as she was upright. She couldn't tell from his expression what he was thinking.

For that matter, she wasn't even certain what *she* was thinking.

Without meeting his gaze, she twisted her hair with a few well-practiced motions and had it pinned into a bun in a matter of seconds.

What a fright she must have looked when he stumbled on her—her hair all loose and tangled, her birthmark on full display and the rest of her face nearly as red and blotchy from her crying. It was a wonder he hadn't turned and left without ever coming near.

But naturally he'd felt sorry for her and had been too much of a gentleman to abandon her to her distress.

She stilled a moment. Is that all that kiss had signified—sympathy?

Of course. How could she have thought, even for a moment, that it had been something more?

"Ready?" His question drew her from her uncomfortable thoughts.

She unfolded and shook out her bonnet. "Yes, of course."

He stopped her before she could place the starched cloth on her head. "There's no need for that."

Callie remembered Simon's conversation with his friends. "Yes, there is." She resolutely pulled the bonnet firmly in place and tied the ribbon under her chin. Just as resolutely, she tamped down the memory of Jack's thumb caressing her there. "You forget, there are the children to consider."

He shook his head as he extended his arm. "I don't think you give them enough credit. They are children, after all. They would adjust to your appearance quite quickly, given the chance."

Callie took his arm, glad she'd let loose all of her feeling on the subject earlier. She could face the matter squarely now, without useless self-pity to cloud her attitude. "Perhaps, when the time is right, we'll give it a try."

Then she straightened her skirt and gave him a serene smile. "Now, as you said, we'd best get back before the children come looking for us."

That evening, Callie closed the door to Simon's room and leaned against it as she let out a tired sigh. Though he grumbled that he'd outgrown the nightly ritual, she still went in to hear his prayers and tuck him in, just as she did with the girls. And every night, his prayers consisted mostly of pleas for God to find a way to help him return to life in town.

Tonight, he'd made his plea more specific, praying that Callie would see Jack's construction efforts as the answer to those prayers and allow them to move "home" when it was done.

After his Amen, the boy had scrambled into bed and turned his back to her, not bothering to so much as acknowledge her when she tucked the coverlet up around his shoulders.

Would she ever be able to get through to him?

Callie pushed away from the door, then hesitated. Should she join Jack for their normal chat tonight?

In spite of her protests this afternoon, Jack had told the children about her birthday and they'd put together a little impromptu celebration. Emma had drawn pictures and Annabeth had picked armloads of wildflowers to decorate the parlor. Jack had dug some cocoa out of the pantry and whipped them each up a cup of cocoa and milk for a treat. Then he'd capped the evening off by insisting that he and the children take care of the kitchen chores while she propped up her feet.

But despite the festivities, there'd been a subtle awkwardness between the two of them ever since that kiss this afternoon. Would being alone together on the moonlit porch ease the tension or intensify it?

Callie squared her shoulders. They'd have to be alone together again sometime.

She loosened her bonnet string. Might as well get it over with sooner rather than later. Besides, if she didn't go downstairs tonight, he'd likely read something into her absence that she'd prefer he not.

And she absolutely refused to acknowledge the little tingle of anticipation that shimmied through her.

Jack straightened when he heard the door open behind him.

He hadn't been sure she'd join him tonight, wasn't even quite sure if he'd wanted her to.

"Thanks for the birthday celebration," she said as she leaned against the rail.

A nice, safe subject. Did she plan to ignore what had happened between them this afternoon then? That's what he'd wanted, but still, he'd give a pretty penny to be able to read her mind at the moment.

"You're welcome," he said carefully. "I'm afraid it wasn't much of a party."

"Actually, it's one of the nicest ones I've had since Julia left Ohio."

She must have seen the surprise in his face, because she quickly added, "Oh, I didn't mean to say my family didn't celebrate with me. But this had more the feel of a child's tea party and it brought back sweet memories."

He grimaced. "A child's tea party, huh?"

"I'm sorry." She grinned, not looking one bit repentant. "Does it bother you to think you had a hand in such an event? I assure you, it was done quite well."

Jack relaxed, comfortable with the bantering tone she'd set. "Just don't let word get back to my demolition team."

She crossed her heart. "You have my word."

Then her expression turned serious. "You know Simon is still set on returning to his old life in town.

He sees this building project of yours as God's answer to his prayers."

Jack shifted in his seat. He'd never thought of himself as the answer to anyone's prayers. "By the time I'm done, he'll have had more time to adjust to life here on the farm."

"I don't know that a few weeks, or even months, will make much of a difference in his feelings."

He heard the wistful tinge in her voice. "What about you? Are you so certain this is really the life you want?"

"More so than ever."

Not the answer he'd expected. "Why?"

She raised a brow. "Disappointed? I thought you wanted to make certain the farm stayed in Tyler family hands."

"That's my reason." He pointed a finger at her. "I asked about yours. Running this place is hard work and you're more accustomed to city ways."

"It's true that my former home was in the midst of a good-sized city with lots of modern conveniences that haven't found their way out here yet. But I spent most of my days inside that house so it's not like I'll miss the sights and sounds. As for the conveniences, I get by quite nicely without electric lights or fancy shops or so-called fine entertainment, thank you. Moving to Sweetgum proper wouldn't provide those things anyway."

She turned and stared out over the darkened landscape. "My reason? I like it out here. I like the feel of openness and of making my own way. I like the fact that it's forced me to draw on skills I didn't know I had. And I like experiencing God's handiwork in such an intimate way." She turned back to him and crossed her arms. "It's also the life Leland wanted for Annabeth and I feel I owe it to him to give it to her."

Leland again. It always came back to his brother. "What about Emma and Simon?"

Callie sat on the bench and picked at something on her skirt. "I've been pondering on that. I still worry about Emma. But I think the change in scenery and routine has been good for her. Once we figure out whatever is truly bothering her, I believe she'll be happy here."

So she still thought there was something bothering Emma, something besides her grief. He'd have to keep a closer eye on the girl. He was beginning to appreciate Callie's instincts when it came to the kids.

"As for Simon," she said slowly, "I just don't know. He seems to have his mind made up and I'm beginning to wonder if we'll be able to change it. The thing is..." She paused, then lifted her head confidently. "I believe, whether he thinks so or not, this is the best place for him right now."

That seemed a strange choice of words. But before he could question her further, she stood. "I think it's time for me to retire. You enjoy the evening."

Jack continued shaving strips off his block of wood. At least it seemed his impulsive kiss hadn't done any permanent damage to the friendship that had begun to take root between them.

Why, he wondered, didn't that give him a sense of satisfaction?

Chapter Twenty-Four

Callie set a pie on the window sill to cool and glanced out toward the work shed, wondering what Jack was up to.

He'd come back from town at lunchtime today and spent most of the afternoon working on some project out there. He'd been evasive about whatever he was up to, but he'd worn a self-satisfied smile when he came in an hour ago looking for baking soda, wood polish and silver polish.

She shook her head and moved back to the oven to fetch the second pie. As if her thoughts had conjured him up, Jack stepped through the back door.

"Where are the kids?"

She placed the pie atop the stove. "I believe the girls are in the parlor and Simon is on the front porch. Why?"

"I have something to show them. Would you call them in here?"

So, they were finally going to learn what he'd been up to. Intrigued, Callie did as he asked. When the four of them entered the kitchen, Jack stood beside the table. He'd thrown a cloth over it and there were several interesting looking lumps beneath it.

"Here we are," she said unnecessarily.

Jack nodded and waved them forward. "Simon and Emma, while we were working in town last week, my crew and I found a few things I thought you might want." With a flourish, he pulled away the cloth to reveal an odd assortment of items.

A penknife lay next to a silver-plated hand mirror and a delicate teacup.

A tin box held three polished rocks and an assortment of marbles. Next to the box was a gold locket, without a chain.

Displayed on a flour sack were a collection of knobs, handles, drawer pulls and other assorted hardware.

And behind all of these items were three wooden boxes of different sizes and designs.

Simon touched the penknife as if it were a valuable relic. "This was Dad's. He used it to trim the wicks on the lamps."

Jack put a hand on the boy's shoulder. "It's yours now."

He turned to Emma who was running a fingertip over the mirror, as if afraid it would break if she applied even the slightest pressure.

"I know that was your mother's," he said softly. "She got it for her thirteenth birthday."

Emma nodded, her eyes glistening.

Callie watched the children's reactions to these rescued treasures and swallowed back the lump in her throat. Every one of these items had been scrupulously cleaned so there was not a smudge or hint of char on them. The silver gleamed. The locket glowed with the warmth of well-worn gold.

The man was a fraud. Anyone who would go to so much trouble to salvage these treasures for the children was no cold-hearted loner. But then again, she'd stopped believing that about him quite some time ago.

She cleared her throat and touched the rim of the teacup. The delicate rose-patterned piece had a soft, pearly luster inside and out. "This is beautiful."

"It's Momma's good china." Emma's voice was hoarse with emotion. "We only used it when company came."

Callie nodded, moving her hand from the cup to Emma's shoulder. "Then it deserves a place of honor. What do you say we clear a spot in the china cabinet for it?"

Emma nodded.

Callie picked up the delicate cup and solemnly carried it over to the china cabinet that stood in the dining room. With great care she shifted a few items around and then set the tea cup where it could be admired with ease.

When they returned to the kitchen, Simon was eagerly examining his rocks and marbles.

Jack pointed to the boxes. "I thought you might like to have something to store your treasures in. These are made from the wooden walls and floors of your house. The hinges and knobs are from the doors and windows."

He looked at Annabeth. "Little Bit, I made one for you, too. I thought you might like to have a memento to remember your Aunt Nell and Uncle Jed by."

Callie met his eyes over the heads of the children and hoped he could read her approval.

Lord, thank You for bringing this man into the children's lives. And mine, as well.

The next few days settled into a routine. Callie rose with the sun to help Jack with the morning chores. Then she woke the children and started breakfast. By the time she had the meal on the table, the children were dressed and in their seats, and Jack was cleaned up and ready to join them. After breakfast, everyone scattered to his or her assigned chores for that day, and Jack headed into town to work on the construction.

As the days passed, though, she and the children saw less and less of Jack. He didn't even bother to come home for the noonday meal. Instead he stuffed a chunk of cheese, a thick slice of bread and an apple or pear in a basket to take along with him.

It was usually late when he returned from town. Once he checked that everything was in order with the animals he washed up and came in for supper.

Even their nightly chats grew shorter. Callie tried to look on the bright side of things. It was probably for the best. After all, this was how things would be when he went back to his old life. She should get used to it now.

But she found very little consolation in that thought.

By the end of the week, however, she was worried about the toll the workload seemed to be taking on Jack himself.

He'd been pushing hard—too hard. Rising before sunup, doing his share of the morning chores, then gulping down breakfast before heading to town. The days had been brutally hot, yet that hadn't slowed him down. By the time he came home in the evenings he looked withered and bone tired.

Callie stood in the kitchen Saturday evening, and glanced at the watch pinned to her bodice for the tenth time. It was nearly dark out and there was still no sign of Jack. She'd long since fed the children and cleaned up their dishes.

What was keeping him? Had he run into problems?

Her head came up at the sound of a wagon.

"Your Uncle Jack is home," she announced. "Emma, would you set him a place at the table, please? Simon, run out and see if you can help him with anything."

Callie nibbled at her bottom lip. This was ridiculous. It was time she had a talk with him. Tonight. Before the fool man worked himself down to a nub.

Jack inhaled deeply as Callie set a plate in front of him. Coming home to a meal like this in the evening had become the high point of his day. He was sure going to miss it when he returned to life on the road.

Among other things.

Funny how that kind of thinking occupied his mind of late. Must be because he was so tired. The Texas summer heat certainly took its toll on a man.

But the work was coming along well. If his luck held and he kept up his current pace, he could finish in under a month.

Callie took a seat across from him. "Shall I say grace for you?"

He paused with his fork halfway to his mouth. The kids weren't anywhere in sight. But apparently that wasn't the point.

With a nod, he set his fork down and bowed his head.

"Heavenly Father, thank You for the bounty You have provided. Bless the meal and the one who partakes of it. May it nourish him and provide him strength and sustenance. Amen."

"Amen." Jack picked up his fork again and shoveled the first bite into his mouth. Cooking was definitely one of Callie's gifts.

"You need to slow down."

He gave her a wary look as he swallowed the morsel. "Sorry if my table manners offend you. I'm still not used to eating in mixed company."

She waved a hand. "That's not what I meant. You can't keep up the pace you've set for yourself. Are you in such a hurry to get back to your old life that you're willing to run yourself into the ground to finish faster?"

He shrugged. "I'm used to working long hours to get a project done."

"But no one's set you a deadline for this. Why are you pushing yourself so hard?"

Jack took another bite of food, watching her closely while he chewed and swallowed. "I want to make sure it gets done by the first of August."

Her brow furrowed. "Why that particular date?"

"It's the timeframe I set for heading back to California."

That seemed to set her back a bit and Jack took advantage of her silence to continue eating. With any luck she'd let the subject drop.

"Still, you can't—

He held up a hand. Seems his luck wasn't going to hold after all. "Look, I'm tired and I'm hungry. Can this conversation wait until tomorrow? It'll be Sunday and we'll have all the time in the world for one of these little chats."

"Very well." She stood. "But don't think I'll let this drop."

The thought had never crossed his mind.

The next morning, when Jack came downstairs, he was surprised to find the stove already stoked, a pot of coffee brewing and Callie seated at the table.

"Well, well, you're up mighty early. What's the occasion?"

"You're fired."

Jack blinked. "What?"

Her chin lifted in that familiar stubborn tilt. "I decided I've had enough practice. I'm taking over the morning chores."

He couldn't suppress his grunt of disbelief.

She smiled. "Not by myself. The children have already learned to help with the evening chores. It won't be such a big jump for them to learn to help in the morning as well."

"They might feel differently."

"As you've said before, they'll adjust." She leaned forward. "Starting tomorrow, you can sleep a little later in the morning."

"Look, I know you mean well, but I think I'm the best judge of how much I can and can't handle. If I—"

"I'm certain you're just stubborn enough to continue this pace, even if it wears you plumb out."

Hah! She was one to talk about stubborn.

"But," she continued, "I'd prefer not to have to nurse you back to health when you work yourself to the point of collapse."

He poured a cup of coffee, as much to give himself a moment to think as anything else. When he turned around, she still wore that determined expression.

"All right. I agree it would be good for the children to take on a bit more responsibility for keeping this place running. So if you think you can manage getting them to toe the mark—"

"And there's something else."

Of course there was. "And that would be?"

"You need to spend more time here at the farm."

He set his cup down with enough force to splash a

few drops onto the table. "You just said you wanted to take on more responsibility for the place."

She waved a hand impatiently. "I don't mean to help with the chores. You need to spend more time with the children." Her expression softened. "They've hardly seen you these past few days. I want them to be able to spend time with you, to develop a real relationship with you—and you with them—before you go running back off to wherever it is you're heading when you leave here."

Whoa. She hadn't really thought this through. "Actually, I thought it would be better all the way around if they don't get too used—"

She lifted her chin again. "You said you owed it to Leland and Nell to see that their children were well-cared for. And also that it was important for blood kin to be close. That's why we ended up in this marriage, remember?"

"Of course I remember. But—"

"Well, you can't see to any of that if you're never here."

Blast the woman, there she went, trying to twist his words back on him. "And I suppose you have something in mind to make everyone happy."

"I do."

That I've-got-it-all-figured-out tone set his teeth on edge.

"Go to town in the mornings," she elaborated. "It's the coolest part of the day, and the children will be busy with their own chores. But come home for lunch, and stay. There are things you can do here, and I don't mean chores."

"Such as?"

"Such as take Simon fishing. Such as teach Annabeth about the wildlife around here. Such as walk in the woods with Emma to find things she can sketch."

Her passion for the children lit a fire in her eyes that was something to see.

She threw up her hands as if exasperated. "Tell them stories about when you and their parents were children growing up here. Let them know you really care about *them,* not just that you feel responsible for them."

She was pushing this just a little too far. "Look, I'm more of the loner type than the jovial fatherly sort."

Her expression rivaled Mrs. Mayweather's for sternness. "Then just pretend." She planted both elbows on the table and laced her fingers. "Those children need you, maybe more than they need me. And you know as well as I do that it's what Leland and Nell would have wanted."

She just didn't play fair.

He stood up from the table. "I'll think about it."

She rose as well and gave him a meaningful look. "And I'll continue to pray about it."

No, she didn't play fair at all.

Chapter Twenty-Five

Callie pinned the last bit of laundry to the line strung under the rafters in the washroom. The rain had started a little over an hour ago, just about the time she'd run the last of the clothes through the wringer. It certainly was nice to have such a wonderful arrangement inside for rainy days.

She wiped her forehead with the back of her hand, glad to have the Monday morning chore over with. She hoped Jack had had sense enough to find shelter to wait out the rain. But knowing him, he was ignoring the weather and still pounding nails into boards.

She stepped into the kitchen and checked the stew simmering on the stove, then went in search of the children.

She found them on the front porch, staring glumly at the water dripping from the eaves. Gil was visiting this morning, so there were four pairs of eyes that turned to her, ready for a distraction.

They looked like woebegone waifs. This wouldn't do at all.

She crossed her arms. "Surely you can find some

way to amuse yourselves even if you can't leave the porch."

"It's been raining *forever,*" Annabeth wailed. "When is it going to stop? I want to take Cinnamon for a ride."

"You'll just have to be patient." Callie gave them a bracing smile. "Come on now, what will it be? A game of jackstraws, perhaps? Or maybe charades?"

"You can read us some of the story," Annabeth suggested hopefully.

"But it's not even lunchtime yet."

Gil immediately followed Annabeth's lead. "Oh, yes, please, Mrs. Tyler. Simon's been telling me about the story and it sounds like an exciting tale."

She stared at the four hopeful faces and her resistance crumbled. "Oh, very well. Emma, would you fetch the book, please?"

Callie read for twenty minutes, then finally closed the book. "That's enough for today. It looks like the rain has stopped and I need to check on lunch."

"That's one rip-roaring tree house," Gil said. "Sure is clever the way they turned bits and pieces of wreckage into a bang-up place to live."

"Yeah," Simon agreed. "I wish we had something like that around here."

Callie paused in the act of getting up.

Gil popped up and placed both hands on his hips. "If we did, we could spend our afternoons planning our own adventures."

"And designing special devices to furnish it with." Simon's voice had more energy in it than Callie had heard in a long time.

"Why not?" she asked impulsively.

The children looked at her as if she'd just sprouted antlers.

"Ma'am?" Gil's one word question hung in the air for a second while all four children seemed to hold their breath.

"Why not build a tree house?" she elaborated. "That big oak out back is the perfect place for one. And Simon, you're good at building things."

The boy's eyes lit up. "Do you think we really could?"

Callie felt her heart warm at the eager look on his face. Maybe, just maybe, he could learn to see the appeal of life in the country after all. "Well, we'd have to ask your Uncle Jack, of course. And I don't think we could do anything as elaborate as the one in the book."

"But we could design it ourselves and add whatever features we like." Simon turned to Gil. "I know Uncle Jack has some old crates in the barn we could use, and maybe some kegs, too. How about your dad?"

Annabeth clapped her hands. "A tree house! I want to help."

Simon crossed his arms with a sniff. "You're a girl."

"Girls can build things, too." Annabeth turned indignant eyes toward Callie. "Can't they?"

"Of course they can, sweetheart."

Simon wasn't happy with that answer. "Gil, help me here. Tell them this is men's work."

Callie tried to soothe the boy's ruffled feathers. "Simon, remember in the book, it wasn't just the tree house itself that had to be built. There were furnishings, too. I was thinking the girls could work on some of those things."

"Sounds fair to me," Gil said quickly.

Simon nodded reluctantly. "I guess so. But no frilly stuff."

"No frilly stuff," Callie promised. "And remember, we need to clear this with your Uncle Jack first."

Too late Callie realized she probably shouldn't have gotten their hopes up before she spoke to Jack about it. If he objected to the scheme, she was going to have some very disappointed children on her hands. Because the four would-be adventurers were already putting their heads together, discussing plans for the tree house.

To her relief, once Jack was able to sort out the gist of the idea from the eager babblings of the children, he gave his stamp of approval to the plan. But he had a few stipulations.

"Before I say yes, there are some ground rules we need to set. For one, your chores come first. No work gets done on the tree house until that's taken care of."

Three heads nodded agreement.

"And I'll have to talk to Gil's dad and make sure he's okay with Gil taking part."

"I'm sure Mr. Wilson will be okay with this," Simon offered.

"Still, I want to talk to him first. Now Simon, you and Gil will be in charge of collecting most of the materials. I'll help where I can, but this is going to be your project. You can clean out a corner of the barn to store things in."

"Thanks."

"If you boys want to come to town with me one morning this week, you can dig through the scrap pile and see if there's anything there you can use."

"Yes, sir!"

"Next time Gil comes around we can all sit down and draw up some plans. Then you can start work."

Once the children were down for the night, Callie stepped out on the porch. It felt good to have this little ritual back.

She'd missed their talks, discussing the children and the day's events, making plans for the coming days.

When had she started looking forward to it so much?

"The children are excited about the tree house. I could hardly get them to settle down tonight."

"I understand it was your idea."

She gave a little half-grin, not certain if that was approval in his voice or something else. "They were talking about the tree house in the book and I saw how excited Simon was. It's the first time I've seen him take a real interest in something other than moving to town. I couldn't help myself." She gave him an apologetic look. "I'm sorry if I put you on the spot."

He shook his head. "Actually, I think it's a great idea. The boy has a natural skill when it comes to using tools, and this will give him a sense of responsibility to go along with it."

"I'm glad Gil will be working with him on this. The two have become good friends. Maybe he won't miss his friends in town so much."

"So, are you going to fill me in on the latest chapter of our adventure story?"

Callie smiled and gave him a quick recap.

"Just another couple of days and we'll finish *Swiss Family Robinson,*" she added when she'd finished. "I think the children will really be disappointed."

"I admit I'll miss it myself."

Callie smiled. "Don't worry. I have some others you'll all enjoy just as much."

"Do you, now?"

She ticked them off on her fingers. "There's *Around the World in Eighty Days* and *Tom Sawyer.* Then there's a new book about a detective named Sherlock Holmes, and one about an undersea adventure. And at least a half dozen others."

"Quite a collection." He gave her a searching look. "These all come from your personal library?"

She reddened slightly. "Actually, I bought them as a wedding gift for Leland. Julia had mentioned once how much he enjoyed reading adventure stories."

His hands stilled and she couldn't quite read the expression on his face. "I thought your grandfather's pocket watch was your wedding gift for Lanny."

She didn't detect anything other than mild curiosity in his tone. But she had a feeling there was something stronger behind the question. "Now, why ever would you think such a thing?"

He ignored her question. "If you didn't intend to give it to Lanny, why did you give it to me?"

This time she heard a hint of accusation. "I told you, it was a keepsake from my grandfather. I—I wanted to give you a gift that fit who *you* are."

"Oh."

She tilted her head to one side, trying to read between the lines. "Is that why you didn't like it? Because it wasn't bought specifically for you? I didn't feel right giving you something I'd bought for Lanny. That seemed a bit wrong somehow. But there wasn't time to order anything, and I really wasn't certain what—"

He cut her off. "It's not that I didn't like it."

"Then what?"

He went back to his whittling and she saw a tic at the corner of his mouth.

"I'm sorry. I shouldn't have asked that."

He paused, then leaned back against the rail and gave her a long look. "No. I suppose I owe you an explanation." He raked a hand through his hair. "It was actually because I thought you *did* bring it to give Lanny."

"Oh." She tried to make sense of that but couldn't quite.

He stuck the knife point into the block of wood. "Growing up as Lanny's younger brother meant I wound up with every item he outgrew. Things he no longer needed or wanted or could fit into became mine. Guess I got a little tired of always ending up with my brother's hand-me-downs."

Of course. She should have realized. "And you thought I was giving you a hand-me-down gift."

His grin had a self-deprecating edge. "Yep. I suppose that was a confoundedly fool reaction, even if it had been true. A grown man shouldn't let something like that get under his skin."

"We can't help how we feel about things." She of all people knew the truth of that. Almost of its own accord, her hand touched his shoulder. "I'm sorry I didn't get you something new, something no one had owned before," she said softly.

He paused a fraction of a second at her touch, then gave her that crooked smile. "Don't go apologizing. It was a fine gift, even more so because it had such value to you."

She removed her hand somewhat awkwardly and he

leaned back. "I suppose it's really me who should apologize to you. I didn't even thank you proper."

She wondered what he thought of her touching his shoulder. Had she given away too much? "Why don't we just call it even then?"

"Okay by me."

Callie decided she really liked Jack's smile, especially when it was focused on her.

Twenty minutes later Callie climbed the stairs to the second floor. She and Jack had stayed out chatting later than usual.

She paused as she passed the girls' room. What was that sound?

There it went again.

Just a hiccup.

She started to move on, then stopped again. That was a muffled sob.

Callie quietly opened the door and slipped inside the room. All was quiet now.

Had she imagined it? Or was one of the girls making sounds in her sleep?

Letting her eyes adjust to the dark, she studied the forms of the two girls. Annabeth was sprawled with abandon across her bed.

Emma, however, was lying on her side, body curled and facing away from the door. Callie crossed the room and stood over her.

"Emma, honey," she said softly, "what is it? Are you sick?"

Emma shook her head, still not turning to face Callie.

"Having a bad dream then?"

Again a shake of the head.

Poor dear. She was probably missing her parents. Should she force her to speak about it?

Callie sat down on the bed and gently pushed the hair from the child's damp forehead. "Won't you tell me what's wrong?"

Emma finally looked up and met Callie's gaze. The despair filling those teary eyes was almost more than Callie could bear.

"Oh, Aunt Callie, I've done something awful."

The broken words tore at Callie's heart. "Sweetie, whatever it is, I know it can't be as bad as you're imagining."

"You don't know." Another sob escaped her. "Everyone would hate me if they knew."

Annabeth stirred and rolled over.

Callie stood and pulled the covers from Emma. "Come on," she whispered, "let's go down to the kitchen so we don't wake your sister."

Emma took Callie's outstretched hand and slipped out of bed. She allowed Callie to lead her from the room, much as a doomed prisoner would follow along behind his executioner.

Callie led her to the kitchen and seated her at the table. "Now you sit here while I fix us a little treat." She kept talking, careful to keep her back to Emma, giving the child time to compose herself. "I believe we have a little cocoa left in the pantry and I think this is a good time to bring it out." She retrieved two cups and filled them with warm water from the kettle on the stove. "The secret to a good cup of chocolate is to add a touch of vanilla and a touch of peppermint oil." After she'd mixed the aromatic drinks, she carried them to the table.

"Before you say anything, I want you to understand that there is nothing you could possibly have done that will make me hate you. And no matter what it is, you know that God will forgive you and call you His beloved."

"But you don't know what—"

"Then tell me."

Emma placed her hands around her cup but didn't drink.

Finally she took a deep breath that sounded more like a sob.

"The fire was my fault."

Chapter Twenty-Six

Callie fought to keep her expression serene. What a terrible burden for a child to carry. "What makes you say that, sweetheart?"

"Because it's true." Emma's voice trembled.

"Tell me what happened."

Emma sniffed, then nodded. "Momma had bought some pretty new candles that smelled real nice. They were supposed to be used for special occasions, but I was grumpy about not getting the new colored pencils I saw at Mr. Dobson's store."

She looked up with pleading eyes. "I was really careful about where I placed the candle, I promise. And it did make me feel better. Then Simon came in to say he was taking me and Annabeth over to see the new foal at the livery and I forgot all about the candle."

Callie touched the girl's arm. "Oh, Emma, that's not what set that fire."

The girl refused to be comforted. "You don't know that," she insisted.

"But *I* do."

Callie and Emma both turned as Jack entered the kitchen.

"Sorry to eavesdrop, but I heard y'all talking when I came inside." He knelt down in front of Emma, taking one of her hands between his. "I talked to Mr. Wilson after I got here. They don't know exactly what caused the fire, but they could tell that it started in the kitchen."

Emma's eyes filled with both doubt and hope. "It did?"

"That's right. And you didn't leave your candle in the kitchen, did you?"

She shook her head.

"So that means your candle had nothing to do with the fire."

"Then it really wasn't my fault?" The weight almost visibly lifted from Emma's shoulders. With a sob, she threw her arms around Jack's neck and buried her head against his chest.

Callie wanted to throw her arms around him as well. The gift he'd just given Emma, the cleansing of her guilty conscience, was beyond price.

Instead of joining the embrace, she stood and went to the cupboard. "What do you say I fix your Uncle Jack a cup of cocoa so he won't have to just watch us drink ours?"

By the time Callie returned, Emma had finally released her hold on Jack.

Callie's heart swelled as she saw a peace in the child's expression that hadn't been there before.

Jack accepted the cup she brought him and she studied the way he watched Emma as he drank. The mix of satisfaction and concern in his eyes was so, well, so *parental,* that Callie was tempted all over again to give him a hug. Why had Julia's letters never mentioned this softer aspect of Jack?

Because, of course, Julia had been in love with Leland, and Leland and Jack had been at odds. But Callie didn't have that emotional entanglement to fog her vision of the man, and she saw the tender protector, the concerned family man he could be.

He really did love these children—she could see it not just in his eyes, but in his whole presence. His life was now tied irrevocably to theirs, whether he realized it or not.

If only he felt as deeply about her…

Jack looked up and met her gaze. She lifted her glass, covering her emotion with a silent salute to his accomplishment.

He smiled back, his expression almost sheepish.

The three drank their cocoas in companionable silence. Then, as Callie carried the cups to the sink, Emma let out a jaw-stretching yawn.

Jack bent over and scooped up his niece. "Time to carry you back to bed, young lady."

Without so much as a murmur, Emma wrapped her arms around Jack's neck, rested her head on his shoulder and closed her eyes.

Callie followed close behind as they exited the room, enjoying the picture they made. As they reached the stairs, Emma's eyes opened the merest crack and she reached behind Jack to stroke Callie's cheek.

"Annabeth was right," she said drowsily. "Your angel's kiss is beautiful."

"Looks like you boys are doing a good job."

The hammering paused and Gil's freckled face peered down at Jack from the unfinished platform above. "Hi, Mr. Tyler. Is it lunchtime already?"

"Not for another hour or so. I just decided to come back a little early today. Is Simon up there?"

"He went out to the tool shed to fetch a crowbar."

Jack made a quick survey of their progress. "You having some problems?"

"No, sir. We just decided to move a couple of our bigger boards to a different spot."

"Sounds like you have it under control then. Once I talk to Simon's Aunt Callie I'll come back by and lend a hand."

Gil gave a friendly wave and disappeared back behind the tree house's floor. A moment later the hammering began again with renewed force.

Jack headed toward the back porch. Might as well let Callie know he was home.

He'd spent most of the afternoon yesterday working with Simon and Gil on the initial foundation, setting several stout hickory posts for support and laying some of the cross beams that would provide the base for the floor. They'd also fashioned a sturdy ladder and nailed it securely to the tree.

He'd then given them a stern lecture on safety and teamwork issues. Once he was certain they were clear on the rules, he'd told them they could work on their own whenever they had the time.

He'd spent another hour dealing with Callie's concerns, assuring her that at less than six feet off the ground, the boys would be okay. He'd survived tumbles from greater heights than that when he and Lanny had run free around this place.

Jack stepped inside the house to find lunch simmering on the stove but no sign of Callie. Following the sound of muffled conversation, he moved to the dining room.

He paused in the doorway. Callie and the girls were

gathered around the table, intent on something Emma was sketching.

"Oh, that's lovely," Callie said. "What color should we make it?"

"Pink and purple." Annabeth's response was immediate and confident. "Oh, and with lots of lace," she added.

Jack found himself smiling, both at the assurance with which Annabeth made her pronouncement and at Callie's attempt to hide a smile.

"Those are lovely colors, sweetheart, but perhaps they're not quite right for a tree house."

Annabeth's lips tightened into a pout. "Why not?"

"Well, because this is supposed to be a home built in the middle of nowhere by a shipwrecked family. I don't think they had a lot of pretty things to work with." She put a finger on her chin, as if giving it careful consideration. "I tell you what. We'll wait until we get to town and look at what fabrics are available at the mercantile, and then we'll decide."

"Yes, ma'am."

Jack stepped farther into the room. "Sounds like you ladies have been doing some serious planning."

Callie put a hand on one hip. "You didn't think we'd let you fellows have all the fun, did you?"

"Hi, Uncle Jack." Annabeth jumped down from her chair and ran to greet him. "We're going to make curtains and rugs and some big pillows to sit on and—"

"Don't spoil all the surprises," Callie admonished. She turned to Jack. "Emma has been sketching out ideas. She's quite the artist. In fact, she's come up with one idea we'd like to get your thoughts on."

"Oh?" Jack turned to his niece. "And what might that be?"

Emma slid one of her drawings out of the stack and passed it to him. The tree and tree house were lightly penciled in with a few strokes that nevertheless conveyed their form perfectly. The main focus of the drawing, however, was a contraption that hung from one of the limbs.

"It's a basket on a rope that we can use to lift and lower things with," Emma explained. "That way we won't have to climb the ladder one-handed."

"That's mighty smart thinking on your part." He sat down next to Emma. It was amazing how much the child had come out of her shell since the discussion of the fire two nights ago. "I see you have the rope pulled over this tall limb and then tied down on a lower one."

She gave him an uncertain glance. "Don't you think that will work?"

"I think it'll work just fine. I have some rope in the barn that's probably long enough." He studied her drawing closely. "And I even have an old pulley out there. What do you think about me and the boys rigging that up while you ladies find us a sturdy basket to use?"

Emma nodded.

"Aunt Callie's going to teach us how to make braided rugs," Annabeth added.

"That sounds like a good idea, Little Bit." He leaned closer and said in a mock whisper, "Maybe you can sneak a little pink and purple in the mix."

Annabeth put a hand over her mouth to muffle her giggle.

Callie stood. "I'd better check on lunch. Emma, why don't you show your Uncle Jack some more of your ideas."

Jack watched her leave, not at all fooled by the excuse she'd given. This was her way of providing the girls time alone with him.

* * *

Callie stirred the pot of stew simmering on the stove.

Why was Jack home early today? Had he really taken her words to heart about spending more time with the children?

He came in a few minutes later and stood behind her. Peering over her shoulder at the food on the stove, he placed his hand on the small of her back as if to anchor himself. It took a concerted effort on her part not to lean back into him.

She cleared her throat. "Things going well in town?" she asked as casually as she could.

"Yep. Why?"

"Just wondering what brought you home before midday."

"Disappointed?"

"Of course not. I only wondered, that's all."

"Actually, I wanted to check on the boys and make sure they remembered my lecture on working safely. I'll go back to my regular schedule tomorrow."

He removed his hand and reached around her to swipe a biscuit from the platter on the back of the stove. Dodging her playful swipe with a dishrag, he headed toward the door. "Think I'll go back out and lend the boys a hand."

"Just a minute."

Jack paused, giving her dishrag a wary glance.

This was more like it. She could handle bantering with him more easily than those intense, confusing emotions.

Callie grabbed a small basket from the counter. "The boys have been working out there most of the morning," she said. "Here's a jar of sweet tea and two slices of last night's gingerbread to tide them over until lunch."

Jack gave her a woebegone look. "Only two slices."

But he wasn't winning any sympathy from her. With an exaggerated sniff, she pointed to the half-eaten biscuit in his hand. "You, sir, chose your treat already."

Jack placed a hand melodramatically over his heart. "Undone by my own greed." Then he gave her a wink. "But for one of your biscuits, it was worth it." Saluting her, he made his exit.

Jack chuckled as he strolled toward the oak. Callie was learning to give as good as she got in the teasing department. He enjoyed these exchanges as much as their evening talks after the kids were in bed.

He was still grinning when he halted next to the tree house ladder. "How's it coming along, boys?"

Two heads popped out above the platform this time.

"Hi, Uncle Jack." Simon gave him a confident smile. "Don't worry, we're laying the boards just the way you showed us yesterday."

"I can see that. Looks like y'all are doing a mighty fine job." He lifted the basket. "Your Aunt Callie thought you two might be ready for a little snack."

"Yes, sir!" Gil's freckled face split in a smile.

Jack handed the basket up. "Go ahead and help yourselves. I'm headed to the barn to look for something the girls need."

"Thanks, Mr. Tyler." Gil already had a sizeable portion of gingerbread in his mouth. "Mmm-mmm."

With a wave, Jack moved on.

"You sure are lucky, Simon."

"What do you mean?"

Jack slowed his steps, then bent down to remove a nonexistent stone from his boot. He was as curious as Simon to hear what Gil had to say.

"I mean I wish I had an aunt like Mrs. Tyler."

"Just cause she sent us out some old gingerbread?" Something in Simon's tone got Jack's back up.

"Hey, this is really good gingerbread." Gil sounded affronted. "But it's not just what a good cook she is. You know what I mean. She can read an adventure story so dramatic-like that you get all caught up in it. And it was her idea for us to build this tree house."

"True." Simon drew the word out as if agreeing in spite of himself.

"Just imagine, a woman doing all that. You wouldn't catch my ma or my Aunt Dora doing anything near as fun, that's for sure."

Simon's response was too muffled for Jack to make out. He straightened and resumed his walk to the barn.

Interesting. Maybe seeing Callie through Gil's eyes would help Simon see her virtues. It sure had Jack mulling over a few of her qualities he hadn't given much thought to before.

As Callie walked along the lane that lead from Mrs. Mayweather's to Main Street Friday morning, her thoughts were on Simon. The boy was helping Jack and his team work on the building today. He'd actually volunteered, offering to help in exchange for some coins to buy a few things he'd had his eye on for the tree house.

They'd all put in a lot of work on that tree house these past three days, but Simon most of all.

Callie had taken this as a hopeful sign. He seemed to be slowly moving toward acceptance of his new lot in life. In fact, he hadn't mentioned moving back to town even once in his prayers last night.

That he'd been willing to forgo visiting with his

friends in town so he could earn money of his own was a major shift in attitude for the boy.

In fact, when they'd arrived this morning, Bobby and Abe had tried to talk Simon into joining them in some escapade or other. She'd been quietly impressed with the way he'd stuck by the commitment he'd made to Jack.

Simon might not ever truly feel close to her the way she hoped, but maybe in time he would come to accept that she wasn't his enemy, and that she had a place in his life.

Callie turned the corner onto Main Street and halted in her tracks. There was some kind of commotion going on over at Dobson's Mercantile.

Mr. Dobson himself stood at the mouth of the alley that ran alongside his store, holding a squirming youngster by the collar of his shirt. Passersby were stopping to gawk and others were starting to drift over, too.

Well, she'd just as soon avoid the crowded scene, thank you very much.

She lifted her skirts to cross the street, then halted again as the scene registered more fully.

Wait a minute.

Releasing her skirt, she quickly marched forward, elbowing her way past the other townsfolk who were trying to get a better look at what was happening.

A moment later she stood face-to-face with the shopkeeper and his captive.

"Mr. Dobson, please release Simon this instant."

Chapter Twenty-Seven

At the sound of Callie's voice, Simon went perfectly still. He slowly looked up and met her gaze with the expression of a doomed prisoner.

The look sent a needle-sharp stab to her heart. Did he think she'd be so quick to judge him?

A hush fell over the crowd as they waited to hear what would happen next. Callie forced herself to ignore everyone but Simon and his accuser.

"Mrs. Tyler, I'm glad you're here." Mr. Dobson pushed his spectacles higher up on his nose with his free hand. "This young vandal has been up to some very destructive mischief."

"I'll thank you, sir, not to be calling Simon names. Now, please release him as I requested and explain to me what all this fuss is about."

If anything, Mr. Dobson tightened his hold on Simon's collar. "This boy of yours has made a mess of my store and terrorized my customers."

Simon turned pleading eyes her way. "I didn't, Aunt Callie. I swear it wasn't—"

"Hush, Simon," she said sternly. "You shouldn't be swearing." Then she gave him a slight nod of encouragement before she turned back to the shopkeeper. "Mr. Dobson, if Simon says he didn't do it, then I believe him."

From the corner of her eye she saw Simon's eyes widen.

Mr. Dobson had a similar reaction, but his expression was accompanied by a stern frown. "That's a fine thing for you to say, madam, but just because you have an affection for the boy, that don't change things. He did it, all right."

"I'm certain you're mistaken. Now, I will ask you one more time to please release my son. Then we can discuss this civilly."

When the man still hesitated, she jutted her chin forward. "I assure you, Simon is an honorable young man and he'll stay right here without coercion until this is straightened out." She stared the man down until he finally released Simon's shirt and adjusted his own cuff with a sharp "Humph!"

Callie placed a hand lightly on Simon's shoulder as she continued to face Mr. Dobson.

"Now, tell me exactly what happened and why you think Simon might be involved so we can settle the matter."

"Perhaps we should get Jack."

His condescending tone set Callie's teeth on edge. While it would be more comfortable to have Jack handle the matter so she could fade into the background, Jack would be heading back to California soon. She had to learn how to handle such situations on her own. "That won't be necessary. Please proceed."

"Very well." His mouth tightened as he tugged at his cuff once more. "A little while ago, this boy and some of his friends set a whole passel of squirrels loose in my store. Those critters took off like Beelzebub himself was after them, scrabbling all over my shelves like furry dust devils, knocking over jars and boxes, and scaring my customers half out of their wits. Why, poor Mrs. Collins had to be revived with smelling salts."

"That's terrible." Callie stifled a grin, chiding herself for the comic image his words conjured in her mind. "But you haven't explained yet why you think Simon had anything to do with this. Did you actually see him release the squirrels?"

"I didn't see any of the culprits' faces, but he was one of them, all right." The man's red face and sharp hand movements highlighted his agitation. "I was busy with customers when I heard the side door open. At first I just figured it was supplies from Erlington. Then I heard whispers and snickering. That's when I went to check things out. Next thing I knew there were squirrels everywhere."

"If you didn't see any of their faces—"

"I'm coming to that." He gave her an officious look. "By the time I made it to the door, the others had run off but Simon was still there." He pointed dramatically to an old burlap sack lying on the sidewalk at their feet. "And he was holding that sack in his hands with a squirrel still trapped inside."

The rumblings from the crowd seemed to support the shopkeeper's story.

Callie ignored them. "Simon, I'm certain you can explain to Mr. Dobson how this came to be."

Simon nodded emphatically, swallowing hard. "Yes, ma'am. I was on my way to Mr. Lawrence's shop to get the sheepskin I wanted. But when I passed by this alley I heard A—" he cleared his throat "—I heard someone running and then I saw this sack on the ground with something moving inside." He raked his fingers through his hair. "I just wanted to see what it was."

There were more murmurings of disbelief. Callie ignored those as well.

But Simon's expression took on a desperate edge. "I give you my word, that's all it was. I didn't let those squirrels loose in Mr. Dobson's store, honest."

"I believe you, Simon." She turned back to Mr. Dobson. "You see, it was all a misunderstanding. I told you Simon is not the sort of person to do such a thing and then lie about it."

The man hooked his thumbs in the armholes of his vest and rocked back on his heels. "Mrs. Tyler, surely you don't believe such a preposterous story."

She drew herself up. "I sincerely hope you are not calling my son a liar."

The man's expression took on a self-righteous edge. "Look, I know the boy has had some hard things to deal with, what with the death of his folks and all, but that's no excuse for—"

Callie felt Simon stiffen, and gave his shoulder a squeeze. "No one is making excuses here, Mr. Dobson. We are simply saying that you are mistaken."

"Mrs. Tyler is correct." Reverend Hollingsford stepped forward from the edge of the crowd. "The boy's telling the truth."

"Reverend?" Mr. Dobson pushed his glasses up again, and shifted his weight. "With all due respect, sir, how can you know that?"

The minister made a slight bow in Callie and Simon's direction. "My apologies for not speaking up sooner. But everything happened so fast, I'm just now sorting things out in my head."

He turned back to the shopkeeper. "To answer your

question, I walked into the mercantile right after the hubbub started. But I remember now that just before I stepped inside—and this was after I heard Mrs. Collins's shriek—I saw Simon walk toward the alley, and he was empty-handed."

Callie felt a swell of vindication fill her chest. "If you won't believe me or Simon, surely you will take the word of the good reverend here. Now, I believe you have something to say to my son."

Mr. Dobson cleared his throat. "Well, I suppose, given what the reverend just said, maybe I was mistaken after all."

He paused, and Callie raised a brow.

The man's face reddened slightly, but he nodded. "Sorry, Simon."

When the boy just stood there with a mutinous expression on his face, Callie gave him a little nudge. "Simon?"

He shot her a quick glance, then swallowed his glower and returned Mr. Dobson's nod. "I accept your apology, sir."

Now that the confrontation was over, Callie was suddenly acutely aware of the crowd gathered around them. The urge to move away from the eye of the storm pressed in on her. "If you will excuse us—"

But Mr. Dobson wasn't quite done. "Just a minute."

She tilted her head. What now?

He frowned down at Simon. "You said you saw someone running out of the alley. Did you see who it was?"

Simon ducked his head and rubbed his palm on the leg of his pants, but not before she saw the quick glance he cut toward the edge of the crowd. Following his gaze, she saw his friends Abe and Bobby watching him carefully.

Simon looked up again. "I never did see their faces."

Was she the only one who noticed he hadn't actually answered the question?

But apparently Mr. Dobson was ready to move on. He turned to the rest of the crowd, quizzing those nearest him to find out what they might have seen.

"Come along, Simon." Callie kept her hand protectively against his back. "Let's find your sisters. It'll be time to head back to the house soon."

Simon didn't wait to be told twice. "Yes, ma'am."

When she turned, Callie spotted Jack standing across the street, looking pleased.

Now why had he just stood there instead of jumping into the fray? Surely he could have handled the situation quicker and with more decisiveness than she had. She couldn't believe Jack had been reticent about facing down Mr. Dobson. So what reason did he have for leaving it in her hands?

Before Simon caught sight of him, Jack turned and headed back to the building site. Following his cue, Callie didn't give any sign she'd spotted him.

Simon was subdued as they moved away from the crowd. He was undoubtedly feeling self-conscious about what had just happened. Thank goodness Reverend Hollingsford had intervened or they might still be at an impasse.

And what hadn't Simon said back there when Mr. Dobson questioned him about who he'd seen? Had the boy actually witnessed his two friends running through the alley, or did he just suspect it had been them?

She felt a strong urge to discuss the whole situation with Jack, to get his take on what they should do next, if anything. But that would have to wait until they were alone.

* * *

"Aunt Callie?"

Callie pulled the coverlet up over Simon's chest, trying not to show her surprise. Simon usually rolled over as soon as he crawled into bed, completely ignoring her. "Yes?"

"Why did you stand up for me today?"

She didn't hesitate for a second. "Because I knew you didn't do what Mr. Dobson said you did."

"But *how* did you know I didn't do it?"

"Because you said so."

"Just like that?"

"Just like that." She smiled at him as she smoothed the covers. "Simon, I'm not your mother, but I am a good judge of character. And while I know you might not be above pulling a misguided prank occasionally, I am absolutely certain you are above lying to avoid the consequences."

"Oh."

"Now, time to get some sleep. You've had a long day today."

The boy searched her face a moment longer, then nodded. "Yes, ma'am." With that he rolled over and shut his eyes.

Callie studied him a moment before shutting the door. For the first time she felt some hope that he might let her be the stepmother she longed to be.

She descended the stairs slowly, untying her bonnet as she went. She hadn't had any time alone with Jack since they left town today. Perhaps now she would get some answers.

Jack studied the block of wood, examining the grain and contours. There was a certain flow to it that was suggestive of a deer or maybe a horse. He absently began shaping the wood with his knife, waiting for Callie to join him.

She'd been magnificent today, a lioness protecting her cub. The fact that she was normally uncomfortable being the center of attention hadn't even seemed to come into play.

He'd have to admit, Lanny had chosen well after all. He should never have doubted his brother's instincts.

Except his brother had planned to relegate her to a spare bedroom. Lanny had wanted a nanny, not a wife.

For the first time in his life, Jack considered his brother a fool.

"You did a good thing today," he said as she stepped outside.

She grimaced. "Actually, it was Reverend Hollingsford who saved the day, not me."

"None of that false modesty now. The good reverend might have pushed the plunger, but you planted the charges and strung the fuse."

She grinned. "An interesting way to put it."

"Just don't go selling yourself short." Jack refused to let her minimize the part she'd played. "You stood up for Simon when he needed a champion. That's something he won't soon forget. And neither will I."

He saw the blush darken her cheeks. But then she tilted her head and gave him a puzzled look. "Speaking of which, how long were you standing there and why didn't you step in?"

"I arrived about the time you were telling Dobson to get his hands off Simon." He shook his head. "That was a sight to behold. Just plain stopped me in my tracks." He couldn't believe the transformation in her from shrinking violet to fierce protector.

"But if Reverend Hollingsford hadn't stepped in—"

"You would have found another way to convince the crowd Dobson was wrong." He gave her a straight-on look. "Believe me, if I'd thought you needed help, I would have stepped in. But I never saw the need."

In fact, if he'd had any concerns about her ability to look out for the family in his absence, they'd been erased today.

A not altogether comfortable thought. Because he'd just realized that it meant he wasn't as needed, wouldn't be as missed around here, as he'd imagined.

And that thought didn't sit well with him at all.

Chapter Twenty-Eight

"Uncle Jack."

Jack tested the saw blade he was sharpening. "Hmm?"

"Does Aunt Callie's face bother you?"

Jack paused and looked up. Simon's earnest eyes were focused directly on him and Jack knew his answer was important.

"I suppose you're talking about her birthmark."

"Yes, sir. I mean, my ma and Aunt Julia were both real pretty. Don't you wish she was more like that? Or at least normal looking."

Conscious of the weight of the moment, Jack chose his words carefully. "Your ma was pretty, all right. But did you ever see that scar she had on her arm, all crooked and puckered-looking?"

"Uh-huh. But that was different."

"Why? You can't deny that it was ugly. Even she thought so. It made her look different from everyone else so she always hid it by wearing long-sleeved dresses."

"But that was just a scar."

"You think it's not the same as your Aunt Callie's

birthmark, but that's only because Nell was your mother and you loved her."

Jack leaned forward. "You're old enough to realize that it's what's inside a person that matters. And your Aunt Callie is a loving, generous woman with a good heart. Besides, there are all kinds of beauty, and your Aunt Callie has a beauty all her own. So, no, her birthmark doesn't bother me, not even a little bit." In fact, he'd gotten to where he hardly even noticed it anymore. There was so much more about her, things to admire and respect.

Simon scuffed a toe in the dirt. "Not even when other people make fun of her?"

So, someone had said something to him, had they? "Well, for one thing, folks around here know better than to make fun of her, or any member of my family for that matter, in front of me. I'd set 'em straight faster than a hummingbird can flit." He let that soak in a moment, then added, "The same way your Aunt Callie set Mr. Dobson straight yesterday."

Simon reddened. "You heard about that?"

"I witnessed it."

That set Simon back. "Then why didn't *you* step in? Did you think I was guilty?"

"Of course not. By the time I got there, your Aunt Callie had it under control. I figured she was doing just fine without me." He lifted a brow. "Don't you agree?"

Simon nodded, and jammed his hands in his pockets.

Jack set the saw down. "Listen, Simon, this is something that shapes the kind of person you are at the very core. Making fun of people, especially for something they have no control over, is a mean-spirited, cowardly thing to do. Any man worth his salt, a man who considers honor not just a word but an actual way of life—would never indulge in such a thing."

"I suppose." The boy studied the ground as if answers to the secrets of life were inscribed there.

"Let me ask you a question. Forget for a minute that she has that birthmark. If you think over everything you know about your Aunt Callie firsthand—the things you yourself have seen her do or heard her say—what would you think about her?"

Simon shrugged.

Jack tried again. "It's simple. Just decide whether your life would be better or worse if she'd never showed up in Sweetgum." He waited, letting the silence draw out.

"Worse, I guess," Simon finally answered.

Jack wanted to clap the boy on the back for taking that small step, but he maintained his solemn demeanor. "So why should a mark on her face, something that's nothing more than a discolored patch of skin, make any difference in how you think about her?" He picked the saw back up. "You don't have to answer me, just ponder on that a bit."

Jack watched from the corner of his eye as Simon squirmed uncomfortably. He waited until the boy looked at him again and then held his gaze with unblinking firmness. "And I hope if ever anyone *does* say something mean-spirited about your aunt in your presence, you'll have the gumption to do the right thing."

Jack watched Simon walk away, hands jammed in his pockets, shoulders slumped as if weighted down. He certainly hoped he'd gotten through to the boy.

Strange. He wasn't certain exactly when it had happened, but discussing Callie's looks with Simon just now made him realize that he truly *did* think of her as beautiful, and not just on the inside. Her appearance was dearer to him than he would ever have believed possible.

He cherished those moments with her on the front porch in the evenings, moments when she unveiled, both literally and figuratively, and was totally herself and totally at ease with him. Whether she realized it or not, that trust was a precious gift, one he'd come to value dearly.

And one he was very much afraid he was going to miss keenly when he left.

Chapter Twenty-Nine

Jack lightly buffed the back of the carved horse with a piece of sandpaper, then rubbed a thumb over the spot. The toy horse was taking shape nicely, if he did say so himself. Annabeth's birthday was in a few weeks and he could almost picture the smile on her face when she unwrapped the package to find this inside.

Too bad he wouldn't be here to see it.

He pushed aside the twinge of regret.

One had to make sacrifices to pursue one's dreams. After all, he had to remember that he'd actually be getting the best of both worlds. He could go off and experience the freedom of his former life, and he could come back here three or four times a year to enjoy a taste of hearth and home.

Yep. What more could a self-made, independence-loving man ask for?

Still, he was strangely reluctant to tell Callie that he had almost finished with the house in town.

When had he become so comfortable with the idea of being part of this family?

Jack swatted at a june bug.

Ridiculous thought. As long as he stayed here he

would never be anything more than Lanny's little brother. And he couldn't go back to that again—he'd worked too hard to establish himself as an expert in his field, someone to be looked up to.

No, the first of August was around the corner and he'd managed to accomplish what he'd set out to do. He'd settled his debt to his family and saw that the kids were well cared for. He'd even provided a fallback plan for Callie, just in case she was overwhelmed by managing the farm.

Better yet, things had settled down considerably over the past few weeks. Simon had lost that chip on his shoulder and was turning into a hard worker, Emma smiled much more these days, and Callie—well, Callie was pulling the whole lot of them together into a true family.

So there really was nothing left to keep him here.

His thoughts turned to Callie—smiling approval at something one of them had done, sitting on the swing reading to the children, humming while she worked at the stove.

The sweet way she'd looked at him when he'd kissed her at the stream—

Stop it! Jack took a deep breath and deliberately turned his focus back to the wooden toy in his hands. He scrubbed the sandpaper across the horse's neck, smoothing away a rough spot, sweetening the curve.

What if Callie asked him to stay? What if she didn't feel ready to handle the farm and the children on her own yet? He couldn't blame her for that, and he definitely couldn't just leave her in the lurch if she felt she needed him. In fact, he'd be honor bound to stay.

He blew away the sawdust. Far be it from him to shirk his duty.

And what if, unlike everyone else, she saw him as more than a poor imitation of the man Lanny had been?

Did *she* ever think about that kiss they'd shared?

The sound of the screen door opening brought his thoughts back to the present.

"I didn't think I'd ever get them settled down tonight."

He heard the smile in her voice.

She sat on the bench, grasping the edges of the seat with her hands and leaning forward as she faced him. "They're having so much fun with the tree house, now that it's finished. Not that you'd think it was complete to hear them talk. They're already thinking of ways to make it even better." She gave a soft laugh. "I told them to give it a few weeks before they start hammering away again."

He likely wouldn't be here to see that, either.

"Speaking of finished," he paused, eyeing the length of one of the horse's legs, "we'll be ready for those curtains you're working on by the end of the week."

"Oh." She caught her lower lip between her teeth, but other than that showed no emotion. "You're ready to wrap up your work in Sweetgum, then."

"Yep. Just some painting and a few other finishing touches left to go."

"So, you'll be leaving us soon."

Her voice was flat, her tone even. What emotion was she trying to hide? Regret? Relief?

"Unless you need me to stay longer." He hoped that came out matter-of-factly.

But she gave an emphatic shake of the head. "I can't ask that of you. It wouldn't be fair." She stood and gripped the porch rail, staring out over the darkened yard. "Besides, the children and I need to learn to make it on our own eventually. More time won't make that any easier."

She turned her gaze upward, studying the stars. "No, we made a bargain and I intend to stand by it. Ida Lee told me her oldest boy Jonah would be glad to earn some extra money helping out once a week after you leave. We'll be fine."

It appeared she had everything worked out. Didn't sound like he'd even be missed.

"Don't worry," she continued with a half-grin. "The farm will still be standing when you come back at Christmas."

Christmas seemed a long time away.

"How soon will you be leaving us?"

"I'll stay long enough to get the furnishings installed, and make sure we have a tenant for the apartment or the storefront, or both." He pulled out his pocketknife to add more detail to the mane. "I've already got a few feelers out to folks who might be interested in renting the place."

"Another week or two, then."

"More or less."

If she felt any regret, she was certainly doing a good job hiding it.

He felt an unfamiliar tightness in his chest. So much for thinking she might ask him to stay.

Callie pulled the brush through her hair, fighting the urge to cry. It had been so hard this evening to pretend she was okay with his leaving, to not break down and beg him to stay.

Only her pride had saved her.

It would have been absolutely humiliating to have him look at her with pity, if not outright horror, when he found out how she truly felt. Admitting her feelings would only distance him from her, not draw him closer.

She had to keep reminding herself that the friendship that had grown up between them was just that—friendship. He'd made it quite clear from the outset that he didn't want to be tied down to either the farm or her.

She stared at her reflection in the mirror. *Foolish, foolish girl. You knew this time would come, that Jack wouldn't stay here forever. How could you have let your guard down so completely?*

She'd played a dangerous game with her heart, pretending that, given enough time, Jack would begin to feel for her what she'd already begun to feel for him.

She should have known better.

Sure, he was more accepting of her disfigurement than other folks. But that didn't mean he could actually develop tender feelings for her.

She should be grateful for the time she'd had and for the fact that they'd become such good friends despite their rocky start. But, heaven help her, she was selfish. It wasn't enough, not nearly enough.

She wanted what she knew she would never have, should never have allowed herself to hope for.

Hadn't her father and sisters warned her that she should focus on making herself useful, that looking for something more in a relationship would doom her to disappointment?

Why hadn't she remembered that lesson when it counted?

She supposed it was Jack's unique brand of kindness and his hard-won friendship, something she'd never experienced with a man before, that had lulled her into thinking he might stay. And to be fair, he'd certainly stayed in Sweetgum longer than they'd originally planned. But it had just been to make certain everything was in order before he left, not because his feelings for her had changed.

She realized that now.

Callie set the brush down, crawled into bed and pulled the covers up to her chin before she lost the battle with her self-control and the tears started flowing.

"We have our first tenant." Jack stepped into the kitchen the next afternoon and plucked a carrot from the bowl on the counter, feeling mighty pleased with himself. With a little help from Mrs. Mayweather, he'd set a plan in motion today that would be his parting gift to Callie, if it didn't backfire on him.

Callie looked up from the stove. "Tenant?"

She wore a starched apron over her dress with a couple of wildflowers pinned to her bodice, and her face was flushed from the heat of the stove. She was the very picture of domesticity, of the heart and glue of a home-sweet-home.

If only he could talk her into taking that silly bonnet off when they were in the house. If only he'd had more time to try to get through her skewed thinking.

Maybe, after tomorrow…

He realized she was still staring at him. "Ben Cooper wants to lease the building in town to use as a photography studio and business office," he explained.

A puzzled wrinkle appeared above her nose. "The undertaker?"

"Yep. Apparently he's done a little bit of that kind of work for funerals already. Says he wants to start capturing some happier occasions, too."

"Oh, that is good news." She set the spoon down and wiped her hands on the apron. "That was a very clever idea of yours, to build a storefront area within the building, I mean."

He grinned. "Not so clever. I just borrowed the idea from what had been there before." He leaned back against the counter and crossed one booted foot over the other. "I also thought, since Ben is looking to get the word out about his new enterprise, that it might be a good idea to have a family photograph taken before I left."

Her eyes lit up. "Oh, yes, let's do. It'll give the children something to remind them of you while you're away."

And I'll have something of you all to take with me as well.

"I'm glad you agree. Especially since I already told him we'd be there at ten o'clock tomorrow morning."

Her hands fisted on her hips, and her brow furrowed. "That was mighty presumptuous of you, sir." The sweet quirk of her lips, however, spoiled the mock stern expression she'd obviously been going for.

He only hoped she was still smiling when she learned of the other surprise he had in store for her.

Chapter Thirty

When they arrived in town the next morning, Jack noted with approval that Ben had finished getting things ready. There was a large sign that read Cooper's Photography and Business Office hanging out front, and the shades were rolled up on the big glass fronted window facing the sidewalk.

A number of townsfolk were gathered around, talking with interest about the new business venture.

Jack halted the wagon right in front and set the brake. "Simon, help your sisters down, please." He jumped down and strode quickly around to lend Callie a hand.

Once she was safely on the ground, he retrieved a box from under the buggy seat. "I bought you a little something."

She gave him a startled look. "What's the occasion?"

He shrugged. "Call it a late birthday present. Or something to remember me by."

She opened the lid and, to Jack's relief, gave a cry of delight. "Oh, Jack, it's lovely." She lifted the hat out of the box, turning it this way and that to examine every ribbon and flower. "I've never owned anything so beautiful."

"Mrs. Mayweather helped pick it out." Jack fidgeted

with the brim of his own hat. "The green ribbons were my idea though. I thought they matched your eyes."

Her expression softened as she fingered the ribbon. "It's such a thoughtful gift."

He saw the moment the realization hit her. Her eyes lost some of their sparkle and regret mingled with apprehension on her face. "But I can't—"

He wasn't about to let her back down. "It would mean a lot to me if you'd wear it for the picture."

"But—"

Jack touched a finger to her lips and saw her eyes widen in reaction.

"When I look at this picture in the coming weeks," he said, not bothering to lower his voice, "I want to see *you* looking back at me, the woman I had all those late night talks with, not some shrinking violet hiding behind a bonnet."

She hesitated and her gaze darted to the nearby crowd.

More than likely a number of them were eavesdropping. At least he hoped so. He didn't want to leave even a faint impression in anyone's mind that he had a problem with the way she looked.

When her eyes met his again he saw her uncertainty was stronger than ever. But he held her gaze, refusing to give in, and finally she nodded.

Pride surged through him, pride in her mettle and in her spirit. He knew the courage it had taken to make that decision. "Good." He reached for the ribbon tied beneath her chin, acting quickly, before she could change her mind. "Allow me."

With deft movements, he untied the bonnet strings and removed it from her head while she held perfectly still. Her gaze was locked onto his as if to a lifeline.

Handing the old bonnet to Emma without breaking

eye contact, he took the new hat and placed it on her head. "What do you think, girls? Full on or at an angle?"

"Definitely at an angle," Emma said with a smile.

"I agree." He set the hat at a jaunty tilt and tied the bow with a flourish.

He ran the back of his hand softly down her blemished cheek, then took a step back to study the effect. "Yes, much better." He offered her his arm. "Shall we?"

Callie nearly melted inside from the sweetness of his touch.

Was this some sort of show he was putting on for the benefit of the town? Or did he truly not mind what she looked like?

All she knew was, right at this moment, she didn't care. Either way, his motives were grounded in a true nobility of spirit. And thanks to him, she'd never felt lovelier in her life.

Callie's courage held all the way up until the actual sitting. Suddenly she became very conscious of the other folks who'd wandered inside or stood outside at the window, watching what was going on.

When Ben tried to pose the five of them, reality flooded back in. What had she been thinking? Why in the world would she want to preserve this hopelessly flawed image of herself?

Ignoring Ben's directions, she turned so that only her good side was showing.

Jack, however, was having none of that.

"I want everyone looking straight at the camera," he announced in his firmest tone. "Just as if they were looking at me." He met Callie's gaze. "Because that's what I want to see when I look at this picture."

So despite her better judgment, Callie swallowed hard, tried to shut out everyone else, and stared at the camera. She imagined it was Jack, way across the country in California, looking back at her. She even managed a wavery smile.

When the sitting was finally over, they headed for the buggy. Callie held tightly to Jack's arm, wanting to shrink away every time they stopped to talk to someone. She felt all those eyes staring at her, judging her by the mark on her face, and pitying Jack for being tied to her.

When they reached the buggy, she offered Simon her seat up front and climbed into the back with the girls before Jack could protest. She told him to let Simon drive them home, that the boy needed to get more practice in.

But the resigned look on Jack's face told her she hadn't fooled him. And moreover, she'd spoiled his pleasure in the gift.

Why couldn't he understand that she had accepted the burden of who she was? She didn't need nor even want to force everyone else to live with it as well.

As soon as they walked into the house, Callie stopped in front of the mirrored hall tree and untied the ribbons under her chin. "Emma," she called as she removed the lovely bit of millenary, "do you still have my bonnet?"

"I think I left it in the buggy," Emma said. "But you don't really need it right now, do you?"

"Well, yes, I—"

"Doesn't it make you feel all hot and stuffy?" Annabeth asked. "Besides, I hardly ever get to see your angel's kiss."

"I know, sweetie, but—"

"But what?" Simon interrupted. "Other ladies don't wear sunbonnets in the house."

That brought her up short. She thought the sight of her birthmark embarrassed Simon.

"It sounds like you're outvoted to me." Jack stood in the doorway, arms folded across his chest.

Callie stared at the four of them and felt something inside her uncoil softly, like a morning glory unfurling at the first hint of sunlight.

Not even her parents and sisters had looked at her that way. With them, she'd always known they were protecting her, were trying to make her feel normal. She'd always felt the need to make herself not only as invisible as possible, but also as useful as possible to justify her place in the family.

The feeling she was getting right now from Jack and the children was that she *was* normal, she was appreciated for who she was, and they truly didn't understand why she'd want to shut herself off.

"Very well." She heard the huskiness in her voice and made an effort to lighten it. "We shall leave the sunbonnets for when I'm out in the sun."

Callie headed upstairs, needing a few minutes alone to absorb the feelings flooding through her. The mix of joy, gratitude and humble appreciation were almost overwhelming.

Thank you, Father, for placing me in the midst of this wonderful family. When I grow lonely or discouraged in the days to come, let me remember this moment and find joy again.

She couldn't bear to put Jack's gift back in its hatbox. Instead, she set it in a place of honor on the top of her bureau where she could see it whenever she was in the room.

It had been such a deliberately kind, meaningful gesture on Jack's part. How could she ever repay him? There wasn't anything she could give in return that could compare—

Her gaze fell on her bedside table.

Actually, there was one thing.

Callie took a deep breath as she prepared to step out on the porch that evening. Then she pushed open the screen door and, bypassing the bench, took a seat on the step beside him.

Jack halted his whittling and gave her a startled look.

"I want you to take this with you." She held the well-worn Bible out to him.

Jack looked down at the book and then his gaze flew up to meet hers. "This is your personal Bible."

She smiled. "I have the Tyler family Bible now. And you can bring this one back to me when you return."

"Callie, I don't—"

"I know. But humor me." She took his hand, turned it palm up and set the Bible there. She placed her own hand on top. "I *want* you to have this. It'll be like taking a part of me with you." *You already have my heart, but that will be my secret.*

They sat like that for a long moment, gazes locked, the Bible sandwiched between their left hands.

Finally Jack nodded. "I'd be honored to guard this for you until I return." He gave her his crooked smile. "I might even read it from time to time."

She held his gaze a moment longer. "I hope so. Because, whenever we do our evening Bible reading here, I'll be imagining you doing the same. It'll be almost like you're in the room with us."

But almost was not nearly the same as actually.

Why can't I be content with what I have instead of always wanting more?

Chapter Thirty-One

Jack leaned back against the seat of the stage, watching the town of Sweetgum roll past the window, still seeing the faces of the four of them as they waved goodbye from the sidewalk outside the Sweetgum Hotel and Post Office.

The goodbyes had been more difficult than he'd imagined. And not just for those he'd left behind.

Strange how different this departure was from that last one eleven years ago. There'd been no one to see him off then, because he hadn't told anyone ahead of time he was leaving. Just left a note and slipped away.

Back then he'd been eagerly looking ahead to new adventures, confident that once he stepped out of Lanny's shadow he'd finally come into his own. And in a way he had. That pushing-forward drive had become a way of life for him, keeping him always moving, always looking to the next job, the next challenge.

And until he read that earth-shattering telegram, he'd never let himself look back.

This leave-taking today, though, had a whole different feel to it. Instead of that sense of anticipation, there was a pull to look back. He couldn't stop thinking about everything he was leaving behind—the homeplace that seemed more like home now than it ever had before, the kids who looked to him to keep their world safe, and most of all Callie, who was so loving and determined and full of the right kind of grit. So much so, actually, that it seemed she no longer needed him.

He tipped his hat down over his face and shifted to a more comfortable position. This strange mood was probably just fatigue and delayed grieving.

He'd no doubt be back to his old self by the time he reached California.

"You have such a lovely voice, dear."

"Why, thank you, Mrs. Mayweather, what a kind thing to say." Callie stepped from the church into the bright sunshine. Jack had been gone for three days and already she missed him almost more than she could bear. It had been hard on the children as well. Did Jack realize how much they'd all come to care for him, how big a hole his departure had left behind?

But she refused to wear a long face and feel sorry for herself—at least not in public.

"Not kind, honest." Mrs. Mayweather fluttered an elegant ivory and lace fan under her chin. "I wish God had seen fit to bless me with such talent instead of a frog-like croak."

Callie was distracted by the discomfort of her tight-fitting bonnet. "I'm sure your voice is quite nice," she said absently.

She ignored the urge to loosen the ribbon. She still wore the poke bonnets when she came to town, of course. But now that she had dispensed with wearing them at home, she found they no longer felt like the part of her they once had.

"Oh, no." Mrs. Mayweather smiled and patted her hand. "No need to worry about my feelings, Callista, dear. I have learned to live with my limitations." She sighed. "It's just that I do love to sing and I must constantly remind myself to hold back so that I don't disrupt the service."

Callie shook her head, certain her friend had blown the problem all out of proportion. "I'm certain you're being much too harsh with yourself."

"Not at all. Sometimes I do feel it is such a trial not to be able to just burst out in song. But the voices raised in the worship service should have an angelic quality to them, not a rasping one."

Callie stopped and turned to face her friend fully. There was no reason Mrs. Mayweather should think of herself in such unflattering terms. "I am surprised that you of all people should say such a thing. Why, isn't your voice the one God saw fit to give you? As such it cannot be displeasing to Him. On the contrary, I imagine it would give Him great pleasure to hear you lift it up in praise."

"Perhaps." The schoolteacher gave a wry smile. "But it would hardly be fair to the rest of the congregation."

"Nonsense." Callie waved that objection aside, determined to make her friend see how foolish she was being. "And anyone who thought the less of you for it would not be in the frame of mind they should be in when in God's house. You should be proud of that which God gave you."

The woman nodded thoughtfully. "What an enlightened way of looking at things." She closed her fan with a snap and gave Callie a pointed look. "You know, that was such a lovely hat Jackson gave you before he left."

She touched her chin with the folded fan, "I wonder why it is you haven't worn it since?"

The schoolteacher's point hit Callie with the force of physical blow. The heat crawled into her cheeks with a relentless sting.

Mrs. Mayweather smiled, aware that her dart had hit its mark. "It is so much easier to see how others should handle life's burdens than it is to handle our own, is it not?"

Callie nodded numbly. Was Mrs. Mayweather right? Had she been hiding behind her bonnet all these years, not out of respect for the feelings of others, but out of vanity?

How many times had she lectured others as she had Mrs. Mayweather just now on how they shouldn't be ashamed of whatever talent or burden God had assigned to them.

She'd been so eager to find the mote in others' eyes that she'd ignored the beam in her own.

Oh, Father, I've been such a vain, self-righteous fool. Lend me Your strength to follow through and do what I now know is the right thing to do.

Jack stepped onto the station platform feeling tired and out of sorts. He wasn't even certain what the name of this town was, only that he needed to switch trains here.

A check-in at the depot window brought the unwelcome news that he'd just missed his connection and would have to wait until tomorrow afternoon for the next one.

Hefting his bag, he trudged to the town's only hotel, which he'd been assured served a decent meal and had clean sheets.

Up in his room, Jack pulled Callie's Bible out of his bag. Reading a passage every evening had become a habit. One that, for some reason, he hadn't wanted to break.

He opened the Bible and found himself in the book of Psalms. He read the first verse he came to, but his mind was too distracted by other thoughts to really absorb the words.

Who was reading the verses at home tonight? Callie? Simon?

Would Callie step out on the porch to look at the stars after she put the kids to bed? Did she miss their talks?

Surging to his feet, Jack strode out of the room. Maybe finding something to eat would put him in a better mood.

The next morning, after a restless night, Jack woke to the sound of church bells. Was it Sunday? Still half-asleep, he felt his lips curve in a smile. If Callie were here she'd give him one of those looks that made him feel guilty for even thinking about not attending services.

Well, why not? He came fully awake and scrubbed his hand across his face as he sat up. He was stuck here until afternoon and he had nothing better to do.

Jack shaved and dressed quickly, then walked the short distance to the local church. The service was just starting when he slipped inside, and he took a few seconds to get his bearings. It was a much larger church than the one in Sweetgum. But he spotted an empty seat on a pew near the back and quietly slipped in. He received a friendly smile from the elderly couple seated next to him, then everyone faced forward as the organ began to play.

The first hymn was one he already knew, so he sang

along. The choir was good, but he missed the sound of Callie's voice.

As the organ stilled, Jack suddenly felt like a fraud. What in the world was he doing? Why had he come here? Was he such a besotted fool that he'd attend a church service just to feel closer to the family he'd left behind?

Not only was this foolish, it was wrong. This was a place for the worthy to come and find love and fellowship, not for the likes of him.

Jack had half risen from his seat when the preacher stepped up to the pulpit and opened his Bible.

"The passage we're going to study this morning is that of Luke 15, the parable of the lost sheep."

There was something about the man's voice, about his earnest expression, that grabbed hold of Jack, made him sit back down and truly listen.

He sat through the sermon, listening to the preacher expound on God's deep desire to reclaim the lost, and His joyful celebration over bringing even the lowest of backsliders back into the fold. The longer he listened, the tighter the vice-like grip in his chest squeezed.

After the service, he almost ran from the building. He shut himself inside his hotel room and before he'd even realized what he was doing, the Bible Callie had given him was open on his lap and he was turning to the passage the preacher had read earlier.

And he continued reading, moving from that passage to barely remembered verses that had been so alive for him in his childhood.

Why had he wasted so much of his life trying to escape something that didn't matter one jot? So what if he wasn't the man Lanny had been? So what if no one in Sweetgum ever thought of him as the best at anything?

To God he was special, the stray sheep that was searched for until found, the prodigal son whose return was not only marked but celebrated.

And if God truly valued him, why should the rest matter?

He might not have gotten the answers he wanted to those passionately uttered prayers so long ago, but that didn't mean God hadn't been listening. And God had gifted him in the here and now by putting Callie and the kids in his life. Only he'd blindly thrown it all away.

Was it too late?

God, I've been such a pig-headed fool, trying to impose my will on Yours, to wrest control over my life from You. Not only did I do a lousy job at it in the process, but I blamed You when things didn't turn out the way I wanted. Are You really willing to give me another chance, a chance to do it right this time? I won't promise I'll get it perfect 'cause we both know I'd never pull it off, but I will promise I'll try with everything I've got.

Chapter Thirty-Two

Jack stepped out of the stagecoach and hefted his bag. He suddenly felt as nervous as a young buck asking to walk out with the town's sweetheart.

It had been ten days. Would Callie be glad to see him? Or just wonder what had gotten into him?

Well, he wouldn't find out by standing here.

Turning toward the livery, he marched quickly down the street, barely pausing to return greetings from the startled townsfolk he passed. He didn't plan to explain his return to anyone until he'd talked to Callie.

He stepped inside the stable to find Jessie combing one of the horses.

"Mr. Tyler!" She patted the horse and stepped out of the stall. "Good to see you back so soon, but I hope that don't mean something's wrong."

"Nope, everything is fine as far as I know." Jack set his bag down. "I want to rent one of your horses to ride out to the farm. I'll get it back to you tomorrow."

"But..." Jessie's brow drew down in a look of confusion.

Jack rubbed the side of his face impatiently. "You do have a mount available for rent, don't you?"

She nodded. “Sure, we have a couple of real fine horses. But, well, if you’re looking for Mrs. Tyler and the kids, they’re here in town.”

“Are you sure?” It was Wednesday so it wasn’t market day. Why would they have made the trip to town in the middle of the week?

“Saw ’em myself not more’n thirty minutes ago. Simon and the girls come by to see Persia.” She nodded toward the corral that adjoined the stable. “If I remember right, one of them mentioned meeting Mrs. Tyler over at Mrs. Mayweather’s place.”

“Thanks.” Jack half turned, then paused. “Mind if I leave my bag here?”

“Nope. I’ll keep an eye on it for you.”

Jack headed back through town, holding himself in check, resisting the urge to break into a run.

As soon as Mrs. Mayweather’s house came into sight though, he felt his resolve falter.

This wasn’t exactly how he’d planned this meeting. He’d much rather speak to Callie in the privacy of their own home. But he was done second-guessing circumstances. If this was how it had to be, then this was how it had to be.

He pushed open the front gate, marched up the walk and climbed the porch steps.

Mrs. Mayweather answered his knock and smiled. “Why, Jackson, how good to see you back so soon.”

It certainly didn’t feel like “so soon.” “Thank you, ma’am. I understand Callie and the kids are here visiting.”

“Sorry, you just missed them. They left not five minutes ago.”

Jack tightened his jaw in frustration. Another delay.

No, this wasn’t the way he’d imagined his return at

all. But if this was some kind of test, he didn't aim to fail it.

"So they're headed back to the farm then?"

"Actually, I believe they planned to stop by the cemetery first."

The cemetery? Not exactly the most cheerful spot for their talk. But so be it. It only mattered that he find Callie quickly.

He tipped his hat. "Thanks."

"Jackson."

Jack had already turned to leave, but he reined in his impatience and turned back. "Yes, ma'am?"

Her smile was warm and knowing. "Welcome back."

Jack gave her a sheepish grin. "Thanks."

This time he took the shortcut through Tom Bacon's cow pasture. And he pitied any bull that tried to get in his way.

He finally rounded the corner of the church house and drank in the sight of the four figures standing in the cemetery.

At last!

But as he drew closer, he frowned. They were all standing around Lanny's grave, even Simon and Emma, and he noticed a large bouquet of fresh flowers had been placed next to the grave marker.

Was Callie still mourning the man she had come here to partner with, the man he would never be?

His steps slowed, then stopped, as all the old insecurities flooded back.

Perhaps returning here had been a mistake.

Then Callie looked up and the unguarded joy that flooded her face reassured him, setting his feet in motion again.

It took a second for the change in her to register. She

wasn't wearing one of her stuffy poke bonnets. Here in town, in full view of even the most casual of passersby, she had chosen to wear a pert little hat that sat high on her head and completely revealed her face.

So, the caterpillar had finally shed the last of her cocoon. And what a sweetly special butterfly she made.

The kids finally noticed his presence, and with whoops, ran to greet him. Callie followed at a slower pace, her gaze never breaking contact with his.

Only when Annabeth grabbed him around the knees did he look down.

"Uncle Jack!" Annabeth's voice was nearly a squeal. "I missed you."

"I missed you, too, Little Bit." He put a hand on Annabeth's shoulder and pulled Emma into the hug as well. He smiled at Simon, including him in the greeting. "All of you."

"Did you come here for daddy's birthday, too?"

Of course. It was Lanny's birthday.

And Callie, being Callie, would make a special event of it, for Annabeth's sake.

"Actually, I came here to find all of you," he said, "but it being your daddy's birthday just makes it all the more special."

"Welcome back," Callie said, smiling.

"Thanks." His arms ached to reach for her, but he managed to refrain. "I like the hat."

She raised a hand to touch the saucy concoction. "Why, thank you kindly, sir. It was one of Julia's. I find I share her taste, in hats, at least."

"Are you here for a long visit?" Emma's voice held a hopeful note.

Jack glanced down at his niece. "I'm not sure yet." He looked back at Callie. "It depends."

He pulled a couple of coins from his pocket. "Simon, why don't you take the girls down to the mercantile and the three of you can pick out some penny candy. Your Aunt Callie and I will meet you at the buggy later."

Simon looked from Jack to Callie, then nodded. "Yes, sir. Take your time. I'll watch the girls 'til you two get there."

Callie couldn't stop looking at him. She still couldn't believe it. He'd come back!

He said he'd missed them. Was that all it was? Dare she hope there was something much deeper going on here?

He offered his arm and she placed her hand there, feeling suddenly tongue-tied.

"Let's have a seat, shall we?" He swept an arm toward the bench beneath the cottonwood. "We have some things to discuss."

Not trusting herself to speak, she nodded and let him lead the way.

A moment later, he seated her on the bench, then sat beside her. "I missed you."

She tried not to read too much into that statement. One could miss good friends. "I missed you, too. The porch feels much too empty in the evenings since you've been gone."

He smiled, then ran a hand through his hair.

"Callie, there's something I need to tell you, a confession of sorts." He took a deep breath. "All my life I've known I was second-best to Lanny, never quite good enough to meet the standard he set. It's the real reason I left Sweetgum eleven years ago. I even think it's why I proposed to Julia. A part of me knew she loved Lanny and I wanted to claim her for myself."

Why was he telling her this? What did it have to do with his reason for coming back? But if it was reassurances he wanted…

"You're not—"

He put a finger to her lips. "Hush and let me finish. I was so jealous of Lanny that I let it eat at me until I lashed out at him. The last words I said to him were said in anger. I'll have to live with that for the rest of my days."

She touched his arm in sympathy, aching to ease his pain, but remained quiet, as he'd requested.

"I had a hunger to find someplace where I could be the best at something, could be respected for myself, the way Lanny was here. I knew it was vain and wrong, and that it was unchristian. So I quit praying, closed myself off to God, and hardened my conscience." His jaw tightened. "And I thought I found what I'd been seeking when I formed my own company and gained the respect of my peers. But I was wrong. You, sweet, dear Callie, helped me to see that."

This was torture. Couldn't he see she wanted something much deeper than his gratitude?

"Over the past few days I've been doing a lot of thinking and a lot of praying."

Callie's pulse jumped. Praying! "Oh, Jack." She breathed more than said the words, giving his hand a squeeze. Suddenly her own desires seemed selfish and insignificant.

He smiled. "Yes, I've finally come to my senses. Thankfully our God is a God of patience and forgiveness, because it took a long time to get the truth of His Word through this thick head of mine. It's not Lanny's standards I need to measure up to, I understand that now. God has given us each our own unique talents and gifts, and we should focus on using them in ways that best serve Him."

"Jack, I'm so happy for you." It was ironic how they'd both had similar revelations that had come to them only after they'd been apart.

He sat there in silence a long time, his gaze distant, his mind seemingly miles away.

Finally, she couldn't stand it any longer. "Jack, I'm very happy you shared this wonderful news with me. But I have to know, was that the only reason you came back?"

He gave a crooked grin. "I can always count on you to fill the silences." Then he sobered and took her hand. "I came back because I couldn't stay away. Not from this place. Not from those kids." He touched her cheek. "Not from you."

She wanted to lean into his hand, but dared not. She didn't want to do anything to spoil the moment.

"Here is where I belong. Because I realized something else while I was away." He squeezed her hand. "Callie, I love you. I think a part of me has loved you since you sat right here that first day, looking so brave and noble with your chin lifted high, letting me stare my fill at your face."

Her heart hitched in her chest and she found it suddenly hard to breathe. He didn't mean it. He couldn't mean it. Yes, she'd finally come to accept who she was, but no man—

"I know I'm not the man you came to Sweetgum looking for, but I'm hoping you can see past that. Because when I'm with you, I feel anchored—not in a hold-me-back way, but in a here's-where-I-belong way."

"No."

She saw surprise and then hurt in his eyes.

He released her hand and shifted his weight away from her. "I see. Well—"

"I mean, no, I won't let you do this. It's not love you feel for me, except perhaps the love of one friend for another. It's very sweet of you, but it won't do either of us any good for you to pretend otherwise."

"Look at me, Callie." He put a finger under her chin and lifted it. "Really look at me. Tell me what you see in my eyes. Is it friendship, or is it the very real love I feel for you from the depth of who I am?"

His jaw worked. "If you don't return that love, if what you feel is mere friendship, then just say so and we won't speak of this again. But don't dare tell me I don't love you. Because if you'll have me, I want to live up to those wedding vows we made—to love and cherish and protect you, until death us do part."

She studied his face, not daring to let herself believe what she saw there. It couldn't be.

Her hand reached up of its own accord and rested against his chest. She could feel the strong beat of his heart, a heart that he was offering to her for the taking.

That crooked smile of his appeared again. "I'm sorry," he said softly. "I shouldn't be pressuring you like this. We can step back for a moment, or as much time as you need, and pray for guidance."

Those words finally released the last of her fears. This is what God had been leading her toward, had been preparing her for. And she had almost been too timid, too wrapped up in her own insecurities to reach out and take hold of it.

"Oh, Jack," she said with a laugh of pure joy. "Your faith puts mine to shame."

She gazed deep into his eyes. "You're not Leland. You are Jackson Garret Tyler, and don't you ever dare apologize to me for that again. Because Jackson Garret Tyler is the man I love." She touched his lips the way he had touched hers earlier. "I love your sense of honor, that heart of gold that you try so hard to hide, and the affection you have for the children. I love the way you look at me when we're talking, as if you truly care about what I'm saying. And I love all the small things you do without any sort of fanfare to make the children and me feel secure and loved."

She moved her hand to his cheek. "And I will love you always, for the wonderful person you are, until death us do part."

With a smile as big as the Texas sky, Jack gently folded her into his arms, bringing her home at last.

Epilogue

Eleven months later

"There," Ida Lee said, adding one more pillow behind Callie's back, "that should make you more comfortable." She gave a little chuckle. "Now, I'd better go tell Jack he can come on up before he wears a hole through the kitchen floorboards and rubs the skin plumb off the back of his neck."

Callie merely smiled, unable to take her eyes from the miraculous bundle cradled in her arms.

A little boy. And he was absolutely beautiful. She gently stroked his cheek, marveling at the softness of his skin, praising God for this wondrous gift.

The object of her attention gave a huge yawn and peeked up at her, as if annoyed by the interruption, before closing his eyes again. Her smile widened. Those were Jack's eyes—jaybird blue and oh-so expressive.

She looked up as the door swooshed open and saw Jack crossing the room, his gaze locked on her, his face reflecting a mix of cautious concern and ready-to-burst joy.

He gently brushed the hair from her forehead and

placed a light kiss where the strands had been. “How are you feeling?”

“Tremendously blessed.” She loosened their newborn’s swaddling cloth. “Meet your son.”

“He’s so small.” Jack eased himself down to sit on the bed beside her, his eyes drinking in the infant with the rapt attention of an explorer who had uncovered an immense treasure. Then he tentatively reached down to touch a tiny hand and the baby reflexively curled his fingers around one of Jack’s own.

Callie watched powerful emotions playing over Jack’s face, and felt her cup of joy and contentment overflow.

Thank You, Father, for this wonderful family You’ve made me a part of.

Jack looked up and stroked her cheek with his free hand. “He’s beautiful. Just like his mother.”

She leaned into his touch, drawing strength and comfort, as always, from his warmth. “But he has his father’s spirit.”

The baby released Jack’s finger and Jack drew Callie’s head against his shoulder. “Mrs. Tyler, are you calling our son a troublemaker?”

She chuckled. “Not at all. I’m just saying I can tell he will be very self-assured.” She studied the baby again. “We need to give him a name.”

“I’ve been thinking about that. What do you think of the name Leland?”

She straightened slightly so she could study his face. Had his suggestion come from some sense of guilt or dutiful penitence?

Jack met her gaze without flinching. “If it makes you uncomfortable, we’ll pick something else. It’s just that, well ” he rubbed the back of his neck, the merest hint of ruddiness tinting his cheeks "—I know I didn't act much like it these past several years, but I always loved and respected my big brother. I'd like to do this for him. And I can't think of a better role model for our son."

Callie's eyes welled. "Oh, but I can," she said softly. Then she leaned her head back against Jack's chest. "However, I believe one Jack in this family is quite enough. I think Leland is a wonderful name. And Matthew for a middle name, perhaps? It means 'Gift from God.'"

Jack nodded, but anything he might have said was forestalled by the clattering of footsteps on the stairs.

"The children have been champing at the bit to come up here ever since Doc Haynie left." Jack grinned. "You should have heard Simon's cheer when Doc said it was a boy."

Callie laughed at the thought.

"Selfish man that I am, I told Ida Lee to hold them off a for a bit so I could have a few moments alone with you."

Callie sat upright again, but didn't leave the circle of Jack's arm. It was her favorite place to be.

She gently stroked the baby's head.

"Leland Matthew Tyler, prepare to meet the rest of your family."

* * * * *

Victoria Bylin fell in love with God and her husband at the same time. It started with a ride on a big red motorcycle and a date to see a *Star Trek* movie. A recent graduate of UC Berkeley, Victoria had been seeking that elusive "something more" when Michael rode into her life. Neither knew it, but they were both reading the Bible.

Five months later they got married and the blessings began. They have two sons and have lived in California and Virginia. Michael's career allowed Victoria to be both a stay-at-home mom and a writer. She's living a dream that started when she read her first book and thought, "I want to tell stories." For that gift, she will be forever grateful.

Feel free to drop Victoria an email at VictoriaBylin@aol.com or visit her website at victoriabylin.com.

Books by Victoria Bylin

Love Inspired Historical

The Bounty Hunter's Bride
The Maverick Preacher
Kansas Courtship
Wyoming Lawman
The Outlaw's Return
Marrying the Major
Brides of the West

Visit the Author Profile page
at Harlequin.com for more titles.

THE MAVERICK PREACHER

Victoria Bylin

Be kind and compassionate to one another,
forgiving each other, just as God in Christ
forgave you.

—*Ephesians* 4:32

To my husband, Michael...

Your faith inspires me, and your love sustains me.

Chapter One

Denver, Colorado July 1875

If Adelaide Clarke had been asleep like a sensible woman, she wouldn't have heard the thump on her front porch. As moonlight streamed through her window, she stopped breathing to block out the smallest sound. Last week a shadowy figure had broken the same window with a rock. She had an enemy. Someone wanted to drive her out of Denver and the boardinghouse called Swan's Nest.

Trembling, Adie listened for another noise. None came.

The thump had sounded like a rotten tomato. The sooner she cleaned up the mess, the less damage it would do to the paint, but she worried about waking up her boarders. The women in her house would fill wash buckets and gather rags. They'd scrub the door with her, but all four of them would tremble with fear.

Whoever had caused the thump could be lurking in the dark, waiting to grab her. Adie had been grabbed before—not in Denver but back in Kansas. Shuddering, she closed her eyes. If she'd been on speaking terms with God, she'd have prayed until she dozed. Instead she counted backward from a hundred as her mother had taught her to do.

Before she reached ninety, she heard a low moan. The timbre of it triggered memories of gutters, bruised ribs and the morning she'd met Maggie Butler. Adie knew about moaning. So did the women in her house. Mary had arrived bruised and angry in the dead of night. Pearl, thin and sick with pregnancy, had appeared at dawn. Bessie and Caroline, sisters from Virginia, had arrived in Denver on a midday train. Bessie had served with Clara Barton in the War Between the States and suffered from nightmares. Caroline had seen her husband lynched.

If a woman needed shelter, Adie opened her door wide, just as Maggie Butler had once opened *her* door to Adie.

She slid out of bed and reached for her wrapper. As she slipped her arms through the sleeves, she looked at the baby in the cradle next to her bed. No matter how Stephen Hagan Clarke had come into the world, he belonged to Adie. Grateful he hadn't been colicky as usual, she touched his back to be sure he was breathing. He'd been born six weeks early and had struggled to survive. Maggie Butler, his natural mother, hadn't been so fortunate.

Comforted by the rise of his narrow chest, Adie hurried down the staircase, a sweeping curve that spoke to the house's early days of glory. She crossed the entryway, cracked open the front door and looked down at the porch, staying hidden as she took in a body shrouded in a black cloak. A full moon lit the sky, but the eaves cast a boxlike shadow around the tangle of cloth and limbs. Adie couldn't make out the details, but she felt certain the person was a woman in need. She had owned

Swan's Nest for three months and word had spread that she rented only to females.

She dropped to a crouch. "Wake up, sweetie. You're safe now."

Her visitor groaned.

Startled by the low timbre, Adie touched the dark fabric covering the bend of a shoulder. Instead of the wool of a woman's cloak, she felt the coarse texture of a canvas duster. She pulled back as if she'd been scalded. In a way, she had—by Timothy Long and his indulgent parents, by the people of Liddy's Grove, by Reverend Honeycutt but not his wife. Adie hadn't given birth to Stephen, but she could have. Timothy Long had accosted her in the attic. If she hadn't fought him off and fled, he'd have done worse things than he had.

Moaning again, the man rolled to his side. Adie sniffed the air but didn't smell whiskey. If she had, she'd have thrown water in his face and ordered him off her porch. Before meeting Maggie, she'd supported herself by cleaning cafés and saloons, any place that would pay a few coins so she could eat. The smell of liquor had turned her stomach then, and it still did.

Adie worried that the man had been shot, but she didn't smell blood, only dirt and perspiration. Judging by his horse and the duster, he'd been on the road for a while and had come straight to Swan's Nest, not from a saloon in the heart of Denver. Maybe he was a drifter or even an outlaw on the run. Adie didn't rent to men and didn't want to start now, but her conscience wouldn't let her close the door.

Neither would her common sense. What if the stranger died? A dead body meant calling the sheriff. Calling the sheriff meant exposing Swan's Nest to scrutiny. A reporter would show up from the *Denver Star*.

The next thing she knew, she'd be answering questions that came dangerously close to revealing the truth about her son and Maggie Butler. Calling for help, even the doctor, put Adie and her son at risk. She saw only one solution. The man had to wake up and leave. Using all her strength, she rolled him to his back. "Wake up!"

He didn't stir.

None too gently, she patted his cheek. Black whiskers scraped her palm, another sign of his maleness and time spent on the trail. She pulled back her hand. "Can you hear me?"

Nothing.

The circumstances called for drastic measures. She hurried to the kitchen, filled a glass with water, then opened the high cupboard where she kept smelling salts. She lifted a vial, picked up the glass and went back to the porch. If the ammonia carbonate didn't wake the man up, she'd splash his face with the water.

Dropping back to her knees, she tried the smelling salts first. They stank worse than rotten eggs.

Her visitor got a whiff and jerked his head to the side. His eyes popped wide, revealing dilated pupils and a sheen of confusion.

"Wake up!" she said again.

He looked at her with more hope than she'd ever seen on a human face. "Emily?"

"I'm not Emily," Adie replied. "Are you ill or shot?"

He groaned. "I'm not shot."

"Are you drunk?"

"Not a drop." His voice faded. "No laudanum, either."

Why had he added *that?* Thoughts of opium hadn't crossed Adie's mind. "Here," she said, holding out the water. "This might help."

He reached for it but couldn't raise his head. Setting aside her reluctance, she put her arm behind his shoulders and lifted. As he raised his hand to steady the cup, she felt muscles stretch across his back. His shoulder blades jutted against her wrist, reminding her again that he had a physical strength she lacked.

He drained the glass, then blew out a breath. "Thank you, miss."

She lowered his shoulders to the porch, then rocked back on her knees. "Who are you?"

"No one important."

Adie needed facts. "What's your name?"

"Joshua Blue." He grimaced. "God bless you for your kindness."

Adie's lips tightened. Considering how God had "blessed" her in the past, she wanted nothing to do with Him. "I'm not interested in God's blessing, Mr. Blue. I want you to leave."

"Blessings aside," he murmured, "thank you for the water."

Adie didn't want to be thanked. She wanted to be rid of him. "Can you stand?"

"I think so."

"Can you ride?" she asked hopefully.

He shook his head. "I came to rent a room."

"I don't rent to men."

"I'll pay double."

The money tempted her in a way nothing else could. Before meeting Maggie, Adie had been homeless. She valued a roof and a bed the way rich women valued silver and jewels. It had taken a miracle—and Maggie Butler—to make Swan's Nest Adie's home. She owned it. Or more correctly, she owned half of it. Franklin Dean, the new owner of Denver National Bank, held the promissory note Adie had signed with his father. The older man had viewed banking as a way to help hardworking people, but he'd died a month ago. His son lacked the same compassion, and Adie had clashed with him the instant they'd met. They'd done battle again when he'd tried to call on Pearl against the girl's will.

Adie's blood boiled at the thought of Dean, all slick and shiny in his black carriage. She'd managed to keep up with her mortgage but not as easily as she'd hoped when she'd signed the papers. Her guests paid what they could and she didn't ask for more. So far, she'd made ends meet. She'd also served broth and bread for supper when the pantry ran low. No one ever complained.

A few extra dollars would be welcome, but she had to be careful. Swan's Nest lay on the outskirts of Denver, several blocks from the saloons but close to the trails that led to Wyoming and places notorious for outlaws. Before she rented a room to Joshua Blue, she needed to know more about him. Double the money could mean double the trouble.

"Are you an outlaw?" she asked.

"No, ma'am."

Adie wrinkled her brow. Human beings lied all the time. Timothy Long had lied to her in the attic she'd called her room. Reverend Honeycutt had lied to the town. Maggie had been as close as a sister, but even she'd had secrets. Adie studied the man on her porch for signs of deception. In her experience, evil men bragged about their misdeeds. Joshua Blue had offered a humble denial. She took it as a good sign, but she still had to consider Stephen. He'd been born too soon and had almost died. She feared bringing sickness into the house.

"What about your health?" she asked. "If you're ill—"

His jaw tightened. "If I had the pox, I wouldn't be here."

"But you fainted."

He grunted. "Stupidity on my part."

"That's not much of an answer."

"It's honest."

Looking at his gaunt face, she wondered if he'd passed out from hunger and was too proud to admit it. She'd had that problem herself. Sometimes she still did. If she skipped breakfast to save a few pennies, she got weak-kneed and had to gobble bread and jam. How long had it been since Joshua Blue had eaten a solid meal?

"All right," she said. "You can stay but only until you're well."

"I'd be grateful."

"It'll cost you four dollars a week. Can you afford it?"

"That's more than fair."

"You'll get a bed and two meals a day, but your room won't be as nice as some. It's small and behind the kitchen."

"Anything will do."

Maybe for him, but Adie took pride in her home. She'd learned from Maggie that beauty lifted a woman's spirits. The upstairs rooms all had pretty quilts and matching curtains Adie had stitched herself. She picked flowers every day and put them in the crystal vases that had come with the house. She thought about brightening up Joshua Blue's room with a bunch of daisies, then chided herself for being foolish. She had no desire to make this man feel welcome.

"The room's not fancy," she said. "But it's cozy."

"Thank you, Miss—?"

She almost said "it's Mrs." but didn't. Necessary or not, she hated that lie. "I'm Adie Clarke."

"The pleasure's mine, Miss Clarke."

For the first time, he spoke naturally. Adie heard a clipped accent that reminded her of Maggie. Fear rippled down her spine, but she pushed it back. Lots of people traveled west from New England. When she walked down the Denver streets, she heard accents of all kinds.

"Can you stand now?" she said to him.

"My horse—"

"I'll see to it after I see to you."

His eyes filled with gratitude. "I'll pay for feed and straw. Double whatever you charge."

Adie had forgotten about his offer to pay twice what she usually asked. She felt cheap about it, especially if he'd fainted from hunger. "There's no need to pay double."

"Take it," he said.

"It's not right."

"It's more than fair," he insisted. "I'm intruding on your privacy in the dead of night. Please…allow me this small dignity."

Adie saw no point in arguing. If Mr. Blue wanted to protect his pride with money, she'd oblige. "Let's get you into that room."

She stood and offered her hand. When he clasped her fingers, she felt strength inside his leather glove and wondered why he hadn't eaten. Grimacing, he pushed to a sitting position and put on his black hat. Using her for leverage, he rose to his full height and faced her. Adie's gaze landed on his chin, then dipped to the Adam's apple above the buttoned collar of his white shirt. She judged him to be six feet tall, rail thin and too proud to lean on her.

She let go of his hand and turned. "I'll show you to your room."

She stepped over the threshold, paused at a side table and lit a candle. As she held it up, Joshua Blue stepped into the room and took off his hat. The candle flickered with the rush of air. Light danced across his craggy features and revealed a straight nose that struck her as aristocratic. His dark hair curled around his temples and brushed his collar, reminding her of crows gleaning seed from her mother's wheat field. Everything about him was black or white except for his eyes. They were as blue as his name. In a vague way, his gaze reminded her of Maggie except her friend's eyes had been pure brown. Stephen's eyes hadn't found their color yet. Adie hoped they'd turn brown, a closer match to her hazel ones.

Blocking her worries, she led her new boarder down a corridor with green and pink floral wallpaper, through the kitchen and down a short hall that led to his room. As she opened the door, she raised the candle. The tiny space looked as barren as she feared. The room had a cot and a dresser, but mostly she used it to store odds and ends she donated to charity or tried to sell herself. Dust motes floated in the gold light, and a cobweb shimmered in the corner of the ceiling. Not even daisies would have lifted the gloom. A mouse scurried away from the glow.

Adie felt embarrassed. "I'll clean it out tomorrow."

"It's fine."

"It's dirty."

"Not as dirty as I am," he said dryly.

She stepped into the room, lifted a rag from the pile on a trunk and swatted the cobweb. It broke into pieces and fell on her face. The vague sensation sent her back to the attic in the Long house, where Timothy Long had threatened to smother her with a pillow if she cried out.

The storeroom had the same smell as the attic, the same dust and collection of unwanted things.

Adie wanted to run from the room, but Joshua Blue was standing in the doorway with his hat in one hand and his eyes firmly on her face. He'd trapped her. Or more correctly, she'd trapped herself. What a fool she'd been. Thanks to Timothy Long she knew better.

Show no fear. Stay strong.

The voice in Adie's head belonged to Maggie. As always, it gave her strength. She coughed once to recover her composure, then looked straight at Mr. Blue. "Do you need anything else?"

He looked pinched. "Do you have another candle?"

His tone made her wonder if the dark bothered him as much as it bothered her. She indicated the top of the dresser. "There's a lamp—"

"I see it."

He lit the match and wick, then adjusted the flame. Adie stepped to the door. As she turned to say good-night, Mr. Blue took off his hat and tried to stand taller. He looked weary to the bone and frail enough to pass out again.

She had no desire to fix him a meal, but he needed to eat. "Would you like a sandwich?"

His face turned pale. "No, thanks."

Adie wondered if he had a bad stomach. "Broth?"

He swallowed as if his mouth had started to water. She could see him thinking, weighing her inconvenience against his hunger. She took pity on him. "How about bread and butter? Maybe with strawberry jam?"

"No bread," he said. "But I'd be grateful for a glass of milk."

Adie knew all about bellyaches. In addition to a cow,

she kept a goat for Stephen. "I have goat's milk. Would that—"

"Yes, please."

"It's in the kitchen."

Holding the candle, she led the way down the hall. She set the brass holder on the table, indicated a chair and opened the icebox where she had two pitchers. The prettiest one, blue crystal etched with cornflowers, held the cow's milk she served her boarders. The other was smaller and made of pewter. She set it on the counter, took a glass from the shelf and poured.

As the stranger lowered himself to the chair, she heard a stifled groan. She turned and saw him sitting straight, but he looked as pinched as Stephen with a bout of colic.

"Here," she said, handing him the milk.

He took it, sipped, then drank more deeply. As he lowered the glass, he closed his eyes and exhaled.

The contented silence reminded Adie of her son after a late-night feeding. She glanced at the clock. Soon Stephen would wake up hungry and she still had to put the horse in the carriage house. If she hurried, she'd be back before her son stirred. If he woke up early, Rose or Pearl would check on him.

"I have to see to your horse," Adie said to her guest. "Will you be all right?"

"I'm much better."

His voice rang with authority, as if he were used to speaking and being heard. Adie could scarcely believe she'd taken him for a meager drifter. With the candle flickering, he filled the kitchen with the shadows of a giant. He frightened her, yet he'd just guzzled milk like a baby. Confused by her thoughts, she set the pitcher on the table. "Help yourself."

He lifted it and poured. "Just so you know, Miss Clarke. I'm an honorable man. You have nothing to fear from me."

As he raised the glass from the table, his eyes found hers and lingered. Adie felt as if he were looking for her soul. He wouldn't find it. She'd left that part of her heart in Liddy's Grove. Ever since, she'd drawn lines and expected people to stay behind them.

"I have a few rules," she said.

"Whatever you say."

"Under no circumstances may you go upstairs."

"Of course."

"Dinner's at six o'clock. If you miss it, you can make yourself a sandwich."

"That's fair." His eyes twinkled. "Anything else?"

If she made the list long enough, maybe he'd leave. Adie searched her mind for male habits she recalled from her days as an orphan. She'd lived with six families in four years. She'd also cleaned saloons and cheap hotels. She knew about bad habits.

"No cursing, drinking or smoking," she said.

"That suits me fine."

"No shouting," she added. "I can't abide by it."

Joshua Blue looked amused. "I'll try."

"If you use a dish, wash it."

"All right."

"I don't want you sitting on the front porch. If word gets out I rented to you, other men will knock on the door."

"I'll keep to my room or the stable. How's that?"

"Fine." Except his courtesy annoyed her.

The man's eyes locked on to hers. "I know where I stand, Miss Clarke. You've opened your home and I won't betray that trust. I have urgent business. Once I see to it, I'll be on my way."

What business? Adie wanted to ask but sealed her lips. If she didn't ask questions, she wouldn't have to answer them. "Then we're agreed."

"We are." He lifted the glass of milk, sealing the deal with a mock toast, a gesture that looked strangely natural considering his appearance.

Adie headed for the front yard where he'd left his horse. In the moonlight she saw a gray mare waiting patiently. Glad to be dealing with another female, she led the horse to the carriage house. The hens twittered as she passed the chicken house. Several yards away she saw her milk cow at the fence marking a small pasture. The cow spent most of her time grazing on the sweet grass, but Adie kept the goat, a cranky thing named Buttons, inside the outbuilding. Her son depended on the nanny goat and she couldn't risk it getting loose.

When she reached the carriage house, she lit the lantern inside the door, then turned back to the mare and inspected the things strapped to the saddle. Her gaze went first to a rifle jutting from a plain leather scabbard. A canteen hung from the saddle horn and a set of saddlebags draped the horse's middle.

Adie felt ashamed of herself for what she was about to do, but a woman with a secret couldn't be too careful. Only her friends knew Stephen wasn't her natural born son. Somewhere he had a father, a man Maggie had loved and protected with her silence. Adie didn't know the whole story, but she'd loved her friend and had admired her.

She felt otherwise about Maggie's powerful family. Maggie had said little about them, but she'd once let it slip that her brother was a minister. Rather than shame him with an illegitimate child, she'd left home. Maggie never mentioned her family's wealth, but Adie had seen her fine things—silk chemises and embroidered camisoles, stockings without a stitch of darning, shoes with silver buttons. Adie had been in awe, but it was Maggie's education that made her envious. Her friend had spoken French, played the harp, knew mathematics and could recite dozens of poems.

Adie's assumption of Maggie's wealth had been confirmed the day she'd died. Bleeding and weak, she'd told Adie to remove a velvet bag from a drawer of her trunk and look inside. Adie had gasped at the glittering gems. Maggie's dying wish still echoed in her ears. She had begged Adie to take Stephen and raise him as her own; then she'd squeezed Adie's wrist with her bloodless fingers.

"Leave Topeka tonight. Break all ties with me."

"But why?"

"Don't let my brother near my son. He'll send Stephen to an orphanage."

Adie had stood alone as an undertaker buried Maggie in a run-down cemetery; then she'd taken the jewelry and backtracked to Kansas City where Maggie had sold a few pieces of jewelry before coming to Topeka. The sixty-mile train ride to the bustling city had given her two advantages. She'd gotten a better price for Maggie's jewelry, and the railroad left Kansas City in four different directions. If Maggie's family found the jewelry, they wouldn't know where she'd gone. If by chance a detective, or Maggie's brother, traced her to Topeka, the man would reach a dead end.

Adie had sold only what she needed for a fresh start, then bought a ticket to Denver because of its size. She wanted to open a boardinghouse, a place for women like herself and Maggie. For two days she'd held Stephen on the crowded train, struggling to keep him fed until they'd arrived in a city full of gambling halls and saloons. Pretending to have Maggie's poise, she'd stayed at a hotel, visited the bank and explained her ambition to the elder Mr. Dean, who had shown her Swan's Nest. The mansion had reminded her of Maggie and she'd bought it, using what cash she had from the jewelry sale and signing a two-year promissory note for the balance.

She could have sold more jewelry and paid for the house in full, but she feared leaving a trail for a Pinkerton's detective. Nor did she want to squander Stephen's inheritance. The remaining jewels—a sapphire ring, a pearl necklace, a bracelet and some glittering brooches—were his legacy from his mother, a gift from the woman who'd given him life but had never held him.

As Adie led the mare into a stall, she felt the sting of tears. Maggie had died three months ago, but she still missed her friend. She also feared strangers, especially men. If Stephen's father tried to claim him, Adie would have to make a terrible choice. On the other hand, she had no qualms about hiding from Maggie's brother. Considering how he'd shunned his sister, he didn't deserve to know his nephew. In Adie's book, he didn't deserve to breathe.

She lifted the saddle off the mare, set it on the ground, then stripped off the scabbard, the canteen and the saddlebags. She set everything aside, filled a bucket with water and gave the horse a measure of hay. Satisfied, she closed the gate to the stall, stepped to the saddlebags and dropped to a crouch. She had no business going through Joshua Blue's things, but she had to be sure he had no ties to Maggie Butler.

With shaking fingers, she worked the buckle on the bulging leather bag.

Chapter Two

As soon as Adie Clarke left the kitchen, Josh drained the glass of milk and poured himself another. He'd been aiming for her boardinghouse when he'd left Kansas City, but he hadn't intended to faint on her doorstep. Before he'd left, he'd seen a doctor who'd told him what he already knew. He had a stomach ulcer, a bad one that could bleed and threaten his life. At the very least, it offered daily torture.

Josh didn't care. He had to find his sister. Ten months ago, Emily Blue had left their Boston mansion with a satchel, her jewelry and Josh's bitter words ringing in her ears. He'd never forgive himself for that night. He'd said unspeakable things, calling her a name that shouldn't be uttered and accusing her of being a Jezebel. He'd made hateful accusations, all the time wearing the collar that marked him as a minister.

The memory sent fresh acid into Josh's belly. He had to find Emily and her baby and make amends. Until he found them, he refused to rest.

Never mind the stomach ulcer. The Apostle Paul had written of a thorn in his flesh. It had kept him humble. The ulcer often humbled Josh, though not as profoundly as it had tonight. Fainting on Adie Clarke's porch hadn't been in the plan when he'd left Kansas City on the word of Wes Daniels, a gunslinger who'd frequented the saloon where Josh had been preaching on Sunday mornings. Wes had told him about a boardinghouse called Swan's Nest.

"It's for women in trouble," he'd said, winking at Josh. "Maybe your sister's there."

Josh had left the next morning. Halfway to Denver, his stomach had caught fire and he'd stopped eating. Pure and simple, he'd fainted on Adie Clarke's porch out of hunger.

As he raised the glass to his lips, he said a silent prayer for Emily and her child. Somewhere in the world he had a niece or nephew he'd never seen. A little girl with Emily's button nose...a boy with the Blue family chin. Josh was imagining a child with Emily's dark curls when he heard a baby cry. High pitched and needy, it cut through his soul. For all he knew, Emily was sleeping right above his head. The baby could be his niece or nephew.

He wanted to charge up the stairs, but his common sense and Miss Clarke's stern rules kept him in the kitchen. Closing his eyes, he prayed for the child and its mother. He knew how it felt to wake up with a bellyache.

Above his head, the ceiling creaked. He heard the pad of bare feet on the wooden planks and imagined a mother hurrying to her child. The footsteps faded, then stopped. An instant later, the baby's wail turned to a hopeful whimper. He imagined the mother taking the baby in her arms, sitting in a rocking chair as she nursed it back to sleep. He listened for the creak of the rockers, maybe the hint of a lullaby. Instead the baby shrieked in frustration. Footsteps scurried back down the hall while the baby's cry stayed in the same room, growing louder. The pacing stopped over Josh's head, paused, then went halfway down the hall. He heard a door open, then another pair of steps, muted now as if two women were trying to be quiet on floors that wouldn't allow it.

When the stairs squeaked, Josh shot to his feet. Adie Clarke knew she'd rented him a room, but the women coming down the stairs would see a drifter in black, maybe an outlaw. Common sense told him to leave the kitchen, but he stood frozen with the hope of seeing Emily.

"Don't move, or I'll shoot you dead." The female voice, shaking with sincerity, had come from the shadow in the hall.

He froze.

"Get your hands up!"

As he raised his arms, his duster pulled open. Josh believed in turning the other cheek, but he wore a Colt Peacemaker on his hip. He'd learned early in his travels that riding unarmed into an outlaw camp caused more of a stir than a cocked rifle. Carrying a weapon was his way of being a Greek to the Greeks. The Colt made him familiar to the rough men with whom he felt called to share the Good News. Unfortunately, the woman in the doorway wouldn't see the gun as a calling card. Josh felt the weapon pulling on his belt and winced. He'd lost weight. If he didn't hike up the belt soon, he'd lose his trousers.

"Who are you?" the woman demanded.

"I'm a new boarder."

"Liar," she said in a stony voice. "Adie doesn't rent to men."

"She took pity on me." Josh peered into the hallway.

He couldn't see the woman, but candlelight glinted off the double barrel of a two-shot Derringer. The weapon shook, a sign of her nerves.

"Where's Adie?" she demanded.

"Tending my horse."

"Why aren't you tending it yourself?"

Pride kept Josh from admitting his weakness. Before he could correct the mistake, the woman hollered down the hallway.

"Pearl! Get Bessie and Caroline! We have an intruder." The gun stayed steady. "Find Adie *now*."

With his hands in the air, Josh heard doors open and the tap of feet on the stairs. In Boston, he'd enjoyed the Women's Auxiliary meetings. The ladies had fawned over him and the compliments had gone to his head. The women of Swan's Nest wouldn't be so appreciative.

Pain stabbed past his sternum and around his ribs. If he'd been alone, he'd have fallen to his knees, clutched his middle and curled into a ball. With a gun trained on his chest, he didn't dare move. The pain hit again. His shoulders hunched as he cringed, causing his arms to drop as if he were going for his gun.

The woman fired.

The bullet slammed into Josh's shoulder. He took a step back, caught his boot on the chair and fell against a hutch filled with china. Plates crashed to the floor and so did Josh. He didn't want to die. He had to find Emily. He'd shamed himself as a man and a minister. He had to make up for his mistakes.

"Don't shoot," he said. "I mean no harm."

The woman kept the pistol trained on his head. "We'll see what Adie has to say."

Josh lay on the floor, clutching his belly and smelling sulfur and blood. He'd seen men die before. In Boston he'd prayed with elderly gentlemen fading in their own beds. In camps west of the Mississippi, he'd seen men die from gunshot wounds, infections and disease. Curled on the floor, he listened to his own breath for sucking air, a sign he'd been hit in the lung, but he heard only a rasp in his dry throat. His heart kept an even rhythm, another good sign.

Judging by the pain, he'd been hit high in the shoulder. Silently Josh thanked God the woman had owned a Derringer and not a Colt .45. He'd live as long as she didn't panic and shoot him in the head.

He heard footsteps in the kitchen and opened his eyes. Bare toes and the hems of robes filled his vision.

"You shot him!" said a new female voice.

"What happened?" demanded another.

Could one of the women be Emily? The voices hadn't matched hers—one sounded Southern and the other was too high pitched—but he'd seen four pairs of feet. Josh wanted to look but realized it would be fruitless. He'd become thin and ragged, but Emily would have recognized him. He closed his eyes in despair.

In a breath of silence, he heard the hopeful cooing of a baby and looked up. The fourth woman had an infant in her arms. The goat's milk, he realized, was for the child. Expecting to be fed, it had settled into its mother's arms but was growing impatient with the delay. The cooing turned to a complaint, then a wail that dwarfed everything in the room, including Josh's pain.

"The baby's hungry," he said.

"Quiet," ordered the woman with the gun.

Josh could barely breathe for the pain. "Please. Feed it."

No one moved.

He raised his voice. "I said feed the baby."

He flashed on the night he'd clashed with Emily.

Three times he'd told her to leave, betraying her love as surely as Peter had betrayed his Lord. Like the fisherman, Josh felt lower than dirt.

The wailing grew worse. The woman with the gun called to one of the others. "Get the milk, Pearl. I'll keep watch."

Emily had loved their mother's pearls, a strand so long it reached to her waist. Was she using an alias to avoid him? Maybe she *hadn't* recognized him. He'd changed in the past year. Even more worrisome, maybe she'd seen him take a bullet and wished him dead.

Bare feet, slender and white, padded across the wood floor. Josh tried to call Emily's name, but his belly hurt and the words slurred to a groan. He watched the woman's feet as she retrieved the pitcher of goat's milk, filled a bottle and warmed it in a pan of water on the stove. The baby, smelling food, shrieked even louder. Wise or not, Josh raised his head. The baby's mother wore a yellow robe, his sister's favorite color, but she had white-blond hair. Emily's hair was dark and wavy like his. He hadn't found his sister after all, but neither was this woman the baby's mother. Her belly promised new life and promised it soon. Closing his eyes, Josh prayed for the mother and child, wishing he'd done the same for Emily instead of driving her away with his foolish pride.

Adie heard a gunshot, dropped the unopened saddlebag and ran for the house. Mary, a former saloon girl, kept a pistol in her nightstand and wouldn't hesitate to use it.

Had Joshua Blue betrayed Adie's trust? She didn't think so. The man could barely walk. It seemed more likely that Stephen had awoken early and Mr. Blue had lingered over the glass of milk. Whoever went for Stephen, probably Mary, had seen Adie's empty bed. Maybe she'd heard the thump on the door and jumped to ominous conclusions.

She ran up the back steps and flung open the door.

"Adie!" The cry came from Pearl. "We thought—"

"I know what you thought." She dropped to her knees at the man's side. "He's hurt. We'll have to call the doctor."

Stephen shrieked. He needed to be fed in the worst way, but Adie feared for the wounded man's life.

Groaning, he rolled to his back, revealing the bullet hole in his duster. When she opened his coat, she saw a red stain blooming on his white shirt. With each breath he took, the blood spread in a widening circle.

Looking at her face, he mumbled something unintelligible.

She hunched forward. "I couldn't hear you."

"I said…feed the baby."

Joshua Blue was lying on her floor with a bullet in his shoulder, bleeding inside and out, and he was thinking of her son. What kind of man put a baby before his own life? Using the hem of her nightgown, Adie wiped his brow. "Be still. We'll get the doctor."

"No." His voice sounded stronger. "No doctors."

"But you need help."

Someone lit a lamp. As it flared to life, Mary stepped closer. Adie smelled the residue of gunpowder and looked up. "Maybe Caroline can go for Doc Nichols."

The man lifted his head. "I said *no*."

His refusal made Adie wonder if he was on the run. It wouldn't have surprised her. Everyone at Swan's Nest had run from something, including herself.

Mary scowled down at her. "Who is he?"

"I rented him a room."

"But you don't rent to men. You promised—"

"This isn't the time," Adie said.

She looked past Mary and saw Pearl at the stove. With her back to the rest of the kitchen, she lifted the bottle out of the pot of water and whisked Stephen into the front room where she could feed him in peace. Adie looked at Caroline. "Where's Bessie?"

"She went to get her nursing kit."

Mary finally lowered the gun. "Maybe she can take out the bullet."

Adie studied the man on her floor. His color had come back and his breathing seemed steady. Maybe they could avoid Dr. Nichols after all. Bessie hurried into the kitchen and dropped down next to Adie. She looked at the wound, checked the man's back for an exit hole, then lowered him gently to the floor. "The bullet's still in you, sir. It'll have to come out."

"Can you do it?"

"I can try," Bessie said. "I'm a trained nurse, but it will hurt."

"Go ahead," he said.

Bessie looked at Adie. "Get that pint of whiskey."

Adie kept it with the smelling salts for medicinal purposes only. Before she could stand to fetch it, the stranger clutched her hand. "I don't want it."

Why would he deny himself a painkiller? Adie was about to argue with him when Bessie interrupted. "It's not for your belly, sir. It's to clean the wound."

He relaxed but didn't release Adie's hand. She felt awkward comforting him, but they were both aware of the coming pain. When Adie didn't move, Caroline went to the cupboard for the whiskey. She gave the bottle to Bessie, then lifted the instruments from the nursing bag, put them in the boiling water and set out clean rags for blotting the blood. Bessie had opened the two buttons on the man's shirt, but it wouldn't pull wide enough to reveal the wound. Using delicate scissors, the kind most women kept for embroidery, she cut the shirt and tugged it back from a small hole oozing blood.

Adie's stomach churned. The hole in Joshua Blue's shoulder wasn't much bigger than a man's finger, but it had the potential to kill him with infection. In his weakened condition, he might not be able to fight it. Adie squeezed his hand. She feared for his health. She also feared for herself and Stephen. She'd just opened the first saddlebag when she heard the gunshot. Later, when he'd fallen asleep, she'd search his things.

"Whiskey, please," Bessie said matter-of-factly.

Adie watched as Caroline splashed whiskey into her sister's palm. As Bessie rubbed her hands together, Caroline dampened a patch of cotton and gave it to her sister. Bessie looked at the man's face. "This is going to hurt, sir."

He closed his eyes. "Just do it."

Bessie took a probe from the instruments Caroline had put on a clean towel. As she inserted it into the wound, Joshua Blue arched up. Bessie pulled back.

"Adie, Caroline. You'll have to hold him down."

The two women moved into position. On their knees, they each held a shoulder. As Bessie went to work, Adie felt the man straining against her hands. She also sensed acceptance. The bullet had to come out.

"I found it," Bessie said.

She removed the probe and lifted a pair of forceps. After a glance at her patient, she inserted the instrument, pinched the bullet and pulled it out. Joshua Blue groaned with pain. Adie wondered which hurt more, his chest or his belly.

Bessie held the bullet up to the light and examined it. "It's in one piece. We're done except for stitching this gentleman up."

He let out a breath. "Thank you."

"You'll do fine as long as the wound doesn't fester. Of course you'll have to rest up for a while."

He grunted. "How long?"

Adie had been wondering the same thing.

"As long as it takes." Bessie took a stitch with a needle and black thread. "Judging by your appearance, you're half starved. You need a week in bed and a month in a rocking chair."

Adie cringed. "That's so long."

Bessie gave her a motherly look. "It's what the man needs, honey. We'll be all right."

Leave it to Bessie to calm the waters. Mary would pitch a fit. Pearl, conscious of her belly, would stop coming downstairs. Caroline judged no one. She'd befriend Mr. Blue without hesitation, posing a problem of a different kind. Adie watched as the nurse stitched up the wound, snipped the thread and wiped the incision with whiskey. She inspected her handiwork, then wiped the man's brow with a clean rag. "We need to get you to bed. Can you walk?"

"I think so."

With Adie on one side and Caroline on the other, he leveraged to his feet. He looked like a kicked-in chimney pipe, but he managed to move down the hall. Adie started to follow, but Bessie stopped her. "I'll see to him. Go hold Stephen. It'll make you feel better."

"Thanks, Bessie."

"By the way," said the older woman. "Who is this man?"

"I wish I knew." Adie told her briefly about finding him on the porch. "He was in pain even before Mary shot him."

"Maybe an ulcer," Bessie said. "I've got a small bottle of laudanum. I'll fetch it for him."

Adie thought of his earlier comment about the drug but said nothing. She wanted Joshua Blue to fall asleep so she could finish going through his saddlebags, but first she needed to check her son.

"Whatever you think," she said to Bessie. "The sooner he heals, the sooner he can leave."

"He needs time," the nurse said gently.

Adie sighed. She'd cook meals for Joshua Blue and nurse his wounds. She'd change his sheets and wash his clothes. But time to heal—what he needed most—was the one thing she didn't want to give. The sooner he left, the safer she and Stephen would be.

As Bessie went down the hall, Adie headed for the parlor where she heard Pearl humming a lullaby to Stephen. She rounded the corner and saw both Pearl and Mary on the divan. Pearl looked lost, but Mary had crossed her arms and was glowering. Adie had hoped to check Stephen and escape to the carriage house, but she couldn't leave without explaining to her friends.

"Who is he?" Mary demanded.

"I don't know," Adie said. "But I'm certain he means no harm."

Mary groaned. "You can't possibly know that."

Adie couldn't be sure, but he'd come to the door sick and weak. "Look at him. He's downright scrawny."

"He's also dressed like a gunfighter," Mary insisted. "I know his kind."

Adie felt naive next to Mary, but she couldn't stop worrying about the stranger. She didn't want to argue, but she needed to set Mary straight. "He fainted on the porch. What else could I do? Leave him there?"

"You could have gone for the sheriff."

To protect Stephen, Adie kept to herself as much as possible. If a Pinkerton's detective visited Denver, he'd go straight to the law and make inquiries. The less the sheriff knew about Adie and her home, the safer her son would be. She gave Mary an impatient look. "It wasn't necessary."

"You're too trusting," Mary insisted.

Pearl sighed. "I wish you hadn't shot him."

"He went for his gun!"

Adie worried, but only for an instant. A man intending harm didn't tell a woman to feed a hungry baby. "He has belly trouble," she said to Mary. "He probably bent over in pain."

Recognition flitted across Mary's face.

Pearl went back to crooning to Stephen, who'd fallen peacefully asleep. Adie envied him. She wouldn't sleep that well until Joshua Blue left Denver. "I have to see to his horse."

Mary pushed to her feet. "I'll help."

"No." Adie waved casually, but her stomach had jumped. She wanted to go through his things by herself. "It's been a long night. You and Pearl should get some sleep."

"If you're sure—"

"I am." Adie forced a smile. "I'll see you both in the morning."

Before Mary could ask another question, Adie headed for the back door. As she turned the knob, Bessie came down the hall. "Mr. Blue wants to see you."

The saddlebags would have to wait but only for a bit. With rubbery knees, she thanked Bessie and went to see Joshua Blue.

Chapter Three

In spite of Josh's protests, the woman nursing him had left a bottle of laudanum on the nightstand. He knew all about the drug and the lies it told. He'd first used it in Boston. With the renown that came with his sermons, he'd gotten an ulcer. The doctor he'd seen, a stranger because he'd wanted to hide his weakness, had given him something to calm his stomach, but it had led to embarrassing bouts of belching, something a man in Josh's position couldn't allow. He'd gone to a second physician, then a third. The last one had given him laudanum. It had helped immediately.

Looking at the bottle, Josh knew it would help right now. If he filled the spoon the woman had left—he thought her name was Bessie—he'd be free of pain. He'd be numb to his guilt, too.

The laudanum tempted him.

The craving humbled him.

Reverend Joshua Benjamin Blue, the best young preacher in Boston, maybe in America, had become addicted to opium. Thanks to Wes Daniels, the biggest sinner on earth and Josh's only friend, he'd kicked the habit three months ago in a Kansas City boardinghouse.

Thoughts of Wes made Josh smile. He hadn't succeeded in saving the gunslinger's soul, but neither had Wes corrupted *him.* They'd had some lively debates in the past few months…a few quarrels, too. Wes had understood Josh's guilt, but he didn't share his worry. As long as Emily had jewelry to sell, Wes insisted she'd be sitting pretty. Josh hoped so. For months he'd been visiting pawnbrokers in search of pieces he'd recognize. He knew from Sarah Banks, Emily's best friend, that his sister had bought a train ticket to St. Louis. Sarah had given Josh a verbal beating, one he'd deserved.

"How dare you cast stones at your sister! I know you, Josh. You're as flawed as the rest us!"

She'd been right, of course. With Sarah's remarks in his ears, he'd traveled to St. Louis, where he'd spotted a familiar brooch in a jewelry store. Emily, he'd learned from the shopkeeper, had sold it and moved on. A clerk at the train station recalled her face and thought she'd gone to Kansas City. Josh's only hope of finding her lay in a trail of pawned jewelry and the Lord's mercy. If he could have moved, he'd have hit his knees. Like Paul, he counted himself among the foremost of sinners, a man sorely in need of God's grace. With the laudanum calling to him, he needed that grace in abundance. It came in the tap of Adie Clarke's footsteps.

Bessie had left Josh a lamp, but she'd dimmed it to a haze that turned Miss Clarke into a shadow. Josh recalled her reddish hair and the glint in her gold-brown eyes. She'd struck him as young and pretty, though he wished he hadn't noticed. He'd dedicated his life to serving God with every thought and deed. He wasn't immune to pretty women, but he felt called to remain single. A man couldn't travel at will with the obligation of a wife and family.

Thoughts of children made him wince. Without Emily the family mansion in Boston had become a tomb. For the first time, Josh had taken his meals alone. Listening to the lonely scrape of his knife on fine china, he'd wondered how it would feel to share meals with a wife, maybe children. Tonight he'd envied the woman who'd fed the baby.

Adie Clarke studied him in the dim light. "Are you awake?"

"I am. I need something."

"Milk?"

"No," he said. "The laudanum…take it away."

Her gaze went to the bottle, then shifted to the cot where Josh lay wrapped in a blanket and wearing a silk nightshirt. Bessie had bandaged his shoulder, extracted the garment from one of the trunks in the storeroom and helped him into the shirt. Even in Boston, he hadn't worn anything so fine.

Miss Clarke stayed in the doorway. "Are you sure? Bessie says—"

"Bessie doesn't know me."

"She's a good nurse."

"I don't doubt it, Miss Clarke." Josh felt ashamed, but the truth set a man free. "Until a few months ago, laudanum had a grip on me. I'll never touch it again."

"I'm sorry."

He didn't want her pity. "I'm over it."

"Of course." She walked to the nightstand, lifted the bottle and hurried for the door.

"Wait," he called.

She stopped and turned, but her eyes clouded with reluctance. "Do you need something else?"

"Would you bring in my saddlebags?"

She froze like a deer sensing a wolf. Why would she

hesitate? Considering he'd been shot in her kitchen, fetching his saddlebags seemed like a small favor. He could live without the laudanum, but he desperately needed the Bible packed with his clothes. "I'd get them myself, but—"

"No," she said. "I'll do it."

"Thank you."

As she headed down the hall, Josh rested his head on the pillow and stared at the ceiling. He hoped she'd hurry. His shoulder ached and his belly burned, but his soul hurt most of all. He thought of David writing Psalms in the midst of battle and loss.

Search me, O God, and know my heart... Love swelled in Josh's chest. He prayed for Emily, the women of Swan's Nest and the baby crying for milk.

Try me and know my thoughts... If an ulcer, a gunshot wound and a craving for opium didn't test a man, he didn't know what did. Would ever find Emily? Was she still alive? And her child… He grimaced.

See if there be any hurtful way in me... He prayed for purity of thought and a generous spirit.

And lead me in Your way everlasting. Amen.

As he finished the prayer, he looked expectantly at the door. Any minute Adie Clarke would be back with his Bible. More than ever, Josh needed the mercy of the God who'd walked the earth in a tent of human flesh. Jesus alone knew how he felt. He alone could bring comfort.

Adie ran to the carriage house. If she hurried, she could look in the saddlebags before giving them to Mr. Blue. On the other hand, she saw a risk. If she took too long, he'd wonder where she'd been. He also seemed more alert than she'd expected. If she rummaged through his bags, he might realize his things were in disarray and she'd have to explain herself.

As she entered the outbuilding, she considered another approach. Mr. Blue wouldn't be able to lift the heavy bags. He'd need her help. If she dumped the contents on the floor, she'd see everything *and* be able to gauge his expression. Adie didn't like being sneaky, but her motives were pure. She'd do anything to protect Stephen.

Not bothering with a lamp, she found the saddlebags where she'd left them, draped them over her shoulder, picked up the rifle and went back to the house. She went down the hall to Mr. Blue's room where she leaned the gun by the door and set the bags against the wall. They'd be in his line of sight but not so close that he could see her expression.

He pulled himself upright so he could watch. "I'm not sure which bag it's in."

Adie didn't ask him what he wanted. The less information she had, the more reason she had to riffle through his things. She lifted the first bag, worked the buckle and dumped the contents on the floor. Pots, two plates and utensils clattered against each other, and a can of beans rolled away. She'd found his mess kit but nothing of interest. She put everything back, then unbuckled the second bag. She could tell from the softness that it held clothing. Before he could stop her, she removed trousers, a shirt and a frock coat, all tightly rolled and as black as coal.

"Keep going," he said. "What I want is at the bottom."

Adie removed dungarees, a denim shirt and two pairs of store-bought socks. She checked the edges for darning, found none and decided Joshua Blue was a single man and always had been. Wanting a reason to check his pockets, she picked up the clothing and stood. "I'll hang up your things."

"I'd be obliged."

Feeling like a fox in a henhouse, she went to a row of nails on the back wall. She turned her back, gave the coat a shake and searched the pockets. She felt a few coins, lint and a scrap of paper. A quick glance revealed notes about a man named Peter and something about catching fish. Seeing no mention of Maggie, Adie slipped the paper back in the coat and lifted a pair of trousers. She repeated her search and found nothing.

She went back to the saddlebag. "What is it you want?"

"My Bible."

She knew very little about Maggie's brother, but her friend had let it slip that he was a minister in a big city. Maggie had never said which one, though Adie had surmised she'd come from New England. Trembling, she looked up from the saddlebag. "Are you a preacher?"

"Of a sort."

"Do you have a church?"

"I do, but not like you mean."

Her hand shook as she checked a pocket. "I don't understand."

"I don't preach in a building," he explained. "I go from place to place."

Adie let out the breath she'd been holding. Maggie's brother had been wealthy. He'd have arrived in Denver in a private railcar, not on the back of a tired horse. He'd have never gone from town to town, preaching to the poor. She relaxed until she recalled his interest in Stephen. Not many men cared about hungry babies. Her nerves prickled with worry. Aware of his gaze, she reached into the saddlebag. She felt past a pouch holding shaving tools, found the book and lifted it from the bag.

The words *Holy Bible* caught the light and glowed like fire, taking Adie back to the evenings she'd spent with the Long family. Old Man Long had often read from the book of Jeremiah. Adie had felt sinful and condemned and confused by a God who treated people so poorly. She'd cast Maggie's brother in the same mold. Even without her promise, she'd have protected Stephen from such a man.

She stood and handed him the Bible. Their fingers brushed on the binding, but their hearts were miles apart. Adie believed in God, but she didn't like Him. Neither did she care for preachers. Carrying a Bible didn't give a man a good heart. She'd learned that lesson in Liddy's Grove. She let go of the book as if it had singed her.

Mr. Blue looked into her eyes with silent understanding and she wondered if he, too, had struggled with God's ways. The slash of his brow looked tight with worry, and his whiskers were too stubbly to be permanent. Adie thought about his shaving tools and wondered when he'd used them last. Her new boarder would clean up well on the outside, but his heart remained a mystery. She needed to keep it that way. The less she knew about him, the better.

"Good night," she said. "Bessie will check you in the morning."

"Before you go, I've been wondering …"

"About what?"

"The baby… Who's the mother?"

Adie raised her chin. "I am."

Earlier he'd called her "Miss Clarke" and she hadn't corrected him. The flash in his eyes told her that he'd assumed she'd given birth out of wedlock. Adie resented being judged, but she counted it as the price of protecting Stephen. If Mr. Blue chose to condemn her, so be it. She'd done nothing for which to be ashamed. With their gazes locked, she waited for the criticism that didn't come.

Instead he laced his fingers on top of the Bible. "Children are a gift, all of them."

"I think so, too."

He lightened his tone. "A boy or a girl?"

"A boy."

The man smiled. "He sure can cry. How old is he?"

Adie didn't like the questions at all, but she took pride in her son. "He's three months old." She didn't mention that he'd been born six weeks early. "I hope the crying doesn't disturb you."

"I don't care if it does."

He sounded defiant. She didn't understand. "Most men would be annoyed."

"The crying's better than silence… I know."

Adie didn't want to care about this man, but her heart fluttered against her ribs. What did Joshua Blue know of babies and silence? Had he lost a wife? A child of his own? She wanted to express sympathy but couldn't. If she pried into his life, he'd pry into hers. He'd ask questions and she'd have to hide the truth. *Stephen was born too soon and his mother died. He barely survived. I welcome his cries, every one of them. They mean he's alive.*

With a lump in her throat, she turned to leave. "Good night, Mr. Blue."

"Good night."

A thought struck her and she turned back to his room. "I suppose I should call you Reverend."

He grimaced. "I'd prefer Josh."

Adie preferred formality. She had her differences with the Almighty, but she'd been taught to respect God and honor His ways. Being too familiar with a man of the cloth seemed wrong. So did addressing a near stranger by his given name. She avoided the issue by murmuring good-night.

Before Mr. Blue could ask another question, she closed the door behind her and went to her bedroom. Too anxious to sleep, she stood next to Stephen's cradle and watched the rise and fall of his chest, treasuring every breath he took. Someday she'd tell him about Maggie Butler and pass on the things hidden in the trunk at the foot of her bed. Maggie's jewelry lay wrapped in a red velvet bag, untouchable, except in a matter of life or death. Adie expected to support herself and her son, though earning a living had proven more difficult than she'd expected. With the loan payment due on Friday, she would have to go to the bank where Franklin Dean would harass her.

Stephen hiked up his legs. Adie tucked the blanket across his back and thought of the other things in the trunk, particularly Maggie's diary. In the last weeks of her pregnancy, the two of them had spent their evenings on the porch of a Topeka boardinghouse. While Adie did piecework, Maggie had taken a pen to paper.

"It's my story," she'd explained. "If something happens to me, I want Stephen to have it when he's older."

Blinking back tears, she recalled the day Maggie had written the last words in the journal. She'd asked for the book, scrawled a final sentence and taken her last breath. Stunned, Adie had lifted the book from Maggie's still hands. Without opening it, she'd buried the journal deep in the trunk.

Looking at her son now, Adie thought of the diary

and trembled. Maggie had lived with secrets. The book, Adie feared, held revelations that could tear Stephen out of her arms. She had no desire to read it. Instead she kept it hidden with the jewelry and the picture of his natural mother. Someday she'd give everything to her son. The book held truths he deserved to know, but its presence made Adie tremble. She had no intention of opening the trunk for a very long time.

Josh opened his Bible to the Psalms. Tonight he needed comfort and he'd find it in the words of David, a man with God's own heart but human inclinations. Josh understood that tug and pull. In Boston he'd been inclined to protect his own pride. He'd been an arrogant fool and he hadn't even known it. Others had, though. As the pages fluttered, he recalled preaching in front of a thousand people. Gerard Richards, the leading evangelist in America, had been in the crowd. Josh had been eager for the man's praise. Instead the famed minister, a stooped man with a squeaky voice, had looked him up and down and said, "You have a gift, young man. But you're full of yourself. You'll be better after you've suffered."

Josh had been insulted.

Now he understood. Emily's flight had knocked him to his knees. He'd fallen even lower when he'd lost everything in a river crossing. It had happened on the Missouri at the peak of the spring flood. The barge pilot had steered into an eddy and lost control. When water lapped the logs, the passengers had all run to the side closest to the shore. The raft tipped, sending everything—people, animals and their possessions—into the racing current.

Josh had made it to shore, but he'd lost the satchel

he'd carried from Boston. The clothing could be replaced, but he'd grieved the Bible. It had belonged to his grandfather, the man who'd mentored Josh until he'd died of apoplexy. Even more devastating was the loss of Emily's letter and the tintype she'd had made a few months before she'd revealed her condition. Josh had tucked them in the back of the Bible for safekeeping, but the river had swallowed them whole.

Stripped of his possessions, he'd found work in a livery. That Sunday, he'd preached to a trio of bleary men who'd come for their horses after a night on the town. They'd each given him two bits for his trouble. Josh had put those coins toward the purchase of the Bible in his hands now. The men had come back the following Sunday and they'd brought a few friends. Josh had preached again. He'd used that collection for laudanum.

Recalling that day, he lingered on David's plea to the God who knew his deepest thoughts. He prayed, as he did every night, that the Lord would lead him to Emily. Before the river crossing, he'd shown her picture to everyone he'd met. Now he could only describe her. He missed the letter, too. The night she'd left, she'd put it on top of the sermon notes on his desk. He'd been preaching through the gospel of John and had reached the story of the adulterous woman and Jesus' famous words, "Let him whose slate is clean cast the first stone."

Sermons usually came easily to Josh, but he'd been unable to grasp the underlying message.

Now he knew why. He'd been a hard-boiled hypocrite. When Emily came to him for help, he'd berated her with words that bruised more deeply than rocks. Blinking, he recalled her letter. He'd read it so often he'd memorized it.

I love you, Josh. But I don't respect you. You judged me for my sins—I admit to them—but you don't know what happened or why. You don't know me or my baby's father and you never will. I'm leaving Boston for good. Someday, Reverend Blue, you'll get knocked off your high horse. I'll pray for you, but I won't weep.

Your sister, Emily.

That Sunday, Josh had taught on the same passage, but he'd changed the message. Instead of focusing on the woman and Christ's command to go and sin no more, he'd talked about throwing stones. In front of three hundred people, he'd admitted to his mistakes and resigned his position. A broken man, he'd packed a single bag and bought a train ticket. Based on Sarah's knowledge, he'd headed for St. Louis, worrying all the time that Emily would travel farther west. Josh hadn't found her in St. Louis, but he'd spotted a piece of her jewelry in a shop owned by a pawnbroker. It had given him hope. Over the next several months, he'd traveled far and wide.

Someday he'd find Emily. He'd hit his knees and beg for forgiveness. Until then, he had to live with his regrets. Exhausted, he blew out the lamp. As always he prayed for his sister's safety. Tonight, he added Adie Clarke to that list. He couldn't help Emily, but here at Swan's Nest, he saw a chance to do some good. What he couldn't give to Emily, he'd give to Adie Clarke and her friends. The thought put a smile on his face, the first one in a long time.

Chapter Four

"Don't let him inside!"

"I won't," Adie said to Pearl.

The two women were in the front parlor. They'd been on the porch when Pearl had spotted a carriage coming down the street. Terrified of Franklin Dean, she'd run inside with Adie behind her. Together they were peering through the lace curtain at a brougham that belonged to the banker. In the front seat sat Mr. Dean's driver, a stocky man dressed in a frock coat and black bowler.

Adie's gaze skittered to the back of the open carriage where she saw the banker folding a copy of the *Rocky Mountain News*. Some women would have found Mr. Dean handsome. He had dark blond hair, brown eyes, a mustache and what her mother had called a lazy smile, the kind that curled on a man's lips with no effort at all. In Adie's experience, smiles were rare and had to be earned.

She didn't trust Franklin Dean at all. She'd felt uncomfortable the instant they'd met, and those suspicions had been confirmed when she'd heard Pearl's story. A preacher's daughter, Pearl had been engaged to the banker when he'd taken her for a buggy ride.

Dean claimed that they'd succumbed to temptation, but Adie knew otherwise. Pearl had told her about that horrible afternoon. She'd protested. She'd pushed him away. He'd pushed back and left her ashamed and carrying his child.

Adie put her arm around Pearl's shoulders. "Go upstairs. I'll see what he wants."

"I can't leave you."

"Yes, you can." Adie made her voice light. False courage, she'd learned, counted for the real thing if no one saw through it.

"But—"

"Go on." Adie pointed Pearl to the stairs. "I can handle Mr. Dean."

The carriage rattled to a stop. With her eyes wide, Pearl stared at the door, then at Adie. "I'll hide in the kitchen. If he tries anything, I'll scream for help. I'll get a knife—" Her voice broke.

Boots tapped on the steps. Adie nudged Pearl down the hall, then inspected herself in the mirror. She'd planned to walk to the business district to pay the mortgage and had already put on her good dress. Thanks to the rent from Reverend Blue, she had enough money for the payment *and* roast beef for supper. She'd put Stephen down for a nap and had been looking forward to a peaceful walk. Quiet afternoons were few and far between. She refused to let Franklin Dean steal her pleasure.

He rapped on the door.

Adie opened it. "Good afternoon, Mr. Dean."

He tipped his hat. "Miss Clarke."

It galled Adie to be pleasant, but riling him would only lead to trouble. She forced a smile. "What can I do for you?"

"May I come in?"

She stepped onto the porch and closed the door. "It's a lovely day. We can speak out here."

His eyes narrowed. "I've come to see Pearl."

"She's not accepting visitors."

"I believe I'm the exception."

No, he was the reason. The July sun burned behind him, turning the street into a strip of dust and giving his face craggy lines. Adie couldn't stand the sight of him. He'd hurt Pearl the way Timothy Long had tried to hurt *her.* He swaggered the way she'd imagined Maggie's brother strutted in his fancy pulpit. She had to convince him to leave.

"Pearl's resting," she said.

"You're lying, Miss Clarke." His lips curled into the lazy smile. "She was sitting by the window."

"How would you know?"

"Am I wrong?"

"It's none of your concern."

Her voice rang with confidence, but her insides were quaking. He'd been too far away to see Pearl through the glass. Had he been watching her house? She thought of the rock that had shattered her bedroom window. Fear gripped her, but she met his gaze as if they were discussing lemonade.

Dean rapped a walking stick against his palm. Over and over, he slapped his own flesh as if he didn't feel a thing. Adie had been beaten with bigger sticks and knew when to keep quiet. She also knew that Franklin Dean wanted to drive her out of Swan's Nest so he could sell the property for a higher price than she'd negotiated with his father. Between silver mines and gold strikes, farms, ranches and the arrival of the railroad, Denver had been dubbed the Queen City of the Plains. Adie's house stood on prime land and Dean wanted it back.

He couldn't have it. She forced herself to appear blasé.

He slapped the walking stick against his palm a final time. Gripping it tight, he smiled as if nothing ugly had passed between them. "I'm rather thirsty, Miss Clarke. I'd enjoy a glass of sweet tea."

"I'm fresh out."

"Water, then."

He wanted to get in the house and corner Pearl. No way would Adie open the door. "I was about to leave for town, Mr. Dean. If you'll excuse me—"

"No, Miss Clarke. I won't excuse you." His eyes burned into hers. "I want to see Pearl."

"Like I said, she's resting."

He glared at her. "The mortgage is due today, isn't it?"

"Yes."

"My timing's excellent," he said. "I'll collect payment and save you the trip to the bank."

"No, thank you." Adie never dealt with Dean when she made her payment. She always visited the same teller, asked for a receipt and stowed it in the trunk. They were that precious to her.

Craning his neck, Dean peered through the lace curtain hanging in the parlor window. Adie turned and followed his gaze to Pearl, her belly large and round, as she peered around the corner and out the window.

He rapped on the glass. "Pearl!"

Startled, the girl slipped back into the hall that led to the kitchen. Dean made a move for the front door, but Adie blocked him. He pivoted, went down the steps and turned down the path that led to the garden behind the house. Adie raced after him.

"Stop!" she cried.

"I have business with Pearl."

"You're trespassing!"

Ignoring her, he strode past the vegetables she'd planted in place of flowers and rounded the corner to the back of the house. He was headed for the door, but he hadn't counted on Joshua Blue blocking his path. The scarecrow in the garden had more meat on its bones, but the reverend had a fire in his eyes that scared Adie to death.

After two days in bed, Bessie's care and a gallon of goat's milk, Josh had felt the need for fresh air. He'd gone out the back door, taken in the garden and stepped into the carriage house. He'd been checking his horse when Pearl had run into the outbuilding. Shaking and out of breath, she'd closed the door and hunkered down behind a partial wall before she'd seen him.

Josh approached as if she were a downed bird. "Are you all right?"

She gasped. "It's Franklin Dean. He—" She burst into tears.

Josh didn't know a thing about Franklin Dean, but he knew about evil men. "Where's Miss Clarke?"

"He tried to get in the house," Pearl said, whimpering. "Adie stopped him."

Josh strode out of the carriage house. As he emerged in the sun, he saw a man headed for the back door of Swan's Nest. Adie was running behind him, ordering him to stop. One look at her face and Josh knew she'd fight this man. Pearl's fear explained why. Her belly testified to a deeper reason, one that made Josh furious.

Stifling his anger, he looked the man up and down. The stranger didn't match Josh in height, but he weighed at least fifty pounds more. The difference came from both Josh's belly trouble and the man's indulgence. Whoever he was, he didn't skip dessert.

Josh blocked the path to the back door. "Can I help you, sir?"

"Who are *you?*" the man demanded.

"A guest."

He smirked at Adie. "I thought you didn't rent to men."

"I don't."

Dean huffed. "I see."

"No, sir," Josh said calmly. "You don't *see.* You're trespassing."

"I'm Franklin Dcan."

He said it as if he expected Josh to bow down.

Adie interrupted. "Mr. Dean owns Denver National Bank. He holds the note on Swan's Nest."

Josh didn't care if he owned the entire town. "That doesn't give him the right to trespass."

"You have no business here, Mr.—"

"My name is Joshua Blue." Josh spoke with his richest Boston accent. "My family—"

"Has shipping interests," Dean finished.

"Among other things."

Dean's smile turned oily. "What brings you to Denver, sir?" He smelled money and it showed.

Josh found him revolting. "It's a private matter."

The banker's eyes narrowed. "So is my business with Miss Oliver."

Not in Josh's opinion. Her belly made the matter between them public. He didn't know the details, but he knew Pearl feared this man. At the sight of her, he'd recalled Emily and felt all the inclinations of a brother. Looking at Dean now, he wanted to deck the man for his arrogance. He settled for being direct. "It's time for you to leave."

"Not until I speak to Pearl."

Short of violence, Josh didn't see a way to get rid of the man. He'd have to outlast him. Josh had his flaws, but impatience wasn't one of them. He'd spend all afternoon with Dean if meant protecting Adie and her boarders.

"Fine," Josh said. "I'll wait with you on the porch until she's ready."

Dean frowned.

Adie interrupted. "I have a better idea, Mr. Dean. I'll tell Pearl you're concerned about her health."

"I am."

"If she's up for a visit, I'll send word to you."

Josh watched the banker's face. He didn't want to leave, but Adie had given him a way out that saved his pride.

"Very well," Dean said. "When you bring your loan payment, I'll expect a note from Pearl."

Adie gave a crisp nod. "I'll speak with her."

Dcan glared at Josh, tipped his hat to Adie and walked down the path to the street. Josh followed him with his eyes, watching as he batted at a weed with his walking stick. When he rounded the corner, Josh turned to Adie. When he'd seen her chasing after Dean, she'd reminded him of a robin chasing down a worm. Now, in spite of the sun on her reddish hair, she looked subdued.

Josh raked his hand through his hair. "He's trouble, isn't he?"

"The worst kind."

"If there's anything I can do—"

"There isn't."

As she straightened her spine, Josh noticed her gown. Instead of the brown dress she usually wore, she'd put on a blue calico that made him think of the ocean. Adie Clarke, he decided, had the same sense of mystery. She seemed calm on the surface, but unseen currents churned in her hazel eyes and turned them green in acknowledgment of the dress.

The door to the carriage house creaked open. Pearl peeked from behind the heavy wood. "Is he gone?"

Adie hurried to her friend's side. "He just left."

"Good riddance!"

Josh thought so, too.

Adie put her arm around Pearl's huge waist. "If you'll excuse us, Reverend. Pearl needs to lie down."

"Of course." Except Adie had a need as well. She had to deliver the mortgage payment. Josh decided he needed a walk. He fell into step with the women, held the door and followed them inside.

Adie gave him a harsh look. "Do you need something, Reverend?"

"No, but you do."

"I can't imagine what."

Josh liked her spirit. After the ordeal with Dean, some women—and men—would have been cowering in the closet. Not Adie Clarke. She'd walk on hot coals for someone she loved. So would Josh. Adie wasn't Emily, but for now he could treat her like a sister. "I'm going with you to the bank."

"That's not necessary."

Pearl dropped onto a chair. She looked exhausted. "He's right, Adie. You shouldn't go alone."

"And I need the fresh air," Josh added.

"But your shoulder—"

"It's much improved." He rolled his arm to test it. His belly still hurt, but he didn't pay attention. It *always* hurt, and it would until he found Emily.

Adie looked annoyed, an expression Josh found refreshing. In Boston, the members of his church had deferred to him. On the open trail, outlaws had put up with him. Adie didn't belong in either camp. She treated him with common sense, as if he were an ordinary man. He also admired her sweetness with Pearl. In spite of the pressure from Dean, she hadn't asked her friend to write a note.

Pearl looked at Josh. "She's stubborn."

He smiled. "I noticed."

"I am not." Adie wrinkled her brow. "I don't need company to go to the bank. Besides, I have errands to run."

"Good." Josh hooked his thumbs in the trousers. "I need to pick up a few things, like suspenders."

He'd hoped to lighten the mood and it worked. Pearl patted her tummy. "I don't have *that* problem."

When her friend smiled, Adie's face lit up with pleasure. "I'll bring you some peppermint candy. Would you like that?"

Pearl's eyes brightened. "I'd love some. It settles my stomach."

Josh had known expectant mothers in Boston. They'd all been wealthy and married, secure in love and protected by their husbands. Franklin Dean had robbed this sweet girl of that sanctuary. Someone else had robbed Adie of a husband. Emily had been robbed, too. Josh felt good about escorting Adie to town. He couldn't change the past, but he could help these women in the here-and-now.

"It's settled," he said. "I'm going with you to the bank."

Adie frowned. "You're pushier than Mr. Dean."

"Only for a good cause, Miss Clarke."

She sighed. "If you insist, but—"

Pearl interrupted. "*I* insist. This is all my fault."

Adie put her hands on her hips. "*Nothing* is your fault, Pearl. Do you understand?"

"Yes." Except she looked down at her toes.

Josh's mind flashed back to Emily asking to speak with him in his study. Like Pearl, she'd mumbled and stared at her feet. Josh would regret his first words until his dying day. He'd called his own sister a foul name. He'd ordered her to give the baby away. And for what? His pride…his reputation. What a hypocrite he'd been. In truth, he'd committed worse sins than Emily. By condemning her, he'd denied her the very mercy Christ had shown him and every other man.

Looking at Adie and Pearl, he felt the full weight of his failings. Men had a duty to protect the women they loved. Mothers. Sisters. Wives. He'd failed on two counts. Not only had he harmed Emily, but his mother had died two years ago when he'd been numb with laudanum. If he'd been clearheaded, he might have convinced her to see a doctor for her dizzy spells. As for the third kind of woman—a wife—Josh had vowed to never marry. Without a wife and children, he could pursue his work every minute of the day.

Even without the inclination to marry, he felt protective toward all females. That included Adie and her friends…especially Adie. Annoyed by the thought, he pushed it aside. So what if he liked red hair? He had a call on his life, and that would never change.

"I'll get my coat," he said to the women.

He went to his room, where he lifted the garment off a nail and put it on. After Adie made the payment, he'd excuse himself for a bath and a haircut. At the barber, he'd ask about pawnbrokers.

He went to the entry hall, where he saw Adie at a mirror, tying the ribbons of her bonnet. She'd lifted her chin, giving it a defiant tilt. She looked too young to be a mother, but Stephen was living proof. As she gave the ribbons a tug, Josh found himself admiring the way she faced problems. She didn't duck the truth, neither did she shy away from facts that couldn't be denied. He wished he'd had a friend like Adie in Boston, someone who'd have made him look in the mirror as she was looking in it now.

"I'm ready," he said.

"Me, too." She lifted a drawstring bag and clutched it with both hands.

Josh opened the door and let her pass. It had been a long time since a woman's skirt had brushed over his boots. In Boston, he'd put that awareness out of his mind. He tried to do it now but couldn't. Losing Emily had made him conscious of the simple things women did to soften a man's hard edges, things like smiling and noticing flowers.

As he followed Adie through the front door, he took in the walkway and manicured shrubs. He'd arrived at Swan's Nest in the dark and hadn't noticed the surrounding area. Another mansion stood catty-corner across the street. As they walked down the road, he saw a third home. Set back on a large parcel of land, it was half-demolished. He wrinkled his brow in surprise. "Why is it being destroyed? The house looks almost new."

"It's five years old."

"Seems like a waste."

Adie stared straight ahead. "It is, unless you plan to build five houses in place of one."

Josh put the pieces together. "That's why Dean's harassing you. He wants Swan's Nest so he can tear it down."

"That's right."

She glanced at the demolished remains, now three hills of ragged gray stone. "Mr. Dean bought that house last month. I knew the couple who owned it."

"What happened?"

"Bad investments." Her lips tightened. "The husband owned a silver mine. When it went dry, they lost everything."

"And Dean bought the house."

"For a song."

Josh thought of his cousin in Boston. Elliot liked money, but he wasn't a squirrel about it. He gave away as much as he kept. Sometimes more. A little competition might do Dean some good.

"Tell me more," Josh said.

"That's all I know." Adie made a show of inhaling and raising her face to the sun. "It's a beautiful day."

Small talk couldn't get any smaller than the weather. Josh gave her a sideways glance and saw the set of her jaw. In his experience, people were quick to talk about news and scandals. Considering Dean's visit and the demolished house, he found the change in subject odd, even suspicious, but he followed her lead.

"Summer here is dry," he said. "It's quite a change from Boston."

"I'd imagine so."

Was it his imagination, or did she look frightened? As they passed a third mansion, a stone monstrosity with turrets and a flat roof, she changed the subject again. She told him about the vegetables she'd planted and why she preferred beans to squash. In other words, she told him nothing. Women usually bragged on their children. Adie didn't mention her son once. Neither did she breathe a hint of how she'd come to Denver.

Josh knew about secrets. He'd kept his own. He'd also ridden with men who said nothing and others who told lies. Adie was intent on building a wall of words. Josh didn't mind. After months of gruff male talk, he was enjoying the singsong quality of her voice and the simple pleasure of walking by gardens filled with flowers.

As they neared the heart of Denver, her chatter faded to stray comments about the shops. She stopped talking altogether when they reached a church. Made of rusticated stone, the building had a tall bronze steeple and massive stained glass windows. He'd never seen such beautiful work, not even in Europe. He looked at the pitch of the roof and imagined a vaulted ceiling and the echo of a choir. He blinked and saw mahogany pews filled with people. He pictured a podium carved with an eagle. He'd used such a podium in Boston. He'd never use one again, but he could appreciate the beauty of the church simply as a man.

He glanced at the double doors, then at Adie. "Let's go inside."

"No, thank you." She clipped the words.

Josh would respect her wishes, but he needed to open the door for himself. He turned up the steps. "I'll just be a minute."

She kept walking.

The church could wait. Adie couldn't. He caught up to her in three strides and saw a glint in her eyes.

"What's wrong?" he asked.

"It's none of your business."

Josh had used the same tone when a church elder questioned him about the laudanum. "I don't mean to pry—"

"Then don't."

"You seem upset."

"Upset?" Her expression turned murderous. "Franklin Dean goes to that church. Pearl's father is the pastor."

He knew that Dean had harmed Pearl. Even if a woman welcomed a man's advances, he had an obligation to protect her, to say no for both of them until the benefit of marriage. As for Pearl's father, had he shunned his daughter the way Josh had rejected Emily? He needed to know. If he could spare Pearl a minute of suffering, he'd tell his story to her father.

"Tell me more," he said to Adie.

She stopped in midstride. When she looked into Josh's eyes, he knew he'd hear the truth and it would hurt.

"He raped her," she said in a dry whisper. "They were engaged. He took her on a buggy ride and he forced her."

Emily's face, tearstained and afraid, flashed in front of his eyes.

"Go on," he said.

Adie's voice quavered. "The next day, Dean went to Pearl's father. He 'confessed' that they'd gone too far and asked for permission to marry her immediately. Reverend Oliver ordered her into the parlor. He made her stand there and listen to that *snake* apologize. Her own father acted as if she'd been as sinful as Dean."

A year ago Josh hadn't listened to a word Emily said. He still didn't know who'd fathered her child, if she'd been raped or seduced by a scoundrel. Maybe she'd been in love. Josh had stayed beyond such feelings until the disastrous river crossing. Cold and shivering, he'd watched husbands and wives cling to each other, sharing tears and kisses. That night, he'd known the deepest loneliness of his life.

Looking at Adie Clarke, he felt that loneliness again. She had a way of standing up to people, including men like himself. He liked her spirit and wondered how it would feel to have her fighting at his side. He blocked the thought in an instant. He had no interest in marriage, no plans to settle down. He had to find Emily.

Adie's cheeks had faded back to ivory. "Pearl left home that night. I found her the next morning, throwing up in my garden."

"Did she ever tell her father?"

"She tried, but he wouldn't listen."

Poor fool, Josh thought. "He needs to know."

Adie huffed. "He said what happened was private and he didn't want the whole church gossiping about his daughter. He told her to get married and keep quiet."

Josh grimaced. "Dean committed a crime. What about the law?"

Adie glared at him. "Who'd believe her? They were engaged. She went with him willingly. Alone."

"But—"

"But nothing." Her cheeks flamed again. "Franklin Dean owns half of Denver. That's why he's still on the elder board. People are afraid to confront him, even the other elders. I don't know if *Reverend* Oliver tried to get him thrown off or not, but I doubt it. From what I can see, he cares more about his reputation than his daughter."

The same shoe fit Josh. "I see."

"Do you, Reverend Blue?"

He bristled. "I know about sin, Miss Clarke. I've seen arrogance, greed and male pride. None of it's pretty."

Her expression hardened. "You don't know what it's like to be Pearl. I do."

Her eyes turned shiny and she blinked. Josh had seen women cry. He'd visited sick beds and spoken at funerals, but he'd never been alone with a woman's tears except for the night he shunned Emily. He'd pushed his own sister away, but the urge to hold Adie flashed like lightning. It startled him. The lingering thunder unnerved him even more. A reaction, he told himself… A man's instinct to protect a woman and nothing more. He settled for offering his handkerchief.

"No, thank you." Adie frowned at the monogrammed linen. "I shouldn't have told you about Pearl."

"I'm not naive," he said gently. "My sister got in trouble, too."

Adie paced down the street, almost running to put distance between them. Josh didn't understand her reaction. She'd already revealed the truth of her son's birth, and he hadn't judged her for it.

He wanted to ask her about Emily, but he knew she wouldn't answer. Instead he caught up to her and walked in silence, recalling the times he'd asked strangers if they'd seen his sister. Most said no without thinking. He'd learned to ask less obvious questions. That's how he'd traced Emily to Kansas City. He'd shown her picture to a clerk in a St. Louis pawnbrokerage. The man had shaken his head. Later he'd recalled a woman asking for directions to the train station.

The bank loomed on their right.

"We're here," Adie said.

He stepped ahead of her and held the door. As he

followed her inside, he saw a teller cage, a cherrywood counter and a clerk in a white shirt. To the right, a waist-high railing surrounded a massive desk. A leather chair resembled an empty throne, and a low shelf boasted art-work. Josh found himself staring at marble sculptures depicting Greek gods, cherubs and women. The mix made him uneasy. Franklin Dean was nowhere in sight, so he stood back as Adie made the payment.

As she tucked the receipt in her bag, he guided her to the door. The instant it closed behind them, she looked jubilant.

"Thank you, Reverend."

"For what?"

"Your rent helped to pay my mortgage."

She made him feel like an errant knight. "My pleasure, Miss Clarke."

"I'm making a roast for supper. I hope you'll join us."

Her hazel eyes shone with happiness. Josh liked roast, but he liked this woman even more. Common sense told him to avoid Adie and her autumn eyes, but supper would give him a chance to ask her boarders about Emily.

"I'd be grateful," he replied.

Concern wrinkled her brow. "Is your stomach strong enough? I could make you a custard."

Babies ate custard. Men ate meat. As kind as it was, Adie's offer irked him. "My digestion's much better."

"Good."

Having supper with five ladies made a bath a priority. "If you'll excuse me, I need to run an errand of my own."

"Of course."

As Adie retraced her steps down Colfax Avenue, Josh headed for the part of town where he'd find a bath-house among saloons and gaming halls. Tomorrow he'd come back to this sorry place and ask about his sister, praying he'd find her and hoping it wouldn't be in an upstairs room.

Maybe she'd found a sanctuary like Swan's Nest. The thought cheered him. It also raised questions. Adie's dress, a calico with a high neck and plain buttons, spoke of a simple life. She worked hard to care for her boarders. How had she come to own a mansion, especially one with the air of old money? She kept one parlor closed, but the other had a marble hearth, cornices and wall sconces. An oriental rug protected the hardwood floor, and the latest flowery wallpaper lined the hall. While most of the Denver mansions were made of stone, someone had spent a fortune to haul in wood for siding.

Most notable of all, a stained glass window adorned the entry hall. Round and wide, it depicted a white swan with an arched neck floating on a lake of blue glass. Swan's Nest struck Josh as a perfect name, especially considering its owner and her female guests. Tonight he'd eat a home-cooked meal in the company of good women. They'd chatter, and he'd listen to their birdsong voices. He wouldn't be lonely for conversation, and he might glean news of Emily.

Two hours later, Franklin Dean entered the bank he'd inherited from his father. A review of the day's business showed Adie Clarke's payment. Irritated, he summoned Horace, his driver, and left for the Denver Gentlemen's Club.

As usual, he'd eat supper alone. He blamed the unfortunate state of his evening on Pearl. Didn't she know how much he loved her? He'd die for her. Sometimes, like this afternoon when he'd seen the foolish preacher at Swan's Nest, he thought he could kill for her.

He hoped the circumstances wouldn't come to that. He knew from experience that dead bodies raised questions. He hadn't meant to strangle Winnie Peters, but she'd started to scream. Why had she done that? Frank didn't know, and he didn't care. He'd left her body in a ravine and paid Horace to remove her belongings from the hotel. No one missed her. She'd come to Denver alone and hadn't made friends.

As the carriage passed through town, Frank considered today's visit to Swan's Nest. It hadn't gone well, and he'd missed Adie's visit to the bank. If it weren't for her, Pearl would be living at the parsonage. By now, her father would have forced her to marry him. Instead she'd found refuge in a mansion that should have belonged to the bank.

Frank scowled at his father's shortsightedness. Swan's Nest was on Seventeenth Street, a dirt road that led to the outskirts of Denver. As the city grew, that street would fill with businesses. In a few years, the land would be worth thousands of dollars. Frank's father had sold the mansion for a song, and Frank wanted it back.

He had to get rid of Adie Clarke and he had to do it soon, before Pearl had the baby and his son was born without his name.

"Horace?"

"Yes, sir?"

"Do you recall the job I asked you to do last month?"

"Of course, sir."

Frank had asked his driver to send Miss Clarke a message, so Horace had thrown a rock through her bedroom window. Miss Clarke had replaced the glass and said nothing, not even to the sheriff.

"It didn't accomplish what I'd hoped," Frank said.

"Another plan, sir?"

He thought of the garden he'd seen on the side of the house. A smirk curled his lips. "I believe Miss Clarke's vegetables need attention."

"Yes, sir."

Horace stopped the carriage in front of the Denver Gentlemen's Club. Frank exited the rig, then pressed a shiny silver dollar into his driver's hand.

Horace's eyes gleamed. "Thank you, sir."

With his walking stick in hand, Frank entered the club where he'd find fine food and drink. Tonight he had everything he needed…except Pearl. Only Adie Clarke stood in his way.

Chapter Five

"Good evening, ladies. May I join you?"

Adie had been about to carve the roast when she looked up and saw Reverend Blue, tall and lean in a black coat and preacher's collar, standing in the doorway. His cheeks gleamed with a close shave and his hair, dark with a slight wave, wisped back from his forehead. Adie nearly dropped the carving knife. The drifter who'd fainted on her porch was nowhere in sight. In his place stood a gentleman. His eyes, clear and bright, shone with mirth. He'd surprised her, and he knew it.

He'd surprised her boarders, too. Pearl's face had turned as pale as her white-blond hair. Mary, her cheeks red with anger, glared at him. Bessie beamed a smile, while Caroline stared as if she'd never seen a handsome man before.

Adie was as tongued-tied as Caroline but for different reasons. While walking to the bank, she'd chirped like a cricket to stop him from asking questions about Stephen. She'd kept her focus until they'd reached Colfax Avenue Church. She hated that building as much as she loved Swan's Nest. She felt that way about all churches, especially ones led by men like Reverend Honeycutt and Maggie Butler's brother.

Looking at Reverend Blue, she didn't see the trappings of such a man, but still felt more comfortable with the drifter.

She indicated the chair on her right. "Please join us."

As he approached, she glanced around the table. If he asked questions, her boarders would answer truthfully. The thought terrified her. They all knew she'd adopted Stephen after the death of a friend, but she'd never breathed Maggie's name. As slim as the details were, Adie didn't want a stranger, especially a preacher, knowing her business.

She positioned the meat fork, lifted the knife and sliced into the roast with too much force. As the cut went askew, the blade cracked against the platter.

Still standing, Reverend Blue indicated the roast. "May I?"

Caroline broke in. "Please do, Reverend."

Irritated, Adie set down the knife and took her seat, watching as his fingers, long and tanned by the sun, curved around the handle. Maggie's hands had been pale, but her fingers had been just as tapered. As he cut the meat into precise slices, her nerves prickled with an undeniable fact. Joshua Blue had carved a hundred roasts. Like Maggie, he'd sipped from fine crystal and knew which fork to use. Her stomach lurched. In the same breath, she ordered herself to be logical. Lots of men knew the proper way to carve meat.

Reverend Blue arranged the last slice on the platter and sat to her right. Adie had no interest in saying grace, but Bessie insisted on keeping the tradition. Tonight the older woman looked at their guest. "Would you give the blessing, Reverend?"

"I'd be honored." He bowed his head. *"Lord, we thank You for this meal, good friends and the gift of your son. Amen."*

He finished the prayer before Adie even folded her hands. Either he was hungry or he respected a woman's effort to serve hot food. She appreciated his quick words. Old Man Long's prayers had been lengthy and harrowing. She'd paid dearly for tonight's meal and wanted to eat it hot.

As she handed him the green beans, Caroline indicated the meat platter. "Take plenty, Reverend. You're still thin from your illness."

He blanked his expression, but Adie caught a hint of annoyance. No man liked being called scrawny, and that's what Caroline had done. He thanked her but still took a reasonable portion.

Bessie spoke over the plink of serving spoons. "How's your shoulder, Reverend?"

"Much better," he answered.

"You were in poor shape the last time we all met. Perhaps introductions are in order."

He glanced around the table. "I know Miss Clarke, and you're Miss—"

"Call me Bessie."

"Bessie it is."

Caroline said her name and beamed a smile. Mary answered with a scowl but introduced herself. Pearl, staring at her belly, spoke in a hush. They'd each offered their given names, expect for Adie. Reverend Blue turned in her direction. Not wanting to be different from the others, she shrugged. "You know my name. It's Adie."

"Short for Adelaide?"

"Yes."

He hadn't questioned the others about their names. Why her?

Caroline handed him the bowl of potatoes. "Where are you from, Reverend?"

"Boston. And you?"

"Virginia."

He turned back to Adie. "You're not from either of those places. I'd guess Missouri."

She would have lied, but her boarders knew bits of her history. "I was born in Kansas."

His interest was piqued. "When did you leave home?"

"Years ago."

He meant Kansas, but Adie thought of "home" as her mother's farm. Her stomach twisted. If Reverend Blue kept quizzing her, she wouldn't be able to eat. She sliced a bit of roast and started to chew. With her mouth full, she wouldn't have to answer his questions.

He lowered his fork. "This might be a good time to explain why I'm in Colorado. I'm looking for my sister."

Adie almost choked.

"She left home ten months ago."

"What's her name?" Caroline asked.

"Emily Blue."

The name meant nothing to Adie. Her stomach settled until the reverend drilled her with his eyes. "Emily was last seen in Kansas City, but I know she bought a train ticket for somewhere else."

Caroline turned to Adie. "Didn't you come here from Kansas City?"

Adie wanted to gag her with the napkin. Instead she blanked her face. "That's only where I got on the train. I was raised on a farm."

"But you've been there," Caroline insisted.

Adie tried to look bored. "It's a big city, Caroline. *Lots* of people pass through."

Mary gave Adie a sideways glance. Of all her boarders, she had the least in common with the former saloon girl, but that changed in a blink. Mary, too, lived with a secret. She saw the trepidation in Adie's expression and looked at the reverend.

"Your sister could be anywhere," she said. "The railroad goes to San Francisco now, or she could have gone to Chicago."

"That's true," he answered. "But I can't give up. I have to know she's safe, even happy."

Adie thought of how he'd considered Stephen's empty belly before the bleeding hole in his own shoulder. He couldn't possibly be the cruel man who'd driven Maggie from Boston.

He looked into her eyes. "It's worse than I've admitted. When Emily left Boston, she was unmarried and with child."

He'd said Emily, not Maggie. Except Adie recalled the day she'd met Stephen's mother. *I'm Maggie Butler now.* Adie had heard "now" and wondered about her past. Her friend, she realized, had changed her name. Adie risked a glance at Joshua Blue, saw Maggie's nose and decided fear was making her see things. She had to change the subject. "How's the roast?"

"Delicious," Mary replied.

Caroline snapped at her. "How can you think about food? I'm worried about Emily Blue."

"And the baby," Pearl whispered.

The reverend turned back to Adie. What did he see? She'd have sold her soul to protect Stephen, but she couldn't lie worth beans. Blood rushed to her cheeks.

"I'm desperate," he said to her. "Emily and I parted with unkind words. It was my fault."

Tremors raced from Adie's chest to her hands. Her throat went dry and the room started to spin. She needed water but didn't dare lift the goblet for fear of spilling it.

Bessie interrupted. "What will you do when you find her?"

"I'll take her home."

"And the baby?" Mary asked.

"Of course."

Pearl raised her chin. "What if she doesn't want to go?"

"I won't force her," he answered. "But I hope she'll listen to reason."

Adie knew all about "reason." Reverend Honeycutt had deemed it *reasonable* for her to leave Liddy's Grove while Timothy Long got nothing but a talking-to. She'd had to fight him off and had earned bruised ribs in the effort. Fuming, she managed a bite of bread.

Caroline's plate sat untouched. "What do you know about the baby's father?"

"Nothing."

"I hope you find her," Bessie said. "A single woman could have a hard time, especially with a baby. Do you have a picture of her?"

Adie went pale.

"Not anymore," he said. "I lost it in a river crossing."

The women mumbled condolences, even Adie though she felt like a liar. She was glad he'd lost the likeness of his sister. Without a picture she could dismiss the similarities between Emily and Maggie as coincidence. At least that's what she wanted to believe. In truth, she was already telling lies. Reverend Blue didn't have a picture of his sister, but Adie had one of Maggie Butler. The tintype, brownish in color, showed an oval of Maggie's face and was framed by white cardboard.

The picture had the potential to end this man's search. If Maggie and Emily were the same woman, it also had the power to rob Adie of her son. Concealing it made her feel dishonest, but she'd made a promise to Maggie. No matter the cost, she had to protect Stephen from his uncle.

"Adie?" Bessie's voice broke into her thoughts. "The reverend asked you a question."

"Your son," he repeated. "What's his name?"

"Stephen."

His eyes turned wistful. "That was my grandfather's name."

How many coincidences could she ignore? Desperate to avoid more questions, she raised her water glass to her lips and took a long sip. The liquid went down the wrong pipe and she choked.

"Raise your arms," Bessie ordered.

The coughing racked Adie's body. Bessie and Reverend Blue both shot to their feet. He was closer and reached her first. Both gentle and strong, he gripped her shoulder and thumped her back.

"I'm—" *Fine.* She choked again.

He patted harder.

Adie shoved to her feet. She needed air that didn't smell like roast and darkness that would hide her eyes as she weighed the facts. She signaled that she could breathe, then headed for the porch, where she coughed until tears streamed down her cheeks.

Josh hadn't meant to upset Adie. Since the trip to the bank, he'd figured she and Emily had walked a similar road. Now he was sure of it. Had she been shunned by her family? How had she come to own Swan's Nest? He also wondered about the father of her child. Any man worth his salt would have married her. Josh wasn't naive about the force of nature. He'd performed a shotgun wedding in Boston and two others since coming west.

He'd have performed one for Emily if he'd had the opportunity. Looking back, he saw signs that she'd been keeping a secret. For years she'd volunteered one day a week at the Greenway Home for Orphans. A few months before their argument, she'd been working three days a week and staying late. One day he'd expected her to be visiting Sarah and had paid a call. Sarah had been home, but Emily hadn't been with her. Three hours later she'd arrived home flushed and vibrant.

"Where were you, Emily?"

"Visiting friends."

"Who?"

"You don't know them."

It had been a clue, and Josh had missed it. He wished now that he'd shown more concern.

He wouldn't repeat that mistake with Adie. He wanted her to know he wouldn't throw stones. Even more important, God loved her. Because of her generosity, the ulcer had started to heal. He wanted to return the favor with food for her soul. He pushed to his feet. "If you'll excuse me, I'd like to speak to Adie."

"Of course," Bessie answered.

He filled Adie's water glass, then carried it to the porch, where he found her on the swing. He'd intended to call her Miss Clarke, but the name no longer fit. In his mind she'd become a friend, a sister like Emily.

"Adie?"

"Yes?" She sounded hoarse.

"I brought you water."

As she sipped, he ambled to the railing. The moon and stars bathed the porch in silver light. When he turned around, he saw Adie's watery eyes. Choking did that to a person, but she looked distraught for deeper reasons. He gentled his voice. "I'd like to tell you about Emily."

"Why?"

"Because you two have something in common."

Tears glistened on her cheeks. She looked terrified.

Guilt stabbed through Josh's chest. Had Emily sat on a similar swing, weeping with shame for what she'd done? He blinked and thought of the women of Swan's Nest. Pearl hadn't once looked up from her plate. Mary had scowled at him all through supper, a sign that she, too, had resentments. Bessie and Caroline looked like sisters who'd walked a hard road. Mostly, though, he wondered about Adie. The thought tripped him like a wire. He didn't want her to be special, but she was. She'd fixed his meals and offered him milk. She had a baby who needed a father, a kind heart and a head full of red hair that defied combs and pins.

Josh had never looked for a wife, nor had he met a woman who inspired such thoughts, at least not until now. Blinking, he flashed back to the times he'd hidden his laudanum bottle. If Adie had found it, she'd have spoken her mind and tossed it in the trash. She'd have held his feet to the fire in a way no one else had dared. Looking at her now, he wondered what it would be like to love a strong-minded woman.

Two seconds later, he squared his shoulders inside his coat and called himself a fool. Only Adie mattered tonight. Later he'd deal with his wayward thoughts. Hoping to appear relaxed, he leaned against the railing and got back to telling Adie about his sister. "Among other things, you and Emily are both alone."

Her lip quivered.

"You both lost families, either by choice or cruelty."

"You're right."

He barely heard the whisper. "I also know you're brave and kind. So is Emily."

She knotted her hands in her lap to hide the trembling. He couldn't stand being her enemy. "I don't know who hurt you, Adie. But I know God loves you."

"God?" Her mouth gaped.

"He's all-powerful. He's—"

"You came out here to talk about *God?*"

"Not exactly."

"Then why?"

"I could see Emily's story upset you."

"Just a little."

It had been a lot, but he let her keep her dignity. "People judge a single woman with a child. I know, because I judged my sister. I'll regret it to my dying day."

"Don't pity me, Reverend."

She spat his title. If she didn't respect it, he didn't want her to use it. "Call me Josh."

She glared at him.

"Why not?" he asked. "It's my name."

"All right," she murmured. "I'll call you Josh."

He liked the hush of it, the way it hung between them like fog. In Boston, he'd avoided being alone with women. When he made calls, he'd brought his sister. He didn't feel that need with Adie. They were equals.

"You remind me of Emily," he said.

"How so?"

"In spite of being robbed of something, you both put

others first. My sister worked in an orphanage. You take care of your boarders."

"Of course I do. They're my friends."

"It's more than that," he said. "I hurt Emily, but she didn't crawl into a hole and feel sorry for herself. She came west to make a new life. You've done the same, Adie. You're both survivors."

She put her hand to her mouth and coughed. "If you'll excuse me, I should do the dishes."

Josh had pressed her as far as he could. "I'll help."

She stood. "No, thank you."

"Really, I'd like—"

"No," she insisted. "You're a paying guest."

Josh knew about drawing lines. This one annoyed him. From what he'd observed, Adie worked harder than the Blue family servants. "Your other boarders help. So can I."

She looked peeved. "Not tonight."

"Then tomorrow."

"Fine." She stood and headed for the door. When she reached the threshold, she turned. Her shadow spoke to him in a hush. "I hope you find your sister."

"So do I."

She stepped into the house, leaving behind the scent of rosewater. Josh hadn't smelled rosewater in years. It took him back to his mother's sitting room where she'd read stories to Josh and Emily every night.

His sister felt close, or was it Adie's presence he sensed? Josh didn't know, but he had a confession to make. Deep down, he envied Adie Clarke. She had a home and a son, good friends and a belly that didn't hurt. Tonight she'd sleep in a clean bed. Tomorrow she'd bake bread. In the past year, Josh had ridden in the rain, slept in muddy caves and eaten snake for supper. He lived with an ulcer and a craving for opium. Like the Apostle Paul, he'd learned how to abase and abound, how to live well or humbly depending on the Lord's provision.

He wanted to say that he'd learned to be content in all things, Paul's declaration to the Philippians, but he couldn't make that claim. Tonight he felt a longing for the soft timbre of Adie's voice. He liked her far more than was wise for a man destined to leave. With an emptiness he didn't want to admit, he sat in the swing, bowed his head and prayed for Adie, Emily and all the women of Swan's Nest, but especially for Adie.

Adie went to the kitchen, saw that her friends had done the dishes and headed to her room. She needed to hold her son to chase away thoughts of Emily Blue. As she climbed the stairs, she thought about Josh's description of his sister and how he'd compared Adie to Emily, calling them both survivors. Maggie had called herself a survivor with pride. Adie would have described her just as Josh had described his sister. Her friend had overcome everything except death.

As Adie neared her bedroom, she heard a creak from down the hall. She turned and saw Pearl looking pale and afraid.

"Are you okay?" Adie asked.

"Can I speak with you?"

"Of course." She went to her room with Pearl, lit the lamp and checked Stephen. His little chest rose and fell in a soothing rhythm. No colic tonight. Relieved, she turned to the bed where Pearl was lying on her side to ease the pressure on her back. She looked as round as the moon.

"I'm scared," she said.

"Of what?"

"Giving birth."

"You'll do fine." Adie sounded confident, but she knew the risks. So did Pearl.

"I want you to promise me something."

Adie flashed to Maggie lying on soiled sheets. Ashen and weak, she'd made the same request as Pearl. She'd asked Adie for a promise. "What is it?"

"If something happens to me—"

"It won't."

"It could and we both know it." Pearl sounded strong, even wise. "If I don't survive the birth, I want you to give the baby to my father. I don't want Frank to even *see* my child."

Adie gripped her hand. "I promise."

"My father's a good man."

Adie wasn't so sure. Reverend Oliver had taken Dean's word over his daughter's. He struck her as stern, but Pearl loved him. "I'll do whatever you ask."

"Thank you." Pearl tightened her grip. "I'm scared."

"It's natural."

"There's more," she said. "Tonight at supper, I saw the reverend's expression when he talked about his sister. He won't stop until he finds her."

Adie thought of Josh's words on the porch. "You're right."

"As long as I'm in Denver, Frank won't leave me alone. If I left—"

"Don't even think about it." Adie recalled her earliest days with Stephen. She'd had Maggie's jewelry but no friends. No mother to take a turn rocking the colicky child. No husband to shoulder the load of food and shelter. "Being alone is harder than you know."

Pearl rested her hand on her belly. "But if I left, no one would know me. I'd have some peace."

"Maybe," Adie said gently. "But you'd have other problems, like paying rent and buying food." *And living a lie.*

Pearl sighed. "Do you think Frank would follow me?"

"I don't know."

"I *hate* it here." Her voice wobbled. "People think the baby is my fault, but he forced me. He—" She clenched her teeth, but tears still rose to her eyes.

Adie gripped Pearl's hand in understanding. Timothy Long had abused her in the Long family's attic, but she'd escaped with her purity and a shred of pride. Thanks to Maggie Butler, she'd been given a fresh start. Pearl deserved the same chance. Adie flashed on the jewelry in the trunk. Maggie would have approved of giving Pearl a nest egg, but Adie couldn't risk selling even a brooch. If the Butler family had hired a detective, pawnbrokers would be the first place he'd look for clues.

Pearl heaved a sigh. "Maybe I'll write to my cousin. She might take me in."

"Where is she?"

"Wyoming." Pearl told Adie about Carrie Hart, the daughter of her mother's sister. Carrie was about Pearl's age. When her parents passed away last year, she'd chosen to stay in Cheyenne where she taught at Miss Marlowe's School for Girls. Pearl hadn't confided in Carrie, but they exchanged occasional letters, and she knew her cousin missed having family close by.

Adie liked her. "Going to Wyoming might be smart."

"Maybe." Pearl bit her lip. "I'd still have to earn money somehow."

"If someone could watch the baby, you could teach."

"Or I could sew at home."

Neither occupation would give Pearl security, but she'd have her dignity.

"Think about it," Adie advised.

"I've been praying for *months*." Pearl wrinkled her brows. "God isn't answering."

Adie knew the feeling.

"I believe, though." Pearl wiggled to a sitting position. "And I like Reverend Blue. You have to admire a man who cares so much about his sister."

"I suppose."

"He's handsome, too."

Adie's cheeks turned pink. "I didn't notice."

"Caroline did." Pearl's eyes twinkled. "She's looking through her recipe book this very minute. She's going to bake him a pie."

The thought irked Adie beyond reason. With his weak stomach, Josh needed simple food, not a crust made from lard. Even more upsetting was the possibility that he'd like Caroline and her pie. What if he stayed in Denver? She thought of Caroline charming him and frowned. "I wish she wouldn't do it."

"Why not?"

"He doesn't belong here."

"I'm glad for it." Pearl patted her belly. "I'm as big as a horse. I might as well eat like one."

Adie smiled. "You don't look anything like a horse. You're beautiful."

With her pale hair and blue eyes, porcelain cheeks and perfect nose, Pearl had the luster of her name. She also had tears in her eyes as she touched the hard roundness of the baby.

"I'm ruined, Adie. What man would want me now?"

"A very special one."

"Do you really think there *is* such a man?"

"I do."

For the second time that night, Adie had lied. She'd told Josh she hoped he found his sister. She did, but only if the woman wasn't Maggie Butler. As for Pearl's question, Adie doubted a man that special walked the earth.

Pearl yawned. "I'm off to bed."

As the women stood and hugged, Adie felt Pearl's belly and thought of Maggie. What would she say about Swan's Nest? Adie hoped she'd be proud.

Thoughts of Stephen's mother led to an awareness of the trunk. As soon as Pearl left, Adie looked at the walnut case with its brass lock. Did Maggie's picture hold the answer to Josh's search? Adie didn't know and was afraid to find out. For now, the trunk would keep its secrets.

Chapter Six

Five days later, a noise in Adie's garden woke Josh from a fitful sleep. Living among outlaws had made him wise to danger and he felt that prickle now. He pushed aside the blanket, dressed and strode down the hall to the back door.

A sweet fragrance made him wince. Caroline had baked another pie, her third this week. Josh had endured baking sprees before, but he'd never been caught under the same roof as the woman doing the baking. Not once in Boston had he felt even a spark of interest. He did now, though not for Caroline. It was Adie who filled his thoughts.

Two days ago, she'd been working in the garden. He'd stood by the carriage house, watching from afar as she arranged the tomato vines. He'd seen her lips moving and he'd smiled. Adie talked to her plants in the same tone she spoke to Stephen. She crooned to them. Josh didn't think the plants felt a thing, but he did. Just looking at her made him feel sharper, more alive. More everything.

Being with Adie brought out Josh's humanity in the best possible way. He enjoyed the way she took care of others, the way she'd cared for him when he was ill. Her independence, a trait he suspected had been honed by loss, made him want to shield her from life's hurts. She stirred him up in a good way, but he hadn't missed the obvious. The sooner he left Denver, the better off he'd be. Yesterday he'd visited several pawnshops, but he hadn't quizzed the patrons of local saloons. He'd do it soon, though. Maybe tomorrow.

In the meantime, he wanted to know more about the noise in Adie's garden. He went out the back door, heard thumping and strode toward the noise, pausing at the woodpile to arm himself with a split of wood. He believed in turning the other cheek but only for himself. If an intruder had plans to hurt Adie, he'd do it over Josh's dead body.

Tense and wary, he rounded the house and saw a bulky shadow trampling Adie's vegetables.

"Hey!" he shouted.

The man bolted for the street. Josh dropped the wood and sprinted after him. He chased the stranger to the end of the block, but he didn't have the wind to catch him. Annoyed, he slowed to a walk, then headed back to the garden.

Moonlight revealed a methodical assault. The man had started in the corner, where he had kicked down the stakes supporting the tomatoes and trampled the vines. Next he'd flattened most of the cornstalks. The strawberries made Josh even angrier. He knew how much Adie liked strawberry jam. Red and ripe, they'd been ready for picking.

Looking at the mess, he felt a strong need for vengeance. Not only did Adie need the garden for food, but she loved it. He'd seen her on her knees, working the loamy earth with her small, pretty hands. At supper she talked about her squash and beans. The man who'd destroyed her garden had done it out of malice, and he'd done a good job.

Josh worshipped the God of mercy. He also revered the God of justice. Looking at the damage, he wanted to see Adie's assailant—or the man who'd hired him—pay for his crime. Was Dean behind the vandalism? Josh's neck hairs prickled. Unless he found a sign that Emily was in Denver, he had no reason to stay. He'd been considering where to go next, San Francisco or maybe Chicago. Tonight's assault changed his priorities. He wouldn't leave Swan's Nest until the vandal was caught.

He looked again at the damage, then fetched a rake from the toolshed. He didn't know much about gardening, but he could spare Adie the sight of the crushed vines.

After an hour, he'd swept the mess into a pile and had shoveled it into the compost heap. By the time he finished, the eastern sky had a lavender glow. Birds were chirping in the lush cottonwoods and he smelled the freshness of a Colorado dawn.

The slap of the back door broke into his thoughts. He turned and saw Adie walking to the carriage house where she'd milk Buttons. He dreaded telling her the bad news, but it had to be done. He put the tools in the shed, then went through a side door that led through the tack room to the main part of the building. Adie had her back to the door. She didn't see him, nor had she heard his footsteps. Josh paused. Buttons could be trouble and he didn't want to startle her.

Neither did he want to take his eyes off Adie. After a scratch and pat for the goat, she dropped to her knees at the animal's side. Her dress, a faded calico with tiny flowers, made a circle on the floor. A high window sent a slice of dawn across her shoulders and neatly pinned hair. Her red hair…even restrained by pins, it looked as spirited as Adie.

When was the last time he'd appreciated the simple beauty of a woman? Maybe never. He'd prided himself on being above such things, but looking at Adie he saw God's handiwork. She had a heart and soul, eyes that changed with her moods and a knack for being wise. The Lord himself had knit Adie in her mother's womb and He'd done a fine job of it.

Even so, Josh couldn't stand by the door and stare. It was unseemly, even rude. Buttons would have to cope. He cleared his throat. "Adie?"

Gasping, she pressed her hand against her chest and faced him. "You startled me!"

"Sorry."

Her brows snapped together. "Is something wrong?"

He stepped closer so he wouldn't have to shout. "Someone vandalized your garden."

"My *garden?*"

He told her about the damage. "I stopped him before he could finish it off. You still have beans and squash."

Her eyes burned. "If Dean's behind this—"

"I saw the man who did it," Josh said. "He was too stout to be Dean, but he could have been paid."

Adie rocked up from her knees. Josh stepped forward and offered his hand. As she took it, Buttons grabbed a mouthful of his shirt and pulled. Instinctively he stepped back, taking Adie with him. They ended up in a tangle with Buttons tearing his shirt. Adie stumbled into his arms. They were face to face, hands gripping each other's elbows. When she gasped, he felt the breath of it.

They stepped back at the same time. Adie grabbed

Buttons by the collar and pulled. “Stop that!” she said to the goat.

As Buttons bleated a complaint, Josh looked down at the rip in his shirt and chuckled. “That’s a first. I’ve been attacked by a goat.”

She scowled at the tear. “I’ll mend it for you.”

“Thanks.” When he left Denver, he’d have a reminder of Adie’s hands working a needle and thread. The thought warmed and saddened him at the same time.

Adie led the goat back to the milking spot. “I’ll finish with Buttons, then check the garden.”

As she dropped to her knees, Josh walked to the door to wait. Slouching against the frame, he took in her profile. She had to be frightened, but the fear didn’t show as she calmed Buttons and finished the milking. As her shoulders moved, he thought of her stumbling into his arms. Awareness had flashed in her eyes. He’d felt it, too, and he’d wondered again what it would be like to court her properly.

Had Adie wondered, as well? Guilt welled in his belly. He had no business thinking about a future with Adie Clarke. As soon as the vandal and his cohorts went to jail, Josh would leave Denver. Somewhere, Emily needed him.

Adie pushed to her feet. “I’m done.”

Josh opened the door. As she walked through it, her skirt dusted his boots and the sun reflected off the crown of her head. With the scent of cotton filling his nose, he waited while she walked to the house. She left the bucket on the first step, then returned to the carriage house. As she looked toward the garden, her eyes dimmed. “I better see the mess for myself.”

“I cleaned up,” he said as they walked down the path. “But it’s not pretty.”

"Thank you."

"I wish I'd caught whoever did this."

When the damage came into view, Adie gasped. Leaving Josh at the edge of the plot, she went to the corn, dropped to a crouch and touched a broken stalk. She stood, propped up a stake and arranged a single tomato vine. When she looked at the remains of the strawberry plants, she pressed her hand to her lips and whimpered. A woman's tears had never dampened Josh's shirt, but he didn't think twice about stepping to Adie's side.

He touched her back. "I'm sorry. I know what the garden means to you."

Instead of turning to him, she stiffened. "I have work to do. I have to replant."

"I'll help." When a tremor shot up her spine, he wanted to bloody Franklin Dean's nose. He settled for glaring at the corn. "We need to call the sheriff."

"No!"

Her reaction didn't make sense. "Why not?"

Adie took three steps away from him. She seemed to be staring across the street, but Josh sensed she was hiding her eyes. "There's no point," she finally said. "Dean owns Denver and everyone in it."

"He doesn't own *me.* I'll hire an attorney. I'll—"

"You'll do *nothing.*"

"Adie—"

She faced him. "Pearl's involved, too. She wants her privacy."

"But—"

"But nothing!"

Josh didn't care for one-sided conversations, but he couldn't force Adie to share her thoughts. "All right," he said. "I'll respect your wishes."

"Good."

"I don't like it, though."

She glared at him. "It's none of your concern. You'll be leaving soon."

"No, I'm not."

Her mouth gaped. "But—"

"I won't leave until you're safe… Pearl, too."

Josh didn't want to butt in to Pearl's life, but someone had to speak candidly with her father. When the time was right, he'd visit Colfax Avenue Church.

Adie stood glaring at him. "There's another problem."

"What's that?"

"You can't stay here indefinitely."

"Why not?"

"Our agreement was for two weeks."

"So we can change it."

"I don't want to. As I said, I don't rent to men. I made an exception, but it's awkward."

Josh couldn't disagree. Between his feelings for Adie and Caroline's baking, he felt like a black swan among five white ones. He had to stifle his tender feelings for Adie but not the urge to keep her safe. "Dean wants to harm you," he said in a sure voice. "If you think I can leave now, you've misjudged my character."

No, she hadn't. Josh had washed dishes and fixed the roof. He'd cleaned up after Buttons and filled the wood box. He had a good heart. He hadn't asked about Emily again, and Adie could almost believe he wasn't Maggie's brother. She'd decided to let sleeping dogs lie, but if Josh stayed in Denver, those dogs would wake up and bark. She had to convince him to leave.

Apart from her worries about Stephen, she didn't like the way he made her feel. When he looked into her eyes, she saw a man full of hope and kindness. He knew how to laugh and when to cry. He didn't resemble Reverend Honeycutt in the least, but he still wore a black coat and believed in God. Adie believed in God, but she wanted nothing to do with Him.

She and Josh lived on opposites sides of an endless fence and she didn't see a gate. Never mind his blue eyes, bright with anger and ready to fight. Never mind the sight of his arms laced stubbornly across his chest. She couldn't let this man fight her battles. Franklin Dean posed a threat to Adie's house, but Josh could take her son. The sooner he left Denver, the safer she'd be. She squared her shoulders. "I still want you to leave."

"I can't."

"Find a hotel."

He lowered his chin. "I'll pay triple."

Oh, how she needed the money.... "No."

"Four times."

Her mouth gaped. The amount would cover half the mortgage. She could afford a new dress.

"Five—"

"Stop." Her greed shamed her. Stephen mattered more, but she desperately needed the money. Every month she lived in fear of selling Maggie's jewelry and being discovered. If Josh stayed at Swan's Nest, she could keep the trunk closed a little longer.

"You win," she said. "You can stay."

He looked pleased.

"But four times the rent is too much."

"I don't think it's enough." His eyes locked with hers. "Our deal was for two meals a day, but I'm getting breakfast, lunch and supper. I have a place to sleep, company in the evenings. I've never had it so good."

Maggie's brother, a wealthy man, wouldn't have been

impressed by Swan's Nest and her humble meals. Josh enjoyed simple things as she did. He'd also saved her garden from total devastation. She owed him her gratitude, if not the truth.

"All right," she said. "We'll keep the current deal."

She considered telling him not to pay double, but she knew he'd argue.

"Agreed," he said.

Why did she feel light-headed? "Are you hungry?"

"Bacon and eggs?"

She smiled. "Biscuits, too."

Together they walked to the house. When they reached the steps, Josh lifted the milk bucket and held the door. As they stepped inside, Caroline came into the kitchen holding Stephen. Adie reached for the baby. Aware of Josh's eyes on her back, she felt goose bumps rising on her back and arms. The less Josh saw of Stephen, the safer she'd feel.

Caroline greeted her, then turned to Josh. "Good morning, Reverend. You're up early."

"It's a fine day."

Caroline beamed. "'This is the day the Lord hath made. We will rejoice and be glad in it.'"

Adie didn't need Caroline to quote Bible verses. Neither, apparently, did Josh. He looked uncomfortable.

Caroline gave a too-cheerful smile. "Would you like breakfast, Reverend? I'd be happy to fry some eggs."

"I'm doing it," Adie said.

"You have Stephen." Caroline lifted a fry pan from the rack on the wall. "He's hungry, plus he'll need a fresh nappy."

Josh gave Adie a look she could read like her own thoughts. He had no interest in Caroline and her fried eggs. Neither would he be the rope in a tug-of-war. "Milk and bread would be fine."

With Stephen on her hip, Adie set the bucket on the counter, then poured a glass of milk for Josh from the pitcher. The baby smelled food and cooed. She would have treasured the moment, except Caroline was buttering bread for Josh. She also had to tell her friend about the garden.

She looked over her shoulder at Caroline. "I have some bad news."

"What happened?"

Adie told her about the vegetables and how Josh chased off the vandal. When she finished the story, Caroline looked at Josh as if he could walk on water. "You're a brave man, Reverend. You could have been hurt."

He looked more annoyed than before. "It was nothing."

"*I* don't think so!" She set a plate of bread in front of him. "Whoever did it could have turned on you."

Mary walked into the kitchen. "What happened?"

Caroline faced her. "Someone trampled the garden. The reverend chased him off." She turned to Adie. "We have to go to the sheriff."

Mary huffed. "It won't help."

"It might," Caroline insisted.

Adie felt Josh's gaze on her cheek. She couldn't protest without sounding desperate. She looked to Mary for help, but Mary shrugged. "I guess it's worth a try."

"I'll go this morning," Josh said.

He looked to Adie for approval. She didn't want to give it, but how could she say no? She thought of using Pearl but felt terrible for the thought. Deep down, she knew Dean had to be stopped and Pearl couldn't do it alone. If Adie didn't step up, who would? As much as she wanted to go to the law, the thought terrified her. What if a Pinkerton's detective had visited the sheriff with questions about Maggie Butler? For all Adie knew, Maggie's brother could have distributed posters with his sister's likeness. Adie held Stephen tighter. With a little luck, nothing in the sheriff's office would link Maggie Butler and Emily Blue. If it did, she might have to flee Denver.

Barely breathing, she watched as Caroline poured coffee for Josh and then herself. She loved her house and her friends, but she loved her son more.

Shortly after breakfast, Josh changed into his black coat and left Swan's Nest. The milk and toast had settled nicely, but he regretted the coffee. His stomach burned as he walked into the flat-front building that housed the Denver sheriff's office.

A man in a leather vest with a badge stood up behind the desk. "Good morning, Reverend. Can I help you?"

"I hope so." Josh introduced himself. "Someone vandalized Swan's Nest last night."

"The boardinghouse on Seventeenth?"

"That's it."

The deputy offered his hand. "I'm Beau Morgan." He indicated a battered chair. "Have a seat."

Josh sat on the wood, then told the story. "I'm worried, Deputy. Someone wants to harm Miss Clarke."

"Any thoughts on who?"

"Franklin Dean paid a call recently. To put it mildly, he forgot his manners."

Morgan's brow furrowed. "He owns the bank."

As if that mattered, Josh thought. Evil men came in all shapes and sizes. Some had money. Others didn't.

"He also trespassed on Miss Clarke's property. I saw it." Josh left Pearl out of the conversation. He wanted to see Dean punished, but he didn't have the right to tell her story.

The deputy wrinkled his brow. "Anyone could have vandalized the garden, but I could have a chat with Mr. Dean."

"I don't think that's wise," Josh answered. "If he's pressured, he might do something even worse."

"Personally, I don't care for the man." Morgan looked as if he'd gotten a whiff of bad meat. "Rumor has it Dean roughed up one of Miss Elsa's girls. I'll ask around town, quietly of course. Can you describe the man you saw?"

"Average height. Stocky build." Josh thought of the chase down the street. "He's fast on his feet."

"Anything else?"

Josh had two missions today. He'd done his best for Adie. Now he could focus on Emily. "It's unrelated, but I'm looking for my sister." He described her and mentioned she had a baby. For the hundredth time, he wished he had the oval tintype.

"I can see why you went to Swan's Nest," Morgan said. "Miss Clarke's new in town, but she's got a reputation."

"For what?"

"Helping women in trouble." The deputy chuckled. "I'm surprised she gave you a room."

"Why?"

"She chased Clint Hughes off with a shotgun. He had it coming, though. The drunken fool nearly busted down her door."

Josh was glad he'd faced Mary's pistol instead of Adie and two barrels of buckshot. He focused back on

Emily. "If you see anyone resembling my sister, I'd like to know."

"Sure."

The men shook hands and Josh went back to the street. He climbed on his horse and rode to Fourteenth Street where he hoped to find a quality jewelry shop. Emily's jewels were worth a fortune but only if someone had the money to buy them. If she'd come to Denver, she'd been wise. What with mining interests, the railroad, commerce and cattle, the city had men who'd want fancy jewels for their wives.

As Josh approached the corner of Broadway and Colfax Avenue, he saw the steeple of Colfax Avenue Church. On a whim, he turned and rode past the magnificent building. He wanted to go inside, but today the doors looked intimidating. Entering the church would send him back to Boston. He'd recall the crowds and the rapture of the choir. He'd also hear the ring of his own voice.

Josh was certain he'd been born to preach. He'd felt the call at a young age and had flourished under his grandfather's mentoring. The question had never been *should* he preach, but where? Not in a church like this. Not anymore. Feeling bittersweet, he clicked to his horse and headed for a row of shops. He spotted a jewelry store and went inside. A balding man came out from behind a black curtain.

"Good morning," he said in a German accent.

Josh glanced around the spartan room with a sinking heart. He saw gold, silver and turquoise but nothing like Emily's pearls or other pieces.

"I'm looking for fine jewels," he said.

"A diamond, perhaps?"

"Possibly. May I see what you have?"

The man came out with a tray of rings on black velvet. Josh didn't recognize a single one, but he felt the heartache shining in the stones. What made a woman sell a precious ring? Need and desperation… His heart pounded for Emily's suffering.

"Thank you, sir." Josh wrote his name on a card. "I'm staying at Swan's Nest. If something new comes in, would you contact me?"

"My pleasure."

Josh left the store and headed into the heart of Denver where he visited three pawnbrokers but saw nothing of interest. The next stop tore him up inside, but it had to be made. He walked into an establishment called Brick's Saloon where a burly man was sweeping the floor. Judging by his size and red hair, he had to be Brick.

The man looked Josh up and down. "Kind of early for preaching, ain't it, Reverend?"

"I'm not here to preach," Josh said. "I'm looking for a woman."

Brick kept sweeping.

"She's got dark hair, the same as mine."

As Josh had hoped, Brick looked him in the eye. "Why do you want her?"

"She's my sister."

The man set the broom against the wall, stepped behind the counter and poured Josh a glass of water. "Here."

Josh took a sip and waited. He'd learned to let people tell their stories in their own time. The barkeep busied his hands by wiping the counter, but his mind seemed to be a hundred miles away. When he'd wiped the last inch of the wood, he looked at Josh. "I have a sister, too."

"What's her name?"

"Jenny."

"Is she in Denver?"

"Nope. Don't know where she went." The man looked as broken as Josh felt. "She ran off with a two-timing rat. My little sister—" The man cursed.

"I'm sorry."

"Me, too." Brick looked at Josh. "You gotta picture of your sister?"

"Not anymore." Josh gave Emily's description.

Brick kept wiping the counter. "Miss Elsa's Social Club is on Walnut, just past Fifteenth Street. If your sister's gone down that road, that's the place to look."

Josh headed for the door.

The barkeep called after him, "Come back again, Reverend. Coffee's on the house."

"I'll do that," Josh replied.

He felt at home with men like Brick. On a whim, he looked back and saw the barkeep neatly folding the towel. "Are you open on Sunday morning?" he asked.

"No, sir."

"Mind if I hold a church service here?"

Brick scowled. "I don't see why. There's lots of churches in Denver."

"And lots of people," Josh added. "Not everyone's comfortable in the same place."

The barkeeper grunted. "I know how it is."

Unfortunately, so did Josh. His Boston congregation had been well heeled and as proud as he'd been. Josh no longer saw "church" as four walls and twenty rows of mahogany pews. Now he held services anywhere, anytime.

Brick shrugged. "I guess there's no harm."

"Then spread the word," he said. "I'll be here on Sunday. The service starts at ten."

Brick grinned. "I'll do that."

Josh left the saloon, climbed on his horse and headed to Walnut. His spirits sank as he neared a mansion built in the style of the South. White and proud, Miss Elsa's Social Club had tall columns, long windows and a veranda where he saw four women sipping tea. He spoke from atop his horse. "Good morning, ladies."

Another woman came through the door. Tall and slender, almost emaciated in Josh's opinion, she wore a gold silk gown. In spite of her rouged cheeks and dyed hair, she looked several years older than the girls on the veranda.

"Good morning, Reverend. I'm Miss Elsa."

He tipped his hat. "I'm Joshua Blue, out of Boston."

"What can I do for you?"

The invitation in her voice was unmistakable. Before he left, Josh vowed to make an invitation of his own. "I'm looking for someone."

The girls on the veranda stared with desperation, as if they were hoping he'd come for them. In a way, he had. Every time he reached out for Emily, he prayed for women in her predicament.

"My sister's name is Emily," he said to the girls. "Maybe you've seen her." For the third time that day, he described her dark hair and eyes.

Miss Elsa's expression revealed nothing. "I can't help you, Reverend. We keep secrets here."

She paused to let her meaning sink in. If Emily had been inside, the madam wouldn't tell him. She'd also implied that she'd keep secrets for Josh. If Miss Elsa thought she could tempt him, she was flat-out wrong. He didn't see pleasure sitting on her porch. He saw four Mary Magdalenes in need of rescue. Josh focused on the girls. They ranged in age from young to bitter. He didn't know which broke his heart more.

He looked each one in the eye, then said, "I'm starting a church. You're all invited to Brick's Saloon on Sunday at ten."

Two of the women sneered. One stared at her toes. He looked at the fourth girl and saw hope.

He focused on the girl with the hopeful eyes. "I hope to see you there."

After a nod to Miss Elsa, he turned his horse down the road and headed back to Swan's Nest. He had a sermon to write. He also needed someone who could carry a tune. He'd sing if he had to, but it wasn't pretty. As he neared Swan's Nest, he thought about refreshments. He wouldn't ask Caroline to bake cookies, but she'd probably think of it herself.

Would Adie come? He hoped so, but he didn't think she would. Last night at supper, Caroline and Pearl had asked him to lead a Bible Study. Josh had agreed and they'd made plans for Thursday. Bessie liked the idea and even Mary said she'd attend. Adie hadn't said a word. She'd made it clear that she didn't think much of churches and the men who ran them. Josh wanted to know why. When the time was right, he'd ask.

Chapter Seven

Alone in the kitchen with Stephen on her hip, Adie tapped her toe as she waited for his milk to warm. Laughter filtered down the hallway from the parlor where her boarders had gathered for Josh's Bible study. He'd stepped outside and would be back any minute. Adie wanted to be upstairs before he came through the door.

As she tested the milk, Mary walked into the kitchen. "You're not going to hide in your room, are you?"

"I'm not *hiding,*" Adie replied. "I'm going to feed Stephen and put him to bed."

"Feed him downstairs."

"He'll make too much noise."

"Nonsense!"

"No, it's not," Adie insisted.

Mary's eyes twinkled. "You know what I think?"

"No, but you're going to tell me."

"I think you like the reverend…a lot."

"Mary!"

"See?" The saloon girl sounded wise. "Women only avoid men they care about. It can be love, hate or fear.

No one hates Josh. He's a gentleman. Even *I* like him. There's no reason to fear him. That leaves—"

"Don't be ridiculous!"

The back door opened in the middle of her protest. Smiling, Josh looked from Mary to Adie. "What's ridiculous?"

Adie turned to the stove to hide the pink stain on her cheeks.

Mary nudged her elbow as if they'd been sharing a joke. "It's girl talk, Reverend. I'm trying to get Adie to stay for the Bible study."

Of all the confounded choices… If she said no, Mary would think she had feelings for Josh. If she said yes, she'd have to sit through a harangue with Stephen in her lap. Adie had heard enough scripture from Old Man Long to last a lifetime. At night the family would sit in a circle while he read. Sometimes he thundered just at her.

Adie couldn't see Josh thundering at anyone. On the other hand, she could imagine Mary teasing her for days. She needed a way out.

She looked to Josh for an excuse. "What if Stephen cries?"

"So what?"

"Babies fuss. Back in Kansas—" Adie sealed her lips. She'd slipped, badly. Emily had been in Kansas.

Mentioning it had to rouse his curiosity, but he looked disinterested. "This isn't Kansas."

Without a bit of hesitation, he walked out of the kitchen, leaving her alone with Mary. Without an excuse, Adie shrugged. "I'll go, but I warned you about Stephen."

Mary's eyes twinkled with mischief, but she kept silent.

Adie lifted the bottle from the pot of water and followed her to the parlor. She saw Caroline and Bessie on the divan and Pearl on a hard chair from the dining room. She preferred it for her back. Josh was sitting in the armchair. Mary gave Adie the rocker next to him and squeezed onto the divan.

When the women were settled, he opened his Bible. "Ladies, shall we pray?"

Adie thought of Old Man Long. She wished she hadn't come, but she couldn't leave now.

The women bowed their heads. Adie followed their lead, but her neck ached with old resentments. In the Long home, she'd worked from dawn to dusk. Once she'd fallen asleep during the Bible reading and Old Man Long had slapped her for showing disrespect. As Josh asked the Lord to open their hearts, Adie's chest ached. She'd been eight when her father went to pan gold and never returned. She'd been twelve when her mother died and sixteen when Timothy Long had trapped her in the attic. Where was God on that miserable night?

"Amen." Josh's voice rang with a joy Adie didn't feel. He looked at her, then scanned the other faces. "Before we start, I have an announcement. This Sunday at ten o'clock, I'm holding a church service."

Pearl looked pleased. "Where?"

"At Brick's Saloon."

"A saloon!" said Caroline.

Mary raised an eyebrow. "What's wrong with that?"

"I'm just surprised," Caroline answered.

So was Adie.

Bessie smiled. "It sounds like you're putting down roots, Reverend."

"No," he said. "I'm just planting seeds. Someone else will tend them when I'm gone." He scanned their faces, stopping when he reached Adie. "You're all invited. In fact, I'm hoping for a little help."

"What do you need?" Caroline asked.

"Cookies would be nice."

"I'll make macaroons."

"Can anyone sing?" Josh asked.

Mary's face lit up with interest, but just as quickly her smile sagged. "I used to."

"Then you still can," he said. "Any hymn would do."

"Can I think about it?" she asked.

"Sure."

He looked at Adie but said nothing. She hid her eyes by staring at Stephen's nose.

Josh went back to business. "I thought we'd talk about a Psalm tonight. Any suggestions?"

Caroline, seated on Josh's left, looked poised in a blue dress with a lace scarf draped around her neck. She'd washed her face and repinned her hair. Across from her, Adie felt like an out-of-place sparrow. Her brown dress had a spot on the bodice, and her hair had become untidy.

Caroline smiled demurely. "You pick, Reverend. I'm sure you have a favorite."

"I do."

Josh closed the Bible and recited words that Adie had never heard.

"O Lord, Thou hast searched me, and known me.

Thou knowest my downsitting and mine uprising,
thou understandeth my thoughts afar off."

His voice went deep and low, slowing as the psalmist described his inability to hide himself from God, then soaring with the awareness of God's infinite presence. He spoke about darkness and light being alike to God, how the writer had been fearfully and wonderfully made in his mother's womb. How many times had Adie marveled at Stephen's toes? She had no trouble believing in God, but she didn't believe He loved His children like an earthly father. She'd lived through too much heartache.

Josh, though, spoke with power and compassion. Adie imagined him in a Boston cathedral and felt both awed and afraid. With the next verse, he focused on her.

> "Search me, O God, and know my heart. Try me and know my thoughts."

Adie didn't want anyone to know her thoughts. She feared being found by Maggie's brother and dreaded losing Stephen. Still focused on her face, Josh's eyes filled with compassion, as if he were confessing his own anxious thoughts, his own worries. His voice gentled to a plea.

> "See if there be any hurtful way in me, and lead me in Your way everlasting."

Still holding her gaze, he whispered, "Amen."

Adie didn't want to hurt anyone, especially not Josh. Sometimes he reminded her so much of Maggie that her stomach knotted. Other times she felt certain that this good man couldn't possibly be the ogre who'd driven Maggie from her home. The trunk held the answer, but she couldn't bear the thought of opening it and losing her son.

Mary looked thoughtful. "Tell us, Reverend. Why is this Psalm your favorite?"

"It keeps me humble."

Maggie's brother didn't know the meaning of the word. Feeling safer, Adie dared to look at his face.

His eyes glistened with the lamplight. "Back in Boston, I was an arrogant know-it-all. Deep down, I'm still that man."

"No, you're not!" Caroline insisted.

When Josh gave her a firm look, Adie felt oddly pleased.

"No, Caroline," he said gently. "I *am* that man. Left to myself, I'm as prideful as ever. This Psalm reminds me that God knows me inside and out. He's with me, even when I stumble. He's with each of you."

Bessie looked wise and Mary seemed hopeful. Pearl was rubbing her belly as if to caress the baby, and Caroline had a worshipful expression Adie found irritating. As for herself, she didn't believe a word Josh had said. Where was God when her mother died in the middle of the night? Adie had been alone at her bedside. She'd tried to dig the grave herself, but the task had been too great. She'd gone to Reverend Honeycutt for help and her life had turned wretched. And what about Maggie? She'd endured a hard labor and then died for her effort. Adie looked down at Stephen. She hadn't been paying attention and he'd chugged half his bottle. He needed to be burped, so she raised him to her shoulder.

Josh watched the baby with stark longing. "God loves my sister, too."

Adie wondered.

"Have you heard anything?" Bessie asked.

"No, but I've been asking around town." He told them about his trip to the saloon and vaguely mentioned Miss Elsa's Social Club. "At least I know where she's *not*."

"That's a help," Mary said.

Caroline looked concerned. "Did she have money when she left?"

"Her jewelry."

Adie's hand froze on Stephen's back.

"Did you check the pawnbrokers?" Mary asked. "That's what I do. I'd sell it and start over."

"I hope she did," Josh answered. "I left word around town that I'm looking for certain items."

"Like what?" Caroline said.

Before Josh could answer, Stephen let out an angry cry. As Adie shifted him to her other shoulder, he lost the contents of his tummy. Sour milk dripped down the front of her dress.

"Ick," said Mary.

Pearl turned green.

Bessie headed for the kitchen. "I'll get a towel."

Caroline stood to help her, but Josh stepped in front of her. "I'll hold him. You go change."

Before Adie could protest, he lifted the stinky, crying baby into his arms and held him as if he'd been given a precious gift. Still in the chair, Adie looked up at Josh, watching as he focused on Stephen and crooned. Would he see Maggie's nose? Her heart-shaped face? Breathless, she waited for a glimmer of recognition. Instead she saw the most generous kind of love. There was Stephen, reeking of spit-up, kicking and crying. Yet in Josh's eyes she saw nothing but joy. Compassion, too. The man knew about stomach trouble. Standing tall, he swayed with the baby in his arms, making silly talk until Stephen quieted.

He looked down at Adie. "He's beautiful."

"Thank you."

"He has your eyes."

Icy tingles ripped down her spine, leaving her numb with fear. Her boarders knew she'd adopted Stephen. Once, during a thunderstorm, they'd each shared a secret. Stephen's adoption had been hers. She'd never described Maggie or told her friend's story, but they knew Stephen's eyes would never match hers.

Mary and Pearl didn't react, but Caroline stared at her.

"Go change," Josh repeated. "We'll wait for you."

Adie wanted to grab her son and run. Instead she calmly walked to her room, where moonlight poured through the window. When she reached the trunk, she fell to her knees and wept. "Help me, Maggie. I don't know what to do."

She'd spoken to her friend's memory, but Adie felt the presence of the God in Josh's Psalm. He could see her now, on her knees and torn to pieces. Adie didn't feel fearfully and wonderfully made. She felt wicked and deceitful for what she'd done.

She touched the lock with her fingertips, pressing until the brass felt warm. If she stood, she could fetch the key from the drawer. With a turn of her wrist, she could be free of her guilt. She'd show Josh the picture, he'd shake his head no and her worries would end. But the risk… If Maggie Butler and Emily Blue were the same woman, Josh would take his nephew home to Boston. Adie would lose her son. She'd purchased Swan's Nest with Maggie's money. He'd have the right to take her home. Where would Pearl go? What would happen to her friends? To her?

Her fingers slid away from the lock. The risk was too great. Determined to compose herself, she stumbled to her feet and put on fresh clothes, dawdling with the hope that Josh would give up and go to his room.

She'd heard enough Bible reading for tonight…enough for the rest of her life. After several minutes, she went downstairs to fetch Stephen.

"Adie's taking her sweet time," Caroline said irritably.

Josh barely heard her. He was holding Stephen and couldn't take his eyes off the boy's face. In Boston, he'd christened babies in front of huge crowds. He'd enjoyed the moment, but his heart hadn't stirred the way it did for Adie's son.

Earlier Bessie had cleaned the child up. She'd wiped his face with a damp rag, then changed him into a baby gown she'd fetched from the laundry room. She'd offered to hold him, but Josh had said no. He hadn't felt this peaceful in months, maybe never. He thought of Adie alone in her room. The Psalm had touched her, he felt sure of it. He hoped it touched everyone. Of the five women at Swan's Nest, Bessie had the calmest disposition, but she also had an air of sorrow. Pearl was the most anxious. Caroline desperately needed someone to love and Mary needed someone to fight. That left Adie. What did *she* need?

A husband.

A friend.

Someone who'd protect her from Franklin Dean and pay the mortgage, a man who'd teach Stephen to fish and to read, to respect all men and fight for the people he'd come to love. Not once in Josh's life had he wanted to be a father, but he did now. Looking at Adie's son, he felt a connection that defied logic. The feeling stretched to Adie, too.

He'd glimpsed her face just before Stephen lost his supper. She'd gone pale. Why? He'd been talking about

Emily, but he hadn't been critical of anyone but himself. If he'd hurt Adie's feelings, he wanted to apologize. As a man, he couldn't stand the thought of her tears. As a minister, he wanted her to be at peace with herself and the Lord. He wanted to speak to her but not tonight. He'd had an upset of his own. She'd looked lovely in the lamplight and he'd caught himself looking twice, even a third time. Adie made him weak in the knees. Before he spent time with her, he had some praying to do.

"Let's call it a night," he said to the group.

Caroline frowned. "We could start without Adie."

Josh held in a groan. Caroline had many fine traits, but he had no interest in her as a woman. Yesterday she'd offered to mend his shirts. He'd said no. He'd also imagined Adie's fingers sewing the tear made by Buttons. Looking at her tonight, covered with the mess from Stephen, he'd imagined the joys he'd forsaken for the benefit of his calling. A wife…a child. He couldn't go down that road, not with Emily missing and his history of pride.

"We'll continue next week," he said to the women.

Caroline smiled demurely. "It's a lovely Psalm, Reverend."

Lovely wasn't how Josh would have described the words he'd just read. David, a gifted poet and powerful king, had known the torment of bad decisions.

Caroline said good-night and headed for the stairs. Mary and Pearl followed. Bessie watched them leave, then faced Josh. "May I speak with you, Reverend?"

"Of course."

"It's about Adie."

He avoided gossip, but people often spoke to him in confidence about family members. The women at Swan's Nest were sisters. "You sound worried."

She lowered her voice. "Be kind to her."

Had he been *un*-kind? "I don't understand."

"I know you don't, but you will. She and Stephen had a hard beginning. Your sister's story hits close to home."

"That's what I thought."

"She's afraid."

"Of what?"

"You, I think."

Josh had seen that same fear in outlaw camps. It lived in the eyes of men who'd murdered and thought they were beyond mercy. Guilt wore a person to bare bones, and he feared Adie lived with that despair. He couldn't stand the thought, especially while holding her son.

"When the time's right, I'll speak to her," he said to Bessie.

"Don't wait."

He felt the same urgency. "I'll do it tomorrow."

"Tonight," she insisted.

Before he could reply, Adie entered the parlor. She'd changed from the brown calico into the coppery dress that matched her hair. The color reminded him of maple leaves. Maples reminded him of home—not the mansion in Boston, but the home in his heart, the place he went when he closed his eyes and laid his humanity at God's feet. Somehow Adie and home had become one thought. The realization shocked him to the core. He had no business thinking of Adie in that way. He had to find his sister and the search might never end.

Looking at her now, Josh knew he wasn't the only troubled soul in the room. Her eyes had a dullness he'd never seen before, and her skin had gone from rosy to pallid. Bessie was right. He had to speak with her tonight.

Stephen had fallen asleep. Without meeting Josh's

gaze, Adie reached for her son. “It’s his bedtime. I’ll take him upstairs.”

Bessie cut in front of her. “I’ll do it.”

“No,” she insisted. “You’ve done enough.”

Josh maneuvered Stephen into the nurse’s arms. “If you don’t mind, Adie. I’d like a word with you.”

She looked ready to grab the baby and bolt, but Bessie had a firm hold. As the women locked eyes, Josh saw compassion in Bessie’s gaze and fear in Adie’s. The nurse didn’t give an inch. Defeated, Adie lowered her arms and turned to Josh with a hard look in her eyes. She was poised for a fight, which he didn’t mind at all. When it came to Adie, he welcomed the challenge.

As Bessie climbed the stairs, he turned up the lamp. He couldn’t change darkness to light, but the wick did a fair imitation. He indicated the divan. “Please, sit down.”

Adie stepped by him and turned down the lamp. “If you don’t mind, it’s too bright for my eyes.”

Josh *did* mind, but for all the wrong reasons. Darkness and light were alike to the Lord but not to Josh. He didn’t want to be alone with her in the shadows. The dark kept secrets. It hid the truth and led down a dangerous road. He considered postponing their talk, but Adie looked like a bird caught in a net, as if she wanted to escape but had nowhere to go.

He sat on the armchair. “You have a beautiful little boy.”

“Thank you.”

“It’s none of my business,” he said gently. “But you seem troubled whenever I mention Emily.”

Her eyes narrowed. “What do you mean?”

“When I say her name, you look pained.”

“I do?”

“Every time. I’m wondering why.”

Chapter Eight

How much did Josh know? Was he toying with her? Maggie's brother would have done such a thing, but Josh wouldn't. From the day he'd arrived, he'd treated her with respect, even kindness. He also wore a black coat and carried a Bible, signs that he couldn't be trusted. Looking at him now, Adie felt more confused than ever. His mouth had settled into a gentle curve, and his eyes held only compassion. No wonder Caroline had baked six pies and three cakes. Josh was a handsome man. Even more frightening, he inspired trust.

So had Timothy Long.

So had Reverend Honeycutt.

Adie prepared herself for a fight. She'd do anything to keep her promise to Maggie Butler. She had to protect Stephen at all costs, even Josh's peace of mind. She homed her gaze to his too-blue eyes. "Emily's story upsets me. I can't imagine."

Except like Emily, she'd been deceived by a minister and forced to leave the town she'd called home. She knew exactly how Josh's sister had felt. She'd lied again.

Judging by the look in his eyes, Josh knew it, too.

She folded her hands in her lap. "I guess I can *imag-*

ine it, but I haven't *exactly* been in that position." With her cheeks flaming, she jerked her eyes away from his. She'd done it again—said too much and raised questions.

"Adie?"

She said nothing.

"Please," he said gently. "Look at me."

She couldn't, not with lies still sour on her tongue. She closed her eyes, but she couldn't escape the sense of Josh's gaze. She heard the slight rustle of his coat, then felt the warmth of his fingers on her chin, urging her to look up. When she finally gave in, she found herself staring into his eyes and feeling a kinship she'd never known. Not with her father… Not with anyone.

He held her gaze but lowered his hand. The warmth of him lingered like the scent of bread. He looked as unsteady as she felt. "I want to tell you about the night Emily left."

Her heart cried no, but she nodded yes. She hurt for this man. She also feared him. Of the two, the hurting weighed more than the fear, at least for now. "I'm listening."

He sat back in the chair. "Talking about Emily hurts worse than giving up laudanum."

"Then it hurts a lot."

His face went rigid. "The story begins three years before Emily left. I'm not bragging when I say I had everything—the biggest church in Boston, respect from my peers. I felt God's hand on my life in a way I can't describe."

"In a good way?" She couldn't imagine.

"The best."

"What happened?"

"I got prideful. Greedy, too. If fifty people came to

hear me preach, I wanted a hundred. I worked to make it happen. I told myself I was doing God's work, but somehow I lost my way. I prayed but didn't listen for answers. I told God what I thought and assumed He'd agree."

Adie couldn't imagine anyone talking to God. Old Man Long had bellowed about sin and salvation in the same tone he used to call the pigs. Josh's faith fascinated her. So did the hard line of his jaw and the hint of whiskers. She saw a man with feelings, hopes and failures, a man who also wore a preacher's collar.

He gave a half smile. "My downfall started with a bellyache."

"The ulcer?"

"A small one, but I refused to slow down. I didn't eat right. Didn't get enough rest. When the pain became intolerable, I went to a doctor. Not to our family physician, but to a man who didn't know me. I didn't want anyone in the church to know I had a weakness." Josh looked her in the eye. "Secrets are dangerous. They're a sign that something's amiss with a person's soul. I know, because I've kept my own."

Her insides started to quake.

"I don't know what your secret is, but I suspect it has to do with Stephen and how he came into this world."

She struggled to breathe evenly. "What do you mean?"

"Emily left home because I shamed her. I cared more about my reputation than I did about her." He raked his hand through his hair, leaving furrows. "She left because I told her to stay with cousins in Providence. I wanted her to give her baby away."

Maggie... Emily... The stories matched again in perfect, undeniable detail.

"I didn't ask her about the father," Josh continued. "For all I know, she'd been attacked and was afraid to tell me. Or maybe she was in love. I hope so. The thought of violence—" He sealed his lips. "I'd rather think she was in love and fell to the oldest temptation in the world."

Adie didn't know Maggie's whole story, but she knew her friend had loved the father of her child. He'd died and she'd been grieving when they'd met. She wanted to offer Josh that comfort, but she couldn't do it without opening the trunk. She didn't want to hear another word about Emily, but she felt compelled to reach out to Josh. "How old is your sister?"

"Twenty-four."

Maggie had been twenty-three when they'd met. Her birthday would have been in April.

"Emily had suitors," Josh added. "But she never said yes to marriage. Before our mother died, she made sure Emily met suitable men. She encouraged her to find a husband, but I didn't. I had the benefits of a hostess without the complications of a wife."

"Maybe she didn't want to marry."

"I doubt that."

"Why?"

"Emily loved children."

So had Maggie. The two women had sometimes talked of marriage. Adie felt intimidated by it, but Maggie had no such reluctance. In spite of her grief for Stephen's father, she'd told Adie that she didn't regret falling in love, only the mistakes that followed. If she'd lived, she'd have married and had more children.

Adie looked for another consolation for Josh. "Maybe she went to the baby's father."

"Or else she's alone somewhere."

"You don't know that."

His eyes burned into hers. "What about you, Adie? Were you alone when Stephen was born?"

Blood drained from her face. "No."

"Losing my sister changed me." He leaned forward in the chair. "I failed Emily. I won't fail you and Stephen."

"I don't need your help."

"I think you do," he said. "Someone trampled your garden. I see you counting pennies."

"Thank you, but I can manage on my own."

She pushed to her feet. Josh stood, too. When she turned, he pinned her in place with his eyes. "I don't know who hurt you, Adie. But I know God loves you. Whatever it is that upsets you when I say Emily's name, put it down."

She wanted to run from the room. She settled for looking down at his boots. She saw creases in the leather, a sign of the miles he'd traveled for Emily.

He shifted his weight. "No matter what happened, you don't have to carry that shame."

The shame of an out-of-wedlock child was small compared to the guilt she felt now. She felt certain Maggie and Emily were the same woman. If her fears proved true, he'd take Stephen back to Boston.

He laced his hands behind his back. "I'm sharing this story for one reason."

Her throat hurt. "What is it?"

"I was a hypocrite and a fool. I've been addicted to laudanum, told lies and had thoughts so hateful they still shame me. In spite of my failings, Christ died for me. He paid the price for *all* of us."

He shifted his weight again. "I don't know who fathered your son, Adie. I don't know what happened to you. But I know this… No one has the right to throw stones at a woman who's made a mistake."

Realization stole Adie's breath. Josh had no idea that she hadn't given birth. Her secret was safe, but that security came at the cost of her integrity. By staying silent, she was lying. Josh had told the truth about secrets. Knowledge of Maggie's diary weighed like a millstone. She couldn't bear his compassion. She didn't deserve it. Fighting panic, she broke from his gaze and headed for the door.

"Adie, wait." He cut in front of her. "I did it again. I hurt you. That's not my intent. I—"

"Stop! Don't say anything else."

She looked up and saw the shadow of his day-old beard. His black hair wisped over his ears and his jaw jutted with determination. He didn't look a thing like Maggie…except for the shape of his eyes and the slant of his nose, the line of his brow and the curve of his mouth. Adie's heart cried no, but her common sense said yes. She stepped around Josh and raced up the stairs. She heard his boots in the hallway, but they halted at the first step. As she fled into her room, the words of the Psalm played through her mind.

Wither shall I go from Thy spirit?

And wither shall I flee from Thy presence?

Josh hadn't come up the stairs, but she felt as if he were hearing her thoughts. With nowhere to hide, she checked Stephen. Instead of calming her, the sight of the sleeping baby made her tremble. Soon she'd have to pay the mortgage. If she had to sell one of Maggie's brooches, Josh would see it in the jewelry shop and he'd know. She also feared that Bessie would tell him about Stephen's adoption. Looking back, she realized why the older woman had thrown them together. She suspected the truth and wanted Adie to be honest. If Bessie suspected the connection, so did Caroline.

Feeling trapped, Adie stared at the open window. "Talk to me, Maggie."

Adie waited for a flash of memory, a sense of what Maggie would say about Josh now. None came, but Adie didn't need her friend to guide her. She knew right from wrong. She also loved her son enough to die for him and she'd made a deathbed promise to the boy's natural mother. Did that promise give Adie the right—the obligation—to hide the journal? Did a secret do harm when it protected an innocent baby? Or was she protecting herself?

She touched her son's cheek. No one could love him as much as she did. Not an uncle or cousins. Nothing mattered more than love… Not money. Not blood. Someday Stephen would ask questions. When that day came, she'd answer them truthfully. Until then, she'd hide the facts of his birth.

The decision calmed her but only until she looked out the window. A month ago someone had hurled a rock into her room. Three days ago a man had stomped her tomato plants. She felt as unsafe as she had with the Long family. Adie didn't know whom she feared more—Josh with his good intentions or Franklin Dean, who wanted her out of Swan's Nest.

Either way, she had everything to lose and nothing to gain from opening the trunk. Some truths, she decided, were best left buried.

At precisely midnight, Frank left Miss Elsa's Social Club through the back door. As instructed, Horace met him with the carriage. Frank smelled liquor on his driver's breath and frowned. He didn't care how Horace passed the evening, but the man had to be discreet. If liquor loosened his tongue, he'd become untrustworthy, a fearful possibility considering the secrets he kept.

Frank didn't need the details, but he had to be sure Horace hadn't taken to blabbing at Brick's Saloon.

He made his voice jovial. "Where have you been, my friend? In good company, I hope."

"At Brick's Saloon, sir."

"I smell whiskey."

Horace chuckled. "I downed a shot or two, but I think you'll be pleased with what I gleaned."

"Regarding Miss Clarke?"

"In a way, sir." Horace turned on Broadway where Frank lived in a new mansion. Made of stone with turrets on the corners, it resembled a castle. Other homes on the street had the same look, but none of them matched his house in size.

"Tell me what you learned," he said to Horace.

"It's about the reverend."

"Joshua Blue?"

"He's starting a church, sir."

Frank wrinkled his brow. "Whatever for? Denver has more churches than it needs."

As an elder for Colfax Avenue Church, the biggest church in Denver, Frank kept track of attendance and collection records. Another church would take a slice of the pie.

Horace chuckled. "It's not *your* kind of church."

"Oh?"

"The reverend's holding services in the saloon. He told the barkeep to spread the word."

"I see."

Aside from objecting to another church, Frank didn't want Joshua Blue lingering at Swan's Nest. The reverend had done more than protect Pearl at Franklin's last visit. He'd declared war. The banker could play that game, too. Horace knew better than to mention Adie's garden, but Frank had heard talk at the café where the blonde named Mary waited tables. Swan's Nest had been vandalized. Adie Clarke had cleaned up the mess and replanted.

What would it take to drive her away? If Miss Clarke left town, Pearl would have to move back to the parsonage. Her father could marry them in a private ceremony. Frank would have possession of his son and of Pearl. He wouldn't need to visit Miss Elsa's Social Club. As always, tonight's visit left him feeling cheated. It was Pearl's fault. If she'd only cooperate, he'd be a good husband. But Pearl wouldn't listen. Not with Adie Clarke filling her mind with lies about respect and love and female independence.

As Horace steered the carriage to the back of the house, Frank looked at the windows, all dark except for his bedroom where a maid had lit a lamp. He couldn't live this way. He needed Pearl.

Horace climbed down from the high seat. Frank got out by himself and faced his driver. "It's time to do more." He didn't need to explain what he meant.

"Any ideas, sir?"

"A fire, perhaps."

Horace raised his brows. "The whole house?"

A fire had hidden benefits. As soon as Franklin took possession of Swan's Nest, he intended to tear it down and build a row of houses he'd sell to entrepreneurs flooding into Denver. If Swan's Nest burned to the ground, the demolition job would be simpler. On the other hand, he didn't want to endanger Pearl.

"Use your judgment," he said. "But Miss Oliver mustn't be harmed."

"What about the others?"

Frank shrugged.

When Horace grinned, moonlight showed his yellow teeth. "You won't know a thing until it happens."

"You're a smart man, Horace."

"That's what you pay me for."

Frank took the hint. Arson cost more than stomping tomatoes. He slipped a five-dollar gold piece into Horace's hand. "Remember. No harm to Miss Oliver."

"Yes, sir."

As the driver led the horse to the stable, Frank had another thought and turned. "One more thing, Horace."

"Sir?"

"When was the last time you went to church?"

Horace snorted.

"It wouldn't hurt you to attend services this Sunday." Frank gave a sly smile. "I hear Reverend Blue is preaching at Brick's Saloon."

The driver smiled back. "That he is, sir. In fact, I think I'll attend."

"Good idea."

As Horace led the horse away, Frank heard the hollow clop of hooves on the dirt path. He entered his house, then headed up the stairs to his empty bedroom, where he blew out the candle and dreamed of Pearl.

Chapter Nine

On Sunday morning Josh strode into Brick's Saloon, saw seven people and rejoiced at the size of the crowd. Brick had arranged the chairs into a square. The barkeep and the girl from Miss Elsa's sat in the second row. Caroline and Bessie had come, but Mary had woken up with a fever. Behind Brick sat three men. Two of them were cowpokes. The third man, a stocky fellow, wore a frock coat and had set a black bowler on the chair next to him. Josh greeted him with a nod. He smiled back, revealing yellow teeth.

Adie's presence would have made him even happier, but he hadn't expected to see her. She'd avoided him since the Bible study and he was worried. For now, though, he had seven souls in his care.

Josh stepped to the counter that Brick had polished. The barkeep had also tacked a sheet over the racy painting above the bottles, a gesture Josh appreciated. As he set down his Bible, he prayed for God to keep him humble.

"Good morning," he said in a hearty voice.

The ladies answered. The men didn't. In some ways,

churches were all alike. No one had sat in the front row. No one ever did, not even in Boston.

Josh felt at home. "Anyone here ever make a mistake?"

The cowboys both grimaced. Josh had never been drunk, but knew a headache when he saw one. Brick looked chagrined, and the girl from Miss Elsa's clutched a hankie. Bessie and Caroline both nodded in support. Josh glanced at the man with the yellow teeth and saw a sneer. Preaching to outlaws had made Josh wise. He judged no man by his appearance, but neither did he turn his back on strangers. He looked straight at the man in the frock coat.

"I've made mistakes," Josh continued. "I make them every day. A year ago I made one so bad it cost me everything. What I'm here to say, friends, is that there's hope. If God can take a man like me—a man who, figuratively speaking, murdered his sister with his anger—then He can touch *you* right where you're sitting today."

The girl from the brothel had tears in her eyes. Brick and the cowboys merely blinked, but Josh rarely saw emotion in the faces of hardened men. Bessie sat with her usual calm, but Caroline, her eyes shimmering with admiration, worried him. She looked like a woman in love and not just with the Lord. As for the man with the yellow teeth, he looked amused.

In Josh's experience, mockers came from two camps. Some had chips on their shoulders. They knew their Bible but had been hurt and wanted to fight. Josh gladly took them on. The second group made his blood run cold. They were hard men who bullied others. Before arriving at Swan's Nest, he'd spent time with the Johnson gang. He'd seen Clay Johnson shoot a dog for wagging its tail at him. Josh didn't know where the fellow with the bad teeth stood, but his instincts told him to be careful. Before he went back to Swan's Nest, he intended to speak with the man. First, though, he had a sermon to give.

The words came to him easily. He told whatever Bible stories came to mind and trusted the Holy Ghost to make them real. Today he told the story about the prodigal son. By the time he finished, Brick and the cowboys were sitting tall and Miss Elsa's girl looked alive with hope. The fourth man yawned.

"We'll close with a hymn," Josh said. "Who knows 'Rock of Ages'?"

Four hands went up.

Josh got ready to embarrass himself. As Wes Daniels once said, he couldn't carry a tune in a bucket. In Boston, he'd had a choir to fill the gap and he had refused to try. Here he had only himself. With no room for pride, he made a joyful noise to the Lord. Noise, he knew, was being charitable.

As the group sang the last verse, the man with the yellow teeth left the saloon. After the final note, Bessie greeted the girl from Miss Elsa's. As Caroline served cookies, Brick filled mugs with strong coffee. The small group lingered, chatting in the awkward way of strangers.

Josh motioned for Brick to step to the side. "Do you know the fellow who left?"

"Sure do. His name's Horace."

"Is he a regular?"

"On and off," Brick answered. "He's Franklin Dean's driver. Dean owns—"

"The Denver National Bank," Josh said dryly.

"That's him."

Josh thought of the man he'd chased out of the garden. They had similar builds.

"He doesn't say much," Brick added.

In Josh's experience, snakes lay in wait. One had spoken to Eve, but most of them struck without warning.

"Hey, Reverend."

Josh turned and saw the two cowboys. The younger raised his voice. "Thanks for the story."

"You're welcome."

Caroline approached him with a smile. "Are you ready to go back to Swan's Nest?"

Yes, but not with Caroline at his side. Josh had never been in this position. In Boston Emily had run interference for him. If she were here now, she would have spoken to Caroline without embarrassing her.

Bessie approached. "Wonderful sermon, Reverend."

"Thank you."

After giving Josh a knowing look, she turned to Caroline. "It's time for us to go."

Caroline frowned. "I thought Josh might like some company."

Until now he'd been Reverend Blue.

"He doesn't need us," Bessie said lightly. "Do you, Reverend?"

Josh didn't want to hurt Caroline's feelings, but he had to discourage her. "Go on ahead. I'll see everyone at supper."

Caroline looked dismayed, but she followed Bessie out the door.

Josh looked in the basket he'd set on the counter. He hadn't taken an offering, but he knew people would give. He saw a surprising amount of money, including two silver dollars. He didn't care about the amount. What blessed him was knowing people valued the message. He picked up the basket, approached Brick and put some coins on the counter. "For the coffee."

The barkeep shook his head. "You don't have to pay me, Reverend. It's my pleasure."

"I'm not paying you. The congregation is."

"I guess they did." Brick smiled. "Will you be back next Sunday?"

"Definitely."

No way could he leave Adie alone in Denver. Dean had sent a spy. Josh took it as a warning of trouble to come.

He put the rest of the offering in his pocket, then headed for Swan's Nest. He knew exactly what to do with the remaining money. He'd give it away to people in need. Right now, Adie and her mortgage payment were at the top of the list. He had a hunch she'd argue with him. Her cheeks would turn pink and her eyes would flash. She'd act tough, but she didn't stand a chance against Josh's good intentions. Just for the joy of it, he added a gold coin of his own.

For the third time that morning, Adie lifted the sugar bowl from the cupboard and counted the money she'd set aside for the mortgage. She needed twenty-two dollars. She had sixteen and some change. Josh had already paid his rent. Without it, she would have been impossibly short. Both Caroline and Bessie owed for the week, but yesterday Caroline had said she'd be short. Adie had fumed. If the woman hadn't been buying sugar for pies, she could have paid her rent. Bessie worked for Dr. Nichols. Sometimes he paid her a wage. Other times he shared what his clients gave him. A chicken, even a plump one, wouldn't pay the mortgage.

Pearl paid nothing. Mary would contribute, but she'd missed two days of work because of a fever.

Barring a miracle, Adie would have to sell a piece of jewelry to meet her obligation. A single brooch would pay the mortgage for months, but Josh checked the jewelry stores every day. She knew his habits because of Caroline. Every night at supper, she asked if he'd learned anything about his sister. Every night, he gave the same answer.

"Not yet," he'd reply. "But I won't give up."

Adie believed him.

With her stomach churning, she put away the money and looked at Stephen, asleep in the wicker basket she'd lined with cotton. He'd gone three days without colic. Every day Adie looked at his eyes for signs they'd turn brown like Maggie's. They were still blue…like Josh's.

Sighing, she stirred the soup. It looked thin, but she didn't want to sacrifice another chicken. She needed the eggs. She'd saved some carrots from her trampled garden, but they didn't make up for meat. Even if she scraped together the mortgage money, she needed feed for Buttons, shingles for the roof and food for six adults.

Footsteps padded down the hall. She looked up and saw Mary, dressed in faded calico with a shawl on her shoulders.

"You should be in bed," Adie scolded.

"I'm better."

"The fever could come back."

If Mary's illness returned, she wouldn't be able to work. If she couldn't work, she couldn't pay her rent. Adie instantly felt selfish for the thought. What had happened to her goodwill? She wanted Swan's Nest to be a haven for women in need, not a place of disgrace.

Mary reached into the side pocket of her dress. "The mortgage is due in a few days, isn't it?"

"On Tuesday."

"Here." She set a handful of coins on the table. "It's all I've got, almost three dollars. I know things are tight."

Adie did some quick arithmetic. She needed another three dollars for the mortgage and spending money for the week. Maybe she could sell some of the linens stored in Josh's room, though she'd tried before and had gotten pennies.

"Will we make it?" Mary asked.

"I think so." Adie stirred the soup. Her boarders knew she struggled to make ends meet, but no one knew about the jewelry.

Mary glanced at the pot on the stove. "It smells good."

"Would you like some?"

"Just a little."

As she sat, the back door opened and Josh walked into the kitchen. "Good morning, ladies," he said as he hung his hat on a hook.

"Hello, Reverend," Mary answered.

Adie focused on the soup. Since the night on the porch, she hadn't been able to look Josh in the eye. Good manners demanded that she offer him a bowl, but she didn't want him to stay in the kitchen. She mumbled a greeting as thin as the broth.

"How was the service?" Mary asked.

"Good."

"I hear Bessie and Caroline enjoyed it."

Josh chuckled. "Maybe the preaching, but we need someone who can sing."

Mary gave a wistful sigh. "I used to sing every Saturday night. People came to the Ridgemont Canary just to hear me."

As Adie ladled soup for Mary, she heard chairs scraping against the floor, then the rustle of cotton as Mary sat first, then Josh. She didn't dare look up. If she kept her eyes down, she stood a better chance of avoiding conversation. Feeling invisible, she listened as Mary revealed to Josh that she'd sung in a fancy music hall in Texas and had come close to joining a traveling revue. Adie wondered what had stopped her.

If Josh wondered, he kept the question to himself. "If you're free next Sunday, I hope you'll sing for us."

Adie had filled the bowl to the brim. She didn't want to look Josh in the eye, but she had to bring the soup to Mary. As she turned, she heard a tremor in Mary's voice.

"Are you sure, Reverend? I'm not exactly…you know."

"I know, all right." He focused solely on Mary. "I'm not 'exactly,' either."

Neither was Adie.

The bowl dipped in her hand. Josh, tall and dark in his black coat, pushed up from the chair and steadied her grip with his long fingers. The sight of him should have filled her with resentment. Instead she saw his clear eyes and felt as if he truly understood the shame of her deception. His hair, slightly mussed from the hat he'd hung by the door, wisped over his ears and collar. The coat matched the raven color and made his features even sharper.

He lifted the bowl from her hands. "I've got it."

As he served Mary, Adie felt shaken to the core. Surely Maggie's brother wouldn't sit in a kitchen with a saloon girl and an unwed mother. He'd been a Boston muck-a-muck, not a man who'd hold church in a saloon. Oh, how she wanted to believe that lie….

Mary took a sip of soup, then gave Adie a pointed look. "The reverend might be hungry."

"I'm fine," he answered.

"Don't be silly," Mary said. "Please, join us."

Josh had gained weight, but he looked thin today. He'd had milk and bread for breakfast, but not a midday meal that she knew about. She feared his company, but she couldn't let him go hungry. "Mary's right. You need to eat."

"Thank you."

As she filled another bowl, she listened to Josh taking to Mary about her choice of hymns. She knew dozens, including a few Adie had liked as a little girl.

"I'll sing, but only if you're sure," she said.

"I'm positive," he replied.

Adie set the bowl in front of him. He looked up and smiled. "Thank you."

Mary ate quickly, then carried her bowl to the counter. "Thank you, Adie. I'm going back upstairs."

"Wait—"

Mary stopped. "Do you want me to take Stephen?"

"No, I just—" She didn't want to be alone with Josh but couldn't say it. She felt foolish. She also knew Stephen would be happier in his cradle. "Yes, take him. That would be nice."

Mary lifted the basket and the baby, then shot Adie a look. "The reverend might enjoy the bread you baked."

Adie wanted Josh to finish his soup and leave, not linger over bread and butter. She frowned but went to the bread box and removed the fresh loaf. As Mary left the kitchen, Adie sliced the bread, put it on a plate and fetched the butter crock. She set everything on the table. Before she could turn, Josh caught her eye.

"I'd like to speak to you," he said quietly.

"What is it?"

"I have something to give you." He stood and indicated Mary's chair. "Please, sit down."

His Boston manners made her nervous, but she couldn't avoid him. She sat and folded her hands. Josh reached into his coat pocket and extracted a handful of coins. As they plinked on the table, she spotted two silver dollars and a golden half eagle. As she looked up with shock, Josh sat back on the chair.

"I know money's tight." He slid the pile in her direction. "You have a need and I believe God wants to meet it. This is for you. It's today's offering from church."

She desperately needed the money, but she felt dishonest taking it from Josh. His generosity would protect her secret. The irony shamed her. "I can't accept."

"Sure you can."

She looked at her lap.

Josh made his voice light. "Don't be shy, Adie. I know your secret."

Startled, she raised her head. "What secret?"

"You're as prideful as I am."

She couldn't swallow. "Is that all?"

"I don't know. Is there more?" He touched her hand. "Whatever's in your heart, it's between you and God. When I look at you, I see an honest, hardworking woman. I'm proud to know you."

Could she feel any lower than she did right now? Adie didn't think so.

Still holding her hand, he kept his voice low. "This gift is between you and God, too. You can toss it in the air if you want, but I hope you'll use it for the mortgage."

He released her hand and picked up his spoon. Unable to speak, she watched as he finished his soup, savoring every bite as if it were worth more than the pile of coins. When he finished, he carried the bowl to the counter, lifted his hat from the hook and went to his room without another word.

Adie looked at his retreating back, then touched the coins with a single thought. Joshua Blue was the kindest, most honorable man she'd ever know. She pushed to her feet and called down the hall. "Josh?"

He stopped but didn't turn. "Yes?"

"Thank you."

As if he wasn't sure he should look, he faced her. As a cloud passed away from the sun, light shot through the window, warming her face and making her squint. Josh faded to a shadow, but she heard his voice.

"You're welcome," he said. "But it's not from me."

The door to his room closed with a soft click. Adie should have been relieved, but she wanted to run down the hall and pound on the wood. Her heart ached with the need to confess.

I had a friend named Maggie Butler. Stephen could be your nephew.

The thought choked her. She simply couldn't do it.

She wouldn't.

She swept the coins into her palm and added them to the sugar bowl. On Tuesday she'd make the payment, but using Josh's money—or God's money—left her bitter. Her soul, already ragged, raveled to a frayed edge. Even worse, her heart ached for Josh. She wanted to ease his burden almost as much as she wanted to protect Stephen from Maggie's brother.

Shaking inside, she closed the cupboard and turned back to the soup. As she gave it a stir, steam dampened her face. She heard footsteps in the hall, looked up and saw Caroline still wearing her Sunday best.

The woman said hello, then helped herself to a glass of water. "Church was wonderful."

Adie didn't want to hear it.

"Josh is the best preacher I've ever heard."

When had *Josh* invited Caroline to use his given name? Adie used it, but they'd become friends. Her conscience lurched with another half-truth. Her feelings for Josh ran far deeper than friendship. The admission made her head spin. She didn't want to love Josh or any man. She couldn't. Not with a life built on secrets, half-truths and bald-faced lies.

Caroline headed for the pantry. "Seven people came to Brick's."

Adie thought of the offering. Someone had given generously, a sign that Josh's words had mattered.

"That's nice," she replied.

"I bet more people come next week."

Adie's felt a stab of fear. He'd asked Mary to sing. Adie had heard her friend's soprano and knew she'd attract visitors. Josh's preaching had filled a Boston cathedral. What if his little church grew each week? If he stayed in Denver, Adie would be afraid forever.

Caroline opened the pantry and removed the pie she'd baked for dessert. Adie had had enough. Looking over her shoulder, she frowned. "We don't need dessert *every* night."

"Josh likes apple pie."

"He's being polite." Adie knew for a fact he preferred pound cake with strawberries. She thought of the squashed berry plants and felt angry all over again.

Caroline eyed her thoughtfully. "You like him, don't you?"

"Of course not!"

She'd answered too quickly. A smile curved on Caroline's lips. "That's what I thought."

"I like him," Adie admitted. "But not in that way."

"I like him, too." Caroline's eyes turned wistful. "I was married once, you know."

To a man of color in the South... Caroline had seen him lynched. Adie felt stricken. Who was she to criticize Caroline's feelings for Josh? Or his feelings for Caroline? If he'd invited her to use his given name, perhaps he had an interest in her. Why not? Caroline had wavy dark hair, green eyes and a bow-shaped mouth. Any man would find her pretty and she had a sharp mind.

Caroline set the pie on the counter. "I know I've overdone it with the baking, but it feels good to *want* to do it."

Adie stirred the soup. "I wouldn't know."

"You've never been in love?"

"No."

Caroline made a humming sound. "It's the best feeling in the world. I remember how it was with Samuel. It was dangerous, but I don't regret a minute."

Adie didn't know what to think. All her life she'd been afraid. She'd worried that her father wouldn't come home and one day he hadn't. She'd fretted over her mother's health and she'd died. She'd feared Timothy Long and Reverend Honeycutt and they'd both harmed her. She understood fear far better than love, yet with Josh she wondered... What would it be like to live with confidence? To feel safe and be free of secrets?

She put the lid on the soup. It would simmer until supper. So would her problems and there was nothing she could do. Until Josh left Denver, she'd be a nervous wreck. Seeing no escape, she went upstairs to hold her son.

Chapter Ten

As he neared Colfax Avenue Church, Josh thought about what to say to Reverend Tobias Oliver. With the success of the little church in Brick's Saloon, he felt compelled to pay a call on local clergy to introduce himself. He'd preached two Sundays and attendance had increased to twelve. Not everyone approved of a church in a saloon, but he'd learned in his travels that a Harvard degree silenced his critics. Like Paul, Josh didn't mind revealing his credentials for the cause of Christ.

He also wanted to speak to the man about Pearl. Of the two missions, the second would be the most difficult. Josh had no business raising such a personal matter, but how could he keep silent? If someone had taken him to task for his hypocrisy, Emily would be safe in Boston and he'd be… Josh didn't know where he'd be. He rued the reason for his travels, but the past year had made him a better man. If Emily hadn't left, he'd have missed the biggest challenges—the biggest blessings—of his life.

Those blessings included Adie. Josh had never been on such a twisting road. He cared for her. Every day his feelings deepened. She also exasperated him with her silence. She hadn't spoken to him in days, but he knew her habits. She hadn't been sleeping well. At night she wandered in the flower garden behind the wounded vegetables. He prayed constantly for her. When he left Denver, it would be with the regret that he'd failed yet another woman.

Today, though, he could help Pearl. He expected to find Reverend Oliver in the church office, but before he reached the main building, he saw a house set back from the street. A wide porch surrounded a stone cottage with a gabled roof. Ivy climbed up the sides and lilacs bloomed at the base of the steps. On the porch sat a man in a black coat, sipping tea as he read a book.

Josh strode down the brick path to the porch. "Reverend Oliver?"

"That's correct."

"I'm Joshua Blue."

"Ah," he said. "The minister from Boston. I've heard of you."

"That's why I've come," Josh said. "I'd prefer to meet face-to-face than listen to talk."

"My feelings exactly."

The older man waved Josh up the steps. After they shook hands, he indicated a chair. As Josh sat, Reverend Oliver went into the cottage. He returned a few minutes later with a refreshment tray. He set it on the table, sat and lifted a flowered teapot with a gnarled hand. He looked at Josh with stark apology. "If my daughter were here, she'd serve cake. All I can manage is tea."

"Tea is fine, sir. Thank you."

In the time between Emily's departure and his own, Josh had been in this man's position. He'd fumbled with teapots and served stale baked goods. Few men appreciated a woman's touch until they had to manage on their own.

The reverend filled Josh's cup and handed it to him. "I understand you're living at Swan's Nest. How's my Pearl?"

His openness took Josh by surprise. "She's fine."

"And the baby? It's not here yet, is it?"

"No."

The man sipped his tea. "It's a tragedy."

Josh saw an opening and took it. "It depends, sir."

He frowned. "On what?"

"What Pearl does next."

Reverend Oliver set down his cup and crossed his arms. "You seem rather sure of yourself."

"I am." Josh settled back in his chair. "I didn't come to speak of Pearl, sir. I came to tell you about myself. I have a sister. About a year ago, she left Boston under circumstances similar to your daughter's situation."

The reverend huffed. "She did you a favor."

"I don't think so."

"Come now, Reverend. You know how people talk."

"I do," Josh said. "I also know that I called my sister an unspeakable name and she left in the middle of the night. She took a westbound train and never wrote. For all I know, she could be dead. The baby—" Josh sealed his lips. "I can't stand the thought of what might have become of the child. Sir, you don't want to know what that's like."

Reverend Oliver stared hard at Josh. "My daughter sinned."

"Do you know that for a fact?"

"It's obvious!"

"Not to me," Josh said quietly. "I don't know who fathered my sister's baby. I don't know if she was seduced or raped. All I know is that she needed help and I threw stones at her."

The old man's eyes narrowed. "It's no mystery what happened to Pearl. I'll be candid with you, Reverend Blue—"

"Please, call me Josh."

"Then I'm Tobias." The old man cleared his throat. "I'm not naive. I know that men and women stumble, even good Christians like my daughter. I've sinned. You've sinned. Frank wants to make things right. I don't understand why Pearl won't let him."

Josh knew, but he couldn't break Adie's confidence. "Ask your daughter."

"I've spoken with Frank," he said confidently. "He came to me after the buggy ride that led to this mess. I blame myself for letting them go alone, but they'd been courting for months. I trusted him."

A wolf in sheep's clothing, Josh thought.

"He confessed their mistake and asked for permission to marry Pearl immediately. Of course I granted it."

"Did you speak to Pearl?"

"Her feelings were evident." Tobias frowned. "If they'd married right away, there wouldn't have been any talk at all."

Tobias wanted to spare himself the embarrassment, but Josh didn't doubt his desire to protect Pearl. Josh had been misguided about Emily in the same way. He'd honestly thought giving up the baby was for the best.

He had another question for Tobias. "Are you aware of Mr. Dean's visits to Swan's Nest?"

"Only vaguely."

"He's been forceful."

Tobias wrinkled his brow. "He loves Pearl. He's concerned for his child."

Josh tried again. "Mr. Dean has proposed marriage. Is that right?"

"It is."

"And Pearl said no." Josh lowered his voice. "Haven't you wondered why?"

Tobias said nothing.

Josh reached for his tea, took a long sip and made a decision. He couldn't break Adie's confidence, but Reverend Oliver had to know the truth. "Sir, do you recall the story of Amnon and Tamar?"

His eyes narrowed. "Of course, it's in Second Samuel. Amnon was a son of David. He took Tamar against her will and died at Absalom's orders."

"That's right."

"What are you implying?"

Josh raised his chin. "Amnon was the son of king, a trusted member of the household. Tamar was innocent."

Reverend Oliver's cheeks flamed. "Are you saying this happened to Pearl?"

"I'm telling a Bible story."

"Don't beat around the bush, Reverend. How do you know?"

Josh prayed to do the right thing. "I can't say, sir. But you need to speak with your daughter. Don't lose her the way I lost Emily."

Tobias's face turned red. "I just assumed… Pearl's mother is gone. I couldn't speak with her about something so—so private."

Josh understood. "It's a taboo subject, but the sin is very real."

The old man shot to his feet. "He deserves to hang for what he did!"

"It's an allegation, sir. Pearl might not want to speak up."

Tobias sat back down. "I'll do anything for my

daughter. She talked about leaving Denver, but I said no. My church is here. My congregation needs me."

"May I offer a suggestion?"

The old man looked as if he'd been punched. "Please."

"Speak with Pearl."

"I will."

"Let her decide what's best."

Tobias looked across the yard to the stone church. Josh followed his gaze and saw a row of stained glass windows. The first depicted a shepherd and five sheep. Josh thought of the women at Swan's Nest. The second showed Christ with children in his lap. The third displayed an empty cross and a rising sun. Red and purple made up the cross. The sun, a yellow circle, gleamed against a royal-blue sky. The fourth window showed the woman at the well. Jesus had personally told her to go in peace, that her sins were forgiven.

Pearl's father looked back at Josh. "Do you think Pearl will see me?"

"I hope so."

He raked his hand through his iron-gray hair. "I'd go tonight, but the elders are meeting. Frank's on the board. If what you're saying is true—and I believe it is—I have to address it."

Josh knew all about church politics. Women got blamed for gossiping, but men were just as prone to talk too much. He didn't miss the chatter at all. "A suggestion, sir?"

"Of course."

"Speak to Pearl first."

"I will." Looking haggard, Tobias took a drag of tea and grunted. "It's not strong enough, is it?"

"No."

He sighed. "Pearl makes perfect tea."

"Come tomorrow," Josh said.

His eyes turned shiny. "I've missed her."

Silence settled between them. Tobias finished his tea, then straightened his back and crossed his arms. "So, I hear you've started a church. Do you intend to stay in Denver?"

"Only as long as I have to," Josh answered. "Unfortunately, there's more to the story about Mr. Dean."

His eyes narrowed. "Tell me."

Josh told him about the garden and Horace's visit to Brick's Saloon. "Miss Clarke believes—and I agree—that Dean wants her house."

"Why?"

"Land values are increasing almost daily. She's also giving sanctuary to Pearl. Until we know who's behind the vandalism, I intend to stay at Swan's Nest."

"A wise call."

"And necessary."

"Then what?" Tobias gave him an assessing look.

"I'll resume searching for Emily."

"And starting churches in saloons?"

"Sure," Josh replied. "Not everyone's comfortable behind stained glass." He wasn't, not anymore.

Tobias looked hard into Josh's eyes. "You've suffered, haven't you?"

His chest felt heavy; then his body lightened with joy. He recalled Gerard Richards telling him he'd be a better preacher after he suffered. How true those words had been.... Without the struggle of the past year, he'd still be an arrogant know-it-all parading in his black robe, speaking in high-minded tones and hiding his bottle of laudanum. Gratitude washed over him. If his story would help Tobias, he had to tell it.

He looked the older man in the eye. "I failed my sister, sir. I prayed every night and memorized scripture. I claimed to love God more than myself, but when my position was on the line, I treated Emily like a leper."

"You succumbed to pride," Tobias said. "I know the temptation."

"It's ugly."

"And unavoidable. Don't despair, Josh. We worship a God of mercy."

"That we do."

Being of one mind, the men stood at the same time. Tobias held out his hand and they shook. "Come some evening for a visit. It's lonely without Pearl."

"I'll do that."

As Josh turned to leave, his gaze landed on the window showing the shepherd and five sheep. He thought of his "sheep" at Swan's Nest and felt a tug he'd never experienced before. He didn't want to leave them, especially not Adie, but he had to go. Somewhere, Emily and her child needed him. Maybe more, he needed them.

Josh walked back to Colfax Avenue and headed for the part of town where pawnbrokers ran shops. He hoped someone had heard of Emily or seen her jewelry, but more likely, he was grasping at straws. The thought filled him with despair. Instead of visiting the stores, he headed for the café where Mary worked. He needed a strong cup of tea, one that didn't remind him of Pearl and Adie, broken lives and people who threw stones.

With the mortgage receipt tucked in her reticule, Adie left the bank and headed for the café to say hello to Mary. She'd avoided Franklin Dean, but a knot had formed in her belly the instant she entered the building. A cup of tea would settle her nerves, plus she had promised Mary that she'd stop by the café.

Ever since the vandalism, Mary had been extra vigilant. She'd told Adie to ask Josh to accompany her to the bank, but Adie had refused. Josh would visit pawnbrokers and she didn't want to go with him. She'd see the hope in his eyes, then the disappointment. All the time, she'd feel guilty.

She turned on to Grant Avenue. At the sight of Franklin Dean's carriage, she paled. She would have turned around, but his driver spotted her. With a cold smile, he tipped his hat. Adie looked away without acknowledging him and found herself looking at Dean himself. He'd just come out of a fancy barbershop. Even three feet away, she smelled his cologne.

"Good afternoon, Miss Clarke."

"Mr. Dean."

He smiled. "May I offer you a ride to Swan's Nest?"

"No, thank you."

As she tried to pass, he blocked her steps. "It's not the least bit out of my way."

He'd told a flat-out lie. Swan's Nest sat on the outskirts of town. No one traveled in that direction unless they lived in the neighborhood. Taunting the banker would fan his temper, so she tried to sound pleasant. "If you'll excuse me—"

"Tea, then."

"No, thank you."

He scowled at her. "You're making this difficult, Miss Clarke. I want to know about Pearl. The baby's due in a few weeks. I have a right—"

"You have no rights!"

His eyes narrowed to snakelike slits.

Adie regretted the outburst. She had a strong will, but she couldn't outstare a man as cold-blooded as the banker. She softened her voice. "The baby's not due for a month. Pearl's doing just fine. When the time comes, Bessie will see to them both."

Adie expected a rant. Instead he reached inside his coat and lifted his wallet. He took out several bills. "Give this to Pearl."

Adie couldn't stand the thought of touching the money. Pearl would be revolted.

He shoved it closer. "It's to pay for a real doctor."

If Adie took the money, Pearl would be indebted to this man. If she didn't, Dean's temper might explode. She risked the explosion. "Thank you, but Pearl's needs are met."

She forced her way past him. Walking as fast as she could, she headed for Mary's café. Behind her she heard the rattle of the carriage, then Dean's voice coming from the backseat. "You'll regret that, Miss Clarke."

"I don't think so."

"Then think again."

He tapped the seat with his gold-tipped walking stick. The driver gave the horses free rein and they picked up their pace, stirring dust as the carriage passed her. Shaking, Adie watched him go, then hurried into the restaurant, where she saw Mary serving a man at a back table. She couldn't see his face, but she recognized the angle of Josh's shoulders. Mary waved her forward.

Common sense told Adie to leave, but her insides felt like jelly. She needed tea and safety. Being with Josh offered both, so she walked to his table. At the sight of her, he stood and gave a slight bow. His fancy manners unnerved her even more and she wished she'd left the café.

He touched her arm. "Are you all right?"

"I'm—I just—"

He pulled out a chair. "Sit."

Mary urged her into it. “I’m bringing tea.”

As the waitress hurried away, Adie took a breath to steady herself. Her chest felt as if horses were galloping inside her ribs. As Josh held her hand, the gallop turned to a dead run.

“What happened?” he said.

“I saw Franklin Dean.”

She told him about the money for Pearl and how she’d refused it. When she described Dean blocking her path, his mouth thinned to a line.

Mary brought the tea but couldn’t stay. Adie lifted a spoon to add sugar, but her hand shook so badly that the crystals showered the table. Josh took the spoon from her fingers, put the sugar in her cup, then added a second spoonful and a dash of milk. He knew exactly how she took her tea, a sign that he’d been watching her every move.

Using both hands, she raised the cup and sipped. If she hadn’t managed on her own, Josh would have held it to her lips. All her life, she’d stayed strong for other people. Josh wanted to be strong for *her.* What would it be like to lean on this man? Adie didn’t want to know. He posed a threat of his own. Shaking, she set the cup on the saucer. Frightened or not, she had to finish her story. “Dean threatened me.”

“What did he say?”

“That I’d regret not taking the money for Pearl.”

Josh’s fingers curled into a fist. “That low-down—” He clamped his jaws.

Adie wanted to do more than call Dean names. “The broken window, the garden… I don’t know what he’ll do next.”

“We need to see Deputy Morgan.”

“I don’t want to.”

"Why not?"

Adie knew about Josh's visit to the sheriff's office. He'd reported the garden incident and nothing had been said about Maggie, but that could change. Besides, what if Josh *wasn't* Stephen's uncle? What if a man as evil as Maggie had described was still looking for her? She wanted as little exposure to the law as possible. She shook her head. "It'll make things worse."

"So will doing nothing."

"But …" She couldn't think of a single excuse.

"We'll go right now."

"Tomorrow." Her insides were still trembling and she couldn't think straight. If the sheriff asked questions, she had to be calm.

Josh's mouth tightened. "Tomorrow it is."

Behind Adie, a plate crashed on the tile floor. She jumped as if she'd heard gunfire.

Josh clasped her hand. The warmth of it stole her breath. It took away the terror of Dean's threats and the coldness of being alone. She raised her gaze and saw the heat of war in his eyes. This man would fight for her. She wanted to fight for him, too. She'd fed him bread and milk. She'd seen him hurting and she'd seen him heal. If she couldn't trust Josh, whom could she trust? Surely he wouldn't pull Stephen from her arms?

He deserved the truth about Maggie and Emily. He'd become a friend, but the possibilities scared Adie to death. Josh had integrity. He'd want to give Stephen his place in Boston and the family business. Adie felt sick with fear, but her guilt weighed more. She couldn't bear it, not while peering into Josh's eyes. Color flooded her cheeks. She looked at her lap, but she couldn't hide from his presence.

He touched her cheek. "Secrets hurt, Adie."

She bit her lip.

"Did someone harm you?"

She cringed.

"Did you fight to protect yourself?" His voice dropped to a whisper. "No matter what you did, I'll help you."

No, he wouldn't. He'd take her son to Boston. He'd hate her for hiding the truth. She'd couldn't tell Josh about Maggie, but she had to say *something* to make him leave her alone. "Someday I'll tell you about it."

She'd opened the door a tiny crack, but it was enough for the truth to shine. If she confessed to Josh, she'd be free of the guilt. Even in his black coat, he was a human being, a man with a good heart.

He squeezed her hand.

She squeezed back and felt strangled. Maybe for now, she'd said enough.

They sat in silence until Mary arrived with two pieces of pie. The dessert reminded Adie of Caroline and how she'd used Josh's first name. His feelings for Caroline were none of Adie's business, but she couldn't stop herself from feeling jealous. Someday Caroline would marry and have children. Adie never would. She had too many secrets. She lifted her fork. "It's apple."

"It's good," he said.

She forced a smile. "It's not as good as Caroline's."

He stopped with his fork midway to his mouth, then lowered it. "I've got a problem, don't I?"

Adie didn't want to jump to conclusions. "What do you mean?"

"You haven't noticed?"

For once she could tell the truth. "Actually, we all have."

"Emily used to be my buffer. She'd spread the word—"

he hooked his fingers to make quote marks "—Reverend Blue isn't interested in marriage."

Adie thought Josh would be a fine husband. "Why not?"

"Lots of reasons."

She waited for details, but he took a bite of pie. It felt good to ask questions instead of answering them, so she smiled at him. "Now who's keeping secrets?"

His lips curved up, but his eyes had a tinge of sadness. "It's not a secret. My work matters to me more than anything. Getting married—having a family—takes a big piece of a man's life. Without that responsibility, I can give everything to my work."

"So you'll never marry?"

"Probably not." The sadness returned to his eyes. "It's one of the reasons I have to find Emily. Her child's an heir to a fortune."

Adie gasped.

Josh looked quizzical. "You're surprised."

Until now she'd thought only of losing Stephen, not about what he'd gain by taking the Blue family name. If Josh claimed Stephen as his nephew, her son would have the finest clothes and a good education. He wouldn't eat broth for supper or wear old shoes as Adie did. The pie in her mouth turned to dust. She sipped her tea, but it had gone cold.

Josh took another bite of his dessert. He looked pleased. "I hope I find Emily soon. I'm going to love being an uncle."

Adie forced herself to smile. "You think so?"

"Definitely. Holding Stephen was the best feeling in the world." Josh set down his fork. "I envy you, Adie. You struggle with money, but you've got a beautiful son and wonderful friends. Someday you'll fall in love. You'll get married and have more children."

Could he torment her more? She had too many burdens to consider marriage. She had jewelry to hide and a secret to keep. Sometimes she wondered about marriage, but she pushed the notion aside. She had Stephen. Being a mother was enough.

Josh broke into her thoughts. "So tell me, *Miss* Clarke, does some Denver gentleman have his eye on you?"

"Not hardly." She decided to turn the tables. "What about you, *Reverend* Blue? You must have broken a few hearts in Boston."

"I don't think so." His gaze lingered on her face. "Sometimes, though, I wonder what it would be like."

His eyes glimmered with a discord that matched her own. Was he lonely? Did he think about sharing sunsets and morning coffee? She did, more than ever since he'd come to Swan's Nest. She was thinking about such things now, but those feelings could only cause trouble. To distract herself, she took another bite of pie. It tasted sweet, but she barely noticed. The way Josh looked at her had been even sweeter.

As he'd said, sometimes she wondered.

Chapter Eleven

"Take it away, Lord. This feeling for Adie—" Josh groaned out loud.

The sun had set hours ago. After supper, he'd helped with the dishes, then gone out the back door to avoid seeing any of the women. He wanted to speak with Pearl but didn't have the heart for it. Tonight his thoughts were on Adie, and he didn't like the direction they'd taken. How could he think about staying in Denver when Emily was still missing? As for the second turn his thoughts had taken, he had no business courting Adie or any woman. He needed to be alone to pray, so he'd gone to the far end of the flower garden.

He stood there now, a man with anxious thoughts. Josh had noticed pretty women before now, but he'd never felt a stirring in his soul the way he did for Adie. When she smiled, he felt joy. When she wept, he tasted salt. Yesterday she'd been afraid and he'd wanted to murder Franklin Dean. No one—not even Emily—had ever inspired such deep feelings.

Neither had he felt a worry like the one in his gut. Adie was in trouble; he felt sure of it. Every time he mentioned going to the law, she balked. For the past hour, Josh's imagination had run amuck. Women traveled west for all sorts of reasons. Having Stephen out of wedlock explained her secrecy but not her reaction to seeing the sheriff. When it came to shame, she had nothing to hide from him. She knew he wouldn't stand in judgment. That's why he'd told her about Emily.

She had something else to hide, something with grave consequences. Had she committed a crime? Josh looked at Swan's Nest and recalled the question he'd considered when he'd first arrived. Even with a loan, how had she been able to buy a mansion? The possibilities made his belly hurt. Maybe she'd been a servant in a fine home. She could have stolen jewelry and taken a westbound train. Maybe she'd been abused and had seen the theft as her only escape. His mind went down a dark alley, a place full of violence and tears. Had she been raped? Had she killed her attacker to save herself?

She'd suffered and the pain hadn't eased. It wouldn't until she faced the past, but at what cost? The thought of Adie going to prison filled him with horror. Stephen would be ripped from his mother's arms. If Bessie or Caroline didn't take him, he'd go to a foundling home. Pearl had problems of her own. Mary had secrets.

That left Josh. He'd never expected to have a family, but he wanted one now. Adie made him feel alive. When she entered a room, his heart sped up. His eyes would find hers and his soul would settle.

"Why, Lord?" he said to the moon. "I can't stay in Denver. I have to find Emily." He kept his eyes on the stars. "After that, you've called me to preach, but where?"

Josh's thoughts ran wild. The Lord was everywhere, including Denver. His congregation at Brick's had doubled in size. The growth indicated fertile ground. He didn't care about the number for the sake of his pride, but it proved he'd planted seeds and they'd sprouted. He wanted to water those seeds and watch them grow.

God had planted another seed, one Josh couldn't deny. He'd fallen in love with Adie. Had a man ever given her flowers? He wanted to be the first. As for the other firsts in a woman's life, someone had taken her innocence and used it to hurt her. Josh cared for Adie's sake but not his own. When he looked at her, he saw virtue and perfect beauty.

Once he found Emily, he could return to Denver and court Adie properly. But when would that be? How much longer was he destined to search? Josh looked at the stars. He saw God's power in every single one and thought of Adie sitting in the café, pale and trembling because of Franklin Dean. Or was it because of *him?* Did she return his affection?

Someone gasped.

Josh looked down the path from the house and saw Adie turning back. In Boston he never met with women alone. He'd been careful to protect his reputation as well as theirs. Adie deserved the same consideration, but he couldn't let her leave. A woman didn't wander alone at midnight unless she had a troubled heart.

"Adie?"

She stopped but didn't turn.

He kept his voicc light. "Can't sleep?"

"I haven't tried." She faced him then. Moonlight revealed her upturned chin. "I wanted some air. That's all."

Josh thought of the times Emily had questioned him about his "stomach medicine." He'd worn a similar look, one that mixed defiance and desperation. Emily had been intimidated by the defiance and had left him alone. He wished she'd seen the desperation and taken him to task. Adie needed help. If she'd let Josh get close, God had the power to turn ugliness to something good.

Before Josh found the words, Adie broke the silence. "About the sheriff tomorrow, I've changed my mind."

His heart plummeted. "Why?"

"He can't help me."

"We don't know that."

"I do," she said. "Now if you'll excuse me—"

"No," he said. "I won't."

The only other time he'd spoken so forcefully to a woman had been the night Emily left. He hated himself for that outburst, but he felt no remorse for being firm now. Adie needed to face the truth.

Her face tensed with outrage, then softened with a yearning Josh understood in his gut. How many times had he hoped someone would find the laudanum and free him from the lie? He suspected Adie felt the same way, but confronting her came with a risk. She could order him to leave Swan's Nest. She might never speak to him again. He found the thought intolerable, but neither could he leave her to suffer.

Honesty required courage. He needed it now. Knowing Adie might come to hate him, he spoke with authority. "Are you wanted by the law? Is that your secret?"

"It's none of your business."

He indicated Swan's Nest with a sweep of his arm. "This house…where did you get the money? Even with a loan—"

"What are you saying?" Her voice trembled.

"I'm afraid for you."

"Don't be."

"Dean could do real harm." He gestured at the vegetable garden. "He's evil, but I'm even more worried about what you're not telling me."

Adie pulled a thin shawl around her shoulders. "There's nothing you can do."

"I can listen."

She sealed her lips.

"If you need an attorney, I'll hire one."

Her mouth gaped.

"Whatever you did, it can be forgiven. I'll help you through it, Adie. If you stole—"

"I didn't." Her voice dropped low. "At least not money."

Her confession confused him. "What *did* you steal?"

She'd stolen the truth. She had it hidden in the trunk. No matter what she'd promised Maggie, Josh had a right to know if Maggie and Emily were the same woman. Adie had robbed him of that opportunity. She'd come to the garden to avoid him and had stumbled into a trap of her own making. Lies led to more lies. She couldn't bear to look at him, but neither could she flee. If she didn't answer his questions now—at least in part—he'd keep asking.

Yesterday Bessie had urged her to tell Josh the truth. Later Mary had cornered her in the laundry room. Caroline hadn't mentioned Stephen's birth, but Adie had seen her looking closely at the baby, then at Josh. No one had told him she'd adopted the child, but the truth could slip. She could lose everything.

"Talk to me, Adie."

He took a slow step in her direction, then a second and a third. She smelled roses, then the starch of his shirt. She tried to put him in the same camp as Reverend Honeycutt but couldn't. Without knowing her mistake, he'd offered to help her. She could have committed murder and he'd look at her with the same understanding.

Adie weighed her choices. She could tell the truth and hope for the best. She could spin a tale about a rich uncle or make up a dead fiancé. Or she could say nothing. The last option appealed to her, but she doubted she had the strength. She ached to be free of the guilt. Even stronger was the desire to free Josh. They stood face-to-face, breathing in the same rhythm and feeling the same confusion. When the tears spilled down her cheeks, he wiped them with his thumb. No one had ever touched her with such tenderness. Weakened, her shoulders rolled forward. She cupped her face in her hands, but a sob still burst from her throat.

With his arm around her shoulders, Josh guided her to a stone bench, where they sat side by side, hips close but not touching. Slowly, as if they were made of wet clay, they leaned against each other.

"Cry it out," he murmured.

But she couldn't. Tears wouldn't cleanse her. Only the truth could set her free and she feared it more than ever. She jerked upright.

He kept his hand on her back. "I don't care what you've done, Adie. You need to confide in someone."

"It's private."

"I'll take your secret to the grave." He touched her chin, forcing her to look into his eyes. "If you can't tell me, take it to God."

She thought of Timothy Long and Reverend Honeycutt, then Maggie dying in spite of their shared prayers. She jumped to her feet and turned on Josh. "Where was God when my mother died? I was twelve and all alone. I tried to bury her myself, but I couldn't."

"I'm sorry."

"Where was God when Timothy Long did what he did?" Her voice shook. "And when Reverend Honeyc-

utt sent me away like trash! Where was God when—"
When Maggie died. She choked back a cry. Just as she feared, the truth had come to a boil.

Josh stood and clasped her hands. She tried to pull away, but he tugged her closer…closer still…until he held her in his arms and she was weeping on his shirt. She wanted to stop but couldn't. Safe in his arms, she wept for the frightened girl who'd been run out of her hometown. Through choked sobs, she told him about that year in the Long house, how Timothy had abused her and how Reverend Honeycutt had sent her away.

His arms tightened around her. "No wonder you feel bad when I mention Emily. I'm sorry, Adie. You deserved better."

So did Josh. He deserved the truth.

He tucked her head against his shoulder. "Timothy Long… Is he Stephen's father?"

She thought of Maggie bleeding out and her deathbed promise. What mattered more? Josh's peace of mind or Adie's word to Maggie? Josh had a good heart. That goodness could compel him to take his nephew home.

She wiped her nose. "Stephen's my son. That's all you need to know."

As she broke from his arms, she noticed the smell of roses for the second time. The fragrance reminded her of Maggie's burial. Across the hedge she saw the remaining vegetables. The single cornstalk had the jangled look of a skeleton. The tomato plants hung in a lifeless tangle, a reminder of Franklin Dean and his assault on Swan's Nest.

Josh stepped to her side. "I know you've suffered, Adie. I know it doesn't make sense."

She sniffed. "No, it doesn't."

"Honeycutt failed you."

Her eyes burned with the memory of boarding the train out of Liddy's Grove. The Honeycutts had arranged for her to work for relatives of theirs in Nebraska. Traveling alone, she'd gotten looks from strangers and had been afraid. The cousins had been decent folk, but Adie had been a servant when she longed to be a daughter, a sister. After a year, she'd left. She'd gone to Topeka where she'd struggled to find work. In the end, she'd been reduced to sweeping saloons and eating scraps.

Everything had changed when she'd seen Maggie Butler, obviously with child, walk proudly into the Topeka Hotel. On a whim, Adie had approached her and asked if she needed a maid.

"No," she'd said. "But I desperately need a friend."

The memory made Adie sniff. She turned to look at Swan's Nest. She hoped Maggie would be proud.

Adie felt Josh standing behind her, gazing at the mansion rising tall and dark against the purple sky. Not a single light burned in the windows, but nothing could hide the house's grandeur. The mansion brought them back to the questions of money and stealing.

He clasped her shoulders, then turned her to face him. His voice, low and strong, filled her ears. "You *know* I'm not like Honeycutt. You can trust me, Adie."

"I can't trust anyone," she insisted. "But I'm telling the truth. I didn't steal the money for Swan's Nest. And I'm not wanted by the law."

"Then Stephen's father—"

"No."

He tightened his grip. "Talk to me, Adie. I care about you."

His confession sent tremors to his hands. Josh looked startled, but his eyes held no regret. Instead he broke a rose off the hedge and handed it to her. "If it weren't for Emily, I'd stay in Denver. I'd bring you flowers like this one."

Adie pinched the stem, raised the petals to her nose and sniffed. She could love this man…except he was a minister and she'd been living a lie. Neither did she share his love of God. She lowered the rose and looked up. Josh clasped her shoulders. His eyes drifted shut as if he were in pain, then he bowed his head and kissed her forehead. She felt cherished, even blessed, until guilt flooded through her.

Angry at herself for the lies and at God for the pain, she stepped back. "You're very kind, Josh. But there's no place for you in Denver." *Or in my life.*

He lowered his voice. "I'm not so sure."

"I am."

"When I find Emily, I'm coming back."

You'll never find her.

Adie pivoted and strode down the path. What she saw filled her heart with terror. Flames were licking the back wall of Swan's Nest.

Chapter Twelve

She had to get to Stephen and wake her friends. Hiking up her skirt, she raced by the vegetable patch, coughing as the air turned into orange smoke. When she passed the carriage house, she saw fingers of flame shooting up the back wall of Swan's Nest. Someone had lit the woodpile on fire. The house itself hadn't caught, but the wood siding and shingled roof made it a tinderbox. Adie ran for the back door, but the heat intensified, forcing her to race to the front of the house.

As she rounded the corner, the door opened and her boarders came out in wrappers and white night rails. They looked like a flock of frightened swans. She searched and found Stephen in Mary's arms.

Pearl cried out. "There's Adie!"

Bessie ran forward and hugged her. "You scared us to death. We couldn't find you!"

"And Josh," Caroline cried. "He's not in his room!"

"I'm right here."

Adie turned and met his gaze. Behind him she saw billows of smoke. A roar filled the night. Had the fire spread to the house? The jewelry… The journal… She had to get them. She needed Maggie's jewelry to survive. Even more important, the trunk held answers for Josh. She broke from Bessie's grip and ran through the front door.

"Adie!"

The cry came from Josh. She heard the pounding of his boots as he ran up behind her. He grabbed her arm, but she broke loose and sped up the stairs. Smoke filled her nose and eyes. An orange glow pushed into the hallway, but she didn't see flames. Her bedroom was at the front of the house, far from the fire but still vulnerable if the roof caught.

She ran into her room and headed for the bureau where she kept the key. She grabbed it, spun around and came face-to-face with Josh.

"Get out!" he shouted. "*Nothing* is worth your life."

"This is."

She crouched in front of the trunk and inserted the key. Clanging bells signaled the arrival of the fire wagon. As she worked the lock, shouts from the street followed the smoke through the window. She heard Pearl sobbing and Mary yelling for her to get out. Josh stared at her in disbelief.

She opened the lid and tossed the contents on the floor. A swatch of fabric she'd used for curtains fluttered into a heap. Leftover yarn landed in a tangle. At last she grasped the velvet bag holding Maggie's jewels, her picture and the journal. She felt Josh's eyes on her hands, watching as she lifted the bag.

The instant she stood, he tugged her out the door and into the hallway. Smoke choked her as they hurried down the stairs. If the roof caught, she'd lose the house. The thought terrified her, but not as much as losing Stephen or even the journal. Without it, Josh would never know the truth about Emily.

When they reached the street, she risked a glance at Josh and saw questions in his eyes. The noise of the crowd, the smoke and the roar of the flames made it impossible to speak, but she knew the night wouldn't end without him hearing the truth.

Lots of women had red velvet bags…or did they? Josh couldn't block the picture of Adie on her knees, risking her life for the sake of a bag that looked like the one Emily had used to hide her jewelry. He'd seen the bag only on occasion, but he recalled the gold drawstrings.

"All able-bodied men! We need help!"

The call had come from the fire chief. Josh wanted to grab the bag and look inside, but the fire took priority. He gave Adie a firm look. "We'll speak later."

Before she could argue, he hurried to the back of the house where the woodpile was engulfed in flames. The chief directed him to the bucket brigade. Other men followed. A few women, too, including Mary and Caroline. Gallon by gallon, they hauled water from the well, passed it down the line and threw it on the fire. As the flames died, the night returned like a dark blanket falling from the sky.

When the fire chief approached with a lantern, Josh accompanied him to inspect the dying embers. Satisfied the fire wouldn't reignite, the chief looked at the back wall of Swan's Nest. Smoke had stained the white paint, but the siding hadn't caught fire. Whoever set the blaze had inflicted more fear than damage. It struck Josh as the kind of tactic Dean would use.

Deputy Morgan joined them. "It's arson."

"You're certain?" Josh asked.

He held up a kerosene bottle. "I found this in the street."

The chief took the bottle and sniffed. "It's kerosene, all right. Even without the bottle, I'd know this fire was deliberate."

Josh had known it, too. "It started fast."

The chief grunted. "Woodpiles don't catch on fire by themselves. Someone gave it a hand."

"Did you see anyone?" Morgan said to Josh.

He flashed on the moments before the blaze. He'd been about to kiss to Adie. She'd been in his arms and he'd felt a rush of love that couldn't be denied. He'd been overwhelmed and hadn't seen anything except Adie turning her back.

"I didn't notice a thing," he said to Morgan.

"I did."

The men turned and saw Pearl with Mary and Bessie flanking her sides. A wrapper covered her night rail, but nothing could disguise her belly. The men looked discreetly at her face.

"What did you see?" Morgan asked.

Pearl, always pale, looked fragile in the moonlight. "I couldn't sleep, so I went to the window for air. I saw a man hurrying down the street. A few minutes later, I smelled smoke."

The deputy frowned. "What did he look like?"

"Short and stocky." Pearl took a breath. "Do you know Horace Jones?"

The deputy raised a brow. "He's Franklin Dean's driver."

"It could have been him."

"But you're not sure?" he asked.

"It was too dark."

The fire chief traded a look with Morgan. Both men knew the repercussions of accusing Franklin Dean.

Pearl looked at Josh. "We could have died tonight. If I hadn't been up and the roof had caught—"

"It didn't," Mary said. "We're fine."

"It's still my fault."

Josh made his voice gruff. "Don't you dare blame yourself. *You* didn't light the fire."

"That's right," Bessie added.

Pearl nodded but only slightly. She looked close to giving birth in the street. Josh turned to the fire chief. "Is it safe to go inside?"

"The fire's out, but I won't say it's safe." His expression hardened. "Whoever set the fire could come back."

The women paled at the implication. The flames had been doused, but the arsonist was running loose. Josh wondered if Adie and her friends would ever feel safe again. As Mary and Bessie led Pearl into the house, he went in search of Adie. He spotted Caroline first. Next to her stood Adie, clutching Stephen and swaying in a gentle rhythm. He searched for the velvet bag and saw it clutched in her hand, dangling below the baby's back and partially hidden.

When Caroline saw him, she whipped a hankie from her pocket and tried to wipe his face. "You're covered with soot."

He brushed her hand aside. "Not now, Caroline." He couldn't take his eyes off Adie and the bag.

Adie avoided him by looking at Caroline, who'd fallen three steps behind. "I guess we can go inside."

"Not yet." He'd waited long enough for answers. He turned back to Caroline. "I need to speak to Adie in private. Would you take Stephen?"

Adie shook her head. "It's late. Tomorrow—"

"Now," he said gently. "Please."

Caroline reached for the baby. "Go on, Adie. It must be important."

He could see the battle in her eyes, but she kissed the top of Stephen's head, then handed the baby to Caroline, who turned to Josh with a wistful smile. "Good night, Reverend."

She finally understood. "Good night, Caroline. And thank you."

As she walked away, Adie looked both terrified and calm, like a prisoner resigned to an execution.

Josh guided her up the steps and into the parlor, where he lit a lamp and turned up the wick. He wanted to see every flicker of her eyes. She flinched, but she didn't turn down the brightness. As she sat on the divan, Josh dropped on to the armchair, watching as she set the velvet bag in her lap. Looking down, she pulled the drawstrings and removed a black leather journal. She laid the book flat, laced her fingers across the binding and met his gaze. "I have a confession to make. Stephen's not my flesh-and-blood son."

His neck hairs prickled.

"His mother was my best friend. She died giving birth. She made me promise—"

"Her name," he said. *"Tell me her name."*

"Maggie Butler."

His grandmother's name had been Margaret. Butler had been her surname. His grandfather's given name was Stephen. Common sense warned him to hear the whole story before he uttered a word, but his temper was flaring bright. He wanted to shout at Adie for hiding the truth. He also saw her suffering and wanted to hold her in his arms.

Her face turned white. "Maggie had an accent like yours. And a brother. A minister… She hated him."

God, forgive me.

Her fingers clutched the velvet bag. "Her brother said vile things. She was afraid he'd take the baby, so she asked me to raise Stephen as my own. She died minutes later."

Grief collided with guilt. The guilt smothered his anger at Adie for hiding the truth. He had no right to throw stones at her. He'd started the entire mess.

With her eyes downcast, she lifted a square of cardboard from the journal and held it out to him. "This is a picture of Maggie."

As he pinched the edge, glare turned the paper white. He slanted it and the whiteness fell away like a drape, revealing a copy of the tintype he'd lost in the river crossing. He couldn't bear the sight of Emily's unblinking eyes. Pressure built in his chest. He didn't want Adie to see him cry, but the tears leaked from the corners of his eyes. Emily was dead. She'd died not knowing he'd changed. She'd never hear his apology.

"Is it—" Adie couldn't finish.

"It's Emily."

Guilt whipped through him and not just because of his sister. Adie had hidden the truth for weeks. Why? Did she think he'd take her son? He couldn't imagine wrestling a baby from its mother's arms. How could she think he'd do such a thing? The thought wounded him as deeply as he'd wounded Emily.

When he looked up from Emily's still face, he saw Adie holding a strand of pearls. "These belonged to Maggie… I mean Emily."

They'd once belonged to the real Maggie Butler.

"I have most of her jewelry," Adie said with pride.

"She told me to sell it to support Stephen. That's how I bought this house."

"I see," he managed.

"I'm not a thief." She raised her chin. "The jewelry belongs to Stephen, not me. That's why I borrowed to buy Swan's Nest. I'm paying my share with hard work."

Josh didn't think he could hurt any more, but Adie's confession broke his heart. Dressed in brown, she looked like a sparrow protecting her nest. Wisps of her maple hair feathered across her temple. Her lips moved, then stopped. She tried again to speak, but her voice cracked. Like a fluttering bird, she moved from the divan to the foot of his chair, dropping to her knees and clasping her hands against her chest. "Please don't take Stephen away from me! I'll do anything. I'll be his nanny. I'll go with you to Boston."

Shaken and miserable, Josh stared as she told him she'd work as a servant, that somehow she'd pay her own way. Before he found his voice, she clutched his hand. "I'm begging you, Reverend."

Reverend? He wanted to be Josh…just Josh.

She bent her neck and sobbed. "Please, don't take my son."

Her tears scalded his soul, but he couldn't be offended. He'd made that threat to his sister. He couldn't make amends to Emily, but he could give Adie peace. She needed to know Stephen was hers. Just as profound, Josh needed *her* to know *him.*

He deepened his voice. "Look at me."

When she raised her face, he cupped her cheeks in his hands. His voice came out rough. "Adie, you *know* me."

She sniffed. "Do I?"

"Yes!" He needed her respect, her faith in his heart. "You *know* what I'm going to say."

Hope filled her eyes. It vindicated him. "That's right. You're Stephen's mother. That will *never* change."

Bowing her head, she broke into a flood of new tears, murmuring "thank you" over and over. Her gratitude embarrassed him. They were simply two human beings, both flawed, battered by life and in need of kindness. He cupped her chin in his palm. As she looked up, her tears glistened and her lips parted again. Instead of thanking him, she smiled.

He brushed her cheek with his thumb. "I should be thanking you."

"Why?"

"You gave my nephew a home. You gave Emily peace when she needed it most."

"She was my friend."

If her smile made him human in a good way, her tears reflected his limitations. He couldn't kiss them away. Only God could put a woman's tears in a bottle and throw it into the sea. Josh had to settle for giving her his handkerchief. He reached in his pocket and gave her the linen. "Here."

Adie wiped her nose, then looked chagrined. "I'll wash it for you."

He didn't give a whit about the handkerchief. He pushed to his feet and offered his hand. She took it and stood. As she tipped up her chin, Josh bent his neck. He wanted to kiss her, but he didn't have the right. Tonight in the garden he'd imagined a future with this woman. He'd expected to find his sister alive and happy and had dreamed of coming back to Denver. Instead he'd found a tintype with eyes that would never blink.

His search had ended, but Emily's death kept him in

chains. She'd died of natural causes, but Josh felt as if he'd killed her. How could he think of his own happiness with her blood on his hands? On the other hand, he had a duty to care for his nephew. Just as compelling for Josh, he'd made a vow the day he'd left Boston. He'd promised to serve God far and wide. Never again would he pridefully pastor a church.

As much as he wanted to tell Adie how he felt, he couldn't speak until he made peace with God and himself. After a tiny squeeze, he released her hand.

Adie picked up the journal and handed it to him. "This belongs to Stephen, but you can read it."

He wanted to know Emily's story but dreaded her accusations. Why hadn't she written to Sarah or their cousin Elliot? Before he'd left Boston, Josh had written a letter to be sent if Emily revealed her whereabouts. If she'd taken that single step, she'd have learned how deeply he regretted his mistakes. Had he hurt her that profoundly? The truth was in the journal. As he'd told Adie, secrets caused pain. Emily's secrets were in the book and she deserved to tell them. He took the journal from Adie and slipped the picture inside the back cover.

Adie sighed. "I wish I'd told you sooner."

"When did you realize?"

"The first night on the porch, when I choked on my water." She went to the divan.

Josh dreaded going to his room, so he dropped back on the chair. They both needed clarity. "I had no idea."

"But before that night, I wasn't sure. You're nothing like Maggie described."

The compliment warmed him, but guilt doused that small flame. "I was, though."

"Not anymore."

"I wish…" He shook his head. "I'd give anything to tell her how sorry I am."

"Maybe she knew."

The journal felt like a brick in his lap. "I doubt it."

"I don't know," Adie said. "At the end, she asked for the book. She wrote something, just a line or two. I've never read it."

A dying woman's words could be anything. Maybe she'd forgiven him.

"Will you read it tonight?" Adie asked.

"I have to." *Will you read it with me?*

The question made it halfway to his tongue before he stifled it. He had to face Emily alone. The cover grew warm in his hands. If Emily had forgiven him, everything would change. He'd be free to stay in Denver. Once Adie made peace with God, he'd be free to court her with whole bouquets of roses.

Please, Lord. Let it be Your will.

Josh pushed to his feet.

So did she.

He saw a new softness around her mouth. The sparrow would sleep well tonight. Slowly, as if she were unsure of herself, she kissed his cheek. Her red hair tickled his jaw, but the kiss held only innocence. She'd offered it with the same gratitude a broken woman had shown to Jesus when she'd anointed his feet with oil. The oil had been her most precious possession. Likewise, Adie's kiss had been a gift—the best she had to offer.

Josh felt honored. For all his mistakes, he'd done one thing right. He'd given Adie a son. "Just so you know, I intend to make this adoption legal. I don't want you to ever worry about someone taking Stephen away."

She stepped back with a sheen in her eyes. "You're a good man, Josh."

His pride puffed up. He had to quell it. "I'm human, Adie. Deep down, I'm as weak-minded as anyone."

Her brow furrowed. "I don't understand."

It seemed plain to Josh. "What don't you see?"

"Mary shot you and you forgave her. Caroline's been forward, but you've been gentle. You've tried to help Pearl. And Bessie…she calls you her friend. If that's not 'good,' I don't know what is."

Her praise was a balm to his conscience. He'd been a protector and friend to the women of Swan's Nest. To Adie, he wanted to be more. He wanted to be a husband. Was there hope? Did she share his tender feelings? He had to know. "Who am I to you?"

She looked into his eyes, then touched his cheek again. Her fingers left a cool trail. "You're the best man I've ever known."

He knew then that Adie, like himself, had been wondering about a future together. The thought made him feel alive, a reaction he had to control. Until he did business with God, he had no right to encourage Adie's feelings. Never mind that he wanted to kiss her and not on the cheek. In spite of his worries, his lips curled with the pleasure of the compliment. "That's the nicest thing anyone's ever said to me."

"It's true."

She sounded defiant, as if she'd fight for him. Josh intended to do whatever fighting was necessary, especially where it concerned Adie and Franklin Dean, but he treasured having her for an ally. She'd make a fine preacher's wife…except she'd stopped talking to God.

Please, Lord. I need Your help.

Josh didn't expect an answer and he didn't get one. Instead he felt a quiet prompting to read the journal. The book held the key. If Emily had forgiven him, he'd be free to stay in Denver. He couldn't court Adie, but he could be her friend. He wanted to kiss her good-night but settled for holding her hand, raising it slightly to take the weight of it. "It's been a rough night but a good one."

Her eyes shone. "Thank you, Josh, for everything."

Before he could change his mind about that kiss on the lips, he left for his room. Everything—his future, his calling—depended on what Emily had written in her journal.

Adie watched Josh leave with the notebook in hand. She hoped Emily had forgiven him in those final words. It was possible. Adie recalled her mother's last hours. For years Thelma Clarke had resented her husband for leaving for the gold fields. In her dying moments, she'd spoken to her daughter of love.

"He hurt me, child. But I love him. I forgive him for leaving us. I hope you can forgive me for dying."

Adie had forgiven her mother easily. She'd saved her anger for God.

As Josh turned the corner, she hoped Emily had let go of her resentment. The thought rocked her to the core. What would she do if Timothy Long tracked her to Denver to apologize? Even if he begged her to forgive him, she'd want to see him pay for what he'd done to her. She felt the same way about Reverend Honeycutt. He didn't deserve to run a church.

Annoyed, she blew out the lamp and walked up the stairs. Voices came from Pearl's room, so she went to join her friends. As she stepped through the door, she saw Mary sitting on the foot of the bed, Pearl propped up on pillows and Bessie at her side. Caroline sat in a stuffed chair with Stephen in her arms. All the windows were open, but the room still reeked of smoke. Tomorrow Adie would wash curtains and use vinegar on the glass. No way would Franklin Dean scare her away from Swan's Nest. She pulled up a chair from the secretary. "How's everyone?"

"It could have been worse," Mary replied.

Adie felt the same way. "Even so, we have to protect ourselves. Any ideas?"

Pearl spoke in a near whisper. "I could leave."

"No!" said all four women.

Bessie looked at Pearl. "It's not just you Dean's after. He wants Adie's house."

Pearl looked pinched. "I think his driver set the fire."

Bessie stood up from the bed. She was the oldest and tonight she looked wise. "We have to fight, ladies."

Mary broke in. "I've got the pistol—"

Caroline grimaced. "Guns don't solve problems. They make them worse. We need to be smart."

Not everyone agreed with Caroline, but no one spoke. This wasn't the time to argue, only to decide.

Bessie started to pace. "I say we keep watch. We'll take turns at night, except for Pearl."

"But I want to help," the girl insisted. "I can't sleep anyway."

Adie held the deed to Swan's Nest, but the house belonged to each of them. She looked at her friends one at time. "I love you all."

"We love you, too," Caroline said. "You've given us a home. We're not going to let a bully take it."

"That's right." Bessie sounded like a Confederate general. "I wish we'd fought for our home in Virginia. Instead we let the Yankees take it over and we paid. I won't play dead now."

Mary's expression hardened. "We'll have to watch both doors."

Even with everyone on guard, Adie knew they all felt vulnerable. It showed in their eyes.

Pearl spoke next. "I don't want anyone to get hurt. Maybe I should speak to Frank."

"Don't," Adie said. "He's dangerous."

"I have to do *something.*" Pearl knotted her fists. "If he believes I won't marry him, maybe he'll stop."

"He'll never stop," Mary said bitterly. "I know his kind."

Pearl sighed. "What else can I do?"

"I don't know," Bessie said. "But we should speak with Reverend Blue. He might have another idea."

At the mention of Josh, Caroline turned to Adie. "He wanted to speak with you. Was it about the fire?"

"In a way." Her lies had gone up in smoke. "You all know Stephen's adopted. My friend, Maggie Butler, was really Emily Blue. Josh is Stephen's uncle."

The room went deathly still.

Pearl broke the silence. "Do you get to keep the baby?"

"Josh says he's mine forever." She told the story of the journal, the picture and the jewelry. "He's going to make the adoption legal. I can't imagine anything better."

"I can." Mary looked smug. "He should marry you."

Adie's jaw dropped.

"Why not?" Mary hugged her knees to her chest. "I've seen the way he looks at you, not to mention the way *you* look at him."

"Me, too," Pearl added.

Caroline managed a faint smile. "I'm pea green with envy, but Mary's right. Josh cares for you."

"You're all being silly," Adie replied. "He's a minister. I don't even go to church."

"You could," Pearl said.

"No."

"Why not?" Bessie asked.

"Come with us on Sunday." Mary added,"I'm going to sing."

Adie crossed her arms. "I don't like church."

"I do," Pearl murmured. "I miss it."

Adie didn't know what to think. Of all the women in the room, Pearl had the most cause to be bitter. Her own father had shunned her. No one from Colfax Avenue Church, people Pearl counted as friends, had even sent a note.

Adie wrinkled her brow. "Why do you like church?"

"I just do," she said.

Mary made a humming sound. "I like to sing."

Caroline chuckled. "It's a good thing you do! Reverend Blue can't sing a note!"

Bessie and Mary tried to stifle their laughter, but it leaked through their lips and came out in guffaws. Pearl caught the bug, but Adie didn't. She'd never heard Josh sing, but she was sure he had a fine voice.

After a joke about a donkey, she'd heard enough. "You're being mean!"

Caroline dabbed at her eyes. "I think Josh would laugh, too."

"So do I," Bessie added.

Adie had never seen Mary look more excited. "It sounds like I've got a job to do."

"Goodness, yes!" Caroline said.

Pearl sighed. "I wish I could go to Brick's, but I'm huge now."

Why would Pearl want to sit in church for two hours,

even one? Reverend Honeycutt's sermons had been as flat as a washboard. The times she'd listened, she'd felt like a shirt being pounded to get out the dirt. Josh's sermons had to be different because he was a different man, but church was church.

Mary eyed her thoughtfully. "Try it, Adie. Come just once."

"No!"

"Whatever you want," Bessie said. "Aside from all that, we need to be thinking of Josh right now."

"Yes," Mary said. "He just lost his sister."

Pearl folded her hands. "We should pray."

All the women—except Adie—bowed their heads.

Pearl took the lead. *"Lord Jesus, Reverend Blue—Josh—is our friend. Tonight he's grieving his sister. Please, Lord. Give him peace. Show him Your love and renew his hope for the future. Amen."*

Adie hoped God heard Pearl's prayer, but she doubted it. She pictured Josh alone in his room, reading Emily's pain-filled words by candlelight.

When Pearl yawned, the women stood.

Adie lifted Stephen from Caroline's arms. After a chorus of "good nights," she went down the hall and put him in his cradle. A faint glow in the window caught her eye and she went to the glass. Looking down, she saw a circle of light and knew Josh was on the porch, reading the journal alone.

Sure that God wouldn't answer Pearl's prayer for comfort for Josh, Adie decided to comfort him herself.

Chapter Thirteen

Josh had considered a myriad of possibilities in his search for Emily, but not once had he imagined her speaking to him from the grave. That would happen when he opened the journal.

Earlier he'd gone to his room. He'd lit the lamp, seen a haze of smoke and coughed. The room had felt cramped, even coffinlike. He'd taken a candle from the kitchen and returned to the front porch, where he'd set it on a low table, hunched forward in a chair and angled the journal to catch the light.

Looking at the black leather, he pictured Emily sitting beside him and imagined the slide of knitting needles. How many times had she listened to him banter about his day when she'd had secrets of her own? Fool that he'd been, he'd prided himself on being a good listener. In truth, he'd been so wrapped up in himself that he hadn't heard a word she'd said.

"Forgive me, Emily."

With that prayer on his lips, he started to read.

November 1874
My dear child,

> You won't be born for six months, but the day will come when you'll want to know who you are. You'll want to know your father's name and why it's not yours. You'll want to know if you have cousins and grandparents. If you have your father's red hair, you'll ask about that, too.
>
> This diary will answer those questions. One thing I've learned, child, is that life is unpredictable. That's why I'm writing to you. If something happens to me—a possibility as I learned from your father's passing—I want you to have your history.
>
> That history will start with your name. If you're a girl, I'm going to call you Julia Louise after my mother. If you're a boy, your name will be Stephen Paul after my grandfather. Together we're taking Grandfather's last name of Butler. I was born Emily Constance Blue, but I no longer want that name.

In the next several paragraphs, Emily detailed her personal history. She told her child that she'd loved to read and liked to play with dolls. She described growing up in a big house with servants, going to church on Sundays to hear Grandfather Stephen and how their mother grew flowers and gave fancy parties for their father's business associates.

Josh read every word, but he could have skipped the first pages of the journal. He'd lived the same life. He'd especially shared the same love for their grandfather. Stephen Blue had given him his first Bible and mentored him through his early years as a minister. He'd died three years ago.

Josh cringed at what the old man would have thought

of his last sermons, then wished fervently that he'd been alive to hear them. Grandfather would have invited him to his study for a little chat. He would have noticed Josh's glazed eyes and confronted him about the laudanum. The opiate had numbed his conscience. He wanted to be numb now, but Emily deserved his full attention.

> I had a good life, my child. I never went hungry, never lacked for warmth or clean clothes. My needs were met, yet I felt a constant emptiness on behalf of others.

Memories marched through Josh's mind. Emily had fed the birds in their backyard, even starlings and crows. In some ways, he'd been one of her flock. When he needed a hostess, she stepped in. She'd accompanied him on calls and had calmed mothers with sick children.

Had she longed for babies of her own? After a month at Swan's Nest, Josh knew he'd been blind to his sister's feelings. Every time Adie picked up Stephen, she smiled. Pearl, in spite of the violence of a rape, looked radiant when she mentioned her baby. He knew now that Emily had wanted a husband and family of her own.

Josh wanted to close the journal but couldn't. Squinting in the dim light, he read the next entry.

> December 1874
> My dearest little one,
> I'll never forget the moment I first saw your father. He was an Irishman, newly arrived from Dublin, a man with a passion for life but not much money. I saw him in front of a café near the orphanage where I volunteered. How I loved to hold the babies! I thought I'd never have one of my

own. I was twenty-three years old and didn't expect to marry.

It wasn't for lack of opportunity. Men had courted me. Or, more correctly, they courted my family's money. My child, if you choose to return to Boston, you'll have a right to a fortune and the Blue family name. That choice will be yours. As for my choice—to leave with nothing but my jewelry—I have no regrets. But I digress....

The day I met your father, I'd just come from the nursery where I'd spent three blissful hours rocking babies to sleep. Someday, child, I'll hold you in my arms. When I do, I'll see Dennis's eyes, maybe his red hair.

A memory flashed like a dream. Josh had been passing by the orphanage at midday and had stopped to say hello to Emily. He'd invited her to lunch but she'd declined. As he left, he'd seen a man with red hair lingering on the corner. Always friendly, Josh had nodded a greeting. The stranger had nodded back.

Josh recalled the moment because he'd been impressed with the man's bearing. His clothes had been threadbare, but he'd worn them with dignity. The Blue family often hired hands for the stables, so Josh had stopped to talk. He hadn't asked the man's name, but he'd learned he'd worked with horses in Ireland and had offered him a job. Something—or someone—had caught the man's eye. He'd politely turned down the job and walked away. A moment later, Emily had arrived. She'd looked down the street at the stranger's back. *"I'm free for lunch after all."*

As they'd headed in the opposite direction of the

man, she'd looked over her shoulder. *"Who were you talking to?"*

"An Irishman in need of a job."

"What did you think?"

He relived that minute as if it were now. *"He seems decent enough."*

"You liked him?"

He'd answered with a shrug and changed the subject to church business. How could he have been so blind? He wished now that he'd put together the clues. Emily wouldn't have asked about a stranger. She'd known the man and fairly well. Josh wasn't a snob. He'd have sanctioned a marriage between Emily and any man worthy of her love. Josh didn't judge worth by class. He judged it by a man's heart.

The thought made him frown. Dennis Hagan had walked away. If he'd loved Emily, why hadn't he spoken up? Where was the man's courage? The thought gave Josh some redemption but not enough to free him. He refocused on the journal and Emily's first glimpse of Dennis.

> I'll never forget that April day. I was walking to the café with Miss Walker, the woman who ran the orphanage, when she met a friend on the street. I went ahead to get our table. Outside the restaurant, your father stopped me and asked if I worked at the orphanage. When I said yes, he gave me a nickel for the children and left.
>
> Nearly every day for a week, he waited outside the orphanage. Each time he gave me a few coins, and with each meeting our conversation stretched until we took to walking along the river. That's where he told me his story.

He'd left Ireland to escape starvation and the shame of poverty. His parents had both perished and so had three of his eight siblings. The others had married or moved on. He'd found employment on a rich man's estate but didn't have the stomach for a lifetime of earning pennies with no hope of his own land, his own business. Ambitious and hungry, he'd come to America.

We fell in love, child.

Josh felt a small measure of peace. Emily hadn't been attacked. She'd fallen in love and given in to the most common of temptations. After his bout with laudanum, he couldn't claim to be above her in any way.

Nor was he immune to the thoughts of a lonely man. Tonight, before the fire started, he'd kissed Adie's forehead in a kind of blessing. His motives were pure, but he felt nature's way between them. Later, when she'd touched his cheek and kissed it, he'd felt the seeds of tenderness sprouting into vines of love. A few months ago, the thought would have troubled him. He'd prided himself on being like Paul, a man who had walked through life alone. Josh's path now felt wide enough for two. When he closed his eyes, he saw Adie's face. He wanted to hear her sweet voice and feel her hand tucked in his.

"Josh?"

Had he imagined her voice? His thoughts had been vivid, but he wasn't crazy. He looked to the door, where he saw Adie peering in his direction. "I'm over here."

She moved from the darkest shadows to the fainter ones made by the lone candle. He wished he'd sat in the swing so that she'd be next to him. Instead she took the chair on the other side of the table. As she looked down at the open journal, her eyelashes fluttered as she blinked to adjust to the dim light.

"Are you still reading?" she asked.

"I'm about halfway."

"How is it?"

"About what I expected."

She waited.

"It's painful," he admitted.

He needed a respite, so he let his eyes linger on Adie. Her presence gave him comfort in a way he'd never experienced. She understood his thoughts. She felt his sorrow because she'd known Emily and had witnessed the reason for his regrets. He needed to finish the journal tonight, but his strength flagged.

Wordless, Adie reached across the table, turned the book in her direction and began to read out loud.

> I didn't intend to lose my heart to Dennis Hagan. He didn't intend to take it. We were as different as boiled potatoes and lemon pie, yet we connected the instant we met.
>
> Oh, my child! To fall in love is a taste of heaven. Even when it's fraught with sacrifice, there's a joy to giving your heart to someone who treasures it. Make no mistake, your father treasured me. Perhaps *too* much, now that I look back. He treated me as if I were a porcelain doll. Only at the end did I become fully human to him.
>
> When you're grown and fall in love for yourself, you'll understand what I'm about to say. We didn't mean to kiss. It happened on a rainy day in the middle of a busy street. A storm struck and he pulled me inside a doorway. I'd say the kiss just

happened, but that wouldn't be true. He asked with his eyes and I said yes with mine. He regretted it. I didn't. He'd said he'd tasted the sweetest fruit and could never taste it again.

That's when I told him I loved him. I was tired of being coy! Tired of hiding my feelings! In the middle of Beacon Hill, I asked your father to marry me.

He said no.

I called him a coward.

He dared me to go west with him.

I told him I'd pack my things and meet him at the train station. He must have believed me because he laughed. "All right, love. You win. We'll marry, but not until I can support you. Will you wait for that?"

Another dare. I took it, but I dared him back.

Josh had wanted the truth about Emily. Now he had it. She'd been in love and she'd been bold. Dennis Hagan had succumbed to every man's temptation. Josh wanted to punch him, but he had no right to throw stones. In different ways, he'd fallen himself. Josh didn't know if Dennis Hagan had regrets, but he knew his own.

He also knew how he felt about Adie. He loved her and wanted to marry her, but reading the journal hadn't set him free. He still felt obligated to Emily. Did that mean preaching for strangers as he'd been doing? He couldn't fulfill that duty with a wife and child. Nor did Adie share his commitment to his calling. Of all the problems, that one loomed the largest.

As Josh raked his fingers through his hair, Adie looked up from Emily's delicate writing. "That's the end of the passage, but there's more."

He needed an answer. He wanted it now. "Keep going."

February 1875
My Child,
You're kicking tonight! Such a sweet feeling… Your father would have been so proud. I'm at the point of the story that's the hardest to tell, so I welcome the sense of Dennis alive in my womb. You, child, are my only comfort as I relive the darkest moment of my life.

Your father took my dare and I took his. I didn't expect to conceive. Does any woman when she succumbs to sin? By the time I realized you were on the way, he'd left for St. Louis. I had the name of his cousin and his solemn vow to send for me as soon as they claimed land and he built a house.

I knew my brother wouldn't approve, so I asked Dennis to write to me at the orphanage and he did. One precious letter and I had to burn it to keep our secret! I wrote back. I told him you were on the way. I waited for weeks to hear from him. I know he'd have sent for us immediately. We'd sinned, but your father was an honorable man. He loved me. He would have given us his name and more.

Weeks passed. I didn't hear from him and was close to panic. My middle was thickening. I had no choice but to face my brother.

Adie stopped speaking, but her eyes skimmed the page. She bit her lip, grimaced, then covered her mouth with her fingers. "I can't read this. It's vile."

"Then it's true."

"Not anymore." She closed the book.

Josh reached across the table and took it. He opened

the book to the last few pages, then looked at Adie. "Aren't you leaving?"

"No," she said. "I'll stay while you read it to yourself."

Her presence gave Josh the strength he needed to go back to that night in Boston.

> To fully appreciate my dilemma, you need to know that your uncle is a famous minister. People travel miles to hear him, though I don't know why! In those final weeks—when I knew you were on the way—I'd listen to him spout about righteousness and obedience and wonder if he had a drop of warm blood in his body. Josh, you see, is perfect.
>
> At least *he* thinks he is.
>
> I love God, too! God loves me. Jesus died for my sins and I know it. Josh doesn't think he has any sins. Well, he's wrong. That night, he became a murderer. The Bible says he who has anger in his heart might as well have committed murder. I've never seen Josh angrier than when I told him about you. I'd mustered my courage and I'd whispered the simple fact.
>
> "I'm with child."
>
> He ranted at me. He paced like a lion about to eat me. He didn't ask me who or why. He ignored the tears streaming down my face. My clearest memory is of the moment he pounded the table.
>
> "Blast it, Emily! I have a reputation to uphold."
>
> *His* reputation? What about *my child?* I was lost and broken and terrified. In the weeks after Dennis left, I'd had time to weigh the consequences of our recklessness. We should have

waited. We should have found another way, one that protected our child. I couldn't feed you without help. I had nowhere to go except to Josh, who turned his back on me. I didn't think I could be more wounded, but his next words filled me with a pain I'd never known.

"Leave Boston, Emily. Give the baby away."

"No!" I cried.

"I'm *ordering* you to leave."

He started blathering about a long visit with cousins in Rhode Island. When I refused, he called me a horrible name. I ran to my room and packed my things. I heard him prowling in the hall. He pounded on my door, but I didn't answer. When the house finally quieted, I crept down the stairs with a valise and my jewelry and walked two miles in the cold to the train station.

Josh looked up at Adie. "Every word is true."

"I don't care," she insisted. "You wouldn't say those things again."

"No, but I said them once."

If he'd learned anything this past year, it was one simple truth. Mistakes could be forgiven, but consequences weren't so easily erased. Stephen proved his point. So did the pain in Emily's journal. Josh had dedicated his life to preaching God's forgiveness because he needed it so badly. He couldn't change the past, but with God's grace he could claim a better future. He wanted that new start for himself. Hoping to find it, he focused on Emily's next words.

After leaving Boston, I sent a note to my best friend. She knew about Dennis, and I didn't want her to worry. I told her my plans. I intended to find your father in St. Louis and make a new life. That night I vowed to never return home, to never speak to Josh again. Even when I stood at your father's grave, I knew I'd keep that promise. Oh, child. The sadness! I found Dennis's cousin easily. He recognized me from the picture Dennis kept by his bed. As gently as he could, he told me your father had died of influenza.

"He'd been workin' too hard, Miss Blue. He saved every penny for you. Wouldn't even see a doctor."

That foolish man and his pride! My jewelry would have supported us for years. We could have married! We could have left Boston together, but he'd made me promise to wait until he'd made his own way. I weep for him every day. You, sweet child, are my comfort, my joy. You're the reason I know God has forgiven my sins. Only a loving God, a good and kind God, would share with human beings the joy of creation. You, my baby, are a miracle.

Know that I love you and always will. Someday I hope to tell you this story in person, but I know the uncertainties of life. If something happens to me, you'll have these words, a picture of me but not your father, and whatever is left of the jewelry.

With deepest love,
Your mother

Josh looked at the bottom of the page and saw writing that wasn't so perfect. These, he realized, were his sister's final words, written on her deathbed when she was bleeding and weak.

Dear Stephen,
My son! The struggle… I'm dying. Know that I love you. Adie is my best friend. She'll be a good mother. She—

So ended the journal, cut off in midsentence just as Emily's life had been cut short by tragedy. With his eyes red rimmed and hurting, both from the fire and the strain of reading, Josh bowed his head.

Dear Lord, don't let Emily's suffering be in vain. I'll serve You wherever, however, You ask.

Sometimes the Lord spoke to Josh through scripture he'd memorized. Other times he felt a quiet certainty. Tonight his heart beat with a new sense of purpose. Startled, he looked at Adie and saw the future with a sudden clarity. She needed a husband. Stephen needed a father. He loved her and wanted to marry her, but how could he? Adie believed in God but didn't share his commitment.

He didn't know what to say or do until she spoke the words that pointed the way.

"I'm going to church on Sunday."

Adie opened her mouth before she could change her mind. As Josh read Emily's words, she'd seen him grimace. Once he'd shut his eyes and groaned as if he'd been struck. She cared for this man. She'd do anything to make him happy.

To his credit, his mouth didn't gape. "I'm glad."

She wondered if she'd lost her mind. "It might be just once."

"Whatever you want."

That was the problem. Adie didn't know what she wanted. Reverend Honeycutt had sent her away. Old Man Long had ranted about hell and judgment. Josh was different, but he worshipped the same demanding God. As the candle sent shadows across his jaw, she saw the straight line of his mouth. She didn't know what Emily had written, but Josh had taken it hard.

She hurt for him. "Emily didn't forgive you, did she?"

"Not a bit. In the end, she hated me even more." He handed her the journal. "This belongs to Stephen."

As she took it, Josh stood and so did she. As he lifted the candle, gold light pulled them into the same circle. A half smile softened his mouth. "Thank you for staying. You made this easier."

"I'm glad."

She hugged the journal because she couldn't hug Josh. The smile climbed to his eyes. He motioned for her to go into the house, then guided her with his hand on her back. When they reached the stairs, he stopped and raised the candle to illuminate the steps. Their eyes locked in the shadows, but neither of them moved. She wanted to tell him that she hurt for him. She wanted to kiss his cheek and reassure him that he wasn't an ogre. She wanted to tell him that she admired him, but she couldn't. Emily no longer stood between them, but his faith did.

He stepped back, then spoke with a hush. "Good night, Adie."

"Good night."

As she climbed the stairs, questions for Josh swirled in her mind. *You've been hurt. How can you still trust God? Where was He when my mother died?* She had to fight the urge to turn around. Josh stayed until she reached her room; then the stairwell went dark. She went to the trunk, where she put away the journal and the jewelry and closed the lid. If she'd been speaking to God, she would have prayed for Josh. She would have thanked the Almighty for Stephen's life. Instead she spoke to Maggie… Emily now.

"He's changed."

Silence.

"You'd like him, Emily. You'd love him again."

Adie knew, because she felt that love now. The admission stole her breath. She'd fallen in love with Joshua Blue. A man…a minister. She'd lost her mind. No matter what the future held, Josh would always be a man of faith. He needed a wife who shared that passion. Could she be that woman? Adie didn't know, but she was willing to find out. This Sunday, she'd go to church in Brick's Saloon. She'd be among friends and she'd listen.

Chapter Fourteen

Late the next morning, Adie heard someone knocking on the front door. Bessie, Caroline and Mary had gone to work in spite of their exhaustion. Pearl had stayed upstairs and Josh was outside, cleaning up the mess from the fire. When the visitor knocked again, she peeked through the drapes and saw a horse and buggy she didn't recognize. Her stomach dropped to her toes. She couldn't imagine who'd come calling, but she knew Franklin Dean had allies. No way would she open the door.

"It's my father!"

She turned and saw Pearl lumbering down the stairs. She was clutching the railing, but Adie worried she'd fall. "Be careful."

"It's him," she said again. "I looked out the window."

Adie was concerned about Pearl's health. They'd had a rough night and the mother-to-be didn't need the upset. "I'll tell him to leave."

"No," Pearl cried. "Let him in."

Against her better judgment, Adie opened the door. The last time she'd seen Reverend Oliver, he'd stood tall in a crisp frock coat. Today he looked haggard. So did the coat.

He took off his hat, revealing thick silver hair. "Thank you for seeing me, Miss Clarke. I heard about the fire. My daughter…is she all right?"

"She's fine."

"And the baby?"

His tone didn't change. He feared as much for his grandchild as he did for Pearl. Adie glanced over her shoulder and saw the mother-to-be coming forward to answer the question herself. Adie pushed the door wide and stepped back.

Pearl froze at the threshold. "I'm fine, Papa. Thank you for—"

Reverend Oliver strode through the door, pulled his daughter into a hug and rocked her back and forth. In a torrent of choked words, he apologized for every mistake of the past months. When Pearl started to cry, he stepped back and gripped her hands in both of his. "Can you possibly forgive me?"

Her face paled. "How much do you know?"

"Everything." He clenched his jaw. "Reverend Blue paid a call on me. I know about the buggy ride and Frank's last visit. Now the fire—" He sealed his lips. "He forced you, didn't he?"

Tears welled in Pearl's eyes. "Let's sit down."

Adie, with a lump in her throat, slipped into the kitchen. As she busied herself with a pot of tea, Josh came through the back door. His shirt, a blue chambray, would need a good scrubbing and speckles of soot darkened his face. Underneath the grime, she saw bluish circles under his eyes. He'd been up all night and it showed.

As their gazes met, she recalled the emotion of the

journal and her sudden decision to go to church. After she'd gone to bed, she'd tossed all night with dreams of Liddy's Grove and Franklin Dean. She'd become so angry that she'd pummeled her pillow and cursed her enemies. Just before dawn, she'd changed her mind about going to Brick's for church. She didn't want to reveal her upset, but she had to tell Josh about her change of heart.

Looking tired but relaxed, he leaned his hips against the counter. "The mess from the woodpile's gone."

"Thank you."

"I'll get paint for the wall."

She swiped at a speck of dust. "I should pay for that."

"Let me," he said easily.

"You shouldn't. You're a guest."

She kept wiping the counter. With the lightness of a bird, Josh brought his hand down on hers and stopped the motion. "Is that what I am, Adie? A *guest?*"

She hung her head.

His voice stayed low. "I thought we were friends."

"We are."

"Then allow me to buy the paint." He raised his hand, freeing her but leaving a memory of his long fingers and a trace of soot. It was a silly quarrel, one that had nothing to do with whitewash and everything to do with Adie attending church. She didn't want to explain why, so she looked for an excuse. "About Sunday… I can't go to Brick's after all. Someone should stay with Pearl."

"I'll ask Bessie."

So much for that excuse. She hunted for another. "I'd feel bad leaving Stephen."

"You can bring him."

"What if he cries?"

Adie knew a lame excuse when she heard one and

so did Josh. He looked her square in the eye. "He can bellow all he wants. I'll hold him myself."

He reached for her hand. The strength of his grip made her feel small and obvious, as if he could see right through her. She looked into his eyes, then wished she hadn't.

He kept his voice low. "You're scared, aren't you?"

"I'm not *scared,*" she insisted. "It's just that… I don't know exactly."

"You've been hurt."

"Yes."

"And you're angry."

Her eyes blazed. "I am, but I don't want to be. Not anymore."

"That fight is between you and God," Josh said. "He's everywhere, but sometimes He's easier to find when a person goes looking."

Adie didn't know, but she wondered about such things. In spite of Pearl's trouble, she had peace. Mary still kept a loaded derringer, but she'd been smiling more and her humor had lost its sarcasm. They both had as much cause as Adie to be resentful, but neither of them held grudges. Neither did Bessie or Caroline. Adie wanted that calm. She also wanted to please Josh. She cared for him. She was raising his nephew and felt obliged to honor his beliefs.

Looking glum, she said, "All right. I'll go."

His eyes twinkled. "It won't be *that* bad."

When she sighed, he laughed. "What? You think I'll bore you to death?" In a deep, droning voice, he imitated a very dull preacher.

When she laughed out loud, his eyes twinkled with pleasure. "You won't be sorry, Adie. I promise."

When she looked into his eyes, she believed him.

A month ago he'd collapsed on her porch. He was still lean, but he had a strength of both body and character that inspired trust. Every man she'd known had let her down, but Josh had stayed true. She'd helped him, too. Between Buttons and Adie's cooking, he'd recovered from the ulcer. The thought pleased her. "Are you hungry? I could make you a sandwich."

"I'd like that."

As she took a fresh loaf from the bread box, she thought about the simple pleasure of bread. She didn't recall many of Reverend Honeycutt's sermons, but she remembered him calling Jesus the bread of life. Adie knew about going hungry and being filled. Sometimes, especially when she'd feared losing Stephen, she'd felt as if her life were nothing but crumbs. Now she didn't. Going to church sounded better by the minute, but only because she trusted Josh and didn't feel intimidated by Brick's Saloon. She'd worked in shabby places just like it. Reverend Honeycutt wouldn't be anywhere in sight.

As she handed Josh the sandwich, she recalled Pearl and her father in the parlor. "By the way," she said, "Reverend Oliver is here."

"I thought he'd stop by." Josh had been about to take a bite, but he lowered the sandwich. "I didn't break your confidence, Adie. But I said enough to make him think twice about Franklin Dean."

"I'm glad you did." After her experience with secrets, she never wanted to keep one again. "Pearl was happy to see him."

"Good."

"He apologized to her."

Josh's expression turned wistful. She knew he was thinking of Emily. "I'm glad."

"Me, too." The voice belonged to Pearl.

Adie turned to the doorway and saw her friend, large with child and beaming with joy. Dried tears streaked her cheeks, but nothing could dim her smile as she looked at Josh. "I can't thank you enough."

He waved off her gratitude. "You just did."

She shifted her gaze to Adie. "Would you both come into the parlor? My father and I have something to tell you."

Had she decided to report Dean to the law? Adie hoped so, but that decision belonged to Pearl. Adie would support her no matter what she decided. She followed her friend into the parlor and sat with her on the divan. Reverend Oliver had the armchair, so Josh sat across from Adie.

The old man looked first at her. "Miss Clarke, I want to thank you for helping my daughter. When I failed her, you gave her a home. If there's ever anything I can do—"

"I was glad to help," Adie said shyly.

Pearl squeezed her hand. "You're my best friend."

Adie felt honored.

Reverend Oliver cleared his throat. "Pearl and I have come to a decision. In fact, we've come to two of them. One concerns Franklin Dean. I'll get to that one. The second concerns the future. As soon as my grandchild's strong enough to travel, the three of us will be leaving Denver."

Adie pulled her friend into a hug. "I'll miss you, but it's what you wanted."

Reverend Oliver told them that he'd sent a wire to his niece in Cheyenne and she'd already answered. She had a large empty house and would welcome their company.

"Does she know about the baby?" Adie asked.

Pearl looked troubled. "I want to explain in person."

"Of course." Adie squeezed her hand. "If you have trouble of any kind, you *know* you can come back here."

Pearl smiled. "I do."

Tobias cleared his throat. "I'm looking forward to the change, but there's a problem."

"What is it, sir?" Josh asked.

"I'm worried about my congregation here in Denver. You're young, Josh. You've got a heart for the Lord and a level head. I'm hoping you'll take my place."

Josh held up his hands, palm-out to signal a hard stop. "Don't even *think* about it."

"Why not?" asked the older man.

"I know my place, and it's not in a big church."

The tension drained from Adie's spine. She could manage a service in a saloon, but Colfax Avenue Church landed her back in Kansas with Reverend Honeycutt. If a church had stained glass, she wanted nothing to do with it.

Reverend Oliver steepled his fingers. "You sound very sure, maybe *too* sure."

"I appreciate the offer, sir. But I can't take your pulpit."

"Can't or won't?"

"They're the same," Josh answered. "I left an established church in Boston. I'll never pastor another one."

"Why not?

"It's a long story, one I'll tell you another time."

"All right," said Reverend Oliver. "But I'd like to challenge you."

"Go ahead."

"Examine your heart, Josh. Are you living to serve God or serving God to avoid living?"

Josh started to speak, but the older man held up his hand. "Don't answer yet. Read Psalm 139."

Adie recognized the psalm Josh had taught at the Bible study. Even *she* knew the substance of it. David had asked God to search his heart. He'd given the Lord his anxious thoughts.

Reverend Oliver stared hard at Josh. "Pray about it, son."

"I will."

His voice carried just a trace of longing, but Adie heard it. She flashed to the day he'd walked with her to the bank. He'd seen the church and had wanted to go inside. She saw that look now and it scared her. She could handle a church of misfits in a dusty saloon, but she couldn't tolerate the spit and polish of Colfax Avenue Church. The women all wore the latest fashions. The men carried watch fobs and gold-tipped walking sticks like Franklin Dean. Worst of all, not a single member of the congregation had called on Pearl.

Reverend Oliver's jaw tightened. "This leads us to Franklin Dean. He has to be stopped."

On that, they all agreed.

"What do you suggest?" Josh asked.

The older man aimed his chin at Pearl. "This is my daughter's decision, but I support it fully."

As Pearl straightened her back, her belly made an even bigger bulge. The baby could arrive at any time. Adie had seen Maggie die in childbirth. She didn't want to lose Pearl. With her thin bones and white-blond hair, she looked too fragile for the rigors of birth.

Frail or not, Pearl set her jaw. "In a perfect world, I'd report Frank to the authorities and he'd go to prison. But this world isn't perfect. A trial would come down to my word against his and he'd win."

She was right. They all knew it.

"He may be the most powerful man in Denver," Pearl

continued. "But he's *not* the most powerful woman. I'm sending notes to the elders' wives. I'm going to tell them to keep their daughters away from him and why. It's not gossip. I *know* what he did to me. If I don't speak up, he'll hurt someone else."

"That's right," Adie said.

Tobias beamed at his daughter with pride. "It won't be easy."

Adie knew from experience that Pearl's stand would come at a cost. Some women would thank her. Others would accuse her of causing her own problems. In the days before Adie left Liddy's Grove, she'd felt the same daggers in her back.

Josh focused on Reverend Oliver. "You told me Dean's on the elder board."

"That's right."

"What do you plan to do?"

"What I should have done months ago." He hammered his fingers against the armrest. "There are some good men on that board, including Halston Smythe. I'll see him tomorrow. If I know Hal—and I do—he won't let the problem slide. I'm also trusting the women to speak to their husbands. With enough pressure, Frank will resign or face a recall."

Pearl spoke up. "I hope the men listen."

"I think they will." Reverend Oliver's eyes turned misty as he looked at his daughter. "If your mother were alive, none of this would have happened. She'd have given me the what-for six ways to Sunday."

Pearl touched her belly. "I miss her."

They sat in silence, each remembering loved ones until Pearl gripped Adie's hand. "I'm worried about you. Frank still wants Swan's Nest."

"Leave that to me," Josh said.

Adie didn't know what to think. "What are you going to do?"

"It's already done." Josh leaned back in the chair. "Even before the fire I sent a letter to a cousin of mine. Elliot's a banker and a good one. Denver's ripe with opportunity, and there's nothing Elliot likes more than being in the thick of things. He's opening a branch of Boston Merchants Bank. Franklin Dean's going to have some competition."

Reverend Oliver lifted his chin. "'Be ye wise in the ways of the world.'"

"That's right," Josh replied. "Elliot's got a gift for making money. He'll drive Dean to the dogs." With his eyes bright, he turned back to Adie. "Even before last night, I asked him to pay off your mortgage. I figured you'd want to negotiate terms, but that's off the table. As soon as Elliot can arrange it, you'll own Swan's Nest free and clear."

The news stole Adie's voice, her breath. Stephen would never go hungry. Emily's dream of a place for women would be secure. If she and Josh had been alone, she'd have hugged him. "How can I ever thank you?"

"Just love my nephew."

"I do."

Her reply reminded her of a wedding vow. Judging by the intensity of his gaze, Josh heard the echo, too. So did Pearl because she hugged Adie and whispered in her ear, "He loves you, Adie. Be brave."

Except Adie didn't feel brave. She had powerful feelings for Josh. She couldn't deny them, but neither could she imagine being a minister's wife. They both had more to say, but the talk would have to wait for a private moment. With her heart brimming, she looked at

Josh and saw him speaking to Reverend Oliver. "Are you headed to the parsonage?"

"I am."

"May I ride with you? I need to send another wire to Boston."

A sad one, Adie knew. He had to tell family and friends of Emily's passing.

Tobias pushed to his feet. "I'd be glad for the company, Reverend. It'll give me a chance to talk you into taking over my church."

Adie shuddered at the thought.

As Josh stood, he gave Adie a sweet look, then followed the older man out the door.

"Oh!" cried Pearl.

Adie gripped her friend's hand. "Are you all right?"

She grimaced. "My back hurts."

In the days before Stephen's birth, Emily had made the same complaint. "We better get you to bed."

Pearl shook her head. "I'd rather walk in the garden."

"I'll go with you."

Adie stood first, gave Pearl her hand and pulled her up. Together they walked out the front door and into the sunshine. As they neared the garden, the perfume filled Adie's nose. She wasn't on speaking terms with God, but she believed in Him. She knew He'd created the heavens and the earth, plants, animals, man and woman.

He'd created *her.*

He'd created Josh, too.

For the first time in years, she felt as if she belonged with someone. On Sunday she'd test the waters at Brick's. If she found peace, she could love Josh freely. Full of hope, she went with Pearl to smell the roses.

Chapter Fifteen

As Tobias steered the buggy down the street, Josh considered the events of the past hour. Adie had accepted ownership of Swan's Nest without a fight. In the kitchen, she'd beaten back doubts about going to church. She'd been relaxed and happy until Tobias invited him to preach. She hadn't liked the idea at all.

Josh didn't know how he felt. At first he'd rejected the thought because he'd be tempted by pride. Seconds later, his blood had rushed. He'd be preaching every Sunday. He could spend weeks on the same subject, watching as the seeds took root and grew. He knew Adie disapproved, but Josh had asked God to direct his steps. He had to be open to anything.

As they passed the piles of stone from the demolished house, Tobias glanced at him. "You belong here, Josh."

Maybe he did. "What makes you think so?"

"Experience."

"Yours or mine?"

"Mine," Tobias said. "Even this old fool can see God's hand. There's nothing better than a church of your own and a wife and family."

"Hold on," Josh said, chuckling. "You've skipped way ahead of me."

"Not really." Tobias turned the buggy down a street with busy shops. "I saw the way you looked at Miss Clarke. She's a fine woman, and I know from Pearl that she adopted your nephew."

Josh didn't mention Adie's troubled faith, but he knew her doubts stood between them. As much as he liked the idea, he couldn't court her until she made peace with God. A minister's wife worked as hard as her husband.

Tobias's voice turned wistful. "My wife and I were married for twenty-nine years."

"That's a long time."

"Not long enough," he said quietly. "Ginny and I quarreled sometimes, but we always kissed good-night. That was our rule."

"It's a good one."

"You should think about getting married, Josh. A good woman keeps a man honest."

Josh thought of his past concerns. "Paul says marriage is a distraction."

"That, too," Tobias said. "But the commotion is worth what you gain. Ginny had a way of speaking her mind. Without her, I'd have driven this church into a ditch."

"She sounds like a fine woman."

"She was, but she's gone." His eyes misted. "Now it's up to me to take care of Pearl."

"Yes, sir."

"My only concern is my congregation. On that score, you and I are in the same boat."

"How so?"

"If you leave Denver, you'll worry about Miss Clarke and that baby."

Tobias had a point. Adie did a good job of running Swan's Nest, but the big house needed constant upkeep. If Josh left, she'd be wise to hire help…or to marry. He blinked and imagined a faceless man bringing her flowers. Only a fool wouldn't see Adie's fine traits, including her pretty red hair. When the right man came along, she'd fall in love and Stephen would have a father.

Josh wanted to be that man. He wanted sole claim to Adie and to raise Stephen as his own flesh-and-blood. The plan had a certain logic, but he worried about Adie's hostility to his calling. Josh had another problem, one just as big as Adie's lack of faith. Thoughts of marriage filled him with joy, but preaching in the biggest church in Denver took him back to the worst days of his life.

Tobias turned the buggy down a narrow street. "What's the *real* reason you're being stubborn about my offer?"

The answer rolled off Josh's lips. "Pride made me a hypocrite. I destroyed my sister's life."

"So you got knocked off your high horse."

"Yes," he answered. "Leading a church like Colfax Avenue might stir up my pride."

Tobias harrumphed.

Josh frowned. "You don't believe me."

"I believe you," he answered. "I *know* you're full of pride. So am I. So what?"

Josh took offense. "I'm trying to be faithful."

"Nonsense. You're acting like a whipped dog."

"Sir?"

"Good men do battle with themselves every day. You know the scriptures."

Of course he did. He'd memorized Paul's famous

words to the Romans. Like every other man, Josh sometimes did what he didn't want to do, or he didn't do what he knew to be right.

"You fell off your horse at a full gallop," Tobias said. "It's about time you climbed back on."

Josh had to admire the man's insight. Tobias had seen his deepest fear and dared him to face it. Josh had a lot of faults, but being weak-willed wasn't one of them. "I'll think about it."

"That's all I'm asking." Tobias gave a crisp nod. "Go home tonight and have supper with Miss Clarke. Hold that baby in your arms and then decide."

Josh laughed. "You argue well, sir."

As the old man steered the buggy down the street behind the church, Josh looked at the stone wall and saw another stained glass window. It depicted a stream meandering through a meadow. A willow tree hung over the banks. He recognized the first of the Psalms and a particular verse, "And he shall be like a tree planted by the rivers of water." For months he'd been like the stream, wandering through a dry and thirsty land. Now he wanted to be the tree, planted firmly in Denver.

Tobias broke into his thoughts. "I'd like to hear you preach sometime."

"Come to Brick's."

"Better yet, you come to Colfax Avenue."

"I'm not—"

"Hold on," Tobias said. "All I'm asking is one Sunday."

Josh liked the idea. He could test the waters and himself, but he worried about his little flock.

"I've got a commitment to the folks at Brick's."

"Invite them."

He couldn't see bleary-eyed cowboys mixing with

society matrons, nor could he imagine the girls from Miss Elsa's in the front row. As for Adie, he doubted she'd set foot in a stone building with stained glass. In the end, though, Josh knew the choice came down to one question. On Sunday morning, where did God want him to be?

Tobias's jaw hardened. "You can preach your heart out, Reverend. Christ drove the money changers out of the temple and he wasn't gentle about it. Franklin Dean defiled my daughter. I'd like to see him taken to task."

"You could do it yourself, sir."

"I'm too angry."

Josh understood. He'd forgiven Dennis Hagan in principle, but his fists still wanted to flatten the man.

When they reached the telegraph office, Tobias stopped the buggy. As soon as Josh climbed out, the older man shook the reins. As the rig rounded the corner, a carriage approached from the same direction. Josh recognized the matched bays that belonged to Franklin Dean. In the seat sat Horace. Josh wanted to haul him to jail with his own two hands, but he couldn't prove the man's involvement. Neither could he link Dean to the crimes. On the other hand, he could take Tobias's offer and preach a barn-burner about two-faced moneychangers.

The thought tempted him, but taking Tobias's pulpit, even for one Sunday, scared Josh as a hot stove frightened a child. He knew his weaknesses. He also knew his strengths. By faith, Peter had walked on water. He'd doubted and sunk, but Christ had lifted him up. Josh felt that same hand on his shoulder, lifting him up and pointing the way to Colfax Avenue Church.

But, Lord, what about Adie?

Even as the thought formed, Josh knew it came from

doubt. If he could trust God to guide his own life, surely he could trust the Almighty to shepherd Adie. A painful calm settled on his shoulders. As soon as he sent the telegram, he'd tell Tobias he'd preach this coming Sunday. Sure of his decision, he went inside the telegraph office, where he jotted a message to the Blue family attorney who'd spread the word about Emily. He paid the clerk to send it immediately, then walked out of the shop, silently praying that Adie would still come to church.

"What is it, Horace?"

"I saw something, sir."

Frank, alone at his dining room table, looked up from the pheasant his cook had prepared. The bird was done to perfection as were the julienne potatoes, baby carrots and snow peas. Later he'd enjoy the cream puffs—both of them since Pearl wasn't here to eat hers. After dessert, he'd indulge in a bottle of wine. If the liquor didn't cure his loneliness, he'd visit Miss Elsa's Social Club. He'd noticed a new girl and had asked her name. Gretchen, blond and blue-eyed, reminded him of Pearl.

Horace was standing respectfully by the door, but his eyes were devouring the delicacies on the table. The man ate well enough back in the kitchen, so he wasn't hungry for food. As for what the food represented—wealth, privilege—Horace wasn't entitled to such things. Frank swirled his wine in the fancy goblet, took a long swallow, then savored it with his eyes on Horace. The driver dared to look peeved. Frank would have ordered him to leave, but he needed his loyalty. He set the glass aside. "What have you learned?"

"I saw Revered Blue this afternoon."

"Where?"

"At the telegraph office. He sent a wire to Boston."

Frank forgot his meal. "Go on."

"I went inside," Horace said. "The operator's a fellow named Reggie. He don't say much."

Frank drummed his fingers on the table. He wanted to tell Horace to get to the point, but sometimes even *he* had to be patient. "I suppose you had a chat?"

"Not exactly." Horace grinned. "Reggie acted like he didn't know the reverend from Adam. I waited till he left the counter. Then I looked in the trash."

"Good work."

"Yes, sir." Horace stepped forward and handed him a crumpled sheet of paper.

Frank opened it and smiled. He'd been hoping for the wording of the wire and he'd gotten it, written in Joshua Blue's own hand.

> Emily is deceased stop Baby is alive stop Letter to follow re trust fund stop.

Franklin understood "trust fund," but who was Emily and where did a baby fit in the story? He looked at Horace. "This is cryptic, to say the least."

"There's more," said the driver.

"Go on."

"I've been going to his church."

Frank sneered. "A sacrifice, I'm sure."

"Not so bad, sir." Horace squared his shoulders. "Three of the ladies live at Swan's Nest. One of them talked to Miss Elsa's girls about Reverend Blue having a sister. He's been looking for her and her baby."

"I see."

"The older lady told the young one to mind her manners. No gossip, she said."

Frank lived for gossip. “Go on.”

“That’s all I know.”

Frank weighed the hodgepodge of information. Emily had to be Joshua Blue’s sister. The only woman to have a baby was Adie Clarke. The baby would be heir to a fortune, which made Miss Clarke a wealthy woman. Frank muttered a curse. If he’d guessed right, and he usually did, Miss Clarke was sitting on a goldmine. He’d never get his hands on Swan’s Nest. He had to drive her out while he could.

He glared at Horace. “The fire wasn’t enough.”

Horace frowned. “I had to be careful, sir.”

“Not anymore.”

“But, sir—”

“No buts, Horace. I want Swan’s Nest and I want it now.”

The driver’s jaw stiffened. “I can’t do it. Miss Pearl—she’s about to give birth. And that little baby, I heard he’s sickly. He could die in the smoke alone.”

Frank frowned. “Horace, are you going soft on me?”

“No, sir.”

“Good.” He swirled the red wine, watching as it caught the light from the candelabra. Intimidating Adie Clarke hadn’t worked, not with Reverend Blue interfering. Frank needed a new plan for a new enemy. “Perhaps we should take a different approach.”

“Like what?”

“Use your connection at Brick’s. Find out everything you can about Joshua Blue.”

“Why, sir?”

“The reverend and I are going to war.” Frank didn’t know precisely how he’d ruin Joshua Blue, but he intended to enjoy every minute of it.

Chapter Sixteen

"How could you?" Adie cried. "Franklin Dean goes to that church!"

She and Josh were alone in the garden. The sun had set hours ago, leaving a distant moon and a sky full of stars. Adie had never felt so foolish in her life. After this afternoon, she'd dared to wonder if they had a future together. She'd fixed a special supper, complete with candied yams because she knew Josh liked them. She'd been as obvious as Caroline, glancing at him during the meal, passing the yams before he asked. After supper, he'd asked her to meet him in the garden.

Her heart had raced. She'd thought of wedding clothes and making promises as pure as white silk. She could handle going to church in Brick's Saloon. Maybe God would find her there. After listening to Pearl's excitement over Cheyenne, Adie had dared to hope for a new beginning for herself.

"God answered my prayers," Pearl had said.

Maybe, but tonight he'd ignored Adie. She'd let her feelings for Josh run free and now it hurt to look at him. Even in the dark, his hair had a shine. She couldn't see his irises, but she knew how blue they were.

"Why?" she said again. "Why can't you just preach at Brick's?"

"I can preach anywhere," he said. "That's the point. It doesn't matter if I'm in a church or on a street corner."

"I don't understand."

Josh took a step in her direction. She turned her back but couldn't escape his voice. "I have to do what God's called me to do. I'm sorry you're hurt, Adie. I was worried you'd take it hard."

"Hard!" She felt betrayed.

"I know you're upset, but when I saw Horace, I knew I had to say yes."

He'd already told her about seeing Dean's driver. "Fine. Do what you want."

"It's not what I want," he insisted. "I have to do what's right."

This was Josh, a man who would live his convictions no matter the cost. She knew what Emily's death had done to him. It took courage to preach at a church that would remind him of Boston and who he'd been. She admired his bravery but didn't share it. She'd been hurt and had no desire to go back to those bitter days. She turned and faced him. "Maybe this is for the best."

"How so?"

She saw no point in being coy. "I care for you, Josh. But we don't have a future."

"Do you mean that?" He sounded incredulous.

She tried to nod, but her head wouldn't move. "I don't know what to think."

"I do."

Two steps brought him to her side. She saw purpose in his eyes, an intent made gentle by the most tender of feelings. He clasped her arms, then drew her closer until her eyelids fluttered shut. Their lips brushed once, twice, but not a third time. He lifted his head and looked her in the eye, leaving her to wonder about their future but only for an instant. The answer cried from her heart if not her lips. She loved this man. She wanted to feed him and kiss him and bind up his wounds, except she couldn't give him what he needed most—a woman who shared his faith.

He touched her hair. "I shouldn't have done that, but I'm not sorry. I love you, Adie."

She gasped.

"I do and God knows it. I can't lie to myself or to Him. Neither will I hide my feelings from you."

"Josh, I—"

He drew her into his arms, cupping her head and tucking her face into the crook of his neck. She felt his fingers on her hair, not in it, though she could imagine him undoing the strands as gently as he'd just undone her heart. The tension left her bones until she took a breath and smelled the starch of his collar. She tried to pull way, but his arms tightened around her back.

"I know you're scared," he murmured. "But you're not a faithless woman. You're not indifferent to the Lord. You're angry. That tells me you care. Strangers don't hurt us nearly as much as the people we love."

He had a point. She'd grown to hate Timothy Long, but he'd charmed her before he'd cornered her in the attic. As a little girl, she'd admired Reverend Honeycutt. She'd prayed every night with the faith of the child she'd been. Adie wanted to cross back over that bridge, but she couldn't stand the thought of forgiving her enemies. Neither could she endure the idea of being under the same roof as Franklin Dean. Christ died for the sins of mankind, but Adie felt no mercy.

She pushed back from Josh. "I'd have gone to Brick's. Colfax Avenue Church is out of the question."

"What's the difference?"

"You *know* the difference!"

"It's bricks and glass, that's all."

"It's Franklin Dean."

Josh's stare matched hers, but it held no malice. "Will you at least think about it?"

"I don't have to." She crossed her arms. "It wouldn't be fair to you."

"To me?"

"Yes." She loved this man. If she couldn't be a full partner to him, they were better off apart.

As he stepped closer, the scent of soap and wool filled her nose. Without touching her physically, his presence surrounded her like a tent. "You need to understand who I am, Adie. I meant what I said. I love you."

"Don't."

"You can't stop me."

"But..." Her voice faded.

His stayed strong. "But what?"

I'm bitter and angry! God doesn't care, not about me. She blinked fast to hide the tears.

Josh gripped her shoulders. "I'm going after Dean with everything I've got. You're going to own Swan's Nest, and my cousin's going to put him out of business. I have a job, too. On Sunday, I need to speak the truth. I'll do it with love, but it's going to get said."

Adie gave a harsh laugh. "I almost want to be there."

"Then come."

The thought grabbed her and wouldn't let go. Dean deserved to hang for what he'd done to Pearl. Seeing him castigated in church would be almost as good as a lynching. "All right," she said bitterly. "I'll go, but I'm sitting in the back."

"You can sit wherever you'd like."

"And I'm not speaking to anyone."

"That's fine." Josh's tone didn't change, but she saw a softening around his mouth, then the curl of a smile. "As much as I'd like to start the courting right now, I'd better save it for later."

Adie didn't know what to think. On one hand, she was furious with him. On the other, she wanted to be kissed. Her confusion must have shown, because Josh lowered his chin, bringing his lips to her ear. "When the time's right, Miss Clarke, I'm going to sweep you off your feet."

He already had.... If only God would do the same. Adie wanted peace but didn't know where to find it. A silent prayer formed in her mind. *Show me, Lord. Open my heart.*

She felt nothing, but the sound of footsteps drew her gaze to the path from the house. She saw Mary hurrying in their direction. "Adie? Josh? Are you out here?"

"What's wrong?" Adie called.

"Pearl's water broke and the baby's coming fast. Bessie says it's breech."

"Oh, no." Adie thought of Maggie. The doctor who'd finally come said the baby hadn't turned. He'd done it with his hands, but it hadn't been easy.

"I'm going for Dr. Nichols." Mary looked at Josh. "Pearl's asking for her father. Will you get him?"

"Of course."

Adie heard what hadn't been said. Pearl could die. Josh squeezed her hand, then strode down the path. Mary followed him at a fast walk, but Adie froze in place. She didn't want to be in the house. Pearl would scream and she'd hear it.

Mary whirled and faced her. "Adie, hurry up! Bessie needs rags and water. It's your job to make sure she has them."

Terrified, she ran after Mary, who gripped her hand. At the corner of the house, Mary veered to the street. Adie went through the back door and added wood to the stove. She pumped water and filled two kettles, listening all the time to the creak of a rocking chair in Pearl's room, directly over her head. It sounded like a blessedly typical night until a low moan mixed with the heat of the stove.

With a lamp in hand, Adie fled to Josh's room where she stored old linens. He'd insisted on cleaning the room himself, so she hadn't been in it since the night he'd arrived. Very little had changed. She saw his Bible on his nightstand and his clothes on hooks. The saddlebags sat in a corner, flat because he'd unpacked the contents as if he planned to stay forever. Adie needed to sort her thoughts, but she couldn't do it now. Pearl needed her. She opened a trunk, removed muslin sheets and carried them to the kitchen. The moaning had stopped, so she went to Pearl's room and knocked.

"Come in," Bessie called.

Adie opened the door and smelled life. Not perfume or the aroma of bread, but sweat and work and pain. She looked at Pearl. "How are you doing?"

She forced a smile. "Good."

Bessie patted her hand. "She's doing just fine."

Except her eyes were as round as coins and her fingers looked like bones clutching at the sheet. She stared at Adie as if she'd never see her again. "Bessie says the baby's breech."

"I heard."

"The doctor will have to turn it."

Adie fought tears.

"Don't you dare cry!" Pearl scolded.

"I'm not." Except her face cracked like a clay pot, and she started to cry. *Why, God? Why does this have to be so hard? Please help Pearl, Lord. Don't let her die. Keep her baby safe.* Adie hadn't prayed with such hope since being with Maggie. She barely recognized that she was doing it now.

Pearl started to pant. She gripped Adie's hand and squeezed the blood out of it.

Please, Lord! Spare her this pain.

The panting slid into a low moan. Gripping her belly, Pearl writhed on the bed. The sight of her sent Adie back to Maggie's bedroom in the Topeka boardinghouse. Her labor had lasted for hours, almost a full day. Adie loved babies, but she had no desire to *ever* go through this torment.

As the contraction passed, Pearl's grip loosened to a touch. Bessie patted Adie's shoulder. "I'll send Caroline down for the water."

As Adie stumbled to her feet, Pearl pulled herself higher on the pillows. "Is my father here yet?"

"Josh went for him."

Pearl swallowed hard. "I need to see him."

Last words, final goodbyes. Adie thought of Maggie's journal and the last desperate scrawl. Someday she'd read it, but not for a long time. Feeling like a coward, she went back to the kitchen and checked the water. Caroline came down ten minutes later. Adie filled two pitchers to the brim. Her friend hugged her, then carried the pitchers upstairs.

Mary and Dr. Nichols arrived next. They went

straight upstairs and didn't come down. Five minutes later, Josh and Reverend Oliver came down the hall to the kitchen. Adie had just stoked the stove. Heat billowed everywhere, turning the room to a furnace.

Reverend Oliver, red-faced from the walk to Swan's Nest, mopped his brow with his sleeve. "How is she?"

"She—" Adie's voice broke. "She wants to see you."

Tobias tramped up the stairs, leaving Adie alone with Josh. With her eyes blazing, she clenched her hands into fists. She wanted to hit something but settled for shouting at him. "I'll *never* go to your church! Your God is cruel and mean and—" She burst into tears.

Josh pulled her into his arms, but she shoved him away.

"She's dying!" Adie cried. "The baby's breech and it's tearing her apart. I can't stand it. I can't—" She broke into sobs. Only minutes later did she realize he'd pulled her close and her tears were soaking his shirt.

"Cry, Adie. It's all right."

At times like this, when his emotions ran hot and God seemed a hundred miles away, Josh sometimes ranted at the sky. Deep feelings weren't a lack of faith and he didn't feel guilty for having them. God understood tears and anger. He shared them.

Adie didn't know it, but her sorrow put her in the arms of the Lord. Josh didn't try to console her with words. He couldn't. Neither did he know if Pearl would live or die. He only knew that God would see them through this long night, just as he'd seen Josh through his opium addiction and losing Emily. As a minister, he'd performed more funerals than weddings. He'd prayed with gut-shot outlaws who'd suffered for days, then cried out for mercy, died and arrived at heaven's gate. Josh didn't know why life had to be so hard, but he knew that Christ had walked this earth as a man. He'd felt every lash of the whip, the sting of the thorns.

"Let's go outside," he said to Adie.

She let him guide her to the porch, where the night air carried the scent of lilacs. As she sat in the chair farthest from the door, Josh pulled a second chair to her side. He didn't know Adie's thoughts, but he knew his own. Reaching for her hand, he silently prayed for Pearl, her baby and women everywhere who'd walked in Emily's shoes.

Several minutes passed before they heard the creak of the door and Tobias joined them. Except for a hint of moonlight, the three of them were in the dark.

"How is she?" Josh asked.

Tobias lowered his tall body on to the swing. It creaked like his old bones. "It's a hard birth."

Adie glared at him. "They're *all* hard!"

What could either man say? Nothing, though Josh added Adie's complaint to his list of questions for the Alimighty when he got to heaven. Why couldn't babies just pop out? He knew the theology of the fall from grace, he just didn't like it. From his point of view, Adam had gotten off easy with the curse of toiling in the fields. The price for Eve—the pain of childbirth—seemed a hundred times worse.

Tobias grunted. "Doc Nichols says the baby might turn on its own. We have to pray."

He bowed his head. So did Josh and Adie.

"I beg you, Lord, spare my daughter's life. Save her baby." He spoke in the solemn tone of a man who'd witnessed death but believed in heaven. Just before saying amen, he paused.

Adie's voice came out in a rasp. *"Do it, Lord. Please."*

"Amen," they said together.

As the night crawled by, Mary made occasional visits to give them news. Adie made tea and toast for the men, but Josh barely tasted it. Every few minutes, moans drifted through the open windows, coming closer together with every hour. Amazingly, Stephen slept through the cries.

As dawn lightened the sky, Pearl's moaning changed to a staccato of shrieks that turned into one long scream. Josh bowed his head. Adie wept into a hankie. A second scream followed the first, then died to silence. Long seconds passed. They heard a slap, then the cry of a very angry baby.

"My grandchild," Tobias whispered.

The screams had meant Pearl was alive. The silence meant she'd escaped the pain but how? As Adie clutched his hand, thoughts of Emily pounded at him. So did the knowledge that Adie had watched his sister die. He squeezed her hand and prayed hard. Long minutes passed before the front door opened.

As the three of them shot to their feet, Josh saw Mary holding the tiniest human being he'd ever seen.

"Pearl's fine," she said.

Tobias collapsed on the chair and bowed his head. "Thank you, Lord."

Josh swallowed a lump, then looked again at the baby. The fruit of Pearl's labor had a smattering of dark hair and a mouth that moved like a baby bird's. "Boy or girl?"

"A boy." Mary stepped to Reverend Oliver and crouched to put the baby at eye level. "Sir, meet your grandson. This is Tobias Joshua Oliver."

Josh had never felt so honored.

Adie squeezed his hand. Side by side, they watched

as Tobias touched the baby's chin, then broke into a smile. "He's going to be a fine man someday."

"Yes, sir," Josh said.

Tobias looked to Mary. "May I see my daughter?"

"Yes, but just for a minute."

As he went into the house, Mary looked at Adie. "Pearl wants to see you, too."

Josh watched her expression. Either she'd see the birth as a gift of life, or she'd be bitter about the struggle. The first reaction would signal healing. The second would leave them a world apart.

Adie wanted to visit Pearl, too. For the past several hours, she'd felt as if her own body were being ripped in two. She needed to see for herself that Pearl was alive and happy.

Only a few minutes passed before Reverend Oliver came back through the door. "She's tired but smiling," he said to them.

Mary motioned for Adie to come inside. They went upstairs, then through the door to Pearl's room. Pale and weak, Pearl reached for the baby in Mary's arms and held him close. On the far side of the room, Bessie and Caroline were chatting with Dr. Nichols. Small talk had replaced Pearl's moans, but Adie saw a wad of soiled sheets and pinkish water in the basin where Bessie had washed the baby.

She turned back to Pearl. Tobias Joshua lay sleeping against his mother's chest, listening to the beat of her heart. Adie couldn't help but smile. "He's beautiful."

Pearl's cheeks flushed with pride. "If it had been a girl, I was going to name her Adelaide Virginia, after you and my mother."

Adie's eyes misted. "That was sweet of you."

"You're my best friend, Adie. I love you."

She clasped Pearl's hand. "I love you, too."

"I'll miss you when we leave. I'll miss everyone, but I have to do what's best for Toby, don't I?"

"Always."

Pearl stroked the baby's cheek. "He was worth it, don't you think?"

"I do."

Adie felt the same way every time she held Stephen, but the realization left her thoughts in a tangle. Adie's greatest joy—her son—had come from Maggie's death. Her greatest hope—a future with Josh—had resulted from a long list of mistakes. If Emily hadn't fallen to temptation, she'd never have become Maggie Butler. Without the loss of his sister, Josh would still be in Boston, struggling with the ulcer and all it meant. They would never have met. Her insides shook with a truth she didn't want to acknowledge. If she was going to blame God for the ugliness in her life, didn't He deserve credit for the beauty? It seemed logical, but logic didn't erase her scars. She'd been hurt and wanted justice.

Suddenly agitated, she stood up from the bed. "I better go. You need your rest."

"I *am* tired," Pearl admitted.

Adie paced to her room, where she heard Stephen cooing in his cradle. When he saw her, he raised his little arms. She picked him up and held him tight. Blinking, she recalled Reverend Oliver's first arrival at Swan's Nest and how he'd clung to his daughter. He'd hurt Pearl terribly, yet she'd forgiven him even before he'd asked. Why couldn't Adie forgive the people who'd hurt *her?*

With Stephen in her arms, she looked in the mirror. She saw a child with Josh's dark hair. Her own reddish curls had pulled loose and were wisping around her face. The colors reminded her of night and the glow of a fire. What had the psalmist written?

Darkness and light are alike to Thee.

Maybe she was closer to God than she thought. With a lump in her throat, Adie spoke to God in her mind. She told Him about the anger and the bitter memories, how she'd cried for days after leaving Liddy's Grove, and how helpless she'd felt. The words came in a torrent that picked up debris until she opened her eyes.

Her prayer didn't lessen her bitterness, but she knew what she had to do. This Sunday, she'd be attending Colfax Avenue Church.

Chapter Seventeen

Adie had come to church. The woman Josh loved had stepped into her own version of a lion's den and she'd done it for him.

Seated on the dais next to Tobias, he took in her appearance as the organist played the opening hymn. Her green dress, a gown he'd never seen, complemented her ivory complexion. A straw hat hid most of her hair but not the hardness of her chin. When she raised her hand to check her hat, he saw lace gloves covering her work-worn hands.

She'd come in her Sunday best and looked ready for a fight. Josh, too, had come to church dressed for battle. This morning he'd put on a heavily starched collar and brushed his coat until it looked new. The attention to his appearance had nothing to do with pride. He'd been putting on a uniform like a soldier going to war. For three days he'd avoided Adie by working on his sermon. As Tobias suggested, he'd chosen the text about moneychangers in the temple and he'd had Franklin Dean in mind.

The banker was seated in the third row on the aisle. A strategic spot, Josh thought. If he decided to walk out on the sermon, he'd command everyone's attention. Adie, too, had picked a strategic seat. She was in the back row, a step from the door. Instead of walking to church with Caroline and Mary, she'd come by herself and had arrived with a minute to spare. As the organist played the closing notes of a hymn, Josh scanned the crowd for people from Brick's but saw no one. He'd expected the disappointment, but it still hurt. He'd hoped at least Brick would make an appearance.

When the hymn ended, Tobias handled the church business of announcements, a scripture reading and the offering. As the ushers left with the silver plates, he stepped back to the podium. "Ladies and gentleman, we have a special guest today. I'm pleased to introduce Reverend Joshua Blue, my renowned colleague from the fine city of Boston."

Tobias droned on, telling the congregation of Josh's education and the crowds he'd gathered. At one time, Josh would have soaked in the praise like a pickle in brine. Today it soured his stomach. He didn't want Tobias blowing his horn. Hearing about the person he'd been gave him a headache. If he and Tobias had been alone, he'd have corrected him. He couldn't now, not in public.

"Ladies and gentlemen," Tobias said with a flourish. "I present the honorable and esteemed Reverend Joshua Blue."

Josh felt neither honorable nor esteemed. He was a man who'd murdered his sister, a human being in need of grace. His insides curdled. How could he preach down to Franklin Dean when he was no better than anyone in this building? No better than the thieves and prostitutes he'd met in his travels? Sure, Dean was a hard case, but Christ had died for him, too. Josh's gaze narrowed to Adie. She'd raised her chin even higher. As much as he wanted to throw verbal punches at Dean—and as much as Dean had it coming—Josh didn't have the right to preach anything but love, grace and the mercy of the cross.

The sermon he'd planned went out of his head. In came the conviction he needed to speak to himself as well as Dean, Adie and everyone else in the sanctuary. When Reverend Oliver motioned him forward, Josh stepped to the podium and opened his Bible to the story of the adulterous woman. Emily would be proud. He doubted Adie would be pleased, but he had to be true to his beliefs.

The man in the pulpit had the dark hair and piercing eyes of the stranger who'd collapsed on Adie's porch, but otherwise she barely recognized Josh. He stood as straight as a steeple, scanning the crowd as he called for prayer.

"Father God," he began, "be with us today…."

She only half listened. This was the minister who'd drawn crowds in Boston and chased Maggie out of her home. It was also Josh, the man who'd kissed her and held her and given her Stephen. Listening to his prayer, she admired his sincerity. She was also aware of the sun pressing through the massive stained glass windows. When she looked at the window depicting a stream and a willow, she felt lost. When she focused on the shepherd with his sheep, she wanted to weep. Worst of all, she could see the back of Franklin Dean's head. She wanted to stand up and tell the congregation that they had vermin in their midst.

Maybe Josh would do the job for her. As he ended the

prayer, Adie looked directly at him. He acknowledged her with a nod, then faced the congregation.

"I'm honored by Reverend Oliver's introduction, but I'm compelled to set the record straight. I'm neither honorable nor worthy of esteem. I'm a sinner saved by grace, a man as flawed as anyone…everyone…in this room."

Adie bristled. She hadn't come to church to hear about her flaws. She'd come for justice. She'd been harmed by Dean and men like him. If she and Josh had been alone, she'd have taken him to task.

Josh started to pace. "There's a story in the Bible that reminds me of who I am."

A natural storyteller, he took the congregation, even Adie, back in time to Jerusalem where a group of men had dragged a woman into the temple. Caught in the act of adultery, she had nowhere to go, no way to hide what she'd done. She didn't deny the accusations. She couldn't. Her disheveled appearance was plain for all to see.

Adie knew the story. She'd always wondered why the men brought the woman and not the man who'd been with her. Josh didn't mention the man, either. Instead he described how Jesus had dropped to a crouch and written something in the sand.

Pausing, he looked from person to person, then asked a question. "What do you think Christ wrote?"

Adie had never thought about it.

"We don't know," Josh continued. "It could have been anything—the woman's name, a list of her accusers. Maybe he drew a cross as a sign of things to come. What we *do* know is what happened next. Jesus stood and said, 'Let him whose slate is clean cast the first stone.'"

He paused again, giving the congregation time to think. "Can anyone here say they have a clean slate? I can't."

Adie didn't give a hoot about having a clean slate. She saw nothing but Franklin Dean's blond head. She hated him. If she'd had a rock in her hand, she'd have thrown it as hard as she could.

Josh went back to pacing. "We've all fallen short. Christ out of love died for each of us. It doesn't matter what you've done. Jesus—through his death on the cross—gives both justice to victims and mercy to those who ask."

Adie fought to keep still. How could Josh preach mercy with Franklin Dean sitting like a toad in the third row? At the end of the dais closest to her, he stopped pacing and sought her gaze. Adie knew the next words would be for her.

"It's hard to imagine such charity. It's even harder to believe that among Christ's final words were these. 'Father, forgive them. They know not what they do.'"

He turned next to Dean. "Every day we have a choice—repent and accept that gift or continue in our old ways."

Josh went back to the podium. "Most of us know what happened to the woman in the temple. One by one, her accusers dropped the stones and left, leaving her alone with the Lord, who gave a simple command. 'Go and sin no more.' I hear that as 'Go and start fresh.'"

Josh closed the Bible. "Imagine…whatever you've done, whatever mistakes you've made, they've been forgiven. That's true for everyone in this building."

Adie couldn't stand another word. When Josh bowed his head to pray, she slipped out the door and ran down the steps. She didn't want to hear about forgiveness and second chances, not with Dean under the same roof. She hated him. She hated Timothy Long, Reverend Honeycutt and everyone else who'd hurt her over the years. If she couldn't sit through a single sermon, how could she even *think* about loving Josh?

She needed time to compose herself. Instead of going home, she headed to the heart of Denver. The shops would be closed and she expected be alone, but as she turned a corner, she saw two young women in front of a hat shop. They were well dressed and she wondered if they'd been to church. Then she noticed the frippery on their dresses and the cut of their gowns. Miss Elsa's Social Club was a block away. Adie wondered if the girls were prostitutes out for a morning walk.

She couldn't look at a soiled dove without thinking of how low she'd sunk before she'd met Maggie. She hadn't turned to such a life, but she'd lived with the threat of it. As she neared the hat shop, she heard a bit of conversation.

"I hate him!" said a girl with a German accent.

Adie slowed her pace. The other girl offered her a handkerchief. "If he's cruel, tell Miss Elsa."

"I tried, but—" She bit her lip. "She said Mr. Dean is a good customer."

Adie stifled a gasp.

The German girl wiped her eyes. "She promised me extra money. The more I save, the sooner I can go home."

Adie knew the risks of speaking with this girl. Even if she held the deed to Swan's Nest, Dean could make her life miserable. She didn't care. She stopped and pretended to admire a hat.

"Be strong, Gretchen," said the girl's companion. "Someday you can leave, but for now—"

"Excuse me." Adie touched Gretchen's elbow. "I'm Adie Clarke. I run a boardinghouse. If you're in trouble—"

Gretchen's eyes widened. "You'd help me?"

"Yes."

"But I don't have money."

"You don't need it," Adie said gently.

The girl's companion hooked her arm around her waist. "Come on, Gretchen."

The girl pulled back. "No!"

"You owe Miss Elsa," her friend hissed.

Gretchen's eyes turned into clouds ready to burst. Knowing the girl couldn't simply come with her—she had clothes and possessions, things that mattered to her—Adie stepped back. "I live at Swan's Nest on Seventeenth Street. Look for the window above the door. It's round and shows a swan."

Her eyes shimmered. "My church back home had pretty windows."

"Gretchen! Let's go." Her friend tugged her down the street, but Gretchen looked over her shoulder.

Tonight Adie would be listening for footsteps on the porch. If the girl knocked, she'd open the door wide. As she headed for home, Adie thought about Gretchen's predicament and her own. In a way, they were both trapped in lives they didn't want. What would happen if Adie ran to God in the middle of the night? Would he open the door the way she'd open it for Gretchen?

She knew the answer. The Lord had died for her. He'd welcome her with open arms. The problem, she had to admit, was the hardness of her own heart. She didn't want to forgive the people who'd harmed her. Until she could cross that bridge, she had no future with

Josh, who, in her opinion, was worthy of more than respect and esteem. He was worthy of love.

Josh didn't see Adie leave the church. He'd been matching stares with members of the congregation, including Dean who'd crossed his arms over his puffed-up chest. When he turned back to Adie, he'd seen the door swing shut behind the hem of her green dress.

She'd been either deeply touched or offended. Josh suspected the latter. This morning, watching her expression, he'd been struck by an odd coincidence. Both Adie and Dean had scowled at him through the entire sermon. Until that moment, Josh had thought of her as the woman being condemned. During the sermon, he realized he'd been mistaken. Adie had a handful of rocks and wanted to throw them at Dean, Honeycutt, every other person who'd hurt her. She had cause, but she wouldn't find peace until she set them down.

Josh had planned to tell the congregation his own story, but he'd preached long enough. He gave the closing prayer, then walked down the aisle with Tobias. As the organist played a rousing hymn, he took in the vaulted ceiling and mahogany trim. Sunshine lit up the windows and made a rainbow of light. To Josh's utter joy, he felt nothing more or less than the satisfaction he'd felt while preaching at Brick's Saloon.

He'd told Adie that he could preach anywhere—a cathedral or street corner—today he'd proved it to himself. He felt as if he'd come home. He could do a good job in this church, but he still had concerns. No one from Brick's had come to the service, and Adie had walked out on him. Their future hung by a thread, but Josh knew who held the future.

He wanted to leave for Swan's Nest immediately,

but he and Tobias had to greet people as they left. Side by side, they shook hands with individuals and made small talk. As Dean approached, Josh made eye contact. The banker shook Tobias's hand but withheld the courtesy from Josh.

"Interesting text, *Reverend*." He used the title with utter disdain.

Josh ignored the slight. "Thank you."

Dean walked away. Josh turned slightly and spotted Horace waiting with the carriage. The driver tipped his hat, not to Dean but to Josh.

Nodding back, Josh wondered what the gesture meant. Horace had come to Brick's three Sundays in a row. The last time he'd stayed for coffee and had asked questions. Josh turned back to the reception line where a well-dressed man was offering his hand. "Reverend Blue, it's a pleasure.

Tobias introduced Halston Smythe, the owner of the Denver Imperial Hotel and a member of the elder board. Two other men stood with him, both longtime members of Colfax Avenue Church. One had a mustache; the other wore a bowler hat.

Smythe looked at Reverend Oliver. "We hate to lose you, Tobias, but I believe we've found your replacement."

"I hope so, Hal." Tobias clapped Josh on the back. "You won't find a better preacher west of the Mississippi, maybe in America."

Josh had to interrupt. "Sir—"

"Don't be modest, Josh," Tobias insisted. "You have a gift."

Maybe, but that gift had come from God. Josh wanted no credit for himself, but he couldn't correct Tobias without being disrespectful. Neither could he let the flattery ride. A question crossed his mind, one that would shed light on his future. He focused on Smythe. "You gentlemen need to be aware. I have a small congregation of my own."

"In Denver?" said the man in the vest.

"We meet in Brick's Saloon."

The gentleman with the mustache frowned. "We weren't aware of your, uh, connections."

Smythe gave a shrewd smile, a sign Josh had an ally. "Don't trouble yourself, Pete. I liked what I heard today."

"So did I," Tobias added.

The man in the vest said nothing.

Smythe focused on Josh. "The elders meet Thursday evening. If you're agreeable, we'll ask a few questions and take a vote."

Josh would have four days to consider the possibilities. "I'll be there."

"Good." Smythe turned to the man in the vest. "I'll speak with the elders. Would you distribute a handbill to the members? I want a big turnout."

"Of course," the man answered.

Josh didn't know what would happen on Thursday night, but he knew he had a fight on his hands. The three elders continued down the walk. When the last person exited the church, Tobias turned to him. "I'm eager to see my grandson. Shall we head to Swan's Nest?"

"Sounds good," Josh replied.

His fight with Dean was nothing compared to the battle he expected from Adie. He wanted to know what she'd thought of his sermon and intended to ask. When the church was empty, Tobias closed the door and they headed up the street. They caught up with Adie three blocks shy of Swan's Nest. Judging by when she'd left church, she hadn't gone straight home. Josh suspected she'd been walking the streets, thinking about the sermon. He knew from experience that living with a hard heart didn't shield a person from pain. It locked the pain inside.

Tobias called out to her. "Miss Clarke!"

Adie pivoted abruptly. "Good morning, gentlemen."

Tobias moved to the right. Josh stepped to her left where his body would shield her from passing carriages. As they neared a rut in the path, he fought the urge to hold her hand to steady her. He didn't have that right, not yet. Unless Adie's heart softened, he never would.

Reverend Oliver winked at Josh. "Tell me, Miss Clarke. What did you think of Josh's sermon?"

Josh wanted to know but not in front of Tobias. The older man meant well, but he didn't understand Adie's struggle.

"Don't answer." Josh tried to sound jovial. "I can't take it back now."

"Nor should you," Tobias added. "You did a fine job."

Josh hoped so, but only one opinion mattered and it belonged to the Almighty. Josh had been faithful today. He'd sleep well, except for dreams of Adie throwing rocks at Dean and Honeycutt.

Silence echoed between their footsteps. Adie stared straight ahead. "The service was very nice."

She couldn't have sounded colder.

Tobias rubbed his chin. "We have seven elders. My guess is a 4-3 split, with you being elected."

Josh frowned. "That's a bad way to start."

"It could be 5-2, maybe 6-1 if Pete's wife talks to him. You won't get Dean's vote, but that's to be expected."

Adie looked at Josh. "Would you take the position?"

She wanted an answer—yes or no—but he didn't know himself. Nor did he want to have the discussion in the middle of the street with Tobias in earshot. Josh had to make his own decision. He liked stained glass. He enjoyed the choir and the massive organ, but he missed the people at Brick's Saloon and was worried about them, particularly Gretchen who'd been quieter than usual at last Sunday's service.

Adie was waiting for an answer, so he kept his voice neutral. "I'd consider it."

Tobias scoffed. "Of course you'd take the position."

"But—"

"If God opens that door, son, don't hesitate."

"We'll see," he answered.

Adie's shoulders stayed stiff. "It was a fine sermon, Josh. I'm sure the elders will offer you the position."

"I don't know."

"I do," she said. "You fit right in." Coming from Adie, it wasn't a compliment. "If you accept, I imagine you'll move into the parsonage."

Josh hadn't thought that far.

"It's the end of the month," she continued. "And I may have found a new boarder. This would be a good time to make the change."

He couldn't believe his ears. "You want me to leave Swan's Nest?"

"Yes."

Tobias interrupted. "Miss Clarke has a point. Pearl's room is empty, and it'll give us time to plan the transition."

Josh didn't even know if there would *be* a transition. He felt as if he'd been slugged in the gut. Swan's Nest had become his home. He enjoyed seeing Adie during the day, working in the garden or rocking Stephen on the porch. On the other hand, he understood the need for distance between them. Josh gave her a target, someone to fight when she needed to wrestle with her own soul.

"It's a possibility," he said. "But what about Dean?"

Adie raised her chin. "I won't let him intimidate me."

"No, but he's still a threat. Elliot arrived a few days ago, but he's still getting settled. Until the mortgage is paid—"

"Josh?" Tobias interrupted.

He did *not* want the older man's help. "What is it?"

"Frank's going to react to your sermon. I won't be surprised if he comes after you instead of Miss Clarke."

Adie's brow furrowed. "What makes you think that?"

"I've preached a lot of years, Miss Clarke. If everybody tells me I've given a good sermon, chances are I've just tickled their ears. But when someone picks a fight, I know the truth has hit home. Frank got called a sinner today. He didn't like it."

Adie had heard the same message. Judging by her scowl, she hadn't liked it, either. When they reached the front of Swan's Nest, Josh indicated the door to Tobias. "Go see your grandson. I'd like a word with Miss Clarke."

Tobias doffed his hat to Adie and went inside. As the door swung shut, Josh faced her. "Do you really want me to leave?"

"It's for the best."

"Why?"

She raised her chin. "I respect your faith, Josh. But I'll never share it. I'll hate men like Franklin Dean until I die."

They were at the crux of their differences. Josh preached forgiveness. Adie wanted vengeance. He didn't blame her, but he knew a simple truth. Withholding mercy caused more pain than it took away. Did he answer as a minister or a man? The minister had words for her. The man wanted to draw her into his arms.

He did neither. "Give it time."

"There's no point." She squared her shoulders. "I'm grateful for everything you've done for me. You know I care about you, but we can't be more than friends."

She had a point about their differences, but Josh believed in a powerful God. The Almighty wouldn't leave Adie hanging by her thumbs and neither would Josh. He reached for her hand. "Adie—"

She stepped back. "I'm sorry, Josh. You're a good man."

He'd heard enough. As a minister *and* a man, he had to fight for her. "I'm not 'good' and you know it."

Her brows snapped together. "I'm *sick* of your humble pie!"

"It's the truth." He had to make his point. "I'm no better or worse than anyone and neither are *you*."

Her voice rose. "What do you mean by *that?*"

"The story today... Who are you, Adie? The sinful woman or one of the hypocrites throwing rocks?"

She gasped.

"It's got to be one or the other."

"I'm neither."

"That's the problem," he said. "You think you're better than Dean and Honeycutt, but deep down, *we're all the same*. God's love is so vast, we can't take it in. We're like bugs. You might be a butterfly instead of a roach like Dean, but none of us comes within a mile of God's goodness."

Josh kept his eyes on her face. Either she'd understand his intent or she'd walk away still clutching stones.

Her hazel eyes glistened, then turned hard. "You've made your point, Reverend. I'm lower than a bug. Now go pack your things."

She'd missed the point entirely. "Adie—"

"I'm tired of your talk. You act like you've got all the answers, but you don't."

"I know that."

"And *I* know why Emily left. She got *fed up* with *you* and your know-it-all ways!"

In the past year he'd endured ulcers, a bullet wound, fevers and nearly drowning. Nothing hurt as much as that verbal stone hitting his heart.

Her lips quivered. For a moment he thought she'd apologize. Instead she turned and ran up the steps.

The sun beat on his black coat, heating the wool until he felt it on his skin. The weight pressed him down, but he knew what he had to do. Adie had ordered him to leave Swan's Nest. If he fought to stay, she'd fight back and they'd end up in a bigger tangle. Her battle wasn't with Josh. It was with God and he had to stay out of the way. Bruised and hurting, he went to pack his things.

Chapter Eighteen

Early Monday morning, Adie went to the carriage house to milk Buttons. As she carried the bucket back to the kitchen, she saw a silhouette in the window. Was it Josh? Hope shot through her before she came to her senses. She'd said terrible things to him. He'd packed his saddlebags and gone to the parsonage, leaving her to explain his absence at Sunday supper. Caroline had remained quiet, but Mary had shot her a critical look. Bessie had come to her aid, saying she felt sure things would work out for the best.

Adie didn't share that hope. She regretted speaking cruelly to Josh, but she had no desire to apologize. She'd been sharp-tongued, but being put in the same camp as Franklin Dean had wounded her. Neither did she like being compared to something as common as an insect. All her life she'd felt insignificant. Josh's high-minded attitude had turned her back into that child.

She would have welcomed a chat with Bessie or Pearl, but Adie couldn't face Mary or Caroline. When the shadow moved past the window again, she saw Mary's blond hair. Before she could turn back to the carriage house, her friend opened the door. She had

Stephen on her hip, making it impossible for Adie to linger in the yard.

"This baby's hungry," Mary said.

Adie smiled at her son, but she felt morose. Stephen looked like Maggie, which meant he looked like Josh.

"I'm coming," she said.

"Good," Mary replied. "I have something to say."

Reluctantly, Adie came up the steps. Mary had already started warming a bottle, so she poured the new milk into a clean pitcher. As Stephen started to fuss, she felt the same helplessness. She wanted to leave but couldn't. Mary would follow if she made an excuse, so she took Stephen, lifted the bottle and sat to feed him.

Once he settled, she looked at Mary. "What's on your mind?"

"You."

Adie said nothing.

"Why did you ask Josh to leave?"

Adie looked down at Stephen. The milk had calmed him. She wished she could find a cure for herself. Instead she had to deal with Mary, a woman who had no patience with half-truths.

"We had words," she finally said. "I didn't like the sermon and told him so."

"You didn't?"

"He let Franklin Dean off the hook."

Mary went to the stove and poured herself tea. "If that's true, he let me off the hook, too. I never told you, but I killed a man."

Adie caught her breath.

"It's true." Mary came back to the table. She took a sip from the porcelain cup, then stared out the window. "I can't bear to talk about it, except to say I made a mistake. A judge ruled it was self-defense, but the man's brother didn't agree. Neither did the town. No one threw rocks at me that day, but more than a few wanted to lynch me. I'm still afraid of the brother. He vowed to track me down."

She shook her head as if to erase the memory, then looked at Adie. "That's why Josh's sermon touched me. I was that woman in the square, standing alone while people said terrible things. I looked around that day and do you know what I saw?"

Adie was afraid to ask.

"I *knew* those people." Mary set down the teacup with a thud. "They wanted to throw stones at me, but I wasn't the only guilty person in that square. Every one of them had a secret."

Looking at her friend, Adie understood what Josh had been trying to tell her. The only person at Swan's Nest without regrets was Stephen, and he couldn't even feed himself. Adie, too, had fallen short. She'd lied to Josh and added weeks to his anguish about Emily, yet he'd forgiven her instantly. Adie didn't know if she could forgive Dean and Honeycutt, but she no longer wanted to throw rocks at anyone, certainly not at Josh. She'd hurt him yesterday. She needed to make amends.

Her stomach churned as she looked at Mary. "I understand now."

Mary smiled. "So what are you going to do?"

"I need to apologize to Josh."

"When?"

Adie sighed. "I don't know. It'll be a hard conversation."

"You love him, don't you?"

"I do, but I can't see myself as a minister's wife."

Mary added sugar to her tea. "A month ago, I couldn't

see myself singing in church. If Josh takes Reverend Oliver's place, I might join the choir."

Would Mary be welcome? Reverend Honeycutt would have slammed the door in her face.

Mary ran her finger along the rim of the teacup. "That meeting is Thursday. Only the elders vote, but anyone can attend. Caroline and I are going. Pearl might if she's up to it. How about you, Adie? It would mean the world to Josh."

"I'll have to think about it."

Mary carried her cup to the washbasin, then went upstairs to get dressed. With Stephen warm in her arms, Adie wondered what would happen at the elder meeting. If they voted for Josh—and let Mary sing in the choir—maybe she could make her peace with loving a minister. If not, she wanted nothing to do with such a place.

On Tuesday at twelve noon, Halston Smythe walked into Denver National Bank and greeted Frank with a handshake. The two men rarely saw eye-to-eye. Frank suspected today's visit would be no different. At the club this morning, he'd heard talk of Reverend Blue and the plan to offer him the pulpit.

Frank objected for two reasons. He didn't want Tobias to leave with Pearl, and he hated the thought of Joshua Blue running Colfax Avenue Church. Tobias hadn't been easy to manipulate, but Frank had managed to do it. Until Sunday, he'd thought Tobias was on his side. Now he wondered. The old man hadn't confronted him directly, but his decision to leave Denver didn't bode well. Frank had visited the parsonage, but the old man had been at Swan's Nest, a sign that he'd reconciled with Pearl.

Frank didn't like being the odd man out. He didn't

like Smythe, either. This morning he'd pump the man for information and send him on his way. Hiding his annoyance, he indicated the chair across from his. "Please, have a seat."

Smythe lowered his round body on to the leather. "I'll get to the point, Frank. Tobias and Pearl are leaving Denver."

"So I've heard."

"Have you heard why?"

The entire church knew about Pearl's pregnancy and his involvement. He'd survived the scrutiny by making subtle threats to members who depended on his bank, and by wearing his broken heart on his sleeve. He played that card now.

"I admit it. Pearl and I made a mistake." Frank deliberately looked morose. "I've begged her to marry me, but she won't."

"My wife tells me the 'mistake' was yours."

"What do you mean?"

Smythe rose from the chair, planted his hands on the desk and leaned so close Frank could smell peppermint on his breath. The man's voice came out in a low whisper. "You know *exactly* what I mean."

Smythe's tone meant one thing. Pearl had been spreading lies. Frank wanted to smack her. He settled for glaring at the elder. "Come on, Hal. You know how things go."

Smythe settled back on the chair. "No, Frank, I *don't*."

"We made a mistake. I want to fix it."

Smythe remained impassive, leaving Frank to wonder what had happened to make Pearl tell lies. Then it struck him. She'd had the baby and no one had told him. He didn't know if she'd given birth to a boy or a girl.

He wanted to go directly to Swan's Nest but couldn't. Thanks to Smythe's visit, Frank had to be on his best behavior.

The elder cleared his throat. "Aside from all that, I wanted to make you aware of the change to Thursday's agenda. We'll be voting on Tobias's replacement."

Pictures of Pearl raced through Frank's mind. He could hardly think, but business came first. He had to finish with Smythe. "Tobias wants this Blue fellow, doesn't he?"

"Yes."

"Does he have support?"

"Quite a bit, including mine." For the second time, Smythe rose from the chair. This time he looked eager to leave. "That concludes church business, but I've also come concerning my account."

Tension eased from Frank's muscles. He knew how to handle money. "What can I do for you?"

"I'd like to make a transfer."

"Buying more land?"

"No," Smythe answered. "Boston Merchants Bank just opened. Sorry, Frank. But the new bank has better rates."

Frank leaned back in his chair. In a city as vibrant as Denver, a new bank didn't surprise him. What made him arch a brow was the mention of Boston. He also wondered why he hadn't heard talk at the supper club. The new banker had come to town in a cloak of secrecy. "Who's running it?"

"A fellow named Elliot Morse. He's a member of the Blue family."

Without the courtesy of a goodbye, Smythe walked out the door, leaving Frank to ponder the events of the past few weeks. They led him to a single conclusion.

Joshua Blue was ruining his life by protecting Adie Clarke, influencing Pearl and starting a rival bank. It couldn't be tolerated.

He motioned for a clerk. As she came forward, he scowled. "Find Horace."

"Yes, sir." She set an envelope on his desk. "This came by courier."

As she left to summon Horace, Frank opened the envelope and found a letter from Boston Merchants Bank and a check for the amount of the Swan's Nest mortgage. Furious, he stared out the window, where he saw Horace walking down the boardwalk. Instead of his usual shuffling gait, the driver was striding with a sense of purpose. Frank drummed his fingers on his desk until Horace arrived.

The driver took off his hat. "You wanted me, sir?"

"Sit down."

He lowered himself onto the chair vacated by Smythe.

"I gave you a job last week," Frank said.

"Yes, sir. I recall."

"What have you found out about Reverend Blue?"

"Not much." Horace shifted in the chair. "People like the reverend. He treats everyone the same, even the girls from Miss Elsa's."

Frank's ears perked up. "He's been to Miss Elsa's?"

"Just once," Horace said quickly. "Not for what you're thinking, sir. He invited the girls to church. Two of them come regular now. The men at Brick's like him, too. I haven't heard a bad word about him, sir." Horace pursed his lips, a sign he was holding back.

"Spit it out, Horace. What else do you know?"

The driver fidgeted on the seat. "I don't like telling tales, sir."

Frank put a silver dollar on his desk. Horace eyed it

but didn't move. Frank didn't like the man's reluctance. He added another silver dollar, then a third. Looking torn, Horace slid the coins across the desk and into his hand; then he met Frank's gaze. "I heard the women talking last Sunday. The reverend had a bad time in Boston."

"Go on."

"His sister got in trouble."

"I want to know about Reverend Blue, not some female."

"It's why he came west," Horace said. "He's been looking for his sister everywhere, in places a reverend don't belong."

"I see."

"There's more," Horace added. "Back in Boston, he used laudanum on the sly, too much of it if you get my drift."

So the honorable reverend was an opium addict. The more Horace spoke, the more evidence Frank had against him. Instead of dreading Thursday's meeting, he started to relish the thought of raking the esteemed Reverend Blue over the coals.

"Anything else?" he said to Horace.

"Just one thing," the driver said. "He had a talk with Brick and me and some of the fellows at the saloon the other night. The Reverend walks like he talks, but he's still a man like you or me. He's not all high-and-mighty."

Frank laughed out loud.

Horace's mouth tightened. "I shouldn't have said anything."

"I'm glad you did." Frank slid a half eagle across the desk. "Take the afternoon off, Horace. You've earned it."

"Yes, sir." The driver turned and headed for the door.

Only after he left did Frank see the silver dollars sitting next to the gold piece. Not that it mattered… Horace had done his job and he'd done it well. On Thursday night, Reverend Blue's dirty laundry would be aired for the world to see.

"Coffee, Reverend?"

"Thanks."

As Brick filled the mug, Josh sat on the bar stool with his black coat buttoned tight and his boots freshly shined. It was Wednesday night and he'd been living at the parsonage since Sunday. He'd had all he could take of Tobias's enthusiasm for the elder meeting, so he'd gone for a walk and ended up at Brick's.

Josh liked Tobias, but he didn't share the man's confidence that he belonged at Colfax Avenue Church. The more Josh thought about it, the more he wondered if he was about to fall into a trap. In the past year, he'd learned to read men and their intentions. Halston Smythe struck him as sincere, but the two men with him had seemed weak. Dean should have been voted off the board a long time ago. The fact he remained showed a serious lack of integrity at the heart of the church's leadership.

Josh would go wherever the Lord sent him, but he'd learned a hard lesson about walking into a lion's den. If he went on his own, he'd get eaten alive. If he went with the Lord, he'd have a story to tell for years to come.

He wanted the story.

He suspected he was about to be devoured.

He sipped the coffee, then looked at Brick, who was wiping glasses with his apron. Josh felt good about the changes in the man's life. He'd taken down the tawdry picture above the bar and replaced it with a mirror. He'd written his sister, too. She might never receive the letter, but Brick had asked for forgiveness. Josh saw a new calm in his eyes.

Brick turned and wiped the counter. "I hear talk you're taking over that big church on Colfax Avenue."

"Maybe."

"Never been there myself," he said. "I'd miss Sunday mornings here."

"So go there," Josh replied.

"No, thanks." Brick kept dragging the rag in wide circles. "Tell me something, Reverend. How do you know what's best? Seems to me you can preach here or you can preach there. You've got a choice."

"That's right."

"So how do you decide?"

"I'll pray about it, maybe ask a friend for advice." Josh drummed his fingers on the warm mug. The barkeep had been in business for a while and had heard a lot of stories. "You're a smart man. Any thoughts for me?"

Brick looked pleased by the respect. "My granny had a saying. 'When you don't know what's right, do what's hard.'"

A customer called for the barkeep's attention. As Brick turned away, Josh thought about his advice. Accepting the position at Colfax Avenue Church would test him to the limits. He'd have to fight his pride every day and he'd hurt Adie's feelings more than he already had. The thought made his chest ache. He'd go wherever God led him, but he had to be sure he belonged in this particular lion's den.

As Josh sipped coffee, the perfect test came to mind. He'd take the position under one condition. The elder board had to vote unanimously to approve him. The more he considered the plan, the more he liked it. Dean would have to vote yes or resign. Either way, the banker would lose his influence over the church. Would Adie see the logic? Josh hoped so, but he couldn't let his feelings dictate his choice.

If the board didn't vote unanimously, he'd face another tough decision. He could stay in Denver and preach at Brick's, head home to Boston or go back to drifting. Josh stared at the murky dregs in his cup. Boston didn't appeal to him and neither did drifting. He wanted to stay in Denver where he could see Adie and Stephen and be a small part of their lives.

Small...

The word rankled him in the worst way. He didn't believe in a *small* God and he didn't want a *small* piece of Adie's life. He wanted to love her with everything he had to give. He'd already paid off the mortgage on Swan's Nest. Starting next month, she'd receive an allowance, one that would pay for roast beef every night.

The only loose end was Dean. Would he leave Adie alone once Pearl left? Soon Pearl and Tobias would leave for Cheyenne. Then what? Josh didn't know, but he was certain of one thing. He couldn't leave Denver until Dean no longer posed a threat to Adie. Short of death or a prison term, the banker wasn't likely to leave town.

As he swallowed the dregs of his coffee, Josh thought of the advice from Brick's grandmother.

Do what's hardest.

At tomorrow's meeting he'd stand his ground. If the elders voted unanimously to hire him, he'd accept the offer. If they didn't, he'd stay as long as Adie needed protection, loving her from afar. Both answers struck Josh as hard, but even more painful was the thought of leaving Denver for good. He didn't want to do it, but staying posed a different threat to Adie. Even if Josh kept his distance, their feelings for each other would grow. Until she made peace with God, Josh would be a distraction at best, an impediment at worst.

He set the mug on the counter, left money for Brick and left the saloon. With his thoughts in a jumble, he went back to the parsonage to pray.

Chapter Nineteen

"Tell us, Reverend Blue. What was your greatest achievement in Boston?"

The question came from Franklin Dean, but the other six elders, seated in a row at the front of the crowded meeting hall, were just as eager for Josh's answer. He'd been asked to stand at a podium placed to the side of the elders. When he looked straight ahead, he saw Dean. If he turned his head to the side, he saw a roomful of people. Mary, Bessie and Caroline had come to show their support, but he didn't know anyone else. He hadn't expected Pearl or Adie.

He'd also had a talk with Tobias. At Josh's request, the older man had refrained from repeating his achievements. He'd given a simple introduction, allowing Josh to set the tone himself. He intended to keep the focus on what he believed and why, not on who he'd been. He also wanted his personality to show. He had a dry sense of humor. If the elders didn't care for it, they deserved to know now.

Josh looked directly at Dean. "*My* greatest achievement?"

"Yes."

"Let's see." He looked at the ceiling as if he were thinking, then back at the board. "I learned to ride a pony at the age of four. I was *very* proud of myself."

Three of the elders chuckled. Three others scowled and Dean looked smug.

Josh flashed a smile. "I mean no disrespect, gentlemen. But I *do* feel strongly about the point I hope to make. There was a time when I'd have stood here and rattled off my schooling, the revivals I've preached and the size of the crowds. That day is long gone. Like the Apostle Paul, I count my achievements as dust compared to what Christ did for us on the cross."

He looked each man, even Dean, in the eye. "My greatest achievement, if there is such a thing, is remembering who I'd be without God's grace."

Smythe and another man acknowledged him with easy nods. The other five listened with a mix of boredom and disdain. Smythe started to ask a question, but Tobias, seated in the front row, stood up. "Reverend Blue is too modest to speak for himself, but his church in Boston grew in size from twenty to five hundred in just a few years."

Josh hated to contradict Tobias, but he couldn't let the remark stand. "That's true," he said to the elder board. "I took pride in filling those pews. Then a friend of mine, a shootist named Wes Daniels, said *he* could have gotten twice that number."

"How?" asked an elder.

"By giving away free drinks."

Half the crowd chuckled. Smythe looked pleased. Josh turned to the audience. "The measure of a minister's success isn't in crowded pews. It's in changed lives."

Tobias shot Josh a look, then stood again. "I agree,

but it's only fair to say that you've changed more lives than most. At one revival alone, the newspaper said you spoke to—"

Josh held up his hand. "I appreciate Reverend Oliver's support, but—"

"Go on, Tobias."

The interruption came from Dean. Behind Josh, people murmured with a mix of approval and curiosity. Tobias had remained standing and was describing Josh as if he could walk on water. When he sat, Dean looked directly at Josh.

"Tell us, Reverend. With all your accomplishments, why did you leave Boston?"

At last they were on Josh's turf. "I'm glad you asked. The story starts with—"

Dean broke in. "Your sister was a woman of low moral character. Isn't that why you left?"

"What?"

The banker looked smug. "There's evidence she committed the sin of fornication—"

"Hold it right there." Josh had been ready for Dean to throw stones at him, but Emily? No way would he let his sister be dragged through the mud. He felt every eye on his face, studying the angle of his chin, the color in his cheeks, watching and waiting for his reaction. He looked at the elders one by one, reading each man's expression; then he faced the crowd. What he had to say would singe a few ears. "My sister was a fine woman. It's true she made a mistake, but the questionable character was mine. She—"

Dean interrupted. "We don't need the disgusting details."

"I think you do," Josh answered.

Three of the elders scowled. Smythe held Josh's gaze,

urging him silently to continue. As Josh opened his mouth, Dean broke in. "Is it true you've suffered from a stomach ailment?"

"Yes."

"And that you used laudanum?"

"Yes."

"To excess?"

No matter how Josh answered, Dean would twist his words. The banker didn't want truth; he wanted ammunition. Josh scrutinized the crowd. Some looked troubled, others sympathetic. No one stood to defend him. Mary, Bessie and Caroline were trading angry whispers, but this church's traditions prohibited women from speaking, a rule Josh thought was mistaken. He glanced at Tobias and saw a frown. In spite of the older man's upset, Josh could breathe easy. He'd told Tobias everything about his past.

He'd have told his story to the elder board, but he could see in their flat expressions that his fate had been decided, probably before he'd set foot in the meeting hall. Dean had poisoned the well against him and he'd done a good job. Josh wouldn't go after him personally, but a few things needed to be said.

He spoke directly to Dean. "You know my story better than I do. By all means, tell it."

Wearing a smirk masked with concern, the banker shared everything Josh had revealed to the congregation at Brick's Saloon, including failings he'd admitted to a small group of men. Horace had been in that gathering and was clearly Dean's source. Josh figured Dean would save the biggest rock for last, and he did.

The banker laced his fingers on the tabletop. "Is it true, Reverend, that you've visited Miss Elsa's Social Club?"

The congregation gasped.

"I sure have," Josh said boldly. "It paid off, too. Two young ladies come to services now." Gretchen hadn't missed a single Sunday at Brick's and had brought a friend. Josh hoped she'd leave Miss Elsa's and felt bad that he hadn't spoken to Adie about offering her a room.

"Men have their weaknesses," Dean said. "But we expect a higher standard from our minister."

Josh also knew from Brick that Dean was a frequent guest at the brothel. He crossed his arms. "Is that so?"

"Absolutely." The banker stared hard. "You live at Swan's Nest, an establishment for single women. Is that true?"

"Yes, it is."

"Some of us find that inappropriate."

Tobias shoved to his feet. He looked ready to choke the daylights out of the banker. "*You* of all people have no right to—"

"I'm pointing out facts."

"Let me help you," Josh said in a full voice. "I left Boston to search for my sister. She was with child, out of wedlock, a woman who made the mistake of falling in love and giving in to temptation. To protect my pride, I drove her out of Boston. Some of you *gentlemen*—" he looked from elder to elder "—would have applauded that decision. I see it as my biggest mistake. Instead of showing my sister the same grace Christ has shown to me, I threw stones at her."

He faced the crowd. "I was a Pharisee, a hypocrite." He told the audience about his laudanum addiction, how he'd sought praise and hidden his mistakes; then he looked back at the elders. "Mr. Dean asked what I considered my greatest accomplishment. Here it is. I learned the hard way—at the expense of my sister's life—that Christ died for all of us. That includes you *fine* gentlemen."

Josh glanced at Tobias. The man looked both stunned and pleased, as if he'd realized he should have given this speech before now.

Josh faced the elder board. "Let me ask each of you, are your lives so perfect that you can sit there and judge me?" He let a full minute pass. "Who's been to Miss Elsa's besides Frank here?"

Two of the men turned red.

"Who drinks too much?"

A third glared at him.

"How about lying?" Josh looked straight at the fifth man. He held Josh's stare and gave a little nod. This man, Josh sensed, understood the point he hoped to make.

Josh gentled his voice. "I don't have anything else to say, only that God loves us just as we are. We're fearfully, wonderfully made. He knit each of us in our mother's womb. He counts the hairs on our heads. We can't hide from Him, ladies and gentlemen. The good news is, we don't have to."

No one said a word.

Josh turned back to the board. "If you still want me for your pastor, I'd be honored to serve, but I have a requirement of my own. Tonight's vote has to be unanimous. As it says in the Bible, a house divided against itself cannot stand. I won't be the cause of dividing this church."

Josh strode down the aisle and out the door. He'd wait outside for the vote, but he felt certain he'd never preach in this building again.

Adie had been sitting on the porch for two hours, peering down the street in search of Bessie, Caroline and Mary. She'd considered going to the meeting, even sitting outside and listening through an open window, but she'd lost her nerve. Ever since her talk with Mary, she'd felt heavy with guilt. She owed Josh amends but didn't know how to make them. Apologizing for her unkind words felt as incomplete as unrisen bread, but neither could she speak the whole truth. She loved him. She wanted to be his wife, but how could she marry a minister when she still felt bitter toward God?

She didn't know, but tonight she had hope. If the elders offered Josh the position, maybe she could see past Reverend Honeycutt and old hurts. Everything depended on tonight's vote.

Hushed voices came from the street. Adie jumped to her feet and saw her friends approaching Swan's Nest. Unable to wait, she hurried down the steps. "Did he get elected?"

"Yes and no," Bessie replied.

What did *that* mean? As the women trudged up the steps, Adie went ahead to the parlor, where she turned up the lamp. Caroline plopped onto the divan. She looked as if she'd seen a wagon accident, one where the horse broke its leg and had to be put down. Mary held her chin high, as if she were back in the town where she'd faced an angry mob. Bessie, as always, wore the placid look of a woman who'd lost everything, survived and knew others could do the same.

Mary sat in the rocking chair. Bessie took the spot next to her sister, leaving Adie to pull up a side chair. No one sat in Josh's place.

"Josh did us proud," Bessie said. "But he won't be taking the position."

"They voted him down?" Adie asked.

"Not exactly," said Mary.

Adie listened as her friends described the first half of the meeting. She could imagine Josh sparring with the elders. When Mary told about Dean's assault on Emily, Adie burned with fury. If ever a man had paid for his mistakes, it was Josh. She hated Franklin Dean more than ever. Neither did she care for the people who'd let the verbal abuse take place.

Adie's conscience spoke in a whisper. *Where were you?* She wouldn't have been allowed to speak in Josh's defense, but she could have supported him with a look, a smile at the right time. "I wish I'd gone."

"It got ugly," Caroline said.

"Did he take Dean to task?" Adie hoped so.

Mary laughed. "Josh took *everyone* to task. By the time he finished, every person in the room knew two things. No one's perfect and Jesus loves us anyway."

Caroline looked at Adie. "Josh walked out, but not before making a demand of his own. He said the vote had to be unanimous or he wouldn't take the position. He went outside to wait. That's when *everyone* started to talk. Women, too."

"Really?" Pearl walked into the parlor. "That's never happened before."

Caroline and Mary made room for her on the divan. Adie glanced at Josh's empty chair and wished she hadn't asked him to leave Swan's Nest. Crazy or not, the accusations had to have left a mark. She couldn't stand the thought of Josh enduring the ordeal alone.

"What did people say?" she asked.

Mary looked grim. "Some criticized him. Others sang his praises. Reverend Oliver and a man named Smythe took Josh's side, but two others said he was a troublemaker."

Adie's mouth gaped. "Josh is the kindest man I've ever known."

"Me, too," Mary added.

Pearl looked pinched. "Did anyone mention Frank and me?"

"Not at the meeting," Mary replied. "But lots of women asked how you are. One said to tell you her husband took his money out of Dean's bank." Mary lifted Pearl's hand and squeezed. "You won, Pearl. No matter what happens, people know not to trust Franklin Dean."

Tears welled in the girl's eyes. "I'm glad."

"Me, too," Adie said with venom. "He deserves worse."

"And someday he'll get it," Bessie answered. "Right now I'm worried about Josh."

"Me, too," Caroline said.

Adie needed to hear the rest of the story. "What was the vote?"

Bessie's lips curved up. "Four to three in Josh's favor."

Josh could have had the position, yet he'd turned it down. Had he done it for her? The thought filled her with awe. If he stayed in Denver, she'd go to the little church at Brick's. She could tell Josh she loved him without dreading the denial she'd see in his eyes. She had to speak to him tonight, so she looked at Bessie. "I need to see Josh. Would you walk with me to the parsonage?"

"I would," Bessie answered. "But he's not there."

"Where did he go?"

"I don't know," Caroline said. "But I saw him heading away from the church."

Adie felt terrible. "Maybe he went to Brick's."

"I doubt it," Mary said. "No one except us showed up. He looked disappointed."

Adie's heart broke again. Josh had faced a mob armed with lies and he'd done it alone. Now he was walking the streets of Denver in the dark. If she hadn't asked him to leave Swan's Nest, he'd be here now. She ached to go after him, but walking downtown, past saloons and brothels, would have been stupid.

Caroline looked grim. "After tonight, I won't be surprised if he leaves Denver."

"He might," Pearl said. "But he'd say goodbye. Either way, he needs us right now."

Bessie gripped Adie's left hand and Mary stretched to take her right one. Before she realized what was happening, the women had made a circle. In unison they arched their necks and bowed their heads. Pearl prayed first. She asked God to be with Josh and calm his heart. Bessie asked for safety. Mary prayed that he'd know how much he'd helped her. Caroline, her voice barely a whisper, prayed for Josh to find love and a home of his own.

Adie's throat felt tight and her fingers hurt from clutching Bessie's and Mary's hands, but she spoke from her heart. *"Bring him home, Lord. I don't understand Your ways. I don't know why—"* Her voice cracked. *"I just know Josh is hurting and he needs You. Amen."*

Adie was hurting, too. She needed to see Josh. She couldn't go to him, but she had a sudden, keen sense of Emily's journal locked in the trunk. If she read it from start to finish—including the end she'd been unable to endure—she'd be with him in spirit.

One by one, the women went in different directions. Pearl headed for the kitchen to warm milk for herself. Bessie and Caroline went upstairs to bed, and Mary walked out to the garden. Adie climbed the stairs to her room, opened the trunk and retrieved Emily's journal. Clutching it against her chest, she went to the parlor, where she dimmed the lamp to a glow. Wanting to feel close to Josh, she started reading from the beginning.

Chapter Twenty

As soon as Tobias told him about the vote, Josh shook the dust from Colfax Avenue Church off his feet. He had no regrets. He'd spoken from his heart and had honored his faith. Never mind the pain in his gut. He didn't like to fight, but some battles couldn't be avoided.

Alone on the dark street, he longed to go to Swan's Nest. He wanted to tell the story to Adie, but he couldn't go to her. He didn't want sympathy tonight. He wanted a wife, a soul mate who'd understand tonight's hullabaloo. If he went to Adie now, he'd be settling for her company when he wanted her heart. Josh had never been good at settling, so he strode in the opposite direction of Swan's Nest. If it hadn't been for Franklin Dean, he'd have left Denver to avoid the temptation of visiting her. He blinked and thought of Stephen cooing in her arms. He blinked again and pictured her in her Sunday best, seated in church with her red hair shining under the straw hat.

"Why, Lord?" he said to the dark.

Living in the shadow of Swan's Nest without courting Adie would be the hardest thing he'd ever done, but he had no choice. He had to stay in Denver until Dean no longer posed a threat. With his heart pounding, he walked to the edge of town, where he stared into the night. Darkness and light were alike to God, but Josh felt like a man in a tomb. He tried to pray, but he felt as if the heavens were brass. Neither did he want to speak with Tobias. The older man would want to rehash the meeting, something Josh had no desire to do.

As alone as he'd ever been, he walked back to the parsonage. As he turned onto Colfax Avenue, he saw the silhouette of the empty church. It rose against the sky with a majestic air, but the windows had no life. Moonlight turned the steeple into a sword, but Josh saw the dull edges.

"Good evening, Reverend."

The voice belonged to Franklin Dean. As Josh turned, the banker stepped out of the alley next to the church. Behind him came Horace, a foot shorter and the exact shape of the man who'd trampled Adie's garden. Side by side, they blocked Josh's path.

His neck hairs prickled. "What do you gentlemen want?"

Dean stepped closer. "You ruined me."

"No, I didn't."

The banker had ruined himself, but that didn't change the rage burning in his eyes. With Horace at the man's side, Josh was outnumbered two to one. He had no desire to take a beating, but he refused to run. Neither could he see Jesus swinging his fists at two thugs in an alley.

Moonlight shone on Dean's jaw. "Do you know what you did to me tonight?"

Josh resisted the urge to mouth off. "It's over, Frank. Go home."

"You humiliated me."

"No, I didn't," Josh said calmly. "I talked about second chances for everyone, myself included."

The banker slapped his walking stick against his palm. "I lost four more customers today. That's eighteen in three days."

"Change your ways," Josh said. "They'll come back."

"You stole Swan's Nest."

"I paid off the mortgage."

"You made Pearl tell lies!"

Josh had seen evil before. He'd spoken to dead-eyed men and heard vile threats. He'd had dreams twisted by opium. Never, though, had he felt the breath of violence on his face. Looking into Dean's bloodshot eyes, Josh knew the man intended grave harm. "We're done, Frank."

He tried to pass the men, but they closed ranks. Dean planted his palm on Josh's shoulder and shoved. "I'm not done with you, Blue."

Josh stumbled back. Blocked by the church on one side and the carriage on the other, he stood his ground. "Drop it, Frank. I'm done with Colfax Avenue Church. Let that be enough for you."

The banker reached inside his coat. With a jerk of his arm, he pulled a derringer and aimed it at Josh's chest. The men were just five feet apart. The gun had two shots. A single bullet would be enough to kill. Josh had nowhere to go, but neither would he raise his hands in surrender. If he died, Dean would be free to head to Swan's Nest. He had to fight but how?

Dean cocked the weapon. "You're going to die, Reverend."

Josh didn't fear death, only the thought of leaving Adie at this man's mercy. "Don't do it, Frank. You'll pay."

"Not before you do." His eyes closed to glimmering

slits. "Just think, Reverend. The instant you've breathed your last, I'm going to pay a call on Swan's Nest. Horace and I are going to beat the daylights out of Adie Clarke and her friends. Then we're going to tie them up and burn the house to the ground. That includes Pearl, except I'm going to take her baby. He's mine and I want him."

Dean meant every word. Josh had to get the gun.

Madness burned in the man's eyes. "Imagine it… Miss Clarke will scream and you won't hear it. That baby of hers—"

"Boss?" Horace stepped closer.

"What is it?" Dean demanded.

"This ain't right."

The banker jerked his head toward the driver. Josh lunged and knocked the gun from his hand. Dean cursed, then took a roundhouse swing. His knuckles slammed into Josh's jaw and sent him flying into a rosebush. As the thorns grabbed at his coat, Dean pummeled his face and ribs. With each blow, Josh sank deeper into the bush. A branch snapped and he fell to his back. Dean kicked him in the ribs, over and over, until Josh grabbed his foot and threw him off balance.

Fighting for breath, Josh pushed to his feet, hauled back and landed an uppercut on the banker's chin. As Dean fell back, Josh spotted the derringer under a second bush. He lunged for it, but Horace reached the weapon first and grabbed it. In the next instant, Josh would live or die. He'd save Adie or she'd be left to face Dean alone. He stared hard at the driver, saw the man's yellow teeth and the glint in his bleary eyes.

Without a word, Horace broke Josh's stare and took aim at Dean. "That's enough, boss. Leave the reverend alone."

Dean stared as if Horace were a stranger.

"Put your hands up," said the driver.

The banker laughed. "You little—"

"I mean it, Mr. Dean." Horace's hand stayed steady. "You've done enough harm to those ladies. You've done enough to the reverend and to me, too."

The fight could have ended there, but Dean took a step toward Horace, then another. He held out his hand. "Give me the gun."

"No, sir."

As Dean grabbed for the derringer, Horace pulled the trigger. Josh saw the muzzle flash like a shooting star. The banker looked down at his chest, then up at Horace as if he couldn't believe his eyes. With his mouth gaping, he crumpled into a heap. His legs jerked once, twice, then went still.

"God forgive me," Horace said. "But I couldn't let him hurt the babies."

"I think God will understand." Josh closed Dean's eyes, then covered the man's head and chest with his coat. Death had a way of stripping a man of all dignity. Josh had no respect for Dean, but he respected the passage of life. After a silent prayer for Dean's eternal soul, he stood and faced Horace. "You saved my life."

The driver looked down at Dean's corpse. "I couldn't let him do it, Reverend. I did enough to Miss Clarke already."

"The garden?"

"The fire, too." Horace looked disgusted with himself. "He paid me, but it ain't right to hurt women and children."

"No, it isn't."

He looked at Josh with wild eyes. "I'll tell the sheriff everything, even if it means jail. I don't ever want to smell smoke like that again. I watched the fire from across the street. I saw the ladies get out, but the baby kept coughing. It was awful."

"It was," Josh said simply.

"And tonight..." Horace looked as if he might be sick. "Mr. Dean would have killed you. I could hang for it, but I had to stop him."

"You won't hang." Josh had the bruises to prove Horace's honorable intentions. "Let's get Deputy Morgan."

They walked two blocks to the sheriff's office. The minute Morgan saw them, he jumped to his feet. They told him Dean was dead, then accompanied him to Archer's Funeral Home, where he woke up the undertaker. While Archer hitched up his hearse, Josh and Horace led Morgan to the body. As they walked, Horace told the story, including his part in the vandalism at Swan's Nest.

As he finished, Archer's wagon rattled to a stop. With the deputy's help, the undertaker lifted the body into the hearse. Horace and Josh stood in silence, watching as the black wagon rattled away.

When Archer rounded the corner, Morgan hooked his hands on his belt. "I'd say *that* problem's solved."

Horace let out a long breath. "Are you going to arrest me, Deputy?"

"Nope."

"But I killed him."

"It looks like self-defense to me. As for the problems at Swan's Nest, it's up to Miss Clarke. She can press charges or drop them."

Horace turned to Josh. "Do you think she'll talk to me?"

Josh wanted to say yes, but he didn't know what Adie would say. He also knew that Horace, yellow teeth and all, had crossed a line tonight. "I'll speak to her first—how's that?"

"Thanks, Reverend."

Morgan yawned. "That's it for tonight, gentlemen. Drop by tomorrow and I'll finish up my report."

As the deputy ambled down the street, Horace turned to Josh. "I have Mr. Dean's carriage. Do you want a ride to Swan's Nest?"

Josh ached all over, but he couldn't stand the thought of touching anything owned by Dean. "No, thanks, Horace."

"You don't look so good. Maybe you should see Doc Nichols."

The driver had a point, but Nichols would send him to bed. "I'll be all right."

Horace pursed his lips. "Can I ask you something?"

"Sure."

"Will you be staying in Denver?"

The ramifications of Dean's death struck Josh like a fresh blow. Adie no longer needed his protection. He was free to leave on the next train, but he didn't want to go. With his ribs throbbing, he wondered how she'd react to both Dean's death and the elder meeting. He also had to speak to her about dropping charges against Horace. If her heart stayed hard, Josh wouldn't be able to court her. If he stayed in Denver, he'd be tested every day. Eventually he'd fall and ask her to marry him. Adie had become laudanum to him. He resisted that temptation by avoiding its presence. If her heart stayed hard, he'd be wise to leave Denver altogether.

Horace was still waiting for an answer. Josh stifled a groan. "I haven't decided yet."

"I hope you stay, sir."

"Maybe I will."

"This Sunday," Horace said. "Will you be at Brick's? Something happened to me tonight. I want to tell about it."

Josh wouldn't miss that moment for anything. "I'll be there."

As the driver went to the carriage, Josh headed to Swan's Nest. Every step jarred his ribs, reminding him of the ulcer and the night he'd collapsed on Adie's porch. They'd come a long way, but the journey wasn't complete. It wouldn't be until he saw her reaction to Dean's passing. He didn't expect her to mourn the man. She'd be relieved just as he was, but Josh hoped she wouldn't dance on his grave.

He also worried that she'd feel vindictive toward Horace and the elders. Josh's battle with Dean had been to protect Adie from bodily harm. The next battle was for her soul. As much as he wanted to fight for her, he couldn't. The war was between Adie and God and she had to win it for herself.

A knock on the door jarred Adie to the marrow. Pearl had gone upstairs an hour ago. Mary had already come in from the garden, leaving Adie alone with the lamp turned low and Emily's journal. She'd started at the beginning and had just reread Emily's declaration of love for Dennis.

The knock came again, louder this time. Adie stepped to the window, peeked through the curtain and saw Josh. She flung the door wide, then gasped at the sight of him. Blood oozed from an abrasion on his cheek. He had a lump on his jaw and his right eye would be swollen shut by morning. Just as startling, he wasn't wearing his black coat. Dirt streaked his white linen shirt as if he'd been repeatedly kicked in the ribs.

Adie grabbed his hand and pulled him inside. "You're a wreck! What happened to you?"

He squeezed her fingers. "Dean's dead."

"Dead?"

"Horace killed him."

Adie gasped. "You were there."

"It's a long story. I'll tell you everything but—" He winced.

"You need to sit." She hooked her arm around his waist so he could lean on her. "I want to clean your cuts. Can you make it to the kitchen?"

"I'm all right."

"No, you're not." Adie didn't have the facts, but the evidence spoke for itself. Dean had accosted Josh. She didn't know if Horace was part of the beating, but she didn't care. Both men had tried for weeks to ruin her life. "I'd like to pound whoever did this to you into the ground!"

Josh stiffened. "Dean got pounded, all right."

She helped him into a chair, then filled a bowl with hot water. After taking a soft towel from a drawer, she positioned a chair across from him and went to work cleaning his cuts. As she dabbed at the blood, he told her about the fight in front of the church, Dean's threats and how Horace had intervened. By the time he finished, Adie felt a rage so profound she couldn't contain it.

She shot to her feet. "I hate Franklin Dean. I'm glad he's dead."

"We owe that relief to Horace."

Adie scowled. "I suppose."

"He saved my life," Josh said gently. "He also confessed to the vandalism and the fire. He's afraid you'll press charges."

She huffed. "I'm not *that* hardhearted. Dean was behind it, not Horace."

"Will you speak with him? He wants to apologize."

"I guess." But her heart wouldn't be in it.

Josh said nothing.

She squeezed his hand. "Tonight's been awful for you. I heard about the meeting, how they attacked Emily and—"

"Adie, stop."

"They said terrible things about you! They—"

He cupped her face in his palms, forcing her to look into his eyes. "I don't hate them. I don't hate Dean, either. I hate what he did. There's a difference."

Adie didn't see it. "He tried to kill you!"

"Listen to me." He spoke with an urgency that made her go still. "I forgive him for what he did to me. It's harder to forgive him for what he did to you, but Christ died for those sins, too."

"I don't care!"

As soon as the words left her mouth, she realized how profoundly she meant them. She pushed to her feet and turned away, but she couldn't stop seeing Josh's bruised face. She heard the scrape of his chair, then felt his hands on her shoulders. She didn't dare turn around. He'd see bitterness in her eyes, and she'd see pity in his. She laced her arms across her chest. "I'm glad Dean's dead. I wish Honeycutt were dead, too. And Timothy Long!"

"Adie—"

She whirled to face him, tearing away from his grip. "Don't you understand? I *can't* forgive them."

"It's not a feeling," he said. "It's a choice. Believe me, I didn't feel particularly charitable while Frank was beating the stuffing out of me. But I knew deep down that he was just a damaged, stupid man."

"He's worse than that," Adie insisted. "He was a monster! I'll never believe otherwise. I don't want to!"

His voice dropped to a hush. "Why not?"

"I just don't." She didn't tell Josh, but hating men like Dean and Honeycutt made her powerful. She felt safe behind that wall, not vulnerable as Josh had been tonight. His bruises proved her point.

"I see." His tone turned brusque, like the sweep of a broom, and he sat back on the chair. "I came tonight for two reasons."

The first had been to tell her about Dean. "What's the second?"

"I'm leaving Denver."

She gasped. "You're *what?*"

"I'm going back to Boston."

"But why?"

"I think you know." He gripped her hands in both of his. "I love you, Adie. I think you care for me, too."

"I do. I love you."

The moment called for a kiss, a claiming of forever. Instead his expression turned bleak. "I can't marry you, Adie. We'd both suffer. You'd dread Sundays and church socials, even knocks on the door. You'd start to hate me. I can't ask you to share that life, and I can't give it up without hating myself."

He kissed her hands, then let her go. "I'm not strong enough to fight what feels so right. I have to leave. The sooner, the better."

She couldn't bear the thought. "But you're hurt!"

"I'll be fine."

"But Boston's so far."

"It's settled," Josh said. "I'm leaving Monday."

He'd be alone on the train. What if his ribs were broken and not just bruised? What if his ulcer flared up? Adie couldn't stand the thought.

He pushed to his feet. "I told Horace I'd be at Brick's on Sunday. I'd appreciate it if you'd tell everyone here."

His eyes held hers; then he kissed her lips, a tender brush, another, and finally a parting that felt like skin being ripped from her own body. He touched her hair one last time, looked into her eyes and stepped back. "If you need anything, see Elliot."

She didn't want to see Elliot. She wanted to marry Josh, except he was right. They couldn't walk the same path unless they served the same God.

His voice stayed strong. "I'll write to you." He kissed her one last time, then walked out the door.

Adie collapsed on a chair and wept. She couldn't bear to see Josh go, but he'd been right to leave. She loved him enough to marry him in spite of her wayward soul, but he wouldn't compromise. He wanted her heart, all of it. Silently she raged at the Almighty for leaving her adrift. Why couldn't she let go of her bitterness? Pearl had been as wounded as Adie, even more so, but she didn't hate anyone. Mary had shrugged off the chip on her shoulder. Caroline and Bessie would never forget the havoc of war, but neither did they dwell on what they'd lost.

"What's wrong with me?" Adie said out loud.

Where could she go for answers? Darkness and light were alike to God but not to Adie. She was lost and alone in the dark. Where was God now? With her heart pounding, she wept until she felt hollow. As the tears cleared, she yearned to be filled with love. She thought of Josh and flashed to the journal she'd left on the divan. Desperate to feel close to him, she went to the parlor, turned up the lamp and opened the book to Emily's final entry, the one she'd refused to hear when Josh read it for himself.

The words were as hateful as she'd feared. *He became a murderer...a lion about to eat me.* Adie blinked and saw Josh's agony as he'd taken in the depth of Emily's feelings. Each lash of his sister's pen had marked him.

The words had once been true but not anymore. If Emily had tried to forgive him—if she'd just written home—she'd have discovered that Josh had changed. He would have moved heaven and earth for her. She and Dennis could have married. When the baby came, she would have had the finest doctors and she might have lived. If she hadn't been so bitter, she—

Adie caught her breath. How many times had she and Maggie commiserated over life's unfairness? They'd called themselves two peas in a pod. Yet tonight, reading the journal, Adie felt nothing but pity for her friend. Emily had died throwing stones at her own brother, a man who'd given up everything to search for her.

Looking at Emily's final scrawl, Adie knew she'd been making a similar mistake. She didn't know if Reverend Honeycutt had changed or if Timothy Long had been punished, but it didn't matter. Her bitterness served no purpose except to poison her own heart. In the end, these men would have to answer to God. That was enough. So was Franklin Dean's demise.

In the deepest part of her heart, Adie felt free. Just as Josh had forgiven her for hiding Stephen's identity, she could forgive the people who'd hurt her. Having been forgiven, she could forgive. She closed the journal and bowed her head. Joy welled in her chest and made her fingers tingle. She felt as spotless as snow...as light as fluffy biscuits and goose feathers and rose petals fluttering to the ground. She didn't have to walk around with rocks in her pocket a minute longer.

Speaking out loud, she forgave her father for loving gold more than he loved her. She forgave her mother for dying and Timothy Long for harming her. Next she prayed for the Honeycutts. They'd failed her, but they'd done their best. She even forgave Franklin Dean, a prayer that came easily because justice had been served. God hadn't moved swiftly, but He'd been thorough.

Last of all, she forgave herself. She'd wasted years of her life being bitter. Even worse, she'd almost lost Josh. She stood and looked out the window. Dawn was on the horizon. She wanted to run to the parsonage and tell him her news, but a thought came that made her smile. It turned into a plan that filled her with joy.

News of Dean's death spread through Denver like fire. On Friday, the six remaining elders came to Josh as a group. They asked him to reconsider his decision, but he'd made up his mind. No charges were filed against Horace. The driver hadn't shared the details with Josh, but he'd visited Adie and had made amends. When Horace said he planned to leave Denver, Josh gave the man his horse and saddle. On Saturday he purchased a train ticket for Boston and left word at Brick's that he'd be preaching one last Sunday.

Josh didn't trust himself to see Adie again, so he spent Saturday writing letters to Bessie, Mary, Caroline and Pearl. He figured at least one of them, probably Mary, would come to the service. He'd ask her to deliver the letters, then he'd pack his things. The train left early Monday and he'd be on it.

Sunday dawned like any other day. Josh put on his

collar and coat, picked up his Bible and walked to Brick's Saloon. His ribs throbbed with every step, but he didn't want to stay in Denver while he recovered. Every step away from Swan's Nest took all the discipline he could muster.

As he neared the saloon, he looked for horses tied to the hitching post. He didn't see a single one. He passed the window and saw empty chairs. When he tried the door, it was locked. He'd been looking forward to seeing Gretchen and the cowboys. Horace had planned to tell his story, and Josh had wanted a final word with Brick. He didn't know the newer folks as well, but he'd hoped to leave with fond memories. Instead he felt lonelier than he'd ever been.

He also had no way to deliver his letters. He thought about dropping them at the post office, but he didn't have stamps and couldn't buy them on Sunday. Seeing Adie would rip his heart from his chest, but he couldn't leave without saying goodbye to the women who'd stuck by him through everything. As he headed for Seventeenth Street, he recalled holding Stephen and making baby talk. He thought about suppers, kitchen sounds and the laughter of women. As he passed the piles of rock from the demolished mansion, he felt a weight in his chest and wondered if it would ever go away.

When Swan's Nest came into view, he looked up at Adie's window. He listened for Stephen calling for his mother but heard nothing. The house usually felt alive as he approached. Today it looked abandoned. Confused, he climbed the porch steps, where he saw a note tacked to the front door. Stepping closer, he saw the words "Come to the garden" written in Adie's hand.

Why would she want to meet him among the roses? Anxious but hopeful, he walked down the steps and passed the plot of vegetables. As he rounded the corner, he glimpsed Adie in her green dress, scurrying away from him. Josh picked up his pace.

As he neared the hedge, he heard a ragtag choir singing his favorite hymn, the one he'd picked that first Sunday at Brick's. He took a dozen more steps and saw a crowd. Brick greeted him with a crooked smile. Next to the barkeep stood Gretchen, the cowboys and Horace. Bessie, holding Stephen, stood between Mary and Caroline. On the other side of the path, he saw Tobias and Pearl. She had her baby in her arms and was beaming. Beau Morgan, wearing his leather vest and a string tie, stood off to the side. Josh didn't know the rest of the people by name, but he recognized faces from Colfax Avenue Church, including Halston Smythe.

A church had formed.

His church… As he searched the crowd, Adie came to stand at his side. Before he could speak, she pressed something cold and hard into his palm. He looked down and saw a rock, gray in color and smooth from years of wind and rain.

She folded his fingers over the stone, then looked into his eyes. "I'm done throwing rocks."

Josh had never heard more beautiful words. "What happened?"

She looked sheepish. "After you left, I read Emily's journal. She could have been happy. All she had to do was forgive you." She plucked the stone from his palm and let it fall to the ground. It landed with a thump.

With her hands open and empty, she looked into his eyes. "I have nothing to offer but my heart. I have a temper and I get angry. I say things I regret. I—"

"I love you just as you are." He gripped her hands

and raised them to the level of his heart. “Will you marry me?”

“Yes!” Joy shone in her eyes. “Right now?”

He laughed out loud. “Nope.”

“But—”

He raised her hand to his lips and kissed her knuckles. “We were standing on this very spot when I promised to sweep you off your feet.”

“I remember.”

“That’s what I intend to do.”

Josh had a good reason for not marrying Adie today. He didn’t think she’d change her mind and he knew he wouldn’t change his. His motives were far less dramatic. He simply wanted the fun of courting her. He wanted to bring her flowers, call her “sweetheart,” buy her supper, and enjoy long walks. In the next few months, they’d share laughter and tears. They’d quarrel and make up. When their wedding day came, Adie would be wearing a beautiful dress and carrying a huge bouquet.

With God and the world watching, Josh plucked a red rose from the hedge and gave it to her. When she looked up and smiled, he smiled back. It was a sign of all the good things to come.

Epilogue

October 1875 Swan's Nest

Josh had been courting Adie for two months when Pearl announced she'd be leaving for Cheyenne in three days. Adie had enjoyed every starry-eyed minute, but she had no desire to wait until June to marry as they'd planned. She didn't need roses and a fancy dress for a wedding, but she very much needed her friends.

As soon as she heard Pearl's news, she walked to the house Josh had been renting and knocked on the door. He greeted her with a lazy smile. "Good morning, beautiful."

Adie blushed but refused to be distracted. "Pearl's leaving. I want to get married tonight."

His eyes popped wide. "But your dress—"

"I'll wear the green one."

"Flowers—"

"I don't need them."

"Are you sure?"

"I'm positive."

With that, he swept her into his arms. "What time? I'll see to everything."

They agreed on seven o'clock, and Adie ran down the street to the café. Mary threw down her apron and hurried with her to Doc Nichols's office, where they found Bessie. They fetched Caroline from the dress shop and raced to Swan's Nest.

"In the parlor," she replied.

And so the preparations began. Food arrived from people at church. Brick delivered a wedding cake. The owner of the local dress shop brought four white gowns, veils, gloves and a note from Josh telling her to pick whatever she wanted. When the clock in the hallway struck seven, Swan's Nest was full of guests and Adie was wearing white, standing in the second parlor with Bessie, Caroline and Pearl. Mary would be singing Adie's bridal march, so she was in the parlor with Reverend Oliver.

Adie had never felt more beautiful in her life. She'd chosen a dress made of satin with a scooped neckline. The high collar and tight sleeves made her feel like a real swan, and the satin rosettes holding the draped skirt reminded her of the flowers in her garden. To set off the simplicity of the dress, she'd chosen a waist-length veil made of the sheerest tulle. It covered her eyes, but she'd be able to see every detail—the candles on the hearth, the asters and greenery lining the aisle made from borrowed chairs.

Reverend Oliver knocked on the door. "Ladies? Are you ready?"

Adie had never been more ready in her life. When she nodded, he went back to the main parlor and Mary started to sing Adie's favorite hymn, a standard called "Just As I Am."

Caroline and Bessie walked down the aisle first. Pearl, Adie's maid of honor, followed and took her place next to her father. As Mary sang the final chorus, every head turned to the doorway where Adie stood alone. Halston Smythe had sent a note offering to walk her down the aisle, but she didn't feel the need. She wasn't alone today. She had her heavenly Father at her side.

She also had her friends. She wanted each of them to be as happy as she was this very minute. Soon she'd be Josh's wife. They'd speak their vows, then he'd kiss her and they'd stand together as man and wife. In a little while she'd toss her bouquet. She didn't know who'd catch it, but she had high hopes for another Swan's Nest wedding.

* * * * *

Andrew shifted Mari in his arms. She had laid her head on his shoulder and her eyes were nearly closed. "I hope you weren't embarrassed by the man thinking that the three of us are a family."

Bethany felt her face heat, but with her bonnet on it was easy to avoid Andrew's gaze. *Ja*, the man's comment had been embarrassing, but only because she felt like they had misled him. Being mistaken for Andrew's wife and Mari's mother made her feel like she was finally where she belonged.

"Not embarrassed as much as ashamed that he thought something that was untrue."

Andrew stepped closer to her. "It doesn't have to be untrue. Have you thought about what I asked you?"

Bethany nodded. She had thought of nothing else since yesterday afternoon. "Do you think we could have a good marriage, even in these circumstances?" She looked into Andrew's eyes. They were open and frank, with no shadows in the depths.

"You and I have always made a good team." Andrew glanced at the people walking past them, but no one was paying

LIHEXP65280

attention to their conversation. "I'm asking you to give up a lot, though. If there's someone you've been wanting to marry, you'll lose your chance if you marry me."

"What makes you say that?"

"Dave Zimmer said that he had proposed to you, and so had a couple other fellows, but you turned them down. He thought you were waiting for someone else."

Bethany tilted her head down so that Andrew couldn't see her face. She couldn't explain what kept her from accepting Dave's proposal a few years ago, other than it just hadn't felt right. Being with any man other than Andrew hadn't felt right. No one else offered the easy camaraderie he did, and she had never felt any love for any other man.

She shook her head. "There is no one else."

"Then you'll do it?"

Bethany pressed her lips together to keep back the retort she wanted to make. He made their marriage sound like a business arrangement. She couldn't tie herself to a man who would never love her, could she?

Just then, Mari lifted her head, roused by her uncomfortable position and the noise around them. She turned in Andrew's arms and reached for Bethany. When Bethany took her, the little girl settled in her arms with a sigh and went back to sleep.

If Bethany didn't accept Andrew's proposal, Mari's grandmother would take her back to Iowa, and she would never see her again. She swallowed, her throat tight. And if she didn't accept Andrew's proposal, she would never know the joys of being a mother. Because if she didn't marry Andrew, she would never marry anyone.

"*Ja*, Andrew. I'll do it. I'll marry you."

Pregnant and abandoned by her Englisher *boyfriend, Dori Bontrager returns home—but she's determined it'll be temporary. Can Eli Hochstetler convince her that staying by his side in their Amish community is just what she and her baby need?*

Read on for a sneak preview of Courting Her Prodigal Heart *by Mary Davis, available January 2019 from Love Inspired!*

Rainbow Girl stepped into his field of vision from the kitchen area. *"Hallo."*

Eli's insides did funny things at the sight of her.

"Did you need something?"

He cleared his throat. "I came for a drink of water."

"Come on in." She pulled a glass out of the cupboard, filled it at the sink and handed it to him.

"Danki."

She gifted him with a smile. "*Bitte.* How's it going out there?"

He smiled back. "Fine." He gulped half the glass, then slowed down to sips. No sense rushing.

After a minute, she folded her arms. "Go ahead. Ask your question."

"What?"

"You obviously want to ask me something. What is it? Why do I color my hair all different colors? Why do I dress like this? Why did I leave? What is it?"

She posed all *gut* questions, but not the one he needed an answer to. A question that was no business of his to ask.

"Go ahead. Ask. I don't mind." Very un-Amish, but she'd offered. *Ne*, insisted.

He cleared his throat. "Are you going to stay?"

She stared for a moment, then looked away. Obviously not the question she'd expected, nor one she wanted to answer.

LIEXP1218

He'd made her uncomfortable. He never should have asked. What if she said *ne*? Did he want her to say *ja*? "You don't have to tell me." He didn't want to know anymore.

She pinned him with her steady brown gaze. "I don't know. I don't want to, but I'm sort of in a bind at the moment."

Maybe for the reason she'd been so sad the other day, which had made him feel sympathy for her.

He appreciated her honesty. "Then why does our bishop think you are?"

"He's hoping I do."

His heart tightened. "Why are you giving him false hope?" Why was she giving Eli false hope?

"I'm not. I've told him this is temporary. He won't listen. Maybe you could convince him to stop this foolishness—" she waved her hand toward where the building activity was going on "—before it's too late."

He chuckled. "You don't tell the bishop what to do. *He* tells you."

He really should head back outside to help the others. Instead, he filled his glass again and leaned against the counter. He studied her over the rim of his glass. Did he want Rainbow Girl to stay? She'd certainly turned things upside down around here. Turned him upside down. Instead of working in his forge—where he most enjoyed spending time—he was here, and gladly so. He preferred working with iron rather than wood, but today, carpentry strangely held more appeal.

Time to get back to work. He guzzled the rest of his water and set the glass in the sink. *"Danki."* As he turned to leave, something on the table caught his attention. The door knocker he'd made years ago for Dorcas—Rainbow Girl—ne, Dorcas, but now Rainbow Girl had it. They were the same person, but not the same. He crossed to the table and picked up his handiwork. "You kept this?"

She came up next to him. "*Ja.* I liked having a reminder of…"

"Of what?" Dare he hope him?

She stared at him. "Of…my life growing up here."

That was probably a better answer. He didn't need to be thinking of her as anything more than a lost *Englisher*.

Don't miss Courting Her Prodigal Heart *by Mary Davis,*
available January 2019 wherever
Love Inspired® books and ebooks are sold.